Juliana looke ̲ **her lips parte**

"The baby?" Jason eased closer.

"Yes, I'm sure that's what it was. The doctor said I might feel something soon—like the flutter of a butterfly's wing. And I just did."

His hand lifted. "Can I…?"

"Yes, of course. But I'm not sure if it's strong enough for you to feel anything yet."

He placed his hand on her tummy, felt the swell of her womb, the warmth of her body, the softness of her breath. And although he couldn't feel any movement whatsoever, he didn't draw away. He just stood there, caught up in her floral scent and in the intimacy of the moment.

* * *

Brighton Valley Cowboys
This Texas family is looking for love
in all the right places!

THE BOSS, THE
BRIDE & THE BABY

BY
JUDY DUARTE

Published in Great Britain 2015
by Mills & Boon, an imprint of Harlequin (UK) Limited,
Eton House, 18-24 Paradise Road, Richmond, Surrey, TW9 1SR

© 2015 Judy Duarte

ISBN: 978-0-263-25157-9

23-0815

Harlequin (UK) Limited's policy is to use papers that are natural, renewable and recyclable products and made from wood grown in sustainable forests. The logging and manufacturing processes conform to the legal environmental regulations of the country of origin.

Printed and bound in Spain
by CPI, Barcelona

Since 2002, *USA TODAY* bestselling author **Judy Duarte** has written over forty books for Mills & Boon® Cherish™, earned two RITA® Award finals, won two Maggies and received a National Readers' Choice Award. When she's not cooped up in her writing cave, she enjoys traveling with her husband and spending quality time with her grandchildren. You can learn more about Judy and her books at her website, www.judyduarte.com, or at facebook.com/judyduartenovelist.

To Betsy Bramblett, a dear friend and fellow author.
I enjoy our times together.
Let's have coffee again soon!

Chapter One

Jason Rayburn had never considered himself an early bird, but as the morning sun began to rise over the Leaning R Ranch, he found himself pouring his second cup of coffee.

If his father hadn't died, he'd be in Houston today—still in bed, most likely, but with thoughts of hitting the gym instead of repairing the barn door. After a good workout, he'd take a shower, then head to the downtown high-rise he owned and take the elevator to the top-floor office of Rayburn Energy Transport, where he was the founder and CEO.

With the recent death of his father, he now controlled Rayburn Enterprises as well, not to mention his new role as the sole trustee of the Charles Darren Rayburn Family Trust.

What a mess dividing *that* was going to be. And that's what had led him back to Brighton Valley.

The Leaning R had been part of his great-grandmother's estate, rest her soul. And Rosabelle Rayburn had left it to Charles with a stipulation—that it be divided equally to his issue upon his death. She'd wanted his children to be in complete and wholehearted agreement about its daily operation and/or division.

Yeah. Right. Jason and his half siblings had never been in agreement on anything. Granny, of all people, knew that. And he suspected it was her last-ditch effort to draw them together in a way she'd never been able to do while she was alive.

But there'd been a reason for that. Jason, Braden and Carly had so very little in common they might as well be strangers.

So that's why he had to get the Leaning R up and running again and ready for sale. Because there was no way his brother and sister would make good business partners. He just hoped he could get them to agree on a real estate agent and a price.

When Jason was a kid, spending summers and the occasional holiday at the ranch, he'd dreamed of being a cattle rancher. But those days were long gone. He was a busy CEO now.

On rare occasions those old dreams might come back to haunt him, but there was a reason for that. He'd spent enough time on the Leaning R with Granny Rayburn growing up that he'd actually felt more at home here than he had anywhere else. Of course, that wasn't the case anymore. He was a city boy now—and eager to get back to his life in Houston.

He didn't have time for reminiscing, especially when some thoughts were so bittersweet they could make a grown man actually choke up like a little boy. Yet as he walked through the house, assessing the work that needed to be done, the still-lingering scents of lemon oil and Granny's trademark lavender hand lotion assailed him in every room. So it was nearly impossible to escape the memories.

But he wouldn't allow himself to lollygag in the past. He had too much to do, and he was determined to get the hell out of Dodge, so to speak, as quickly as he could. In the meantime, he'd set up a home office to work remotely. The corporate world didn't stop spinning just because he had to handle some family business.

He would have to hire a couple of extra ranch hands to help Ian, the foreman, get things done. But that didn't mean he wouldn't have to work along with them. He didn't mind the physical labor. It actually drew him back to the time when his great-grandma was still alive, when he was a boy who loved to ride the fence line with the cowboys who'd worked on the Leaning R.

Too bad Granny wasn't here to fix him silver-dollar pancakes for breakfast or to tell him about more of Grandpa Dave's escapades.

He glanced at the faded blue wallpaper with pictures of straw baskets holding wildflowers. Now yellowed with age, the colors had once brightened Granny's kitchen.

Damn, but he missed that sweet old woman. She'd been the closest thing to a mother he'd ever had.

The coffeepot gurgled, and he took one last sip of his morning brew before dumping the remainder in the sink. It wasn't Starbucks, but at least it was caffeine.

He glanced at the cat-shaped clock on wall, its drooping black tail swishing back and forth with each tick-tock. Time to get moving. He had a lot to accomplish today.

Headlights flashed through the kitchen window, and tires crunched on the gravel drive as a vehicle pulled into the yard and parked. He wasn't expecting anyone this early, but it wasn't as if this was the Wild West and he needed to protect his homestead.

Looking out the kitchen window, he watched a woman climb from the small pickup, her hair pulled into a topknot. Instead of heading for the front door, she went straight for the back entrance—just as though she owned the place.

Carly?

His half sister had said she'd come out and help him inventory the household furnishings for an estate sale—the most difficult part of the job, which he had yet to face. But he hadn't been expecting her until tomorrow. What was she doing here now—and at the crack of dawn? She'd never been an early riser, at least not that he could recall.

Jason was already in the mudroom when the door swung open and Carly stepped inside.

"This is a surprise," he said. "You're a day early. Want some coffee?"

"No, thanks. I can't stay."

"What's going on?" he asked.

"I just got offered a singing gig—an important one—and I have to leave town for a few weeks. But I wanted to let you know that there are some boxes in the attic that Granny was keeping for me. I don't want you to throw them out or sell them. That's why I agreed to help you inventory things, especially since I think you're being way too hasty in selling the ranch."

He knew how she felt. But it made no sense to keep the Leaning R going when there was no way the three of them could work together. And he had enough on his plate already.

"You could let Braden run things," she added.

Hell, he and Braden rarely spoke. How in the world were they supposed to be business partners? That was one reason he was in a hurry to get the estate settled— so the three half siblings could each go their own ways. Not that he wouldn't keep in touch with Carly. But with her heart set on singing and acting, that just went to show that they had nothing in common except the DNA they'd inherited from their old man.

"I also have some things to drop off for Braden," Carly added, "but since he's not home, I'm going to leave them here for him to pick up."

"What are you talking about?"

"Braden asked a friend to drop off some stuff with me. I've had it a week, but I'm leaving and already gave notice at my place. So I don't want him to worry about where it is if he needs it."

Jason kept in closer contact with Carly than he did

their half brother. When they'd been kids, Jason had blamed Braden for the divorce that had sent his mom into an emotional tailspin. Of course, as he grew older, he realized Braden had been as much a victim as he'd been. But you couldn't fix a relationship that had never really developed.

"Slow down," Jason said. "Where is Braden?"

"I'm not sure. I think he's in Mexico. It was all pretty cryptic. His friend pretty much just dropped the painting off, along with a couple of boxes. He said it was important that I keep it for him."

"Why can't you leave it at Braden's ranch?"

"There must be a reason why he wanted me to hang on to it. Braden's supposed to explain more when he comes to pick it up. He said he'd owe me one—but now he'll owe you."

Jason was about to object, but it wouldn't hurt to have his half brother indebted to him, even if none of this made any sense. "Did he say when he'd be back?"

"As soon as he can, apparently. A few weeks at the most."

"What the hell? I want to get this property listed for sale. I can't be away from my office while you and Braden are out traipsing around and going on with your lives. It's not fair. And who's going to help me pack up all this stuff?"

She blew out a ragged breath. "Talking to you is just like talking to Dad. I knew you'd never understand."

Her words struck like the flat of a hand against his cheek. For as long as Jason could remember, he'd been trying to win his dad's approval, by following in his footsteps, by attending the same college, becoming a business major, starting his own company. Yet he'd never meant to become a carbon copy of the man.

"Try me," he said.

She merely rolled her eyes—big and blue, just like her mother's.

Jason didn't blame her for being skeptical. He and Carly had never been particularly close. For one reason, at twenty-four, she was six years younger than he was. She'd also been into music and the arts, while he'd been more interested in sports and, later, getting his MBA.

But since the three half siblings would have to compromise during the division of the estate, a task that seemed nearly impossible considering they couldn't figure out a way to be in town at the same time, it was imperative that they learn to find some kind of common ground.

"Tell me about your singing gig," he said.

She unfolded her arms and cocked her head slightly to the side, studying him as though she'd never met him before. Then she slipped her thumbs into the front pockets of her jeans, rocked forward and smiled. "I'm starring in a nightclub near the Riverwalk. It's a six-week run, but it could work into something bigger— *better.*"

She made it sound as if she'd been asked to star on Broadway.

So what would it hurt for him to pretend that she had?

"That's great, Carly. I hope things work out for you."

She paused a beat, then tucked a loose blond curl

behind her ear. "So you're not going to fight me about storing Braden's stuff while he's gone?"

He hoped that didn't mean holding off the sale longer than he'd planned, but if he really thought about it, his relationship with his half brother was in far more need of repair than his and Carly's. And if that meant doing Braden this favor now, then how could he refuse?

"Can you stick around until I find someone else to help me go through the household items?" he asked.

"I'm afraid not. I start tonight, and I have to get back to San Antonio for a wardrobe check this afternoon. It's a long drive."

Crap. How was he supposed to go through the house on his own, plus supervise the ranch work—and hold down the fort at Rayburn Energy, as well as Rayburn Enterprises, without help?

Besides, he'd been hoping Carly would agree to go through the household items. It was hard for him to do it. Everything he saw, everything he touched, reminded him of Granny, and…well, it was hard. Damn hard. And Carly would know better than he would what should be kept and what should be tossed or sold.

"I'm going to have to find someone to help," he said. "And quickly. If they can live in, then all the better."

A slow grin stretched across Carly's face, and he was struck by how pretty she was, even without any makeup. She'd always favored her mother, a popular country-and-western music star and who'd retired recently to marry a state politician. But he hadn't realized how much until now.

"I know someone who'd be perfect—and she's looking for work."

"Who?"

"Remember my friend Juliana Bailey?"

Red hair, pigtails. Big brown eyes and a scatter of freckles across her nose. "The one I used to call Bird Legs? What about her?"

"She's been working in Wexler at an art gallery since graduating from the junior college, but she was laid off recently. Now she's back in town and waiting tables part-time at Caroline's Diner. But she needs to find something that pays better. I'm sure she'd do a great job. And maybe, if you were happy with her, it might work into something more permanent—and in the city. I know she'd love to find something outside of Brighton Valley."

"I wouldn't want to give her any false hope about working at either Rayburn Energy or Enterprises. I leave the hiring up to the HR department. It makes my life a lot easier if I don't get involved with the personnel. But I definitely need some temporary help here on the ranch, and I'd be willing to make it well worth her time."

"You won't be sorry. Juliana is bright, professional and...well, whatever it is HR departments are looking for in new hires. I'm not sure why that company in Wexler let her go. They'd have to be crazy or going out of business, because she had to be their best employee ever."

"You don't have to sing her praises. I'm a little desperate right now."

"Good. I think she's working this morning. I don't have her new number, but you could stop by Caroline's and talk to her. I know she's been staying with her mom and grandmother in a small apartment near Town Square, so she'd probably work for room and board and a fair salary."

Seriously? "You think she'd be interested in a simple offer like that? Even if it's only temporary?"

"Well, that and the opportunity to at least have a chance at an interview with the HR department at one of your businesses. It wouldn't hurt to ask."

"Okay, I will."

"Thanks, Jason. You won't be sorry."

For some reason, he was sorry already. But he set his mug on the counter and followed Carly out to the yard, catching up to her about six feet from the pickup. "How many boxes are there?"

"Two—one containing some ceramic stuff and another with paperwork. There is also a painting." She opened the tailgate, then reached for a box. "Here. Can you carry this one into the house?"

Jason took the carton she handed him, although he had half a notion to drop the damn thing on the ground—or take it and dump it off at Braden's ranch, which was ten miles down the road.

"Have you tried calling him?" Jason asked as he and Carly carried the boxes back into the house.

"Several times, but apparently he doesn't have cell reception wherever he is."

"Didn't you think to ask what he was doing down there?"

"Braden's not much of a talker."

That was the truth. And he certainly wasn't likely to confide in Jason. Hell, they kept each other at arm's distance as it was. And as much as Jason would like to change that—as much as he now *needed* to change that—he couldn't very well build or repair their relationship all by himself.

They deposited the boxes on the kitchen table, then returned for the paintings. He was supposed to be documenting all the stuff in the house so they could get rid of it—not adding more clutter. If he wasn't so determined to mend his relationships with his siblings, he'd…well, he wasn't sure what he'd do.

But damn his father for dying and leaving him with a dysfunctional family and a messed-up estate to complicate his life when he had his own business issues to deal with.

And damn Braden for being so secretive and only making things worse by going MIA when his family needed him most.

Before he could voice any further objections, Carly was behind the wheel of her red Toyota pickup and heading down the road just as dawn broke over the Leaning R.

Now what?

He might as well head into town and get breakfast at Caroline's. He needed some help, and it appeared that he was going to have to snag Caroline's newest employee away with a better offer—room, board, a small salary and the hope that something better might be in the cards for her.

He didn't want to even consider what he'd do if she didn't accept his offer.

For a woman who'd once thought she'd left small-town life behind, Juliana Bailey seemed to have returned to Brighton Valley with her tail between her legs. Not that anyone knew that yet.

As far as the small-town rumor mill went, she'd been laid off at her job at an art gallery in nearby Wexler and had moved home to the two-bedroom apartment her mom and grandma shared above the drugstore. She currently slept on the sofa bed and made the short, one-block walk to Caroline's Diner, where she'd picked up part-time work at a job destined to only last a few more days—at best.

She had a game plan, though. And that was to get out of town before her secret came out. In the meantime, she held her head high and bustled about the diner with her order pad in hand and wearing an oversize apron that matched the yellow gingham café-style curtains in the windows facing the street. She'd always been fashion conscious, but not as of late.

Loose blouses and an apron tied above the waist hid a multitude of sins, namely a growing baby bump, a secret that would be impossible to keep much longer.

Thankfully, no one other than her obstetrician, Dr. Selena Ramirez-Connor, knew that she'd been deceived by a man who'd neglected to tell her he was married. But if she wanted to protect her mom, who happened to be a church secretary, and her grandma, who worked at city hall, from her scandal, she'd have to get out of Brighton Valley quickly.

Trouble was, Juliana had just moved into a nicer place near La Galleria in Wexler, and when she'd decided to leave town, she'd had to use her savings to get out of her lease. So she didn't have enough left to move to the city, especially since she didn't have another job lined up yet. And with a baby due in five months... well, she was strapped right now.

As she refilled the coffee of the lone diner at table three, an elderly gentleman with thinning hair, she caught a whiff of greasy sausage swimming in the runny egg yolks on his plate. Her tummy swirled like a mop in a slop bucket, and for a moment she thought she'd have to have to run to the restroom.

She blinked her eyes and swallowed as the brief bout of nausea passed.

For the most part, the morning sickness that had plagued her for nearly six weeks straight had ended. But there were still a few random moments, like this one, when she wasn't so sure...

"Thanks, hon," the diner said. "I don't s'pose you have any of those caramel cinnamon rolls left, do you? Margie said they were made special yesterday, and I was hopin' to have me another today."

"I'll check and see. If they're gone, I can get you one of the oatmeal spice muffins."

"Sure, that'll do."

Juliana had no more than turned from the table when the bell on the front door jangled, alerting her to a customer's entrance. She didn't normally give the arrivals much notice because Margie, the other waitress, was quick to greet the many diners who flocked to Caroline's for the food as well as the local gossip.

And the news that passed quickly from one person to the next, helped along by Margie, was another reason this was a bad place for Juliana to work if she didn't want to bring any undue embarrassment upon Mom and Grandma.

But for some reason, Juliana glanced at the doorway now, only to note a stranger. Well, not exactly a stranger, but a face she hadn't seen in years.

Jason Rayburn—who else could it be?—had grown up and filled out in the manliest way.

He was tall—six foot or more—with dark hair that was stylishly mussed. Even though she'd heard the wealthy exec was staying in Brighton Valley, she hadn't expected to see him dressed in faded denim and a chambray shirt. It almost made him appear to fit right in, when he was as far from one of the locals as a man could be.

She'd followed his success and found him somewhat intriguing. Actually, the entire Rayburn family was pretty newsworthy around here—including both Carly and Braden. Maybe that's why folks found them interesting. They had the same father, but they couldn't be any more different.

She knew Carly and Braden well. Jason, though, was more of a lone wolf. A wealthy and successful one, from what she'd heard.

He'd gone into business with his father right after

college. And he'd rarely come back, except for Granny Rayburn's funeral. But he'd left town nearly as quickly as he'd come in.

He scanned the small diner. When his eyes zeroed in on her, a smile stretched across his handsome face, creating a pair of dimples and sparking a glimmer in his green eyes.

As he sauntered toward her, as lean as a cowboy and as cocky as a man used to staking his claim on just about anything he had a mind to, she nearly dropped the coffee carafe.

"Well," he said, flashing a boyish grin and sending her heart rate topsy-turvy, "if it isn't Bird Legs."

She couldn't help but return his smile. "If I remember correctly, I threw a rock at you the last time you called me that."

"Yes, you did. I'd been bad-mouthing my brother, Braden, and you felt the need to stick up for him. And if I recall, you missed me by a mile."

"That's true, but I scared your horse."

"Thankfully, I'm a good rider."

That he was, although the mare had gotten skittish and Juliana had been sure he was going to get thrown. But she hadn't liked him picking on Braden, who'd been her friend and sometime riding buddy.

She lifted the glass carafe, which bore more brown stain than coffee. "I'm brewing a new pot. If you'd like to grab a seat, I can pour you a fresh cup."

"Sounds good. Thanks. Which tables are yours?"

He wanted her to be his waitress? Okay. Why not?

She nodded toward the yellow-gingham curtains. "Any of those by the window."

"All right."

She retrieved a menu, as well as a fresh pot of coffee, and took them to him. "Here you go." After upturning the white mug on the table in front of him, she filled it. "Cream or sugar?"

"Just black."

"Okay. I'll give you a minute to decide what you'd like, then I'll come back."

"Thanks. It won't take me long."

She felt his eyes on her back as she returned the carafe to where it belonged. Yet she feared there was more heat radiating from his stare than the coffee warmer.

Margie, who'd worked at the diner for as long as Juliana could remember, sidled up next to her and snatched the carafe labeled decaf. "Isn't that Jason Rayburn?"

"Yes, it is. I talked to Carly not long ago, and she said he's staying out at the Leaning R while he's getting it ready to sell."

"That's what I heard." Margie was up on all the local gossip, whether it was accurate or not. "But he's grown up since I last seen him, so I hardly recognized him. He doesn't favor Braden much, does he? But he does have the look of a womanizer."

"Why do you say that?" Juliana asked.

"Looks too much like his daddy to not be. And you know what they say. The apple doesn't fall far from the tree."

Charles Rayburn had grown up on the Leaning R

with his paternal grandparents, but it had been his maternal grandfather who'd paid for his college and who'd set him up in business. At that point, he'd pretty much left Brighton Valley in the dust. Or so they said.

"I'd better get his order." Juliana stepped away from Margie and made her way back to where Jason sat near the window.

The morning sun cast a glare on the dull brown Formica tabletop, but it had nothing on the sunny smile Jason tossed her way when she asked, "What'll it be?"

"Huevos rancheros. I haven't had that in ages."

"You got it." But instead of turning and walking away, she took a moment to bask in the glimmer of those meadow-green eyes. What color would a city girl call them?

Enough of that now. She had to get over her fixation on a palette of colors ready to spring to life on a blank canvas. She'd have to postpone her dream of becoming an artist.

And a romance gone bad made any other fantasies out of the question, too. So she returned to the kitchen and placed Jason's order. As much as she ought to keep her distance, she had a job to do.

"Can I refill your coffee?" she asked when she passed his table a few minutes later.

"Yes, thanks." He eyed her for a moment, as though assessing her.

Was he considering how much she'd changed? Did he like what he saw? Again, she chastised herself for letting her thoughts veer in that direction, even though it seemed only natural to wonder as his gaze caressed her face, her hair, her eyes.

"Carly told me you were working here," he said.

"Just a couple days a week. I was laid off at the art gallery in Wexler and plan to find work in Houston. This is just a temporary position to help tide me over until I find something permanent in the city."

"Well, I'm glad you were working today."

The way he continued to study her made her wonder if he'd come in just to see her—and not to order breakfast. But she quickly dismissed the idea. "I'm glad I was here, too, Jason. It's nice to see you, again. How long has it been? Ten years?"

"Something like that."

She smiled and nodded toward the kitchen. "I'll check on your breakfast."

Fortunately, Caroline was just placing his plate on the counter. So Juliana picked it up, along with a couple of warm flour tortillas and a small dish of butter. Then she placed his meal in front of him.

"Did my sister tell you I was staying out at the Leaning R?" he asked.

"She mentioned it."

"Did she tell you why?"

"She said you plan to sell the place." And that she wasn't any happier about the decision than Braden was. But Juliana knew enough to keep that to herself.

"I also need to inventory everything and get it ready to sell. It's a huge job, and I need to hire someone to help me. Carly mentioned that you might be interested in the position."

"That depends." Juliana definitely needed the extra money.

"If you're talking about the pay, I'd make it worth your time."

She placed a hand on her tummy, a movement that was becoming a habit, then let it drop. In truth, she was thinking more about the time it would take for her to get the job done. She only dared spend a few more weeks to a month in the area before her baby grew too big to hide. "What do you have in mind?"

"Can you take a leave of absence from here? I'd need you full-time for about three weeks."

She wasn't even working four hours a day as it was, and she suspected Caroline had only offered her the position as a favor to her grandma.

"I'd be willing to pay you a thousand dollars a week," Jason said.

Her pulse rate shot through the roof, and she struggled to keep her jaw from dropping to the floor. That was more money than she could expect to make anywhere. And it would certainly help her relocate to Houston and give her time to find another position.

"There's a guest room at the ranch," he added. "You can either commute each day or stay there, if you'd like. Whatever you're comfortable doing. But it's going to take a lot of work and time. Granny was sweet as can be, but she wasn't very organized."

Not that Juliana wanted to stay out at the ranch with Jason, but the sooner she got out of her mom's house and away from downtown Brighton Valley, the better her chances were of keeping her pregnancy secret.

Still, she was torn about accepting the offer. After all, the man's father had had a reputation for loving and leaving the ladies, which meant Jason might not be honorable, upright or honest. And she'd just gotten out of a relationship with a man like that.

Besides, what would the townspeople say if they thought she was shacking up with Jason out at the Leaning R?

But the generous salary he was offering her was too tempting to ignore.

Besides, if things worked out and she proved herself handy and competent, he might recommend her for an office position at Rayburn Energy in Houston, which would be her ticket out of Brighton Valley for good—and before word of her fall from grace got out into the rumor mill.

All the reasons she ought to turn him down ping-ponged in her brain. She'd fallen for a womanizer's lies and didn't want to cross paths with another one. And as Margie had said, the apple didn't fall far from the tree.

But the money he was offering her would allow her to leave town sooner and give her time to find another position in Houston.

"So what do you say?" he asked.

"When do you want me to start?"

Chapter Two

Jason had barely returned to the Leaning R and gone though a couple of cupboards when his office called with a list of several critical issues he needed to handle. He dealt with each one, which took no less than an hour.

When a pause sounded on the line, he realized that the last crisis had been averted—for the time being, anyway—so he adjusted the cell phone pressed against his ear, sat back in his desk chair and blew out a sigh. This was why he needed extra help on the ranch. He couldn't run a company and get the place ready to sell, even if he could get his siblings to agree. Not by himself.

"By the way, Mr. Rayburn," Marianne, his executive assistant, said, "we received a billing from a company called DII, which stands for Discreet International Investigations. They're charging over three thousand dollars in services, plus fifteen hundred in expenses."

Jason stiffened. "What in the hell was that for?"

"From what I understand, it's a private investigation firm that did some research for your father in Mexico about four months ago. Braden had them send the bill to the office and told me that it was a legitimate expense."

"Who gave Braden the right to authorize a payment like that?" And even more importantly, why had his father hired a PI? Did that have anything to do with his reason for being in Mexico when he died?

"I'm not sure, sir. That's why I didn't want to forward it to the accounting department without running it by you first."

"Thanks, Marianne. Put a hold on it for now. I need to check into this." After the line disconnected, Jason called his brother's cell phone. The unusual ringtone indicated Braden was still in Mexico, but he didn't answer.

For the next couple of hours, Jason continued to sort through cupboards while stopping every so often to try his brother's number with no success. By the time a car drove up and parked near the front of the house, he was madder than hell and ready to fight at the drop of a hat.

Funny how just being in this house had him lapsing into the Western vernacular. He'd be saying "Howdy" and "y'all" if he didn't get back to the city soon. He glanced out the window, only to spot an attractive red-head climbing from a white Honda Civic.

Juliana.

His frustration dissipated as he left his work in the kitchen, as well as the mess he'd strewn about the living room, and met her on the front porch.

An attitude change wasn't so difficult once he saw her face-to-face, though. How did a woman become prettier in a matter of hours?

She'd shed her apron, for one thing. And she looked a lot less frazzled, for another. Maybe that's because he was seeing her in the light of day instead of the diner.

The afternoon sun glistened off the gold strands in her copper-colored hair, which hung loose about her shoulders. Her eyes, a caramel shade of brown, glimmered under a fringe of long, dark lashes. She still bore a light scatter of freckles across a turned-up nose. But in a most attractive way that made a man want to memorize each one.

She wore a cream-colored gauzy top, and while it wasn't the least bit formfitting, he found it sexy in a feminine way.

Rounding off her ensemble was a pair of shorts and sandals that revealed neatly manicured toenails.

"I'm glad you're here," he said, his gaze traveling up—taking in her pretty face, then tempted to travel back down again.

Damn, get a grip. He was glad to have her here. He needed the help. But he didn't need her to realize that she'd also brought in a ray of sunlight to what had started out as a dreary day.

"Here," he said, "let me take your bag."

"It's not heavy."

"Maybe not, but for some reason, I've been doing quite a bit of reminiscing these past few days. I think it's a side effect of being here at the ranch. And I can't help but hear Granny's voice urging me to remember my manners."

"Then by all means," she said, handing over her suitcase while hanging on to her purse and a small canvas tote bag. "I wouldn't want to disappoint her."

His movements stalled for a moment, long enough for Granny's voice to hover in his memory. *You're a good boy. You know right from wrong, Jay-Ray. Don't disappoint me like your daddy did.*

But he shook it off as quickly as it came. He'd done his best to make both his great-grandmother and his father proud. Trouble was, he wasn't so sure he'd pleased either one.

He led Juliana through the living room, winding through the mess he'd made, and into the hall. He'd thought about giving her one of several guest rooms, but decided upon Granny's bedroom, which was bigger and had a private bathroom.

"I thought you'd be more comfortable in here." He placed her suitcase on the lavender floral quilt that draped the queen-size bed.

"Thank you. This will be fine." She set her purse and the tote alongside her bag. Then she glanced around the room, which he hadn't entered in years — until he'd come in last night to change the sheets, dust and air things out.

He wasn't sure why he hadn't come into Granny's room before then. Too many memories, he supposed. Even the furnishings, the white eyelet curtains, the embroidered throw pillows, still held a whiff of Granny's powdery lavender scent. It was enough to draw a boy farther inside—and to make a man withdraw.

Juliana walked toward the south wall, which displayed a gold-framed portrait of Granny that appeared to be fairly recent. She'd only been gone for three years, and it couldn't have been painted too long before that.

"That's a perfect likeness," Juliana said. "She looks just as I remember her—the eyes, the nose, the smile."

Jason followed her, taking note of the expression that had been caught on canvas and thinking the same thing. "It's like looking at a photograph, yet it's softer. And almost real."

"Did she have it commissioned?"

"I assume she did. I don't remember seeing it before last night." But then again, he hadn't been home for any notable visit in years.

"The artist is quite talented." Juliana stepped closer and read the signature in the corner. "I used to work in a gallery, but I've never heard of Camilla Cruz. I don't believe she's local."

That was odd. Then where had Granny met her? Jason supposed it didn't matter, so he shrugged it off. "I'll tell you what. Why don't you unpack and freshen up. Afterward, you can meet me in the den—I've set up a temporary home office in there. It's two doors down on the left. As soon as you're settled, we can go over your job assignment."

"Sounds great. I won't be long."

True to her word, Juliana only took a few minutes to put away the clothing and toiletries she'd brought with her. Then she met Jason in the oak-paneled room with a bay window that provided a view of the front yard and the big red barn.

He had an all-in-one laser printer, fax and scanner that took up a table near a built-in bookshelf on the far wall, as well as a laptop computer that sat next to an old-style PC with a big, bulky monitor that had been outdated years ago.

"I see you brought your own office setup."

He glanced up from his work and smiled. "I tried to talk Granny into updating her computer system a couple of years ago, but she refused. My dad bought it for her about fifteen years ago and installed it. She'd gotten so used to that dinosaur that she couldn't see parting with it. But I need something a lot more high-tech for what I do."

She nodded then moved into the den. "So where would you like me to start?"

He glanced at the laptop screen and clicked the mouse, just as the printer roared to life. "I created a spreadsheet to inventory the items inside the house. If you make a note of them on paper first, we can input the data into the computer afterward. Some of the items are antiques, so we may need to research their value."

"What about the sentimental value?"

He looked at her as if she'd uttered words in a foreign language. "Carly mentioned that. I suppose some people are more prone to form emotional attachments to things like furniture, but I don't. And I doubt my brother does, either."

"You're wrong." She bit her lip, wishing she could take it back. She hadn't meant to be so judgmental, even if she had wanted to defend Braden. "I'm sorry, it's just that I don't think you know your brother very well."

Again he paused for a beat. "You're right about that—Braden and I haven't been close. And if you grew up here in Brighton Valley and heard the local gossip, then you probably know why."

Not for a fact, but she was aware of the rumors. And Braden had said enough to allow her to come to a few conclusions of her own. Their father, Charles Rayburn, had been married to Jason's mother when he'd had an affair with Braden's mom, during which Braden had been conceived. Jason's mom had sued for divorce, but for some reason, Charles had never married Braden's mother.

"Your family connection may not be one of your own choosing," she said, "but you're brothers just the same. I'd think that would account for something, especially after having that relationship for more than twenty-five years."

"Believe it or not," Jason said, "I'd like things to be different between us."

"Have you told Braden that?"

"If we could find time to spend an hour or two

together, I probably would." He got up from his seat, crossed the den, pulled the empty spreadsheet from the printer and handed it to her. "This is pretty self-explanatory."

Okay, so he was done discussing his feelings about his brother. That was fine. It wasn't any of her business anyway. So she scanned the document and nodded. "When do you want me to get started on this?"

"Now, I suppose."

"Do you plan to break for dinner?"

He glanced at the clock on the desk. "I guess we'll have to. Sometimes I forget the time and work until my stomach growls, but that's not fair to you."

"Would you like me to cook something?" she asked.

"That wasn't part of the deal, but sure. If you don't mind. You may have to hunt and peck to find something decent to fix, though. I have some lunch meat and sandwich fixings, but I haven't done any real grocery shopping."

"I'll see what I can come up with."

"We can trade off kitchen duties," he added. "But on my nights, we'll probably call out for pizza. I'm not much of a cook."

"That sounds fair to me." She tossed him a smile, then headed for the kitchen.

Before she stepped foot into the hall, he stopped her. "I have a question for you."

She turned and waited in the doorway.

"How do you know Braden so well?"

"We were neighbors before my grandma's ranch went into foreclosure. He and I used to be riding buddies back then. I guess you could say we were friends and confidants."

He merely studied her for a moment, as though he found that difficult to believe. Or maybe as if he might be a bit envious.

But of whom? Her or Braden?

From the way those meadow-green eyes were boring into her, she couldn't be sure.

Juliana set out a delicious, mouthwatering spread of tuna rice casserole, sliced tomatoes, homemade biscuits and Granny's canned peaches. Jason sat in awe at her domestic capabilities, especially when she didn't look the least bit like a homebody.

She'd probably meant to keep her long, wavy red hair out of the way while she'd cooked, because now she wore it in a sexy topknot, with wisps of escaped curls dangling along her neck and cheeks. He would have guessed that she might have done it on purpose to tempt him—if she'd also changed out of that attractive gauzy blouse and put on a slinky tank top instead.

But she hadn't. She'd also kept on that pair of knee-length shorts that revealed shapely calves. While they were modest and a far cry from a revealing pair of Daisy Dukes, there's no way he'd ever call her Bird Legs again.

Now they stood at the sink, washing the last of the dishes, a chore he'd always done while staying on the Leaning R and seemed especially fitting this evening.

"Did I tell you how much I enjoyed dinner?" he asked.

"Yes, several times. And you're welcome—again." She tossed him a dazzling smile. "But I'm going to have to go shopping tomorrow to pick up something from the meat market. There wasn't much to choose from, other than the sandwich fixings you had in the crisper, tuna, biscuit mix and your great-grandmother's canned goods."

"Those peaches were a real treat. And I can't remember the last time I had tuna. To be completely honest, I might have passed if it was offered on a menu. But it was actually really good. Where did you learn to cook like that?"

"My mom taught me. She's a whiz at making a meal out of whatever she can find in the pantry."

Jason rarely talked about his past, but for some crazy reason, he found himself saying, "You're lucky. I lost my mom when I was just a kid."

"How old were you?"

"Ten."

"I'm sorry. At least you were old enough to have some memories of her."

Not too many good ones. The years he'd spent living only with his mom hadn't been all that happy. She'd been emotionally broken and damaged by his father's cheating.

When he'd eventually gotten a stepmom and was able to move in with her and his dad, Carly's mother had been too busy with her singing career to stay home with her own baby, let alone with a boy who wasn't hers. So Jason had been sent off to an elite boarding school.

But that was okay. It had been good for him. Everyone had said so. Everyone except Granny, anyway. He'd once overheard her tell his father what a mistake he was making. But when that summer was over, he was sent right back to Thorndike Prep as always.

Still, he did have those vacations...

Thankfully, Juliana didn't ask a lot of questions, and Jason was glad. He'd never been comfortable with anyone expressing their touchy-feely emotions or expecting him to talk about his own, especially when it came to his mother.

Granny had tried to step in and take on a maternal role, but it wasn't the same. Hell, his mother hadn't even been a real mom. He supposed he was one of those kids who'd pretty much grown up on his own in a lot of ways. He just hadn't been without any of the essentials or all the shiny extras—houses all over the place, private school, fancy cars...

But he didn't want to think about any of those lonely days and crappy memories, not when he had a beautiful woman at his side. So he said, "I have a bottle of merlot in the pantry. How about a glass of wine?"

"I'd rather have a glass of juice, if you don't mind. And under the circumstances, let's call it a debriefing. We can also create a game plan for tomorrow—or set up a calendar for trading off meal duties. But to tell you the truth, I don't mind cooking. I'm not fond of cleaning up, though."

If he was being honest with himself, as well as with her, he'd rather create a game plan for *tonight*, complete with romantic music, maybe a slow dance under the stars. But Juliana had put a stop to that by setting them both back on track. And he ought to thank his lucky stars that she had. Sexual harassment training was a priority for everyone in upper management at Rayburn Energy, and he'd best keep that in mind.

He offered her a platonic smile—his best attempt at one, anyway. "You're right. That's what I meant. Grab two goblets, then make yourself comfortable on one of those chairs on the porch. I'll get the wine and juice."

Moments later, he took the uncorked bottle of wine and a quart of orange juice outside. After filling their glasses, he took a seat, joining her under the soft yellow glow of the porch light.

He took a sip of his merlot and glanced at the barn door with the chipped paint and broken hinge that dusk couldn't hide. He'd have to ask Ian McAllister, the foreman, to fix that next. Then they'd have to paint it, along with the corral nearest the house.

Juliana glanced out onto the ranch, which still needed so much work to be the kind of place Granny had called home, a ranch she'd be proud of if she were still alive.

He tried to look at the family homestead through Juliana's eyes. He was going to have to hire more hands than Ian to help out around here. It was going to take an army to get it back into shape, even though they had only a handful of cattle left in the south forty.

So why hadn't he recruited those extra men yet? Why was he dragging his feet?

"What are you going to do with the Leaning R?" Juliana asked.

"Granny wanted me, Braden and Carly to run it as three equal partners, but I can't see how we can do that." Jason reached for the bottle of juice and replenished her glass. "Unlike most siblings, Braden, Carly and I never agree on anything—the food we eat, the clothes we wear, the books we read."

Even their memories of childhood and Daddy Dearest were as different as the three women who'd given birth to them.

Since Jason was the only one who didn't have a mother, he'd been closer to their father. Not that he and his dad had done any of the usual father-son activities, like playing catch or going camping. His father had been way too busy with his corporate obligations.

Interestingly enough, they both attended charity functions benefiting the Boys Club and other youth programs, to which Charles and Jason both contributed financially. It was, he supposed, the closest they came to having a typical relationship. But Jason wouldn't complain. He shared more with his dad than either Carly or Braden did. And while he hadn't cried when he'd gotten word that his father had died in a car accident in Mexico a few months back, he'd still grieved.

Jason and Juliana sat quietly for a while, lost in the night sounds on a ranch that had seemed like a ghost town when Jason had arrived last week.

When he'd driven up that first day, there hadn't been any cattle grazing in the pastures along the road, no Australian heeler named Mick to greet him. The barn, once painted a bright red, had weathered over the years and was in such disrepair that instead of asking Ian to take care of it, he'd thought he probably ought to hire a carpenter or two.

But it wasn't until he'd noted the boarded-up windows on the house, unlocked the front door and entered the living room that the old adage struck him and he had to agree.

You really couldn't go home again.

Whenever he'd visited the Leaning R before, he'd always expected to catch the aroma of fried chicken or roast beef or maybe apple spice cake—whatever Granny had been cooking or baking that day. But this time he'd been accosted by the musty smell of dust and neglect.

The first thing he'd done was to pry the boards off the first-floor windows and let in the morning sun. Then he'd called a cleaning service out of Wexler to put the place back to rights—or at least, as close to it as possible.

Jason had only spent school breaks and summer vacations on the Leaning R, but it had been his one constant. And the one place that held his warmest childhood memories.

Still, his plan was to put it on the market before summer was out—if he could get both Carly and Braden to sign the listing agreement. He hadn't expected an argument from Carly, but he'd gotten one. And he expected one from Braden—whenever the erstwhile rancher finally showed up. Then again, he'd never been sure about anything when it came to his half brother. The two of them were only three years apart, but they'd kept each other at arm's length for as long as Jason could remember.

Granny had tried to encourage a friendship whenever Braden came to visit, which was usually on Christmas or holidays. But Braden had a mother and family of his own. Maybe that was why Jason sometimes resented him coming around.

Either way, Granny couldn't create a closeness between the brothers that wasn't meant to be.

But why stress about any of that when he had pretty Juliana seated beside him?

He took another sip of merlot, savoring the taste.

"So what're your plans after this?" he asked. "What's next for you?"

"I'm going to get a job in the city—Houston, maybe."

"Not Wexler?"

"No." The word came out crisp, cool. Decisive.

Hmm. Bad memories?

She'd been laid off, Carly had said, and was only back in Brighton Valley temporarily.

Financial problems? Bad investments? Taken advantage of by a con man? Or maybe a lover?

It was too soon to ask. Still, he couldn't help wondering.

Either way, Wexler's loss was his gain. Or so it seemed, especially when he was sitting outside with a beautiful woman and finding even more solace under the stars.

There was also a lovers' moon out tonight, casting

a romantic glow over the Leaning R. His hormones and libido were pumped and taunting him to make more out of their time on the porch than a quiet chat, but common sense wouldn't let him.

Juliana had made it clear that she didn't want to cross any professional boundaries. What if she quit and left him alone to deal with the mess by himself?

He stole a glance at her, and when he caught her looking his way, she quickly averted her gaze. But as his attraction and interest continued to build, he realized it wouldn't take much for him to reach out and touch her.

Or, at the very least, to ask her why she was adamant about not returning to Wexler.

Juliana hadn't meant to stare at her employer, but he'd been so deep in thought that she couldn't help it.

Okay, so she hadn't just noted the intensity in his furrowed brow. She'd also been checking out his profile and the way his hair appeared to have an expensive cut, yet was stylishly mussed. In that Western wear—the worn jeans and chambray shirt rolled at the forearms—he looked like a Texas rancher. And a handsome one at that.

She tried to imagine him in a designer suit, seated at a board meeting in a high-rise building that looked out at the city skyline. He surely had to be quite impressive. Either way, Jason Rayburn was the kind of man who could turn a woman's head.

He'd certainly turned hers. But she didn't dare let her attraction get out of hand.

"Would you like some more OJ?" he asked.

"No, thank you. I've had plenty already." In her condition, she had to use the bathroom a lot more than usual. And after all the orange juice she'd had already, she'd be lucky if she could make it through the night without waking at least once.

"This probably isn't any of my business," he said, "but do you mind if I ask you something?"

She'd always been fairly open and up-front, although she'd learned to be a lot more cautious recently. "It depends on what you want to know."

"I get the idea you'd like to relocate. I can see why you might want to live in a bigger city. But I also sense that you couldn't leave Wexler fast enough. And that it might be due to bad memories."

She stiffened and leaned back in her chair. Her hand slipped protectively to her tummy. Instead of removing it, which she did whenever she'd found herself doing so in public, she opted to let it linger in the yellow glow of the porch light, allowing her baby the loving caress it deserved. "You're right."

"About the bad memories?"

"That the reasons aren't ones I want to share."

Silence stretched between them like a balloon she'd blown too full. Just before the tension popped in her face, she added, "But yes, there are some bad memories, too."

"Related to your employment?"

The man didn't quit, did he? She turned to him, caught his eyes drilling into hers. Why the sudden inquisition? Shouldn't his questions about her background and previous employment have come up earlier?

Did she owe her new employer, albeit a temporary one, an answer to that line of questioning?

Maybe and maybe not. But a brief yet truthful response might help to quell his curiosity and put this awkward discussion to rest.

"Yes and no," she said. "But if it eases your mind, I didn't lie or steal. And when I left on my last day at work, my personnel file was unblemished. I wasn't fired or laid off, though. I actually quit. If they have any complaints about me as an employee, it's that I didn't give a proper notice."

He nodded, and before he could quiz her any further, she added, "Just so you'll feel better about hiring me and trusting me with your family business, I had a romance that went south rather suddenly, and I wanted to put as much distance between the two of us as I could. Brighton Valley is just a pit stop before I take off for good."

"I'm sorry," he said.

"About my breakup?"

"About quizzing you and making you feel uncomfortable. But for the record, I'm actually glad you left the guy and his memory behind."

A slight smile tugged at her lips, but she tried to tamp it down. All she needed was to lower her guard to the point of doing or saying something she'd regret. And if she'd learned anything out here in the moonlight, she was going to have to stay on her toes around a man like Jason Rayburn.

If he were like his brother, it wouldn't be an issue. She knew Braden as well as she knew anyone in Brighton Valley. His mother's family had been ranching in these parts for years. His grandfather was on the town council for a while. And his mom was involved in the women's auxiliary at the Wexler Community Church. He came from decent people. In fact, she often wondered what his mom had ever seen in his father—especially if what she'd heard about Charles Rayburn was true.

In spite of herself, Juliana risked another glance at Jason, watched him take a drink of his wine, then stare out into the night sky, where a full moon and a splatter of stars glistened overhead.

But the stars weren't the only things sparking. Her pregnancy hormones were surely coming into play and had to be triggering unwelcome romantic thoughts, which were totally inappropriate. She blamed it on her recent betrayal, the stillness of the evening and, yes, maybe a growing attraction.

For all those reasons, she couldn't continue to sit outside with him tonight. It could only lead to trouble—or at the very least, temptation.

She had a job to do—one that paid better than could be expected. And she intended to make the best of it.

Even if she didn't land an interview or a possible position with Rayburn Energy or Rayburn Enterprises, she could use a good recommendation, because she wasn't likely to get a very good one from the gallery.

In fact, after the details of her romance and breakup became known within local art circles—and they certainly could have by now—she knew better than to ask for any kind of reference at all.

Chapter Three

Juliana had lost track of how many sheep had jumped over her bed that night—surely a flock that would make a Basque sheepherder rich.

Blaming the two goblets of orange juice she'd drunk while on the porch with Jason for her need to get up every couple of hours, she gave up the struggle for sleep just after midnight. She remembered reading somewhere that warm milk might help, but there wasn't any in the refrigerator. Chamomile tea was another option, although she didn't recall seeing anything like that in the pantry.

A trip to the market was definitely in order, especially if she was going to do any more cooking while she was on the Rayburn ranch. Since she was wide-awake, she figured she might as well head to the kitchen and start a grocery list.

With that in mind, she rolled out of bed and pulled her robe from the closet. She didn't bother with slippers. As she took a moment to stroke the slight bulge of her womb, she pondered the phrase *barefoot and pregnant*.

How fitting was that?

As she opened the door, she noticed the light on in the den. Had Jason forgotten to turn it off when he went to bed?

She padded down the hall. When she turned into the doorway, she spotted him seated at the desk, glaring into the screen of his laptop. She studied him for a moment.

He'd run his fingers through his hair numerous times this evening. Yet even mussed, it didn't appear the least bit scruffy. Compliments of a highly paid stylist, no doubt.

He frowned as he stared at his laptop, his brow furrowed. Yet even the intensity of his expression didn't take away from his appeal.

She had no idea how long she stood there gazing at him, admiring his handsome profile, as well as his work ethic. A couple of minutes, she supposed.

Finally, he looked up and noticed her watching him in the doorway. "I'm sorry. Did I wake you?"

She smiled. "I never really went to sleep. What are you doing?"

"Problem solving. At least, that's what I'm trying to do. We're working on a marketing strategy that hasn't been coming together for us, and I've been racking my brain to figure out what's missing."

"I wish I could help."

"So do I, but the best brains at Rayburn Energy, including the head of the marketing department, haven't been able to agree on the best layout." He pushed away from the desk. "I'm not sure if I should put on a pot of coffee or call it a night."

"I'd think caffeine is the last thing you need right now."

He tossed her a boyish grin. "You're probably right. Too bad we don't have any ice cream or cookies."

"I'll put dessert on my grocery list. That is, if you want me to do any shopping for meals tomorrow."

"I hadn't thought that far ahead, but now that you mention it, I suppose we'll have to find time to eat during the day. I don't mind calling out for food, but if you want to pick up groceries, that's fine with me."

"We can play it by ear. But I'll whip up something for dinner tomorrow." She glanced at the clock and smiled. "Make that tonight. So what'll it be? Chocolate or vanilla?"

"If you're talking ice cream, let's go with rocky road. I like nuts."

"I'll keep that in mind as I start that list." She reached for the black leather cup on top of the desk that held pencils and pens. "Do you have any paper?"

He took a pad that rested near the laptop and handed it to her. "Here you go." Then he returned his gaze to the screen that had him so perplexed.

"Can I take a look at it?" she asked. "Maybe I can help."

Jason bit back a smile, which had been better than

the chuckle that almost slipped out. The problem had stymied experienced execs with MBAs. Juliana had no experience in the business world.

Okay, so she'd worked as a sales clerk at an art gallery in Wexler. But still, she didn't have the background that would provide her with the experience or the expertise she needed to actually know what she'd be looking for.

But what the hell.

He rolled back his chair, making room for her to see the screen. Then, using the mouse, he showed her the latest artwork and the graphics the marketing department had sent him earlier this evening.

"I see what you mean," she said. "Something's definitely missing. It doesn't have any spark."

She had that right. And while everyone knew something was missing, no one seemed to know quite what that something was.

"I think," she said, "if you merged the wording of number three with the graphics of number four, then used the background of number one, it would be a lot closer to what you're looking for."

"Maybe so," he said. "I'll give that some thought. Thanks."

As she stood beside him, he caught a whiff of her scent—something soft and exotic. He wasn't sure what he'd been expecting her to be wearing. Something down-home and country, he supposed. Something more suited to Brighton Valley. But then again, she was city bound. Why wouldn't she have a more sophisticated air? But did her scent come from her perfume or lotion? Or perhaps from her shampoo?

He glanced at her wild, bed-tousled curls, which gave her a sexy look that the frumpy cotton robe couldn't hide.

What a contradiction she seemed—country vs. city. Lady vs. vixen.

Once again, his attraction built to the point he found it impossible to downplay or ignore, especially at this late hour, with several bedrooms down the hall to choose from.

Unable to help himself, he reached out and twined a loose red curl around his finger. "Has anyone ever asked you if your hair color is real?"

She sucked in a breath, yet she didn't pull away. "Yes, they have. And it is."

"I know it's real. I remember you when you were a girl. It's just that the shade is so…remarkable. Most people might question whether it was possible for something that pretty to be natural."

Their gazes met and locked. For a moment, he could have sworn their breathing stopped.

Then she took a step back, and as her hair tightened against his finger, he let it uncoil.

While he might have released their physical connection, something else held them taut. Something he could almost reach out and touch.

She bit down on her bottom lip, then placed her hand over her stomach. He'd seen her make that nervous gesture before, which seemed to be unique to her. Other women nibbled a nail or twisted a strand of hair around a finger seductively. But he'd never seen another stroke her belly.

He found it kind of cute—the gesture, as well as the fact that he made her nervous.

She took another step back, clearly uncomfortable with the heat sparking between them, and nodded toward the doorway. "I'm going to start that grocery list now. And then I'll try to get some sleep. Otherwise I won't be worth a thing tomorrow."

He sensed that she was the kind of woman who'd be worth her weight in gold—either as an employee or a lover. But he damn well couldn't have her as both. So he let her go.

As he heard her bare feet pad down the hardwood floor, he glanced back at the screen, which displayed the artwork the head of marketing had sent him. He tried to imagine the changes Juliana had mentioned, realizing they did have some merit.

The woman might not have a business background, but she did have some experience with art—if you could give her points for working at what had to be a two-bit gallery in a town that wasn't much bigger than Brighton Valley.

After giving her suggestion some thought, he shrank the screen and signed into his email account.

Doug,
Do me a favor. Try using the background on number 1. Then merge the text of sample 3 with the graphics on 4. Let me see what that looks like.
Jason

Then he hit Send. He wasn't an artist, so he'd have to see the sample to know if it would work the way Juliana seemed to think it would. But it certainly sounded as though it might be a lot closer to what they were looking for.

If that was true, Juliana would have more than paid for her keep already. Of course, it was early yet. They still had a ranch full of memories to pore through.

And less than three weeks to do it.

In spite of getting very little sleep last night, Jason woke early and started breakfast. By the time Juliana walked in, freshly showered and ready to start the day, the coffee had finished brewing and the bacon sizzled in Granny's favorite cast-iron skillet.

"Something sure smells good," she said. "I thought you weren't a cook."

"I'm not, but I was a Boy Scout. So some things are easy. But I'm usually better frying bacon on a campfire." He tossed her a smile. "I'm also good at making s'mores."

She laughed, which lent a flush of pink to her cheeks and lit a glimmer in her caramel-colored eyes.

Damn, she was pretty—even casually dressed in blue jeans and a blouse she hadn't taken the time to tuck in, the bottom button still undone.

"Besides," he added, "I didn't want you to think that you going to starve while living out in the boondocks. And the truth is, I'm pretty good at fixing breakfast."

"That reminds me," she said, "I'll need to make a

grocery run sometime today. That is, unless you want to do it."

He reached into his pocket, withdrew his wallet and peeled out several hundred dollars. "Will this cover whatever you have on the list you made?"

"That'll be more than enough." She folded the bills in half, then tucked them into the front pocket of her jeans. "My plan is to get started with the inventory and packing. Then I'll take a break and go to the market sometime this afternoon."

"That sounds good to me." He nodded toward the coffeepot. "It just finished brewing. Would you like a cup?"

"No, thanks. I'll finish the orange juice instead."

He pulled the OJ from the fridge. Then he emptied the carton into a glass he withdrew from the cupboard and handed it to her. "You'll have to add juice to that list."

"Will do." She turned and moved about the kitchen, taking time to check out the scarred oak table and chairs, as well as the various plaques, pictures and cross-stitch hangings with upbeat sayings Granny had used to adorn the walls.

Jason hadn't wanted to spend any more time in this room than he had to. If he wasn't careful, it would be too easy to become nostalgic and reflective here, mostly because he could almost feel Granny, could still hear her speaking to him, especially with so many of her favorite sayings nearby.

He glanced over his shoulder at Juliana. She was looking closely at a decoupage plaque. He couldn't actually read the words, but he knew what that one said. It was a Bible verse.

He hadn't meant to memorize it, but for some reason, it had stuck with him for years and he'd never forgotten it. He probably never would.

Granny had pointed it out to him the day before he'd left for prep school in California. She'd said she had claimed that particular proverb as God's promise to her. For that reason, she said that she knew Jason, unlike his father, would grow up to be his own man. And that he'd always choose to do what was right and true.

For a moment, Jason thought Juliana might read it out loud. She didn't, though. Yet she didn't have to. He could almost hear Granny saying it to him again. *Train up a child in the way he should go, and when he is old he will not depart from it.* Proverbs 22:6.

Still, Juliana continued to study it, as if pondering the wisdom of it.

"Did you know my great-grandmother?" he asked.

Juliana turned to him and smiled. "Just about everyone in Brighton Valley did. She was a warm and caring woman. I think she was a lifetime member of the PTA, even though she hadn't had a child in school for ages. She was also very involved in the Brighton Valley Community Church. When my mom was recovering from surgery, she and a couple other ladies brought meals to the house on a regular basis."

"What about when Granny was sick? Before she died. Did anyone from the church bring meals to her?"

"I'm not sure. As far as I know, she kept her illness to herself."

Jason certainly hadn't heard a peep from her about any ailments. But then again, she'd never been one to complain. Her doctor must have known something, though. "You don't think she told anyone how sick she was?"

"No, I don't think so."

Still, her family should have been aware of it. And they should have done something—visited more. At the very least, one of them should have been with her at the end so she didn't have to die alone.

A stab of guilt shot through him. Had she thought that her family hadn't come through for her like they should have?

More importantly, had she thought Jason hadn't?

Sure, he'd called regularly and sent money. He also had made a point to come to visit on Christmas and her birthday. Not always on the actual day, but close enough to count.

At least, he'd always thought so. But now, standing in her kitchen, surrounded by her furnishings, by her memory, he wasn't so sure.

Juliana moved on to the far corner of the kitchen, where Jason and Carly had set the boxes and the painting that belonged to Braden.

"What's this?" she asked. "Did you get sidetracked and leave this stuff here?"

"Actually, that can stay where it is. It belongs to my brother. He's supposed to come for it when he gets back from Mexico."

She reached for the painting, a Southwestern style of an old church at night, with a crescent moon and bright stars overhead.

"This is very good," she said.

"Yes, I suppose you're right. But I've never been a huge fan of that particular style. I do like the bright colors, though. It would look good in a ranch-style home."

That's probably why Braden had bought it. Jason returned his focus to the bacon, removing the last strip from the pan and turning off the flame.

"Wow," Juliana said. "That's weird."

Jason turned and leaned his hip against the kitchen counter, the tongs still in his hand. "What is?"

"It was painted by Camilla Cruz."

At that, he set the utensil down, turned away from the stove and made his way across the kitchen to the oak table, where Juliana had placed the painting to get a better look.

"The same artist who did Granny's portrait?" Jason asked.

"Yes. The signature is the same. See?"

He leaned in closer to take a better look at the script. "That's really strange."

"I wonder who she is."

So did Jason. Obviously, Granny and Braden both knew her. Or at least one of them did. "Maybe you were wrong about her not being a local artist."

"I suppose she could be," Juliana said.

She seemed to think that she was an art expert, but

Jason wasn't convinced. After all, she'd only worked at a gallery in a relatively small town—and for just a couple of years at most. She was lovely, though.

As she leaned closer, her head angled next to his, her exotic scent snaking around him, he was willing to concede any credentials she wanted to claim.

She glanced closer at the delicate script of the signature. "It's a Hispanic surname. Do you think it has anything to do with why Braden went to Mexico?"

"No, I doubt it. This is Texas. A lot of people have Hispanic surnames. I'm sure Braden is in Mexico because he's following my dad's trail."

Juliana straightened, taking her scent with her.

"Are you sure my brother never mentioned anything to you about where he was going or why?" Jason asked.

"Sorry. I haven't talked to him lately."

Jason glanced at the box of pottery, as well as the other box that had been sealed shut with packing tape. If his brother had been missing in Mexico, with foul play suspected, he would have had every right to tear into the cardboard lid and try to solve the mystery of Braden's whereabouts. But as far as he knew, his brother was alive and on some international escapade, the details of which he'd either neglected or flat-out refused to share with Jason.

And the fact that he was so completely out of the loop didn't sit well with Jason at all. And it only seemed to make the chasm between the two brothers deeper than ever.

* * *

"Are you going to make me eat dinner alone?"

Jason glanced up from the work he'd spread all over the desk in the den and to the doorway, where Juliana stood, her red curls swept into a sexy topknot.

Yet as his gaze traveled from her pretty hair and face to her kissable lips, his eyes and his hormones were thwarted by one of Granny's full-size aprons, a red-checkered background printed with green apples.

If there was something to be said about Juliana Bailey, she was certainly an unpredictable novelty. Yet the contradictions she presented still drove his libido crazy.

"Aren't you hungry?" she asked.

She was talking about food, and while she had him thinking about a different kind of hunger, he realized his stomach had been empty for hours. "Yes, I guess I am."

"Good. I set a table out on the back porch. I decided you need to get outside for some fresh air. You've been cooped up in the house all day."

So she'd taken it upon herself to look after him, huh? "What time is it?"

"Nearly seven o'clock. And definitely time for a break. Something tells me that if I didn't keep an eye on the clock, you'd continue to work until your stomach put up a fuss."

A grin stretched across his lips. "Isn't that how most people know when it's time to eat?"

"I suspect those who get ulcers do, but I have a little more self-awareness than that. Have you always been like this?"

"As far as I can remember."

"Even as a kid? Were you the last one to come in at night for meals?"

His smile deepened as he recalled the days when he'd lived on the Leaning R. "Granny used to have to ring an old cowbell."

"What about after you left the ranch? Who reminded you to eat then? Who took care of you?"

His smile faded. "The cafeteria workers at prep school—and the other staff. Mostly I was lucky enough to fend for myself."

She tossed him a skeptical smile, then rose and headed to the kitchen, the apron bow hanging along her swaying hips and taunting him until she disappeared out the door.

Maybe he hadn't always done the best job of hiding his needs or his loneliness as a kid, but he'd grown up and he'd survived. All in all, it had been for the best, because that's how he'd learned to become strong and self-sufficient.

He shut down the laptop, tidied up his files, then headed down the hall. Moments later, he caught the whiff of a familiar aroma. At least, he thought it was. If he didn't know better, he'd think that Granny was whipping up a batch of her Swedish meatballs.

Before Juliana could remind him to go outside to the table she'd set, he followed the smell to the kitchen, where he found her standing in front of the stove and preparing to spoon the meal from a pot into a serving bowl.

"What are you doing?" he asked.

She turned and smiled, her golden-brown eyes glimmering. "I found some of your great-grandmother's old recipes this morning, and while thumbing through them, I saw that she'd made notes on them." She lifted the worn and stained card that had been resting on the countertop. "This one says, 'Jason's favorite. Serve with noodles and green beans.' So I checked in the pantry and made a list of everything else I would need to surprise you."

She certainly had.

"This is amazing," he said. "*You're* amazing. I don't know what to say."

She smiled and turned completely around, her back to the stove and countertop. "You don't have to say anything."

But he did. And a simple thank-you wasn't enough. Employees often bought him a bottle of scotch or bourbon for Christmas. A lover might buy him an expensive dress shirt and silk tie. Or maybe tickets to a show *she'd* been wanting to see. But no one ever had gone out of his or her way to surprise him in such a heartwarming way. No one except Granny, anyway.

The fact that Juliana had no reason to do it stroked something deep inside him, and without any conscious thought, he closed the gap between them.

As his gaze locked on hers, his expression must have been pretty intense because she asked, "Is something wrong?"

"No, not at all." He'd just realized that her beauty went far deeper than her flaming hair and golden-brown eyes.

When they were just inches apart, he reached up and ran his knuckles along her cheek. Her breath caught, yet she didn't flinch.

"This is one of the nicest things anyone has done for me in a long time," he said.

She offered him a crooked grin, as if trying to downplay her thoughtful gesture. "You haven't tasted it yet. I might have missed a step or skipped an ingredient. It probably won't taste at all like you remember."

"It's the thought that counts."

She didn't step back, but then again, he supposed she couldn't, because he had her backed up against the counter. She brushed a loose curl from her brow, broke eye contact and gave a little shrug. "I just did it on a whim. It was no big deal."

"Maybe not to you, but it feels like a big deal to me."

At that, he snagged her gaze again, and whatever it was that drew him to her seemed to be affecting her the same way, because her lips parted.

And for some crazy reason he might regret later, he lowered his mouth to hers.

Chapter Four

The minute their lips met, Juliana knew she should turn her head and push Jason away. Yet she couldn't help herself and leaned forward and accepted his kiss as if she didn't have a care in the world.

How could she form a single thought, or voice a protest, when her head was spinning from the scent of his woodsy cologne and the sweet taste of his breath as his mouth opened and his tongue sought hers?

When his arms tightened around her and his hands slipped up and down her back, he nipped at her bottom lip, and she all but melted into a puddle on the floor.

Within a heartbeat, the kiss exploded with a passion she hadn't expected, and her common sense—what was left of it—scrambled to take control of her addled brain.

Jason Rayburn was her employer, for goodness' sake. And even if the two of them were willing to overlook that simple little fact, there was another little something she'd better not overlook—a little *someone*.

She splayed her hands on his chest, felt his heart pounding under her fingertips as she pushed against him. Then she finally turned her face and tore her lips from his.

Her ragged breath betrayed her conscience when she tried to offer an explanation for why she'd let him kiss her in the first place, not to mention allowing it to go. "I'm sorry. I don't know what I was thinking. That was completely inappropriate."

"You're probably right, but you have to admit, it was pretty nice."

"Maybe so, but I don't want you to get the wrong idea." She nearly tacked on *about me*. But she left it off, figuring he could make whatever leap he wanted. That he was wrong about her, about what the kiss might mean, about where any of this might be headed.

A boyish grin slid across his face. "I agree that we probably shouldn't get involved, but there's definitely some strong chemistry going on between us."

She took a step to the side, putting more space between them than the counter at her back allowed. "We have a lot of work to get done in a short period of time. So we need to stay on track."

"You're right." He studied her for a beat, then turned toward the stove. "Dinner smells delicious. Would you like me to set the table?"

She ought to be relieved that he seemed to have

put the kiss behind him so easily, but it left her a bit uneasy—and maybe even envious, since she wasn't sure she could do the same thing.

And she'd been right. All during the meal, she'd fought the urge to study the man seated across from her.

As he dug into the Swedish meatballs and noodles, he complimented her several times, completely glossing over the amazing kiss they'd shared just minutes before. Yet here she sat, her cheeks still warm and no doubt flushed.

But just because she'd been swept away momentarily by the unexpected kiss didn't mean she would let it happen again—or that she'd complicate her life with a man right now.

Jason had no more than dished up a second helping of meatballs over noodles when he said, "You have no idea how much I appreciate you fixing this meal. It was always my favorite—and one I never expected to taste again. To thank you, I'd like to take you out to dinner on Saturday night. There's a little Italian restaurant that just opened up downtown. I'm not sure how it's going to compete with Caroline's Diner, but it's only open for dinner. And it's probably a little too fancy for most of the Brighton Valley locals."

"You don't owe me anything." Juliana lifted her napkin and blotted her mouth as if she could block her thoughts from coming out. Surely, he wasn't asking her out on a date. But that had to be what he was doing. Hadn't he listened to a word she'd said? She didn't want to get involved with him—or with anyone.

Of course, neither did she want to jeopardize her temporary job—and a lucrative one at that—by putting up too many flashing red lights and roadblocks, especially when she'd kissed him back in a way that could only have been taken as a full-on green light. No wonder he sensed a contradiction.

"I'm afraid all my clothes have been packed in storage," she said. "I only brought jeans and casual tops. I don't have anything the least bit fancy, so going out to dinner isn't an option. Besides, if you feel like providing a meal in return, why don't you just pick up a pizza and bring it home one night?"

"I suppose I could do that."

She forced one of her best bright-eyed smiles, then focused on her plate, doing her best to ignore the romantic ambience she hadn't meant to set into motion.

Romantic ambience? Here on Granny's back porch?

Not that there was anything wrong with the cozy quarters, but there weren't any candles or flowers or music. The only thing remotely romantic was the thudding beat of Juliana's heart.

And the lingering memory of a heated kiss she wasn't likely to ever forget.

After they'd washed and put away the dinner dishes, something Jason again helped Juliana do, he asked if she'd like to return to the porch for coffee, a glass of wine, juice or…whatever.

"I'd like to," she said, "but I didn't get much sleep last night, so I want to turn in early. And since I have a doctor's appointment in town tomorrow afternoon,

I'm going to set my alarm clock so I can make up those hours first thing in the morning. I hope to get started on packing the hutch in the dining room—unless you'd rather I started somewhere else."

"No, that's fine." He wondered if she was only making an excuse to put some distance between them and their obvious attraction, but he decided it was best to let it drop. He needed her help with the inventory. He also knew better than to get romantically involved with an employee. His father had made that mistake once, only to be slapped with a charge of sexual harassment. The lawsuit had resulted in a lengthy litigation and a large settlement, a mistake Jason had no intention of repeating. But then again, his old man had probably been guilty as charged, and this situation seemed completely different.

Trouble was, now that Jason had kissed Juliana, he didn't know what to do about it. He'd have to do something, though. A man didn't just ignore a smoking-hot kiss with a beautiful redhead and write it off as if it hadn't happened.

Besides, ignoring the whole thing had damn near killed him during dinner, especially when her rosy cheeks let him know she'd been thinking about it, too.

Still, as Juliana left the kitchen and headed to her room, it was way too early for Jason to turn in. He didn't feel like watching television or holing up in the den, just steps away from where she'd be lying in bed. So he walked through the living room and headed out to the front porch, where the stars sparkled overhead and a somber country-and-western tune filled the night air.

He made his way to the wooden railing and peered at the small guesthouse, where the sole ranch hand, Ian McAllister, sat outside in one of two chairs, his guitar in his lap, his fingers strumming the strings.

Years ago, Reuben Montoya had been the foreman on the Leaning R and had done a fine job of running things. Then about five years ago, there'd been a family emergency, and Reuben had had to return to his home-town, a small village located somewhere near the coast in Baja California. Granny had hired several different men to take his place, but she'd had to let each one go because they'd fallen short of the benchmark Reuben had set. Finally, she'd taken on Ian. From what she'd said several times, Ian had pleased her. "He's got an inborn skill at ranching," she'd said, "and a way with sick or injured critters that's pert near better than any vet I've ever seen."

But when Granny passed, the Leaning R ownership had transferred to Jason's father, who hadn't made any secret that the ranch wasn't a priority to him. He could have given Ian free rein to make a go of things, but for some reason, he'd refused to even consider it. In fact, he hadn't even allowed Ian to hire on any new hands whenever one of the men quit and went on to work for other spreads. And without any qualified cowboys to help him, Ian had been limited to what he could do alone.

Jason was surprised the man had stuck around this long. But then again, he was a cowboy. And those guys had an interesting code of honor, even the younger ones in their midthirties, like Ian.

If Jason were inclined to turn things completely around, he'd let Ian see what he could do with the place. But Granny had wanted at least one family member to live on the ranch and oversee things. And that wasn't likely to happen. Braden had his own place ten miles down the road, Carly was dead set on building a singing career to surpass that of her mother's and Jason wasn't about to set down roots in Brighton Valley. His corporations were based in Houston—and so was his life.

As Ian's haunting melody filled the summer night, Jason swore under his breath. It was too early and too nice of an evening for him and Ian to be outside by themselves, bogged down by melancholy thoughts or sad music. So he strode into the kitchen, grabbed a couple of longneck beers from the fridge and crossed the yard.

When he reached the patch of lawn in front of Ian's place, the music echoed to a slow stop, and the cowboy glanced up. "What's up, boss?"

"I thought you might like a beer and some company. If not, I can leave the drink and go on my way."

Ian tossed him a lopsided grin. "I rarely drink these days." Then he took the Corona and nodded at the empty chair beside him. "But singing makes me thirsty and lonely. So thanks. And have a seat."

Jason didn't normally come out looking for Ian after dark. Nor did he have time to make chitchat. When they did talk, it was to line Ian out for the day or to get his opinion about something to make the ranch more valuable to a buyer. But for the most part, there'd been so much going on at both Rayburn offices that Jason had let Ian continue to handle most of the daily ranch decisions on his own.

"I owe you an apology," Jason said. "Not only have I done very little to help you, but I haven't gotten around to hiring those extra men I promised."

"I can find a couple of hands. All you have to do is say the word."

Jason took a swig of his beer. "I'll make it a priority tomorrow, although I may not get to it until mid-morning."

"No problem." Ian tilted his own bottle and took a drink.

But that didn't assuage Jason's guilt. The man had been shouldering a lot for the past year. Yet he hadn't complained.

"If you're going into town," Ian said, "I have a few supplies that need to be picked up at the feed store."

"Will do."

The two men sat like that for a while—like drinking buddies mellowing out after a hard day's work. Yet they weren't buddies. They weren't…anything.

In fact, Ian probably knew Braden a hell of a lot better than he knew Jason, since they were both locals and ranchers. They had a lot more in common.

Had Ian been making comparisons between the half brothers?

The fact that he might have—and that Jason might have come up short—didn't sit well. And while Jason hadn't actually planned to come out here and strike up a friendship or to quiz the guy, neither seemed to be bad ideas now.

"I hear my brother is in Mexico," Jason said.

"Is that right?"

Didn't Ian know where Braden had gone? Or was he trying to avoid an inquisition?

"I figure he's got a good reason," Jason added, just in case Ian thought he was being set up. "And that he'll clue me in when the time is right."

"He didn't mention anything to me," Ian said.

For some reason, Jason believed him.

So much for the theory that the two Brighton Valley men were tight.

Ian, who'd been balancing his guitar in his lap, set the instrument down. "How's your sister doing?"

"Carly? She has a singing gig in San Antonio, so she's pretty excited about that."

"Glad to hear it. Maybe this is her big chance."

Jason wondered how Ian knew Carly. But then again, his sister had come by to visit regularly while Granny was still alive. And she still dropped by to check on the place occasionally. Apparently, Ian did more talking to Carly than he did to Braden. But Braden was so damned tight-lipped, and Carly...well, she'd sure been a jabber box, at least when she was a kid.

A grin tugged at his lips. He remembered the day when she and Bird Legs had come in from the swimming hole. They'd been all whispers and giggles back then. Juliana sure had changed, hadn't she?

His thoughts drifted from the past back to the present. Damn. Who would have guessed that the gangly little girl would have grown up to be such a shapely beauty?

He glanced at the house, at the window of the room that had once been Granny's, and watched the light go out. So she really was going to hit the sack early.

Had she heard Ian playing the guitar? Would the music lull her to sleep? The tune had certainly had a mesmerizing effect. He wondered what the words were.

"That was a nice song you were playing earlier," Jason told the foreman. "I don't think I've ever heard it before. Not that I'm a country fan these days. Is it a new recording or one that's been out for a while?"

"Actually, I wrote it myself."

"No kidding?"

Ian shrugged. "It's just a cowboy lullaby to put the little dogies to sleep."

"I'm no expert, but it sounded good to me. You probably shouldn't waste your talent on a bunch of cows."

Ian didn't comment. He just lifted his longneck and took another drink.

Had Carly ever heard him play? If so, had she encouraged him to do something with his music? Not that it mattered. Ian obviously liked being a cowboy and was content to play for himself. And Carly wanted to be on a stage. They had different dreams, different life paths.

Jason glanced at the house, where the porch light cast an amber glow, while Granny's bedroom remained dark. His and Juliana's paths had merged temporarily, but they'd soon go in opposite directions, too, just as Ian's and Carly's had.

But they were together for the time being…

Jason avoided commitments and anything long-term. You certainly couldn't blame him for that. Hell, just look at his father's track record.

Of course, that didn't mean he was opposed to a one-on-one relationship as long as it remained mutually beneficial. And right now, Jason was between lovers.

So was Juliana.

He might have made it a point not to get involved with employees or business associates, but Juliana was only a temporary hire.

Would it be wrong to see what developed between them—for as long as it lasted?

Jason had planned to run into town before lunch, but as luck—and the home office—would have it, he didn't get a chance to leave until after two o'clock.

As he was heading out of the house, he didn't spot Juliana in either the living room or the kitchen. He suspected she was getting ready for her doctor's appointment, so he left without telling her goodbye.

Although he would have preferred to stick around and finish the last project he'd been working on, he'd promised Ian he would hire some help, and he didn't want to let him down. So he snatched his hat from the hook by the back door, grabbed the keys to the ranch pickup and took off.

His first stop was Lone Star Hay and Feed, which had once been owned by Del Grimwood. Apparently the man had retired a few years back and sold the business. So Jason introduced himself to the new owner, a middle-aged man named Paco Ramirez.

He'd just hit End on a business call that hadn't gone well when he spoke, so his words came out a little more abrupt than he'd meant them to. "My father was Charles Rayburn, and his grandmother, Rosabelle, owned the Leaning R. I'm in charge now, so I've been staying out there—temporarily."

Paco shifted his stance, then crossed his arms. "I thought the world of your great-grandmother, and I knew your father. I went to high school with him. I also know Braden and his mother's family well. But just so you know, I judge a man by his character—not his bloodlines."

Jason hadn't meant to come across as high-and-mighty, but before he could apologize and tell the man he'd had his mind on his other business issues, Paco added, "Your father may be highly respected in California and in the business world where he once ran, but his reputation in this neck of the woods wasn't much to shout about. But I won't hold that against you—just like I didn't hold it against your brother."

Had his father left that bad of an impression on the townspeople?

Jason always figured his father had considered Brighton Valley to be a Podunk town that he'd outgrown. But did it have more to do with the fact that he'd gotten Braden's mother pregnant while he'd been married to Jason's mom?

That must have been a scandal that tarnished his

reputation, although he'd never missed a child support payment, as far as Jason had been told.

"I'm sorry, Mr. Ramirez. I didn't mean to be rude or to give you the wrong impression. Rest assured, I'm not like my father."

"I'm glad to hear that," Paco said. "What can I do for you?"

"I'm looking for some temporary hands on the Leaning R. Do you know anyone who'd be interested?"

Paco stroked his chin. "Does Ian still work for you?"

"Yes, and I need to find help for him."

"In that case, my oldest boy is looking for a summer job. He's only seventeen, but he's strong, a good worker and knows cattle and horses."

"Great. When can he start?"

"Tomorrow morning, I suspect."

"I'll tell Ian to expect him. What's his name?"

"Jesse."

Jason lifted his hat and readjusted it on his head. "Do you mind if I post an ad on your bulletin board?"

"No, go ahead. I'll keep my ears open, too. Temporary help isn't always as easy to find as a permanent position. But just so you know, Jesse's friends are all football players. They're good kids—strong, too. And they're not afraid of hard work. They're probably your best bet."

"Thanks. You might be right about that. Maybe your son could round up his buddies and bring them out to the ranch. I'd really appreciate it, and I know Ian would, too." Jason reached into his hip pocket and pulled out the list Ian had given him. "I also need to pick up these things while I'm here."

Twenty minutes later, he'd paid Paco and loaded the last of the sacks and boxes into the back of the ranch pickup. Then he was on his way into town.

His next stop was Nettles Realty, a small office on the shady, tree-lined main drag. He pulled into an empty parking stall near the drugstore, then crossed the street and entered the bright red door of the only real estate agent in town.

Granny had been friends with Helen, Ralph's wife. She used to work with him, but she'd gotten sick about the time Granny died. She was better now, but from what Jason had heard, Helen remained at home these days and Ralph worked alone.

Ralph was close to eighty years old and probably should have retired a long time ago, but he often quipped that he was no quitter. He was still spry and sharp. He also knew the area better than anyone else.

Jason greeted the snowy-haired gentleman who sat at a big oak desk cluttered with files and stacks of paper with a handshake. "I'm Jason Rayburn, Ralph. We talked on the phone a couple of days ago."

"Good to see you, son." The old man got to his feet. "I'm glad to get the listing, although I'm sorry to see the Leaning R sold. That ranch has been in your family for years."

A pang of guilt twisted Jason's gut. Harold and Molly Rayburn, Granny's in-laws, had been newlyweds when they'd homesteaded the land. They'd raised a family there. At least, they'd tried to. Harold and two of their children had died of the Spanish influenza early in the twentieth century. Dave, the only surviving child, had inherited the Leaning R and married Granny.

But Jason shook off his discomfort and pressed on. "The place isn't ready to show any prospective buyers yet, but I hope to have it clean, emptied and close to presentable within the next two weeks."

"What are you going to do with the furniture?"

"I have a woman helping me inventory it. Whatever Braden and Carly don't want, I plan to sell."

"Some of those things are antiques," Ralph said. "They might actually make the house show better, so keep that in mind."

"All right." After thanking the real estate agent for his time, Jason left. As he stepped out onto the sidewalk, the hearty aroma of Italian sausage, tomatoes, basil and garlic taunted him, and he glanced to the right at Maestro's, the new restaurant he'd wanted to try. A man in black slacks and a white dress shirt was spreading white linen over the black wrought-iron patio tables in preparation for the diners who preferred to eat outdoors.

Before Jason could cross the street and head toward the space where he'd parked his truck, a woman exited a store to the right. He didn't pay her any mind, but he did catch a glimpse of the mannequin in the window display of the Mercantile, the only dress shop in this part of town. It modeled a sexy black dress that was both formfitting and sleek.

An idea struck, and a smile spread across his face.

Juliana had mentioned that she didn't have anything suitable to wear to an eatery like Maestro's. What if he bought the dress for her as a surprise? He could call it a bonus. And he'd tell her the dinner was in celebration of getting a price for the ranch and finding a listing agent.

He wasn't sure of her size, but his sister had mentioned once that she was a six. And they were about the same height and shape.

What the hell.

Ten minutes later, a sales clerk who knew Carly and believed Jason was making the purchase for her had rung up the dress and placed it in a plastic bag with the Mercantile logo. After draping it over his arm, he left the store. He probably should have taken it to the pickup, but instead, he carried it with him to Maestro's, where he made dinner reservations for next Saturday evening at seven o'clock.

And speaking of dinner, since Juliana had a doctor's appointment, cooking wouldn't be on her to-do list today. So Jason would just stop by Caroline's Diner and pick up something to take home.

Rather than head to his truck first, he decided to place the order and then put away the dress while he was waiting for the food to cook.

It seemed simple enough, especially since Caroline's was just another couple of doors down from the Mercantile. Once inside the diner, he figured he'd make it quick by ordering the daily special, which Caroline displayed on a chalkboard near the register at the door. She always listed the offering as "What the Sheriff

Ate." Today it read: fried chicken, mashed potatoes and gravy, sweet corn and peach cobbler à la mode.

Jason placed the order with a middle-aged brunette waitress whose name tag read Margie.

"I know the special offers mashed potatoes," Margie said, "but you can have French fries if you'd rather."

He gave it some thought before asking, "What do you suggest?"

Margie leaned against the counter and grinned, clearly happy to offer her opinion. "Most folks prefer the mashed potatoes. It's a house specialty since Caroline always makes her gravy from scratch. But I wanted to let you know there was an option."

He tossed her a smile. "I'll go with the local preference."

"You won't be sorry. And how 'bout I just send the peach cobbler for dessert? I don't think the ice cream will travel too well. But if you have any back at the ranch, it'll be a nice finishing touch."

"When I used to come here as a kid, I always chose the German chocolate cake. I don't suppose Caroline has any of that today."

"You're in luck. We've got a couple of slices left." Margie jotted down his order. "It shouldn't take too long to get this ready. Why don't you have a seat?"

The door swung open before Jason had a chance to acknowledge Margie's words or tell her he'd be back in a few minutes. He glanced over his shoulder as Juliana walked in, her hair long and glossy, the curls dancing over her shoulders.

He didn't know who was more surprised to see the

other, but it was all he could do to hide the logo on the plastic bag that announced he'd been shopping at the ladies' store down the street.

Juliana had just left the doctor's office and stopped by the diner to pick up her last paycheck. But when she spotted Jason, her breath caught and her knees nearly buckled.

She'd known he'd gone to town, but she hadn't expected to run into him at Caroline's.

"Hey," he said, all decked out in cowboy casual, his thumbs tucked into the front pockets of his jeans. "It looks like you had the same idea I did."

"What was that?"

"To pick up dinner to take home. But I beat you to it." He smiled, which sent her heart skittering through her chest like a cat chasing its own tail. "How did your doctor's appointment go?"

"Doctor's appointment?" Margie asked. "You were just at the doctor a while back, Juliana. It couldn't have been two or three weeks ago. Is something wrong?"

A response wadded up in Juliana's throat.

Jason glanced at her, then at Margie. The poor guy had no idea that the sweet but gossipy waitress, like a Brighton Valley Lois Lane, had been listening to their conversation. And that she was ready to take note of every single word she'd heard and add her own spin to it.

But Juliana knew she'd better steer the subject in a safer direction before Margie began connecting dots and spreading her assumptions.

"My last visit to the clinic was a month ago, Margie. And this was just a recheck. Everything's fine."

Margie cocked her head, and her grip on the pencil seemed to raise and tighten. "What was the doctor rechecking?"

"It was…uh…sinus infection. All clear now." Juliana flushed and lowered her eyes. Doggone it. She considered honesty a virtue even more than most people, but now she had to add liar to her sinful résumé.

She placed her hand on her tummy, which she realized only served to draw attention to the growing bump. Then she let her fingers trail to her side and down along her thigh. As she did so, she stole a peek at Jason, wondering if he'd heard the deceit in her voice or spotted the guilty flush on her cheeks.

Instead, he seemed to be fiddling with the plastic shopping bag he'd rolled around his arm. Was he hiding something of his own?

Guilt was a funny thing, wasn't it? It seemed to make one suspicious of others.

"Well," she said. "There isn't any reason for us both to hang around and wait for the food. I think I'd better head back to the ranch. I got so much work done earlier today that I don't want to lose my momentum."

Nor did she want to stick around in Brighton Valley until Margie and everyone else in town uncovered the secret she was trying so hard to hide.

Chapter Five

Juliana continued to inventory the household items for the next several days. Jason helped when he could, but he spent the mornings in the office dealing with issues having to do with either Rayburn Energy or Enterprises.

Quite frankly, it was difficult for her to keep the two entities separate—especially when she wasn't privy to any of his telephone conversations and he rarely confided in her, anyway. At least, he hadn't since that first night when she'd made some suggested changes to the artwork his marketing department had been considering.

After eating a sandwich for lunch, he often went out onto the ranch to help Ian and several teenagers who'd come to work repairing the barn, the corrals and one of the outbuildings. The Ramirez boy and his friends were doing a good job. Both Ian and Jason seemed pleased with them.

In the evenings, Juliana cooked dinner, which Jason appreciated. At least, he complimented her on her efforts and asked for seconds. He also invited her to join him on the porch afterward. But ever since that heated kiss, she'd found one excuse or another to avoid being alone with him.

The only problem was, she was getting tired of going to her bedroom early each night and looking—and feeling—like a hermit. After all, sparks aside, she did enjoy his company. Maybe she could just…ignore those feelings in favor of some good old-fashioned conversation by starlight.

So tonight, after dinner, when he asked if she'd like to go out onto the porch, she finally agreed.

It must have surprised him because he broke into a smile. "That's great. But before we do, I have something I want to give you."

Now it was her turn to be surprised. "What is it?"

"Wait here."

When he disappeared through the doorway into the main part of the house, she pulled out a kitchen chair and took a seat at the antique oak table.

He returned before she knew it with a long plastic bag covering what had to be an article of clothing, because it hung from a coat hanger. It also had to be the same thing he'd been carrying when she'd run into him at Caroline's Diner.

"What's that?" she asked.

"A bonus for all the hard work you've done."

Her head tilted slightly to the side. "I don't understand."

He handed it to her. "Take it out."

She reached for the hanger and noted the Mercantile logo. He'd apparently purchased something for her, and she had no idea how to respond. But she probably ought to look inside before saying anything. So she removed the plastic, revealing a stylish black cocktail dress, a slinky, formfitting number that would have looked amazing if she still had a waistline. But there was no way it would possibly fit now. And even if it would, she couldn't accept it.

"I talked to Ralph Nettles about my plan to sell the ranch," he said, "and even though it isn't officially listed yet, I want to celebrate by going out to dinner tomorrow night—at Maestro's."

The gift and the invitation to help him celebrate jumbled her thoughts and robbed her of speech.

"Since you didn't have anything suitable to wear," he added, "I picked this up for you. Consider it a bonus for a job well done."

Was he serious?

A sweet but cocky grin suggested he was. And while his motives might be genuine and sincere, they reeked of those of the once-charming Alex Montgomery, the art dealer who'd swept into the gallery one day, set his sights on her, promising her the moon, then left her holding a handful of lies.

"I'm sorry." She passed the dress back to him. "I can't accept this. And I won't go out to dinner with you, either. I don't feel right about socializing with a coworker or an employer."

His grin faded, and an expression of remorse took its place. "I'm the one who's sorry. I didn't mean to offend you—or to come on too strong. I find you attractive, Juliana, and I wanted to spend some time with you away from work, away from the ranch. I'd like to get to know you better. But I don't want you to feel awkward or uncomfortable about it."

She bit down on her bottom lip, believing the first person to learn her secret should be her mother, but wondering if her new boss deserved a better explanation than the response she'd just given him.

"It's not what you're thinking," she said. "There's more to it than that."

A boyish grin, this one more confident than cocky, slid back into place. "You mean I didn't offend you or come on too strong?"

"No, I'm...flattered."

His smile deepened, and he moved forward.

She lifted her right hand to slow him down—or rather, to fend him off. "I'm pregnant."

He took a step back, as if she might be contagious, and she nearly laughed. In fact, she might have if a flood of tears hadn't filled her eyes to overflowing.

"Oh, jeez, Juliana. I'm sorry. Now I'm the one who feels awkward."

She might have let the chuckles flow, hoping to get some control over the emotions that had been bubbling inside her for the past four and a half months. But there really wasn't anything funny about it—other than the adorable look of utter embarrassment on the gorgeous CEO's face.

"Besides my doctor, you're the first in town to learn the news. I plan to tell my mother next, although the fact that I'm not married to the baby's father and will be raising my child on my own is sure to crush any excitement about being a new grandma. She has pretty high moral standards, and my situation will be sure to scandalize her if and when it gets out. I was hoping to tell her, then leave town. If we keep it a secret and I return a few years down the road, I can create a make-believe story to explain the baby by then."

"So that's why you plan to leave Brighton Valley so soon."

"You heard Margie at Caroline's Diner quizzing me a couple of days ago." She placed her hand on her growing womb, stroking the rounded slope. "As you can see, if I want to keep this a secret, my time in Brighton Valley is nearly up."

"Who's the father?"

"An art dealer who recently purchased stock in the gallery I worked in."

"Does he know about the baby?"

She paused for a moment, wondering just how much she cared to reveal. She was still reeling from the fact that the man she'd thought she loved had been living two different lives—one as a married father of three and the other as a footloose womanizer.

But that would mean she couldn't read people very well and that she'd been completely taken in by a lying jerk. And she hated to admit that her judgment was so poor.

"I made a big mistake by getting involved with the wrong guy," she admitted. "He wasn't the man he claimed to be. He knows about the baby, but he's not interested. In fact, he wanted me to 'get rid of it' and referred to it as a rug rat. But I refused. So for that and several other reasons, he'll never be a part of my life or my baby's."

"What about child support?" Jason asked.

"I'm going it alone. But don't worry. I'll be fine." And she would be.

She swiped a hand across her eyes. Her words might project confidence, but unfortunately, her over-productive tear ducts might not be as convincing.

Jason was stunned. He hadn't expected Juliana to turn him down—or to give him such a compelling reason. He should thank his lucky stars that he had the perfect excuse to run—and not walk!—away from all of that. Yet his...what, his heart? His conscience? Whatever it was seemed to hold him back and wouldn't let him hightail it too far away just yet.

His father had been a womanizer and had left Braden's mother in a similar situation. And while he might not have gotten other single women pregnant, he'd surely hurt them or made them feel as though he cared less for them than he'd first led them to believe.

And now, those women had a face. A lovely one, with flushed, tear-stained cheeks.

"What will you do to support yourself?" he asked.

"I'll find a job. In the meantime, I have this." Juliana swept her arm in front of her, indicating the work he'd given her at the ranch. "I also dabble in art and left a few pieces back at La Galleria in Wexler on consignment. Hopefully, they'll sell. Loren, the original owner, is going to forward the money to my mother. And she'll pass it on to me."

"So you're an artist," he said.

She gave him a halfhearted shrug. "I'd planned to be. Someday. But going on to a four-year university didn't work out. And now I'll be looking for employment I can depend on to support me and a baby."

He felt the urge to offer her a position at Rayburn Energy, but bit back what could only be considered an overzealous attempt to right his father's wrongs. All he needed was to have Juliana within arm's distance day in and day out. Or for her to feel beholden to him in some way. That would really muddle things at the office.

She slipped the dress back into the plastic bag and handed it to him. "Thanks for thinking of me. I certainly appreciate your generosity. But now you can see why I can't accept it."

"Keep it anyway. I'm sure you'll be able to wear it someday."

Her smile didn't reach her eyes, which glistened with tears that he feared could overflow again at any moment. "After the baby gets here, I doubt that I'll have an opportunity to go anywhere for quite a while, let alone to a place where I can wear something this nice."

The truth of her words filled the air, and so did

the unfairness of her situation. She'd be financially strapped and carrying the responsibility of her love child alone. And she was too young, too pretty, too...

He studied her a moment, caught up in... Hell, he had no idea what was swirling around him. It seemed to be the same attraction he'd felt earlier, but it couldn't be.

Was it respect, then? It had to be. That and maybe something more.

"That guy," he said, "the baby's father. He was a fool."

Her smile brightened. "Thanks. My ego needed to hear that."

Unable to help himself, he ran his knuckles along her cheek, and their gazes locked. Then, as if he'd lost all shred of good sense, he brushed a kiss across her lips.

Just to show his friendship, he told himself. His support.

But his arms seemed to have a rebellious mind of their own as they stole around her waist and drew her close. The kiss deepened, promising to light up the room in a burst of heat, just like before, but Juliana ended it almost as quickly as it began.

"I'm sorry," she said. "This isn't going to work."

"I know. I'm the one who should be sorry. I didn't mean for that to happen. It just did, and it was out of line."

Out of line? He'd been out of his mind, too. What had provoked him to kiss her again? She'd given him the perfect opportunity to cut bait and to get back on an even keel.

She placed her hand, the fingers splayed, at the base of her throat and took a step back. "I think it's best if you find someone else to finish up the inventory. I'll help out until my replacement arrives."

She was right, of course. But what was he going to do if she quit?

His gut clenched at the thought of her leaving. How odd that he'd feel that way about losing an employee who could be replaced.

Especially one who was expecting another man's baby.

Jason slept like hell that night and woke early the next morning. Rather than face Juliana and discuss the inappropriate kiss that had probably ruined a successful working arrangement, he fixed a cup of coffee, went into the den and began his day by checking email and catching up on the issues going on at the Houston office.

One of the first messages he received was from Doug Broderick, his right-hand man.

Jason,
I've attached the graphics with your suggested changes to the art layout. Craig, the marketing director, was impressed and thinks you're really onto something. I agree. What do you think of it now?
Doug

Jason studied the revised graphics, realizing Juliana's suggestions had made a big difference and provided that spark the artwork had been missing.

How about that? he mused.

Should he mention to Doug where the idea had come from? It wasn't as though he wanted to steal the credit for himself, but how deep did he want to get involved with Juliana?

Craig had suggested a shake-up in the marketing department to get some new blood. What if he wanted to interview the woman who'd taken one glimpse at the art layout and solved their dilemma within seconds with a simple suggestion?

Juliana needed a job, but she'd already told him she thought it was best that he find someone else to work for him. He couldn't very well sing her praises to the art department then. And that wasn't the only reason.

Granted, she had an innate talent and would be a great addition to an art department someday. But according to Carly, Juliana had never finished college. And she herself admitted that she only dabbled in art. So she wasn't entirely qualified for the position with his company at this particular time.

On top of that, there was the personal dilemma that was impossible to ignore. With the obvious chemistry they had—and the passion that was ready to ignite every time he got within arm's length of her—he couldn't very well risk passing her in the hall or bumping into her on the elevator, now could he?

Still, he wasn't about to use her suggestion without offering her any compensation. He knew the struggle she'd be facing over the next months—and possibly years.

Hell, maybe he could tell her that he'd set up a scholarship foundation for single mothers intending to finish their education. And that he was giving one to her.

Now there was an idea. He could call it the Charles Rayburn Love 'Em and Leave 'Em Foundation, created in an effort to make things right for jilted women around the world. And he could provide the first scholarship to Juliana.

Jason blew out a ragged sigh. Actually, all kidding aside, that wasn't entirely out of the question. He'd have to give it some thought. In the meantime, he had an email to answer.

Doug,
It looks great. I thought that would work. Tell Craig to run with it and see what his crew can come up with now.
Jason

He felt a momentary twang of guilt for taking any credit at all for her idea, but he hit Send anyway. If he hadn't seen the merit, he wouldn't have suggested it to Doug in the first place. Besides, he was going to lose Juliana anyway. Hadn't she told him last night that she'd be leaving?

That reminded him. He'd need to find a replacement—even if he doubted he could find anyone who'd come close to filling her shoes.

He'd no more than moved on to the next project on his to-do list when her voice sounded in the doorway.

"Excuse me," she said, "I hate to bother you, Jason, but I found something you need to see."

He glanced up from the file on his desk and spotted a black leather briefcase in her hand. His father's? It sure looked like it. "Where'd you find that?"

She entered the den and made her way to the front of his desk. "In one of the guest rooms. It was sitting up next to a wing-back chair. I looked inside to see if I could tell who it belonged to, and I found some files and papers that must be your father's. So I thought you'd better go through it instead of me."

That meant his dad had stopped by the ranch recently—before going to Mexico three months ago. Why had he done that?

Had Ian seen him? If so, Ian hadn't mentioned it. But then, Jason hadn't asked. He'd had no reason to believe his dad would have come here.

Jason opened the briefcase, but it didn't take long to realize what Juliana had pieced together. The brief-case had, indeed, belonged to Charles Rayburn. He'd either left it here on purpose, intending to return, or he'd forgotten it.

"Did you find anything else in that room?" he asked. "Any clothes or toiletries?"

"I haven't gone through the closets or the bathroom yet. But I'll go and look now."

"Thanks. I'd appreciate that."

And he would. He was overwhelmed with chores to do around here, both inside and out. And while he'd let Ian do most of the ranch work, and Juliana handled things in the house, that reminded him. How was he going to get everything done if Juliana left?

Braden was still in Mexico, and if Carly's show was a hit, who knew when either of them would step up to relieve him or help out. He could hire someone to replace Juliana, but they'd created such a comfortable working relationship—at least, when he wasn't tempted to kiss her.

After Juliana returned to the guest room where she'd been working, Jason sorted through the briefcase, releasing the spicy scent of his father's aftershave, as well as a hint of the peppermint breath mints he'd favored.

For a moment, Jason felt like a boy again, stealing a peek into his father's domain, hoping for a minute or two of the man's time. But his father was gone. As usual. This time permanently.

As he read over the files, he realized they were all recent. Most of them needed to be back at Rayburn Enterprises. He probably should ship them overnight.

Footsteps sounded in the hallway as Juliana returned. "The closet was empty. So was the bathroom. It looks like the briefcase was all he left."

She leaned against the doorjamb, her hair a tumble of red curls. For a moment, he forgot about his father, his work, his responsibilities to the trust or his siblings. Instead, he studied the lovely young woman who'd crossed his path and momentarily upended his world.

Her baby bump, if you could call it that, barely showed through the blousy green top she wore. Yet it gave her an intriguing appeal—the kind a man could come home to.

But he quickly shook it off. "I'm going to have to send the paperwork back to the office. Do you know where I can find the nearest FedEx or UPS place?"

"The only one I'm aware of is in Wexler, a couple of doors down from the art gallery where I worked."

Jason suspected there was one in Brighton Valley, which would probably be closer, but rather than search on his iPhone, he decided to drive into Wexler. While he was there, he might even swing by La Galleria and check out the deadbeat dad who'd fathered her baby.

He had no idea why it mattered who the guy was and what he looked like, but for some crazy reason, it did.

Forty-five minutes later, Jason left the Wexler FedEx office. But before climbing into his pickup to return to the ranch, he walked a couple of doors down the street to La Galleria, the place where Juliana had worked.

He paused at the glass door for a moment, tamping down a last-minute reluctance to enter, then proceeded to walk in.

Two salesmen stood inside, ready to help an interested buyer. The one behind the register was short, balding and in his fifties. He didn't seem to be a likely baby daddy possibility.

The other was the right age—midthirties, dark hair and not bad-looking, if you liked flashy dressers. His pearly white smile suggested he'd had some expensive cosmetic dentistry.

"Good afternoon," Smiley said. "Let me know if I can be of any help."

"I'm just looking," Jason said as he browsed the artwork on display.

Juliana had mentioned that she had a couple of paintings on commission, so he bypassed the pottery and statues and focused on the art that hung on the walls instead. He had no idea whether he should be looking for oils or watercolors or a particular style, so he focused on the signatures instead.

Surprisingly, he found one. It was a cowboy riding the range. The man was in the distance and wore a black hat, so there weren't any facial features to discern. But the trees were well done, as was the bay gelding he rode and the meadow on the hillside.

It wouldn't go with the decor of his condominium or his office in the downtown high-rise, but Ralph the real estate agent had suggested he make the ranch appealing to buyers. The painting would look good over the mantel in the living room.

The price was five hundred dollars. He wondered how much of it Juliana would get. The bulk of it, he hoped.

"I like this one," he said.

Sensing a sale, Smiley slid up next to him. "Nice choice. The artist also has two other paintings here."

"I'd like to see them."

Smiley moved to the left and pointed to one of a swimming hole that looked a lot like the one in Brighton Valley. A blonde girl with pigtails sat high on a branch, where a rope had been tied. It had swung over the water, and there was a big splash on the surface of the pond, as if another child had dropped underwater.

Just like in the first painting, the face was turned away and too far in the distance to recognize. It had to be the old swimming hole, although he didn't remember so many wildflowers on the grass. Juliana must have added them for effect. It was a nice touch. The cowboy had been riding near a meadow, too. The fact that she appreciated flowers and color didn't surprise him.

"And this is the third piece she has displayed," Smiley added, pointing to a picture of an outhouse with a crescent moon carved on the door.

Now that was unusual, although what drew a smile to Jason's lips were the saddled Appaloosa and the Australian shepherd seated on its haunches, apparently waiting patiently for their master to finish his business inside the outhouse.

Jason wasn't an art aficionado, so he couldn't comment on the quality or on Juliana's skill. But he thought they were good—if you liked Western art.

"What do you know about this artist?" he asked.

"She has talent," Smiley said.

"Is she local?"

"Yes."

"How many of her pieces do you have?"

"Just three right now, although I can get more for you."

Don't bother, Jason nearly told him. *I don't need a middleman, especially you.*

A woman entered, and Smiley turned to her. "Hey, baby. I'll be with you in a few."

"That's all right. The kids and I can meet you at the hamburger place."

"You go on and have dinner with your family," the older man said. "I can lock up the gallery, Alex."

So, Smiley had a name. As well as a wife and kids. Was that what Juliana had meant when she'd said that her baby daddy wasn't the man he'd claimed to be?

Of course, Jason didn't know for sure that Smiling Alex was the guy who'd misled her and asked her to get rid of the baby.

"Thanks, Loren." Alex stepped away from Jason and made his way toward his family." You don't mind locking up for the night?"

"No. I'll take care of things. You go on. The kids are probably hungry."

"These rug rats are always hungry," he said, mussing the hair of the tallest boy.

Maybe he was the baby daddy after all. Either way, Jason still didn't care for him.

When Alex and his family left, Jason asked, "Do you work on commission?"

"Alex and I are co-owners," Loren said, "so it doesn't matter. And as for the artist you were asking about, she used to work here up until two months ago. I was sorry to lose her, but I suppose it was just as well. Once Alex purchased half the stock, he moved his family to Wexler, so we would have had to cut her hours anyway."

"So," Jason said, "I take it Alex isn't from around here."

"No, he was an art dealer who used to come to town regularly. But his wife got tired of all his traveling and asked him to settle down. He decided Wexler would be a good place to raise his kids and asked me if I'd like to sell half my stock in the gallery. I was thinking about retiring in the near future, so I agreed."

"When did his wife and kids move here?"

"Just a few weeks ago. Right before Juliana left. I'll sure miss that girl. She was like a daughter to me."

Who else could Alex be but Juliana's ex and the father of her baby? He was a real piece of work. He reminded Jason of his father. But Charles Rayburn had taken care of his kids—at least financially.

"I'll take all three of these paintings," Jason said.

Loren grinned. "Great. I'll ring them up."

The cost would be more than a thousand dollars, which was quite a bit to grace the walls of a ranch house Jason intended to sell. But he was determined to add to Juliana's coffers.

And to give her another reason not to step foot in La Galleria again.

Chapter Six

Perspiration gathered at Juliana's brow and neck, dampening her curls, so she left the list she'd been compiling in the dining room and headed to the bathroom to pull her hair into a ponytail. Then she proceeded to open the windows and turn on the fans, something she should have done much earlier in the day.

The muggy summer heat had filled the house until it was almost unbearable, and she was going to take a shower so she could cool off.

As she headed for the bathroom, the phone rang and she changed directions so she could answer. It was Jason.

"I hope you haven't started cooking anything for dinner," he said.

Apparently, it was her turn tonight. She glanced at

the antique clock on the mantel. It was already after five, but she hadn't even given it a thought. In fact, she wasn't going to do anything before cooling down and taking a rest. And there was no way she'd be getting near a stove or an oven. "Not yet, but don't expect anything fancy. I'm thinking a sandwich or a bowl of cereal is about all I have the energy for."

"Don't worry about it. I'm going to bring something home. Do you like Chinese food?"

"That sounds great."

"Good. I'll be there in about forty-five minutes."

When the line disconnected, she grabbed a towel from the linen closet, then took a long, refreshing shower. Afterward, she lay down and closed her eyes for a short catnap.

She'd no more than rolled out of bed and entered the living room when she realized she'd dozed longer than she'd planned. Jason had already returned. He stood near the hearth, unwrapping a painting.

"What's that?" she asked.

"I went shopping while I was in Wexler." As he cast aside the brown paper that had protected the artwork, he revealed the painting she'd done of Braden.

Not that Jason would recognize his brother's favorite horse—or any of the places where Juliana and Braden used to ride.

"What do you think?" He lifted the painting. "I need to sell everything in the house, but Ralph Nettles suggested I should have a few things here to attract the buyers. I thought some Western artwork on the walls might do the trick."

Juliana crossed her arms. "I don't understand."

His smile faltered. "I stopped by the art gallery while I was in Wexler."

"I can see that. But why?"

"I was just curious about the type of things they carried. And I liked this painting."

Apparently, since he'd paid the five-hundred-dollar price.

"I also knew you could use the sale," he added. "So it was a win-win for both of us."

Something didn't seem right. Juliana might have been gullible before Alex Montgomery waltzed into her life and spun his web of deceit, but she'd learned to be skeptical and wasn't about to accept a handsome man's explanation at face value anymore—especially if she had reason to believe he might have an ulterior motive.

Why had Jason gone into La Galleria? Was he snooping into her past? Was he trying to play on her vulnerabilities and buy her affections?

Staying here on the ranch, helping him out, wasn't working out the way she'd hoped. And while she needed the money, she couldn't risk getting caught up in another…what? Dead-end romance?

But what if she was making more out of it than it really was? What if he'd only been trying to help her out? She'd been overly trusting once. Was she too skeptical now?

He set the painting of Braden aside and reached for a smaller one he'd leaned against the brown recliner. "I picked up this one, too."

As he unwrapped his next purchase, she realized

he'd also chosen another piece she'd left on consignment at La Galleria—the one of her and Carly at the old
swimming hole. Well, it wasn't actually *her*. She would
be the child who'd splashed underwater. But the blonde
in pigtails on the branch was Jason's younger sister.

Didn't he realize that?

Maybe not. Her back and hair were the only things
that showed. Juliana didn't paint faces. At least not
when her subjects were people she knew.

"Is this the old swimming pond?" he asked.

She smiled and nodded. "I wondered if anyone in
Wexler would recognize it."

"Most kids around here would," he said. "But I don't
remember any wildflowers."

"There are usually a few scattered about, but I added
a lot more. I like color in my paintings."

"It's a nice touch. I thought the house could use a
little pick-me-up, too, especially when Granny's things
are gone."

So he was determined to resell her paintings along
with the house. She supposed it didn't matter that he
didn't plan to keep them for himself. After all, she
would receive her commission. But part of knowing
that her art had sold was believing the buyer had liked
them enough to place them somewhere special, to sense
the love she'd felt when she'd created them.

As Jason tore into the brown-paper wrapping of the
third frame, she knew what he would uncover—the last
remaining painting she'd left at La Galleria—the one
of the old-style outhouse in a meadow.

Ironically, all the paintings were linked to the

Rayburn family. Not that she'd done it on purpose. It's just that her family ranch was gone, so she'd used the backdrops that were most familiar to her—Granny's ranch and Braden's.

The meadow where Braden rode his bay gelding was where she'd sometimes ridden with him, while the swimming hole was where Braden used to take her and Carly to swim.

And the outhouse?

That was the wildest connection of all—and really, just a figment of Juliana's imagination. Granny had once told her and Carly that Harold Rayburn, her father-in-law, used to have an Appaloosa mare and a cattle dog that followed him everywhere he went. *Why, folks said the poor man couldn't even go to the outhouse by himself,* Rosabelle had said. *Those critters would wait outside till he came out.*

The memory had just stuck, she supposed.

So while Jason was ridding the house of family memories, he was unknowingly replacing them with other Rayburn images on the walls.

Did she dare mention that to him?

In spite of what he planned to do with the Leaning R, it seemed as if the Rayburn family was destined to maintain some kind of claim on it anyway.

Jason had no more than opened the first takeout carton when Juliana swept into the kitchen like a cool summer breeze.

"I was just thinking," she said, "it's awfully warm in here. Why don't we eat outside tonight?"

"Good idea. Let's use paper plates, so there won't be any cleanup. And if you're comfortable with chopsticks, we won't even have to wash silverware."

Juliana tossed him a pretty smile. "Chinese food doesn't taste nearly as good if you eat it with a fork."

He studied her for a moment. She'd been wearing jeans when he'd left for Wexler. And now, in bare feet and a yellow sundress, she looked as fresh as the proverbial daisy. Or maybe a field of wildflowers. She smelled like it, too. Something floral. Jasmine, maybe?

"I don't blame you for showering," he said. "If I weren't so hungry and didn't want the food to get cold, I'd take one, too."

"I couldn't help it. I was busy and forgot to open up the windows. It got so warm and stuffy in here, I thought I'd melt."

In the summer, the old house could get hotter than blazes some afternoons if you didn't open things up and get the fans going early. Thank goodness Granny's room had a swamp cooler in the window.

Jason wondered if he should talk to Ralph about putting in an air-conditioning unit. Would that make the property any more appealing to a buyer? That was the first thing he'd want to add to the place, along with updating the kitchen and bathrooms. But then again, some people might like the authentic appeal of an old-style ranch house.

"I saw some citronella candles in the mudroom yesterday," Juliana added. "Maybe I should set them out on the porch to keep the bugs away."

"I'll set the table while you're fighting off the mosquitoes."

Five minutes later, they were seated outside, chopsticks in hand. The flames of four candles lined the wooden railing, flickering to fend off any winged insects out for blood. Yet it added an unintended romantic aura, too. And to make matters worse—or rather, nicer, depending upon how you looked at it—Ian chose that moment to sit on his own porch and strum his guitar, serenading them with a country love song.

"I didn't know Ian was a musician," she said. "Or that he could sing."

"He plays to relax sometimes."

"He's very talented."

Jason thought so, too, but he wasn't sure he should comment for fear it would make it sound as if he'd planned a romantic dinner under the stars. Of course, Juliana was the one who'd suggested eating outside.

A slight breeze kicked up, cooling the air and making the night even more pleasant. Yet as hungry as he was, he couldn't help but gaze at Juliana.

She was dressed casually this evening and had pulled her hair, a mess of damp red curls, into a ponytail that rode high on her head. She wasn't wearing any makeup, but she didn't need any props to draw a man's eye. She had a natural beauty that must have blossomed sometime during her teen years. He wished he could have been around to see the transformation. It must have been something to watch unfold.

In the candlelight, she seemed prettier than ever.

It was going to be tough to keep his hands—and his lips—to himself.

As she dug into the helping of chicken chow mein on her plate with a pair of chopsticks, she said, "Mmm. This is really good. Did you pick it up at Chin's Dynasty in Wexler?"

"That's the place." Her former boss, the man who'd rung up the sale for Smiling Alex, had suggested it.

Jason hadn't planned to talk to her about the gallery or about the men who worked there. Yet now that the subject had come up, he couldn't stop the niggle of curiosity from building until it urged him to say, "I met the newest owner of La Galleria."

Her movements stilled, the empty chopsticks dangling between her fingers as though they might fall onto her plate.

"Did you know he was married?" Jason asked.

"Of course not!" Shock and anger splashed across her face, yet he'd bet his question had hurt her, too.

In the background, Ian played another song about love that would last forever and ever. But there wasn't anything romantic, sweet or eternal about the conversation Jason had just broached.

He wished he could reel the question back. It really wasn't any of his business. Yet for some crazy reason, he wanted to know the details—needed to know them.

Juliana lay down her chopsticks, picked up her napkin and blotted her lips. "I told you he wasn't the man he led me to believe he was. If I'd known he was married or in a committed relationship I wouldn't have given him the time of day. But I thought I was the only woman he was seeing, the only woman he cared about. I didn't even know he had *children*."

"I'm sorry," Jason said. And he was. He might not make long-term commitments, but he never lied to the women he dated or made promises he couldn't keep.

A few moments passed, yet Juliana hadn't commented on his apology—nor had she picked up her chopsticks again.

"Do you still love him?" he asked.

"No. I loved the man I thought he was, but not the jerk he turned out to be. And once I learned the truth about him, I quit my job and left town."

"So you leaving your job had nothing to do with his family moving to Wexler?"

The look she shot him could have humbled a lesser man.

Hell, it humbled him. "I'm sorry," he said again. "I didn't mean to question your ethics or to stir up old wounds. I was just…curious. And concerned."

"Don't be. I'm going to be just fine."

"I'm sure you will be." But that didn't mean he wouldn't like to punch the married baby daddy's lights out.

"I don't owe you or anyone an explanation, but I ended things when I told him about the baby and he wanted me to get rid of it."

By the way she caressed her tummy, by that dreamy look she'd get whenever he did, he could see why the guy's callous solution would upset her.

"When I told him I wanted to keep the baby, he decided to come clean about his wife and family. I guess he figured I'd realize how a pregnancy would complicate our lives. But it wasn't just a complication to me. His revelation made me nauseous, and I'd never suffered any morning sickness up to that point."

The whole thing knotted Jason's gut, too, and he pushed his plate aside.

"I was making plans to give my notice because Alex was an art dealer who frequented the gallery often, and I wanted to avoid him. But when he purchased half the shop and moved his family to town, I hurried the process."

"Does your boss know any of this?"

"Fortunately, Alex had always insisted upon keeping our relationship quiet, although I thought it was because he was a private person—not because he didn't want my boss to find out about us. Hopefully, no one knows how foolish I was to get involved with him in the first place."

Jason could understand her embarrassment. He reached for a fortune cookie and handed it to her. "I have a feeling things are going to be looking up for you from here on out."

"I hope so. Things couldn't get much worse than they were two months ago." She tore into the cellophane, cracked open her cookie, read her fortune and laughed.

"What's it say?"

"'The right choice isn't always easy, but when you make it, your heart's dream will come true.'"

"See? What did I tell you?"

"Okay, smarty-pants." She handed him the remaining cookie. "What does yours say?"

After reading his, he slowly shook his head. "You can't believe this."

"What is it?"

"It's the same as yours."

"No way." She reached for his cookie. When she read his fortune, her jaw dropped. "That never happens."

"Are we supposed to pinky swear or something?" he asked.

She laughed. "That's too weird. I guess we can blame it on the cookies being mass-produced in a factory."

"Or fortunes being mass-printed, I guess." As Jason packed up the carton of sweet-and-sour pork, the house phone rang.

"I'll get it," Juliana said. "I was going to take the dirty plates and napkins to the kitchen anyway."

She answered on the third ring. "Hello?" She paused. "Braden, is that you? I'm sorry, there's a lot of static on the line."

The minute Jason heard his brother's name he got to his feet and headed into the house. Juliana hadn't confirmed it was Braden or not, but on the outside chance that it was, he wanted to talk to him.

"I'm here because I'm helping Jason with the inventory," she said, pausing again, apparently listening to the voice on the other line. "I know. And I will. Let me get your brother." Juliana handed him the receiver. "It's Braden. But there's a bad connection."

Without bothering to say hello, Jason asked, "What's going on?"

"I should ask you that," Braden said. "What's Juliana doing there?"

"Carly had to go to San Antonio for a singing job, and she suggested that Juliana help me at the ranch."

"Yeah, well, watch your step with her. She's a good girl from a decent family."

Jason bristled. "What do you mean by that?"

"Nothing, except she's not your usual type. So I hope you won't take advantage of her."

"I don't intend to." Did Braden know about Juliana's pregnancy? She'd said no one else did, but he sounded so protective. Maybe he knew about her breakup.

If so, was he staking some kind of claim on her?

Jason didn't like thinking that he was. Nor did he like the sense of jealousy that shimmied over him.

The telephone line crackled, and before he lost the connection, he had a few questions for his brother. "Why are you in Mexico? And what's the deal with Dad hiring a private investigator?"

"He was looking for Camilla Cruz," Braden said. "And I'm following up on that."

Before Jason could quiz his brother further, the line buzzed, then went dead. "Dammit." He hung up the phone and turned to Juliana. "Did Braden ever mention Camilla Cruz?"

"The woman who painted Granny's portrait? No, why?"

"Braden is in Mexico looking for her. Apparently,

my father was doing the same thing. The connection was so bad, I didn't get a chance to ask anything else."

"Why don't you do an internet search on the woman and see if you can learn more about her?"

"Good idea."

Leaving the food and the flickering candles on the porch, they went into the den. Jason's laptop was only hibernating, so they didn't have to wait long to run the search.

Juliana stood at his side, her scent snaking around him and reminding him they'd become a team of sorts. At least, they had while working at the house.

He'd yet to come clean about the helpful suggestions she'd given him for that art layout, though. Again, he told himself that was for the best. They had different futures mapped out for themselves, in spite of what the fortune cookies might have implied.

Besides, she was pregnant. And Jason wasn't cut out to be a family man.

As the search engine screen opened up he typed, "Camilla Cruz, Artist" into the search line, then waited to see what popped up. Her website hadn't been updated in two years, but there was a bio page.

Camilla Cruz, a thirty-six-year-old artist, was born in San Antonio and showed talent at an early age. Her father worked on a cattle ranch in Texas and poured his life savings into art classes for her. She later opened galleries in Guadalajara and Mexico City, but had sold them recently and retired.

At thirty-six? That was odd.

After checking a few other sites, the only new bit

of information they picked up was that she had died of breast cancer in San Diego last year.

"It seems a simple internet search could have given my dad and Braden the answers they needed," Jason said.

"Maybe it merely provided them with more questions."

Juliana was probably right. Why had the woman been so important? If Granny were alive, he'd ask her. She would have known the answer. As it was, he was in the dark until he could get through to Braden again.

On a whim, he reached for his iPhone and dialed his brother's cell. But it only rang through. He must be in some remote location. Where had Braden's search taken him? And what else had he learned about Camilla Cruz and their father's interest in the woman that he hadn't been able to share before the line disconnected earlier?

"Braden's obviously not in one of the bigger Mexican cities," Juliana said.

"Did he say anything else to you?" Jason asked. "Before you handed me the receiver?"

Actually, he had. But Juliana didn't think Jason would appreciate knowing Braden's exact words. *Be careful of my brother. He's too much like my father.*

"You mean about Camilla?" she asked.

Jason studied her for a moment, as if he knew she was holding something back. "Did he say anything at all?"

She gave a little shrug. "Not really. He didn't want you to take advantage of me, that's all."

Jason stiffened. "I wouldn't do that."

"I guess Braden isn't so sure."

Probably not. Braden didn't know much about Jason. But then, how could he? They'd never spent much time together. And even when they had, they'd kept each other at arm's distance.

"Are you and Braden close?" he asked.

Juliana wasn't sure what he meant by that. "We're good friends. Neither of us had brothers or sisters…" She paused, realizing her mistake. "Well, he didn't have any living in his house. So we leaned on each other in some ways. You know what I mean?"

"I'm afraid not. I didn't lean on either my brother or my sister."

"That's too bad. You missed out. Carly's a lot of fun and a very supportive friend. And Braden's…" She let it go. Apparently, there was bad blood between them, and she wasn't sure she should get involved in trying to mend that. She wouldn't be around long enough.

Jason glanced down at the desk, although she suspected he was looking right through the files and papers he'd left in piles there.

Was he thinking about the relationships he had with his siblings? Did he wish they got along better? Or was he okay with things the way they were?

If so, it was his loss. She'd meant what she said about Carly and Braden.

For a moment, Jason looked a bit like a lost little boy, a child who'd had everything taken away from him. Yet that couldn't possibly be true. He'd grown up in the lap of luxury and had everything money could buy.

Or was that the problem? Did he realize the best things in life couldn't be purchased?

She wanted to tell him everything would be okay, but how could she possibly promise him a thing like that when she was doing her best to convince herself of that very thing?

Yet her hormones—and not just the new maternal ones that were pumping inside her—were nearly overwhelming, urging her to reach out, to touch him.

She placed her hand on his shoulder, felt the heat of his body, the strength of him. When he looked up and caught her eye, something sparked between them, connecting them in a way that went beyond words, beyond touch.

He must have felt it, too, because he reached up and covered her hand with his, melding her to him. It was both exhilarating and unnerving at the same time, and her heart scampered in her chest like a frightened puppy that didn't know if it should find a way out or a warm, cozy place and stay put.

Who was Jason Rayburn? Rigid, decisive CEO? Or a strong man who'd been wounded as a child?

Either way, she couldn't remain connected to him or to his ranch. She slid her hand out from under his and nodded toward the doorway. "We left the candles burning outside. I'm going to blow them out."

"I'll help."

"You don't need to."

As she padded down the hall, his footsteps sounded

behind her. Both Carly and Braden had told her that Jason, like their father, was self-centered and unapproachable. But she had a feeling that wasn't true. Too bad she couldn't stick around long enough to...

To do what? To learn more about the man behind the myth? To fix things between the siblings? She was afraid that would take more time than she had—as well as a miracle. And she didn't have any of those up her sleeve, either.

In the past week, she'd gotten a lot of items inventoried and packed away, but there was still a ton to do. She hated to leave him high and dry, but there was no way she could continue working for him under the circumstances. He stirred her emotions, which were far too vulnerable, thanks to her maternal hormones. Okay, so her feminine ones were swirling around and complicating things, too.

Not that she believed there was any truth to Braden's warning. She really didn't think Jason would try to take advantage of her. He seemed to be just as perplexed by their attraction as she was. But she couldn't risk getting involved with anyone right now. Her feelings were too raw, and her future was up in the air.

As she blew out the candles on the porch railing, Jason gathered up the leftovers, as well as the empty cartons.

"I'm going to toss the fortunes," he said, "unless you want to keep yours."

"Maybe I should keep them both to prove that they're not as unique as people might think."

"And to remind you that you'll be getting your heart's wish, now that you decided to dump Smiley."

"Who?"

"Sorry. I made up a nickname for him. Well, a couple of them, actually. But that's the only one that's appropriate to say in mixed company."

She laughed. "I have a few names I've called him, too. But no, go ahead and throw away the fortunes. I don't need to keep them as a souvenir. I don't put any stock in that sort of thing."

"Neither do I. Besides, I try my best to make the right decisions every day."

"The fortune cookie was talking about *choices*. That's different."

"I can't see how."

"A decision is made with your brain. But a choice is made with your heart."

He gazed at her for a moment, his eyes zeroing in on hers and sending her pulse soaring. "I thought you majored in art, not linguistics or philosophy."

"Believe it or not, Braden's the one who taught me the difference."

"No kidding? How did he do that?"

"I told you there was a lot about your brother you didn't know."

"That's not news to me, Juliana. My brother and I are practically strangers."

"It doesn't have to be that way. You have a choice."

"So does he."

"But someone has to choose to make the first move." With that, Juliana tucked three candles in the crook of her left arm, grabbed the last one and headed into the house.

If there were anything mystical involved, it would seem that she and Jason had each received the proper fortune this evening. They both had critical choices to make—about what was right. And while he had yet to make his, she'd already made hers, which really hadn't been difficult at all. She'd chosen to keep the baby, to break up with Alex and to move to Houston.

Her heart's dream had always been to become an artist or to work with art somehow. But unfortunately, that wouldn't come true for a very long time.

Chapter Seven

On Saturday morning, Ralph Nettles stopped by the ranch to take a look at the property and give Jason his thoughts on an asking price.

"I haven't been inside since your grandmother's funeral," Mr. Nettles said as he eyed the stacks of boxes Juliana had packed and labeled after she'd carefully listed each item on the spreadsheet. "It's a shame you're not going to keep it in the family."

"My great-grandmother wanted one of us to live here and oversee the ranch, but my house and businesses are in Houston. My sister wants a singing career and is in San Antonio now, but she plans to travel. And Braden can't run two places at once."

"That's true." The white-haired man nodded slowly and stroked his chin. "Braden's granddad hasn't been well, and so your brother will be busier than ever, especially if Gerald passes."

Juliana knew that Gerald Miller had been under the weather, but she hadn't known that it was that serious.

"What's wrong with Mr. Miller?" Jason asked.

"Cancer. I've seen him a few times when I take my wife to see her oncologist. Gerald doesn't talk much, but he told her, at his age, he wasn't going to fight it. He didn't see the point. And I can't say as I blame him. That chemo can take a lot out of a man, especially if it isn't going to do the trick for very long."

Juliana wondered if Braden knew. If so, he hadn't said anything to her. And even though he was fairly private, she suspected he would have mentioned something. She also wondered if Mr. Miller would appreciate Mr. Nettles sharing the news of his illness or his thoughts on treatment with them.

She didn't think so.

"That's too bad," Jason said.

"Sure is. They don't make too many folks like the Millers. They're good people."

That was true. Juliana glanced at Jason, saw his brow furrow. Had Mr. Nettles's assessment surprised him?

"Why don't I show you the rest of the house," he suggested to the Realtor. "Then I'll take you out and give you a tour of the ranch."

"You aren't going to make me saddle up, are you?" Mr. Nettles chuckled. "I used to be a pretty good rider, but these days I'm a little rusty."

"Don't worry," Jason said. "We'll take the Gator. I

also have some aerial shots you can take back to the office."

As Jason and the Realtor left the room, Juliana went back to the work at hand. The men had no more than stepped out the back door when her cell phone rang. It was her mother.

"Hi, honey. A Mr. Alex Montgomery from La Galleria called looking for you."

Juliana had expected Loren, her boss, to call about Jason's purchase, but not Alex. "What did he have to say?"

"Your paintings sold. He wanted to know where to mail your commission check."

"On my last day at work, I left your address and phone number. I instructed my boss to mail my checks to you. So there was no reason for Alex to call and ask." In fact, she'd gone so far as to change her cell number so he couldn't contact her directly. In spite of what she'd told him, he'd had some crazy idea that she might want to see him again anyway—on the sly, of course. And to protect her reputation. As if she'd consider such a thing.

"I'm sorry," her mom said. "You told me that you left on good terms, so I couldn't understand why you wouldn't want to take his call."

A wave of nausea rolled through Juliana's tummy, threatening to send her rushing to the bathroom. But she swallowed it down and cleared her throat. "You didn't tell Alex where he could find me, did you?"

"No, but he seemed so kind and pleasant on the phone. I thought you'd be eager to talk to him yourself, especially since he has a buyer interested in purchasing more of your paintings."

Alex was a charmer, all right. And he'd just sweet-talked her mother into doing exactly what Juliana had asked her not to do. If she'd had a heart-to-heart with her mom when she'd first returned home, her mother would have understood and given him heck—in a pious way, of course. But Juliana hadn't leveled with her yet.

It wasn't like she planned to keep the baby a secret forever. She'd tell her mom the truth—every bit of it. She just wanted to wait until she was settled in Houston and could prove that she'd be all right, that she wouldn't need a husband or a father for her baby.

"I didn't want Alex to contact me here at the Rayburn ranch," Juliana said. "I'd prefer not to talk about my future work while I'm committed to another project."

Okay, so that was only partially true.

"But honey, isn't it great? One man took all three of your paintings, and Mr. Montgomery thinks he can sell him more."

What neither Alex nor her mother knew was that she could sell that same buyer paintings directly—and without a commission—if he actually had reason to stage another ranch house for potential buyers. But Jason Rayburn wasn't interested in her style of art. Not for himself, anyway.

"I hope you're not upset with me," her mother added.

How could Juliana ever be mad at her mom? The woman was practically a saint and had a heart of gold. "No, it's okay."

"So how is the job on the ranch going?"

"It's coming along fine. I should be done soon, then I'll search for work in the city."

"I wish you'd reconsider and look for a job around Brighton Valley. I'm sure you can find something here. I can post an ad in the church bulletin to see if anyone in the congregation is aware of an opening."

Just what the church secretary needed her daughter to do—parade herself around town, unwed, barefoot and pregnant. Sure, times had changed. Not everyone would point their fingers at her. But her mom didn't need to be embarrassed about Juliana's short sight when it came to choosing a mate worthy of a lifetime commitment.

"I actually have a few potential job opportunities already," Juliana said. "And they're all in the city. But I'll let you know if I need your help."

A double click sounded, letting her know another call was coming through. She took a peek at the display. Sure enough, it was Alex's cell number. She'd love to let it go to voice mail, but he'd just keep trying until she answered.

"Listen, Mom, that's Alex now."

"I'm sorry for letting him know how to contact you."

"That's okay. I love you. Talk to you soon." Then she switched over to the incoming call.

"Hey," he said when she answered. "Why did you change your number? You weren't avoiding me, were you, baby?"

"Just looking for a brand-new start. That's all."

"No need to do that. Listen, I'm not sure if your

mother told you or not, but I sold all three of those paintings. The buyer loves your work. How soon can you bring me something else?"

"I'm not interested in working with La Galleria."

"But I have a buyer on the hook. You're losing money by dragging your feet and being stubborn."

"So be it."

He paused a moment, as if plotting his next move. "Did you take care of…the little problem?"

The jerk. "I took care of it." But not the way he'd expected her to. She'd gone to see a doctor and was due to have a baby girl in late December. And she would continue to take care of *her* daughter for as long as she needed her. "Not to worry, Alex. All is well."

"Good. I'll be happy to reimburse you. Let me know how much you need."

"I don't need anything from you. *Ever.* Not a dime, not a phone call, not anything."

"But what about the buyer? I have his name, remember?"

"And I'm not interested. *Remember?*"

Then she did what she should have done the moment she'd heard his voice the very first time he'd asked for a date and suggested they keep it their "special little secret."

She hung up the phone and disconnected the line.

On Monday afternoon, Jason left Ian and the boys painting the barn and drove into town to pick up a few supplies at the hardware store. He'd noticed the engine knocking a couple of times on the way in and thought he ought to stop by Harv's Auto Repair and have him take a look at it.

If he were going to keep the ranch, he'd actually consider buying a new truck since this one was nearly twenty years old and had more than its share of wear and tear. The odometer showed fourteen thousand miles, but it had clearly made at least one lap around— maybe two.

After picking up the items on his list, he returned to the truck. But when he turned the key in the ignition, the damn thing wouldn't start. The lights worked, so he knew it wasn't the battery. He sat behind the wheel for a moment, then blew out a sigh.

Moments later, he'd dialed 4-1-1 and had Harvey Dennison on the line. "This is Jason Rayburn from the Leaning R. I'm parked on Main Street in the old Dodge pickup, but I can't get it to even turn over. Can you come out and have a look at it? I think it might be the starter."

"Nope. That's not it. We replaced that a couple of weeks ago. It's also got a new battery and an alternator. I'll come and bring the tow truck."

"So you're familiar with the engine?"

"Yep. Told your great-grandma it was time to buy a new one, but she passed on before she could do that." The mechanic blew out a sigh. "By the way, son, I'm sorry for your loss. Rosabelle Rayburn was a fine woman."

"Thank you." Not many days went by that he didn't hear someone in town tell him how much they thought of Granny. "Do you have any idea what's wrong with the truck?"

"I worked on it a couple of times for Ian. Told him what I told Mrs. Rayburn. But he said your daddy wasn't going to put any more money into the ranch. I'll do my best to fix it one more time, but it's going to need a new engine. That's for sure."

"Well, do what you need to do. I'm parked about two doors down from the hardware store. Since no one's going to steal it, I'll leave the keys on the floorboard."

"All righty, son. I'll be there in about an hour."

At least Jason wouldn't have to worry about getting a parking ticket, but he was stuck in town until he found a ride home.

He hated to bother Ian, who was knee-deep in the corral repair and overseeing the boys' painting. So he dialed the house.

Juliana answered on the third ring.

"Hey, it's me," he said. "The truck broke down while I was in town. Can you come and get me?"

"Sure. Where are you?"

"On Main Street, by the hardware store. But if you haven't had lunch yet, you can meet me at Caroline's. I'll wait to order until you get there."

Silence stretched across the line.

"What's the matter?" he asked. "Did you already eat?"

"No. It's just that I...well, I was trying to stay out of the public eye since I've started to show."

And Caroline's was a gathering place for the locals.

"If you feel better about it, I can order take-out and

meet you at the car when you arrive. But why don't you come on in? You aren't showing all that much yet. Besides, I doubt anyone will notice anything except how pretty you are."

He hoped she didn't think he was feeding her a line—or trying to sweet-talk her into doing him this favor. Every time he looked at her, he forgot she was pregnant. And when he remembered, he actually found it amazing to imagine a little one growing there.

"All right," she said. "But I can't get there for at least a half hour. Maybe a bit more."

"No problem. I'll wait for you at Caroline's."

After disconnecting the line, he crossed the street and entered the local diner. The lunch crowd was long gone, which ought to make Juliana happy. Her pregnancy was apparent to him now that he knew, but he couldn't imagine that anyone else would spot it so easily, especially since she wore loose clothing.

He suspected she'd be a loving mother. And while her child wouldn't have a father, Juliana would more than make up for that loss.

"I'll be right with you," Margie called from the kitchen. "But feel free to take a seat anywhere you want."

He had his choice of chairs at the counter or any of the tables, but before he could take a step toward a corner booth, Shannon Miller entered the diner.

Braden's mother seemed surprised to see him, although she had to know he was in town. She'd always been an attractive woman, a shapely brunette with green eyes and a sprinkle of freckles across her nose.

From what Jason had heard, she'd been a real knockout as a teenager, but she'd downplayed her beauty after she'd had Braden.

She'd only been eighteen at the time, which made her about forty-five now. Her hair didn't have any gray, although he wasn't sure if that was because of her age, her genes or her hairdresser.

"Hello, Jason." She offered him a smile. "I heard you were back in Brighton Valley."

"Good to see you, Shannon." He'd like to talk to her, to ask some of the questions he had for Braden. Maybe he should he invite her to join him. "Are you meeting someone?"

"No, I only stopped by to pick up some of Megan's muffins. I'm hosting my book club tomorrow morning and don't have time to bake anything myself."

"They must taste good if you drove all the way into town to buy them."

"They are. But this wasn't my only stop. I had to meet with the family attorney and make sure everything is in order. My dad has been pretty sick, but I didn't know how serious it was until now. He's been keeping it to himself."

Her smile faded, leaving her looking worn, troubled. After Jason had talked to Ralph Nettles earlier and learned about the conversation the men had had at the oncologist, Jason had connected the dots and assumed the worst.

Did Braden know? Maybe not, because if he did, he'd probably come home and leave the Camilla Cruz mystery alone, at least for the time being. He'd always been close to his mom and his granddad.

Jason had never really talked at length to Braden's mother. He'd told himself that he'd never had a reason to. He supposed that's because he felt as if he'd be disloyal if he did. But he wasn't sure to whom. His mom, maybe? His dad? Himself?

But Shannon Miller seemed like a nice woman who'd been through a lot—thanks to his father. And now she was facing more trouble. Besides, she might have some answers for those questions he hadn't been able to ask Braden.

"Can I buy you a cup of coffee?" he asked.

She paused for a moment, then said, "Yes, I'd like that. Thanks."

He led her to the corner booth he'd been eyeing before. They'd no more than taken a seat when Margie arrived with a carafe of coffee and filled both mugs that had been waiting on the table for the next diners.

"With your father sick and Braden gone, you must be pretty stretched," Jason said.

She sighed and tucked a loose strand of hair behind her ear. "It's been tough. I've been tempted to call Braden and let him know about my dad, but I haven't done it yet."

Good luck trying to get through to him, Jason thought. "Did he tell you why he went to Mexico?"

"He wanted to find out what Charles...or rather, your dad, had been doing there."

Jason knew that much. "Do you know anything about a woman named Camilla Cruz?"

"Just that she was Reuben Montoya's daughter."

Granny's previous foreman? The news took a moment to register. Jason knew Reuben well, but he'd never met Camilla. Or, if he had, he didn't remember her.

"Why do you want to know about Camilla?" Shannon asked.

"Because that's who Braden was looking for in Mexico. At least, he was following Dad's trail, and that's who Dad was looking for."

Her brow furrowed, but she didn't speak. Instead, she lifted her mug and took a sip of coffee.

"Do you have any idea why Dad would have been looking for Camilla?" Jason asked, prodding.

"No, other than the fact that she was young and beautiful."

Jason knew what Shannon was implying. Charles Rayburn liked pretty women. But something told Jason the mystery wasn't that simple. His father had never had to chase after a woman before or hire a PI to find her. Jason would be more inclined to think the woman had stolen something from him and he'd wanted it back.

"Did Braden mention anything to you about Dad hiring a private investigator?"

Shannon took another sip of coffee. "Braden's pretty tight-lipped."

"Even with you?"

She smiled. "Your brother is a man of few words, but when he speaks, it's from the heart. Genetically speaking, he received the finest qualities of both sides of the family."

Jason had to chew on that for a minute. Was that a loving mother defending her son? Or was it the truth?

Sadly, he didn't know Braden well enough to determine the answer for himself.

Shannon reached out and placed her hand over the top of his. "I'll bet you received the best qualities of both your parents, too, Jason."

Their gazes met, and he saw something warm and tender in hers. Something kind and almost…loving? Not that he wasn't happy to hear her say it—or that he didn't want to believe her. But at the same time, the unexpected words and maternal touch unbalanced him.

"I didn't know your mother very well," Shannon added, "but I was sorry to hear of her death. I felt somewhat responsible, although I think we were both victims in a sense."

"I felt responsible, too," Jason admitted, "even though I was only ten. Dad had me in therapy for a while, and I came to realize she made her own choices. She could have taken her medication and seen her psychiatrist regularly. She'd had issues long before Dad and you…" He paused, not wanting to point fingers at her or anyone. There wasn't anything anyone could do to fix things now. It was all in the past.

"I was young and rebellious back then. And I made a mistake. But fortunately, I didn't compound it by marrying Charles."

"He asked you?"

"Yes, after your parents' divorce. But I realized he didn't really love me. I'm not sure he was able to fully love anyone. But while I'm sorry about the scandal and the embarrassment it caused my parents and Granny, I'm not sorry about the pregnancy. Braden turned out to be a real blessing in my life, and I have no idea what I'd do without him."

When she withdrew her hand, a sense of loss threatened to leave Jason more unbalanced than ever.

A couple of times, when he'd been at Granny's for Christmas, Braden's mom had sent gifts to him and Carly. His sister had always accepted hers happily. But Jason hadn't known what to do with his, especially since Shannon often gave him things like board games that were meant to be played by two or more.

Had she been trying to encourage the two brothers to play together, to become friends? Looking back, as an adult, it seemed that way.

He wondered why she'd never married. He could see why she wouldn't accept his father's proposal. But had there ever been another special man in her life? He wouldn't ask, of course, but he was curious.

Granny had said that Shannon had devoted her life to Braden and then, after her mama had died, to her daddy. And if Granny had been embarrassed or upset by the scandal, she hadn't held it against either Braden or his mom. She'd always had a loving heart—and a forgiving nature.

"I'm sorry that my father wasn't the man he should have been," Jason said.

"It's not your fault. You can't make up for his short-comings."

Like making a lifetime commitment to a marriage, he supposed. Or to a woman in general.

"Your father saw his value in his success," she added. "But there's more to life than money, stock hold-ings and property. There's love and family."

"That's true, but you can't live on love alone. You do have to be able to pay the mortgage."

"I agree," she said. "And while your father had his faults, he had good qualities, too. He had a love for children, even if he didn't spend any time with his own. He financially supported many organizations that benefited underprivileged kids."

Jason agreed. "It would have been nice to have had more of his time, but you're right. He always did have a soft spot for kids. And he put his money where his mouth was."

"He also sent his child support checks regularly. Some men aren't that generous or supportive. Braden could have had it much worse."

It sounded as if Braden might have had it much bet-ter than Jason had. He'd had less of Charles, more of Granny—and a mother who'd loved him. Shannon had also lived long enough to be there for him. And unlike Carly's mom, Shannon hadn't put her dream of being on the stage ahead of her child.

Braden was lucky to have her.

Something told Jason that Juliana's baby would be just as fortunate. All she'd be missing was the finan-cial support.

But maybe it was best if they steered clear of the touchy subjects, like Charles Rayburn. So Jason let the conversation drift naturally to a reminiscence of Braden as a child and Granny, who'd been as loving and maternal as Shannon.

Still, he continued to glance at the door, waiting for Juliana, who took much longer to arrive than the estimated thirty minutes. But Jason didn't mind. Not when he finally saw her walk in.

She'd taken time to style her hair, although the curls still fell long and loose along her shoulders. She'd also put on makeup. Apparently, his comment about looking pretty had caused her to take some extra time with her appearance. Not that she didn't set his heart racing in faded jeans and bare feet.

As she swept into the small-town eatery in her yellow sundress and a pair of sandals, he had an almost overwhelming urge to take her in his arms and welcome her with a hug and a kiss.

And while he managed to tamp down the sudden impulse to embrace her, he couldn't seem to wipe the silly smile from his face as he stood and made room for her to join him and Shannon at the booth.

Juliana had expected to find Jason seated at a table waiting for her, but she hadn't expected to see him having coffee with Braden's mother.

Apparently, by the look on her face, Shannon Miller was taken by surprise, too.

"I'm sorry I'm late," Juliana said as she slid into the corner booth.

"No problem." Jason returned to his seat.

Shannon didn't say a word, but she lifted a brow.

"I've been working for Mr. Rayburn," Juliana told her.

"And doing a great job," Jason added. "I don't know what I'd do without her."

"Your mother told me that you'd been laid off at the art gallery in Wexler," Shannon said. "I was sorry to hear that. I know how much you liked your job."

Not as much as she'd wanted to continue her education, but that would have to wait until the baby was older. "I'll be moving to Houston soon and will find something similar to do there."

"You don't have anything lined up yet?" Shannon clasped both hands around her mug. "Shouldn't you wait until you have a job before you leave your friends and family behind?"

"I have something in the works," Juliana said, although that wasn't quite true. She hoped Jason would put in a good word for her at Rayburn Energy. But if not, she'd find something else. How hard could it be?

But just in case, she probably should start an online job search when she got back to the ranch.

"Thanks for the coffee," Shannon said as she slid out from the booth. "I really enjoyed our chat, Jason. I hope you'll stop by the ranch while you're in town. You're always welcome."

"I'll do that."

She went to the cash register, where Margie rang up an order she'd boxed for her.

"I meant what I told Shannon," Jason said. "You've

been a huge help to me, Juliana. I know you said you think it's best if you moved on, but I'm going to tempt you to stay."

The *temptation* was what made her want to leave. As their gazes met and locked, there was no reason to explain because whatever buzzed between them kicked up again, making conversation unnecessary.

A grin tugged at one side of his lips. "I guess that wasn't the right word. What I meant to say is that I'd like to make you an offer you can't refuse."

She couldn't help but smile. "I'm almost afraid to ask what it is."

"The way I see it, we only have another week or two of packing left. I'd like to offer you a bonus if you'll stick it out and finish."

"You're paying me enough as it is, so you don't need to do that."

"I know. But I want to."

She'd prefer a position at one of his businesses in Houston. Would she be out of line if she asked?

"I'm going to provide a nursery for you," he said.

She glanced to her right and left, hoping no one in the diner had heard him. Had he forgotten that she hadn't wanted word of her pregnancy to get out?

"What's the matter?" he asked.

The diner was empty, which he apparently knew. And Margie was nowhere in sight. But still, her secret was too precious to risk.

She leaned forward, narrowed her eyes and whispered, "Would you please lower your voice?"

"No one heard me. And that's all I plan to say."

"*I* heard you."

"I've been watching the door and can assure you no one is within twenty feet of us."

She blew out a sigh, not appeased. "To answer your question, I'll consider staying. But the bonus you offered is out of the question."

"Why not? The stuff you're going to need will be expensive, and—"

"That's *enough*! We'll talk about that later."

Now it was his turn to look around the diner and check for eavesdropping waitresses or townspeople, although the place was still empty and Margie had yet to return from the kitchen.

He didn't say anything more, and she was finally able to mull around his offer. His generosity was touching—and unexpected. Yet she couldn't help but be offended by it, too. It felt as if he was trying to buy her.

But the move was going to be costly. And so was preparing for a baby. Why couldn't she just accept it as a bonus and go on?

"Do you want to eat?" he asked.

"Not unless we can change the subject."

"Deal."

Good. A temporary reprieve from the problem at hand. She could think about the dilemma as well as both temptations—the man and his over-the-top financial offer—later.

With the issue temporarily tabled, another cropped up when Margie approached with two menus.

"Well, what a nice surprise," the waitress said.

"Looks like that new job turned into an unexpected... *friendship.*"

Her wink suggested that the town rumor mill was already cranked up and ready for action.

Chapter Eight

They'd no more than started back to the ranch in Juliana's white Honda Civic when Jason addressed the elephant in the room—or rather, seated on the console between them. "I wouldn't have mentioned the word *nursery* if I hadn't been absolutely sure there was no one around who could hear me."

"I realize that now," Juliana said as she drove down the tree-shaded main drag of town. "And I'm sorry for freaking out, but it threw me into panic mode. I wasn't sure why you brought it up in the diner—or how much more you were going to say."

"That's all I was going to bring up. And I realize you want to tell your mother and grandmother first. But the baby isn't going to get any smaller. How long are you going to keep this a secret?"

"Until I'm settled in Houston and can assure them that I'm doing well."

Jason studied her stiff form as she gripped the wheel and stared straight ahead. It really wasn't any of his business when she told people, but it seemed to him that she was *afraid* to tell.

"Will they be angry with you?" he asked.

"They'll be…disappointed."

"Because you're not married?" In this day and age, he'd think that people would be more accepting of that sort of thing.

"Yes, but the details behind it are so…embarrassing. I *never* would have gotten involved with a married man. Or a liar, for that matter. But Alex led me to believe… Well, I could blame him for being a jerk, but I fell for it. I should have been more skeptical."

"I'd think that most people assume they can trust their partner. And that may not always be the case."

He wondered whom she was really trying to protect—her mother? Or herself? But he didn't think it was up to him to assume the role of her shrink.

"Maybe someday I'll find a man I can trust."

"I'm sure you will." At least, he hoped she would. She deserved the white-picket-fence dream and everything that came with it. "And that brings me back to my offer. Buying a crib and setting up a nursery will be expensive. And I can afford to help."

"I have a little money put away, so it won't break me. Besides, I plan to go to a thrift shop and pick up a secondhand crib."

He reached across the seat and trailed his fingers

along her arm, felt her tremble at the touch. Yet she didn't pull away.

Did she realize he'd come to care about her, to want the very best for her and her baby? That he'd...be the friend she needed in her corner?

Right. Because friendship makes your blood heat every damn time she walks into a room.

Shrugging off the unbidden thought, he insisted, "I have faith in you. I know you can handle anything life throws your way. But you'll have to do it on your own, and it'll be a struggle—no matter how capable you are. So why *not* accept help when you can?"

She merely stared at the road ahead. After a couple of beats, she glanced across the seat. When their eyes met, tears had gathered in hers, making them glossy.

"Did Braden's mom have anything to do with you making that offer?" she asked.

The question caught him by surprise. "Does Shannon know you're pregnant?"

Juliana, who'd turned back to watch the road, shot another glance his way, her eyes wide, all signs of tears gone. "No! You're the only one who knows about that. And now I wish I hadn't said anything at all."

"I'm sorry you feel that way."

She veered slightly to the right to correct their course, then shook her head. "You still didn't answer my question about Braden's mom."

"Why would she have anything to do with my offer?" He paused, realizing what Juliana might be implying.

Both women had gotten pregnant by married men.

And while Shannon had gone through her childbirth and motherhood with the support of her parents and was able to live out on the ranch, away from town, Juliana was heading to the city—on her own.

Of course, Juliana had a widowed mother and grandmother in her corner, if she ever told them she was expecting, but he doubted either of them had the financial resources to allow her to stay at home and take care of her baby. She'd have to get a job and find reliable day care.

"I'm sorry," she said, "it's just that I'm having a difficult time sorting through the motive of such an overwhelmingly generous offer. Do you really want me as an employee that badly?"

"Yes, I do. But it's more than that."

"What is it, then? Are you a white knight determined to help unwed, pregnant damsels in distress?"

As the accusation tore into his conscience, he turned in his seat and faced her profile. So he'd been right. *That's* what she'd meant about Braden's mother having something to do with his offer.

Shannon had told him he couldn't make up for his father's shortcomings, something he already knew. Now Juliana seemed to be suggesting the same thing. "Can't I just be a nice guy?" he asked.

"Yes, and I'm sorry for sounding so skeptical. I'm afraid my experience with Alex has left me with a bit of scar tissue. Besides, I'm vulnerable right now, and it would be easy to mislabel any feelings I might have."

"I can understand that." He supposed, in some ways, they were both damaged goods. But this was one subject he'd rather let drop, at least if it was going to poke at any excess baggage he might have.

"By the way," he said, "Shannon's father isn't doing well. Apparently, it's serious enough that she's thinking about asking Braden to come home from Mexico."

"Hopefully she can get a hold of him if she needs him."

Jason thought on that for a moment. "I'd like to do something for her, although I'm not sure what. Do you think they need money?"

"Probably, but Braden has access to his trust fund, doesn't he? So they should be okay financially. Besides, just telling Braden that you're sorry and letting him know that he can call on you if he needs anything would go a long way."

She had a point. Their father had set up separate trust funds for each of his children years ago, money they could use to attend college, purchase a house or spend as they saw fit. And as trustee to the family trust, Jason had added more to those trusts according to the instructions in the document.

But Jason felt compelled to offer to help anyway. And while throwing cash at the first sign of a problem was the kind of thing their father might do, it really didn't sit right with him. Some people needed a pat on the back, a hug or a heartfelt word.

Jason had been one of them, especially when he was a kid.

So why did it seem easier to offer money than a kind word? Had he been too emotionally damaged to see the forest for the trees? As much as he liked to think he'd grown up to be different from his father, it certainly seemed that way.

Rather than stir up any more deep-rooted memories, he kept quiet for the rest of the ride back to the ranch.

After Juliana parked near the barn, they climbed from the Honda. Instead of heading to the house with her, he turned toward the barn. "Thanks for the ride home. I need to talk to Ian and check on the boys."

"I'll be working in the guest room where your father stayed. That's what I was doing when you called. There wasn't much to inventory or pack, so I expect to be finished soon. It's nice to move on to a new room. It makes me feel as though I'm making progress."

Did that mean she planned to stick around until the job was done? He hoped so.

The truth was, he could find a qualified replacement fairly soon, especially if he called the home office and asked Doug to send someone out from Houston.

But when all was said and done, he didn't want to work with anyone else. He and Juliana had become a team. And he liked having her around—more than he cared to admit.

Juliana's talk with Jason left her just as unsettled as ever about staying on the ranch and completing her job assignment. Not only was her cowboy boss gorgeous, she could imagine him in a business suit heading an executive board meeting with grace and style. And his generosity was making it impossible to think of him as the type of man she needed to avoid.

Still, as she proceeded to the guest room to finish

the packing she'd started earlier today, she couldn't make sense of it. He was already paying her far more than that type of temporary position called for. Why?

Was it because he felt sorry for his sister's down-and-out friend and this was a way of doling out charity and having her think she had somehow earned it?

Or was there a trust factor involved? She was handling the family heirlooms and personal possessions, which held sentimental value, which could make the job worth more to him than an hourly wage.

Of course, there was another possibility, something she hadn't considered. He'd said he was too busy to do the inventory himself. And that certainly appeared to be true. But what if it was more than that? What if the task was too difficult, emotionally speaking, for him to tackle on his own?

No, that couldn't be it. Unlike Braden and Carly, selling the ranch didn't seem to bother Jason at all. So maybe he didn't have a sensitive streak.

Then again, he wanted to do something for Braden's mother, which was sweet. Maybe, like he'd said, he was just a nice guy and wanted to do something kind for her and the baby.

That being the case, it had been rude of her to turn him down—at least, after she'd implied that he had ulterior motives for making such a generous offer.

She blew out a sigh. But hadn't she thought the best of Alex? Hadn't she believed his lies and reasons for keeping their relationship a secret?

We don't want anyone thinking that I'm using you to cinch the deal to purchase half the gallery. And once

I'm a co-owner, we don't want anyone to think you're vying for extra perks. Let's keep things special and private—just between the two of us.

Yeah, right. He hadn't wanted his wife to get wind of his shenanigans. And he hadn't wanted anyone to tell Juliana about his marital status. She should have seen a red flag then, but she hadn't.

She snatched the packing tape from the top of the bed, then sealed the cardboard box she'd filled right before Jason had called asking for a ride home from town.

With the closet and dresser drawers empty, she moved on to the nightstands. There wasn't much to enter on her spreadsheet—a book by James Patterson, two business magazines, a travel guide of Mexico... Now, that was interesting, especially since this was the room Charles had stayed in last.

She set the reading material aside and reached for a red flashlight, which was missing a piece in back. As she pulled it from the drawer, one of the batteries fell out on the floor and rolled under the bed. She laid the other parts on top of the comforter, then dropped to her knees and peered under the ruffled bed skirt to retrieve the runaway battery.

Instead, she spotted a blue plastic container the size of a shoebox. She slid it out and studied it, wondering what it was doing there.

Since her job was to go through every nook and cranny in the house to determine which items should be kept and which should be thrown out, she popped open the lid. Inside she found several invoices, a letter and copies of an agreement for the lease of a storage unit in San Antonio, as well as the key.

It didn't take long to realize she'd uncovered a clue to the mystery Jason and Braden were trying to solve.

The invoices were in both Spanish and English. It appeared that they were from a Mexican art dealer to Charles Rayburn for the delivery of several paintings and statues.

The storage locker in San Antonio belonged to Charles, too, and he'd paid for it a year in advance.

At the sound of the front door opening and closing, Juliana called out, "Jason? Can you please come here? I found something you need to see."

Moments later, he entered the guest room, tall and lean—a Texas cowboy on the outside, but a wealthy businessman to the bone. "What's up?"

"Look what someone stashed under the bed." She got to her feet and handed him the box.

"What's this?"

"Your father was involved with an art dealer in Mexico and apparently took possession of some paintings and statues. He also seems to have a storage unit in San Antonio. From the size of it, he must have planned to buy and sell those pieces in the States."

"I don't understand. He never said a word about it to me. And we usually met for lunch on Wednesdays." As Jason riffled through the box, his brow furrowed, Juliana inhaled his woodsy scent. She watched his expression morph from confusion to disbelief to…disappointment?

"Do you think Braden knows about this?" he asked.

"I have no idea, but he must have stumbled onto something. I wonder if Camilla Cruz has anything to do with it."

"She must—if my dad was looking for her." Jason set the box on the bed, then crossed his arms and gazed at Juliana. "Do you think they could have been involved in anything illegal?"

"Anything is possible, but those invoices appear legitimate to me. They talk about art sales and shipments, so I think it's on the up-and-up."

"Braden has to know something. Could he and my dad have been involved in an import business? It doesn't seem likely, but he knew Reuben, Camilla's father. So he must know her, too. And if he has a stake in it, he might be down there trying to tie up loose ends."

An expression crossed his face, like a boy who'd found out all his friends had been invited to a campout and he'd been excluded.

She placed her hand on his back, felt the heat of his body, the bulk of his muscle as it quickened and tightened with her touch. "There's only one way to find out. You'll have to ask Braden when he gets home."

"There's a faster way than that." He tossed her an impish grin. "We can drive to EZ Storage in San Antonio, find unit number four-twenty-two, use this key and have a look ourselves."

We? He was including her in the Rayburn family mystery? "You want me to go with you?"

"You're the art expert, aren't you?"

Her hand trailed down his back, lingering a

moment before she removed it completely. "I wouldn't say that, exactly."

"You know a lot more about the subject than I do."

That might be true. "But what if it turns out to be a wild goose chase?"

"Then we end up having a nice dinner and a stroll along the Riverwalk. We might even get a chance to see Carly's show—if she's working. Besides, as long as I'm stewing about this thing, I'm not going to be able to focus on anything else. So pack your bags. We'll leave first thing in the morning."

She probably ought to be a little uneasy about taking such a long drive with him—and spending the night. But she couldn't help the zing of excitement that rose up inside her. And it wasn't entirely due to uncovering a mystery that now included art dealers and paintings. And while she knew better than to let her thoughts wander in too far of a romantic direction, she wasn't sure what he had in mind.

"Are you springing for two rooms?" she asked.

"Sure."

Then he winked, sending that little zing soaring.

Nice guy? Or handsome CEO with an ulterior motive?

"Can you be ready to leave by eight?" he asked.

When he smiled, in spite of any apprehension her brain tossed out in warning, her heart did a swan dive in her chest.

And she found herself nodding—and planning what to take on an overnight trip.

* * *

The next morning, Jason showered and packed. After brewing a pot of coffee, he poured himself a cup, then took it into the den while he emailed the home office. He had to tell his staff that he'd be traveling for the next thirty-six hours or so and that he'd have limited availability if they needed him. Doug, his right-hand man, could handle things in his absence.

Since he had an address for EZ Storage but no idea where to find it, he also wanted to check Mapquest to determine the best exit he should take off the interstate.

When the house phone rang, he reached for the receiver, although he was more focused on the computer screen than the person who was calling. So he answered with a rather ambivalent "Hello."

At the sound of his sister's voice, he released the mouse, sat back in his chair and perked up. "Hey, Carly. How's the singing gig?"

"So far, so good. But how are things at the ranch? Did you ever get a chance to talk to Juliana?"

"Yes, and I hired her. You were right. She's doing a great job."

"I'm glad to hear it. That makes me feel better about leaving you in a lurch."

At least Carly seemed somewhat sympathetic to his plight. "Do you feel any better about me listing the ranch?"

"I still hate the idea of letting it go, but the truth is, I can't be there all the time."

"And neither can I—or Braden."

"Speaking of Braden, he called me early this morning. His grandpa was hospitalized yesterday afternoon. It's pretty serious, so Braden is coming home sooner than he planned. He asked if I'd set up a family meeting this weekend or soon afterward."

Damn—it seemed as though Braden was in for a real shock when he arrived. A pang of sympathy for his brother struck hard. "I'm sorry to hear about his grandfather. I'll check in on his mom and see if she needs anything."

"Gosh, Jason. That'd be really sweet. I'm sure she'd appreciate it, especially if Braden can't get back right away."

"What would stop him?"

"I'm not sure, but he's in some small village and has to catch a ride to a bus stop. Then it's nine hours to the nearest airport."

"Where's his truck?"

"When I asked, he told me it was a long story."

Well, that was one Jason would definitely like to hear, along with a few others. "So when are you available for that meeting?"

"I'm off on Mondays. I'll see what I can work out. I assume we'll meet at the Leaning R."

"That's probably best. And just so you know, I'll clear my calendar on any day you two can swing that meeting."

"I'll ask Braden how next Monday will work for him and let you know."

Silence filled the line, then Carly asked, "Is Ian still working for you?"

"Yes, why?"

"I don't know. I thought he might have gotten tired of holding things together on the ranch without any family support."

The same thing had crossed Jason's mind, but the guy didn't seem to be one to give up easily. "Well, for what it's worth, he has my support now."

Again, she paused. "I'm not sure if he told you, but he'd be willing to supervise the Leaning R if we wanted to keep things going. At least, that's what he told me a while back."

Jason didn't respond. He knew how Carly felt about selling the ranch to strangers, but that didn't solve the problem of having a family member live on the property—or having to spend the better part of his or her life there.

"You can ask around," she added, "but from what I gathered, Ian knows cattle. And Granny thought the world of him."

Jason had asked around. The vet and a few neighboring ranchers spoke highly of the man. And even if the three siblings decided they could trust Ian to run things for them, holding on to the Leaning R meant meeting regularly with Braden and Carly. And before Jason could even comprehend something like that, he'd have to see how things played out on Monday.

After telling Carly goodbye, he returned his focus to the screen, made a mental note of the exit he'd have to take, then shut down the laptop. He'd no more than risen from his seat when Juliana walked in.

"Who was on the phone?" she asked.

"Carly. She said Mr. Miller is in the hospital and

Braden is coming home early. We've tentatively set up a family meeting next Monday."

"Does that mean we're not going to San Antonio?"

"On the contrary. I'm just as eager to see what's in that storage unit. The more information I have about my dad's trip to Mexico and his search for Camilla, the better prepared I'll be for that meeting."

She nodded, then leaned against the doorjamb.

Damn, she was beautiful, with the mass of red curls tumbling along her shoulders and those golden-brown eyes. He scanned the length of her, the way she crossed her arms over the swell of her belly. He'd figured he might be turned off by her pregnancy, but instead, he found it appealing in an unexpected way.

"Do you know whether the baby is a boy or a girl?" he asked.

She blessed him with a bright-eyed smile, straightened and ran her hand over her womb. "It's a girl."

He returned her smile. "That's nice. I hope she has your hair."

"I hope so, too." Something about the way she smiled, the way her eyes sparkled, let him know she'd been imagining what the little girl would look like. And right this moment, he couldn't help getting caught up in that same wonder.

"Your hair is beautiful," he said. "I can see you two at the playground together—mother and daughter."

"You know, I really don't care what color her hair is. The reason I said that is because I'd like her to be all mine and not bear any resemblance to her father. But either way, I'm going to love her. In fact, I already do."

"She's going to be a lucky kid."

"Thanks. I'm also going to teach her to be honest and loving and kind. So even if she ends up looking like her dad, she won't be anything like him."

They stood like that for a moment, caught up in something tender and sweet—something he felt blessed to be a part of, although he wasn't quite sure what it was.

She gasped, then glanced down at her belly.

"What's the matter?" Jason moved toward her, afraid she'd suffered some kind of pain. Afraid something was wrong, that the little red-haired girl—or the blonde or brunette...did it even matter to him?—was in jeopardy.

Juliana looked up, her eyes wide, her lips parted. "She moved."

"The baby?" He eased closer yet.

"Yes, I'm sure that's what it was. The doctor said I might feel something soon—like the flutter of a butterfly's wing. And I just did."

His hand lifted. "Can I...?"

"Yes, of course. But I'm not sure if it's strong enough for you to feel anything yet."

He placed his hand on her tummy, felt the swell of her womb, the warmth of her body, the softness of her breath. And although he couldn't feel any movement whatsoever, he didn't draw away. He just stood there, caught up in her floral scent and in the intimacy of the moment.

And while he'd missed the miracle she'd just experienced, for some wild and crazy reason, he felt a part of it just the same.

Chapter Nine

Before leaving for San Antonio, Jason decided to stop by the Miller ranch.

He doubted Juliana would mind, but he ran the idea past her anyway.

"I'd feel bad if we left town without checking in on Shannon and her father first," Juliana said, "especially with Braden out of the country."

Ten minutes later, they drove into the Millers' yard just as Shannon was locking the front door, the strap of her black purse hanging over her shoulder.

"We didn't come to visit," Jason said as he and Juliana climbed from the car. "We just wanted to see how things were going."

Shannon stepped off the porch and met them in the yard. "The doctor admitted my dad to the hospital last night. He's in the ICU. I stayed there until just after dawn and came home to shower. You caught me as I was heading back."

"I'm sorry he isn't doing well," Juliana said. "Did Braden get home yet?"

"No, but he finally has better cell phone reception. The only problem is, his battery needs to be recharged, and he can't do that on a bus. But at least he'll be able to call again—eventually."

"How are you holding up?" Jason asked.

"I'm okay." Her red-rimmed eyes suggested otherwise.

Jason slipped his arm around Juliana. "Is there anything we can do to help?"

"That's nice of you to offer, but our foreman has things under control here. And Dad's doctor, Tom Hawthorne, is an old high school friend of mine. He's been very supportive, so we're in good hands."

Jason reached into his pocket and pulled out a business card. "Here's my contact information. Juliana and I will be out of town until tomorrow night, but if you need anything, let me know. I'll make sure it gets done."

"Thanks. I appreciate that." She tucked the card in her purse. "I'd better go. I'm hoping to talk to Tom when he makes his rounds this morning."

"Go ahead. We need to take off, too." Jason watched her head for her car, his arm still wrapped around Juliana. He wasn't sure why he continued to hold her close. It hadn't been a conscious move, although he supposed it was a sign of unity, of the team they'd become.

As Shannon slid behind the wheel of her silver Ford Taurus, Jason let his arm slide lower on Juliana's back until he slowly drew away.

"Come on," he said, "we'd better get on the road."

As they climbed into her car, neither of them said a word about him slipping his arm around her as if they were a couple. Just to make sure the subject didn't come up, he turned on the radio, and after a few miles, they fell into a casual conversation that lasted the rest of the six-hour drive.

When they arrived at EZ Storage in San Antonio, they had to ask for help in locating number 422. Come to find out it was a climate-controlled unit in a special building.

Using the key Juliana had found back at the ranch, they unlocked the door and gazed at the numerous paintings, ceramics and other Southwestern-style pieces of art that filled the unit.

"Wow," Jason said as he gazed at the stored items, each numbered and listed on invoices and checked off on a master list. He turned to Juliana, who seemed just as surprised as he was by the sight. "What do you think?"

"The paperwork seems to be in order, so it appears your father was involved in a legitimate import business—or at least he planned to be. Some of these things are high quality—and expensive. I'll use my connections to see if I can find out what he planned to do with them. If he was going to open up a shop or planned to sell them, I should be able to get more details for you."

"Are those connections at La Galleria?" Jason asked, hoping she wouldn't go through Alex.

"No. Fortunately, I've met a lot of people in the past two years who can help me."

He was glad to hear that. He'd rather hire an art expert or appraiser he didn't know than have Juliana cross paths with that jerk again.

As she continued to study the inventory, Jason walked through the storage unit, noting each of the paintings. Not all of them were signed by Camilla, but several were. One of hers sat away from the others. It was a portrait of two bright-eyed children—a boy and a girl about three years old—in front of a Christmas tree, loaded with presents. They were cute kids, and she'd captured something in their expressions—that same vivid, undefinable quality she'd captured in the portrait of Granny.

"Hey," Juliana said as she knelt beside a small box she'd found toward the rear of the storage unit. "Look at this."

He joined her and dropped to his knees beside her. "What'd you find?"

She lifted an envelope, showing him a letter she'd been reading. "It's from Camilla to your father."

"Were they involved in some kind of business venture?" he asked.

"Apparently, their relationship went much deeper than that." She handed him the note Camilla had written in a distinct, flowery script. "They were in love."

"That's hard to believe." He glanced at the letter,

then stared at the other envelopes inside the box. "My father never loved anyone but himself."

"I think these letters may prove otherwise."

He read the one she'd given him.

Dear Charles,

I'm sorry to leave in the middle of the night like this, but I had to go and didn't want to talk to you any more about my decision, especially in person.

It's not that I don't love you, because I do. But like I told you before, your history with women concerns me. I've been betrayed before, and I don't want to go through another heartbreaking divorce.

I so want to believe that what you say is true, that I'm different from the others, that you've never felt this way before, that you'll love me forever. You asked me to stay on the ranch and to give you time to prove it. I wish that I could, but I can't.

My sister is sick, and I have to go home. She has small children who need someone to look after them. Please understand. Perhaps at another time, I'll come back to Texas, and we can see if you feel the same way.

As for me? I love you and always will.

Camilla

"See what I mean?" Juliana asked. "He wanted to marry her, but she turned him down."

"I don't blame her. Look at his track record. I'd be

afraid, too, especially if I'd been betrayed and didn't want to go through a second divorce." Hell, as it was, Jason had been afraid to lower his guard and love the man, himself. And he was just his son.

Juliana leaned back, resting her bottom against her heels. "Well, either way, I find it sad and bittersweet."

"You mean because our internet search revealed that Camilla died two years ago?"

"That, too."

He studied her for a moment, the way she bit down on her bottom lip, the way she studied the other letters in the box. Then she turned to him, her pensive gaze filled with starry-eyed wonder. "Aren't you curious about whether they ever got back together? Whether he proved himself to her?"

Even after being betrayed and hurt by the man she once trusted with her heart, Juliana was still a hopeless romantic.

Jason cupped her cheek and smiled. "I can see why you would be, but he didn't marry her. So does that answer your question?"

"But he went looking for her in Mexico. And he was storing her paintings—and apparently buying them. I think there's a lot more to the story than meets the eye."

He brushed his thumb across her cheek, felt her silky-soft skin. She really did deserve to get married someday and to live happily ever after—if such a thing were even possible. But he wasn't sure if there was a man on earth who deserved her.

"I'm sure you're right," he said. "There's a lot we don't know." A lot they'd never know.

She placed her hand over his, holding their connection. "You're a good man, Jason Rayburn."

Was he? Deep inside, where he was reluctant to let even his own thoughts wander, he wanted to believe her, but he feared he was too much like his father—unable to love someone in the way they deserved to be loved.

Lord knew he tried his best to shake any similarities he might have to his father, any flaws in character he may have learned along the way, and he tried to do the right thing. So to have Juliana recognize his good qualities set off something warm and fluid in his soul.

Unable to help himself, he brushed a kiss across her lips—gentle at first, but the growing desire he felt whenever she was near took over, and he drew her close, running his hands up and down the slope of her back.

She pressed into him, and when her lips parted, his tongue swept inside her mouth. As the kiss intensified, passion threatened to explode right there in the rented storage shed.

Had he ever wanted another woman more?

When they came up for air, he continued to hold her close. His knees ached, yet he didn't want to let her go.

"What do you say we head to the hotel?" he whispered against her hair.

"We definitely need to get out of here." She drew back and got to her feet.

Her flushed cheeks suggested that she'd been just as aroused by the kiss as he was, but she cleared her throat and said, "That kiss may have given you the impression that I changed my mind about…things. But we do have two rooms, right?"

So much for her being as moved as he was.

"Yes," he said. "That was the deal."

He just hoped she didn't think he'd pulled a fast one when she found out that those two rooms were adjoining.

True to his word, Jason checked into two rooms at El Palacio, a five-star hotel with a view of the river.

While he was giving his credit card to the hotel clerk, Juliana wandered over to an impressive water fountain in the center of the lobby. It was an old-world style with a colorful tile mosaic undoubtedly made by artisan craftsmen.

Still, as she carried her overnight bag back to the registry desk, she marveled at the swanky lobby, the impressive decor and the courteous staff. Apparently, this was the way the rich and famous traveled. Not that she stayed in cheap accommodations, but El Palacio was in a class by itself.

When she approached Jason, he held the key cards in one hand and was returning his cell phone to his pocket with the other.

"I called Carly while you were checking out the fountain," he said. "I was hoping we could see her show, but she had to call in sick tonight. She has some kind of stomach bug, so she won't be performing."

"That's too bad. It would have been nice to see her on the stage. She has an awesome voice."

"I agree," he said. "So what do you want to do about dinner?"

"I'm pretty hungry, so anything sounds good."

"There's a steak house on the top floor with a view of the river. Why don't we try that?"

She'd brought the black dress he'd purchased for her. It actually fit, although it was formfitting in the waist, so her condition wouldn't be a secret. But who would know her six hours from Brighton Valley?

Thirty minutes later, she walked out of the bathroom, content with her appearance, just as a knock sounded on the adjoining door. When she opened it, Jason's eyes widened. He didn't speak right away, and she placed her hand on her tummy. "I'm sorry. Maybe I should wear the sundress."

"Please don't change. You look amazing."

"I know, but my pregnancy is so obvious. I feel a little—self-conscious."

"I understand why, since you haven't told your mother yet. But who's going to see you here? Besides, I think it's something to be proud of. You have that glow expectant mothers are supposed to have. I've never noticed it on other women, but you've definitely got it. Especially tonight."

Could she believe him? She certainly wanted to. And by the way his gaze caressed her, it was pretty hard not to.

She'd taken special care with her hair, pulling it up into a twist, which showed off the pearl earrings Grandpa had given her for her sixteenth birthday. She'd also put on some lipstick and mascara—nothing fancy.

When she'd looked in the bathroom mirror, she'd been pleased with her reflection—from the waist up, anyway.

To be honest, she was proud of the swell of her womb, the proof that her daughter was growing strong and healthy. But she'd been hiding it for so long...

Jason took her by the hand. "Come on. Let's go."

They left their rooms and took the elevator to the top floor, to Ernesto's, the steak house where Jason had made reservations for two.

The hostess, a tall brunette in her early forties, reached for two leather-bound menus and smiled. "Follow me, Mr. Rayburn." Then she led them to a linen-draped table with a view of the city lights and the river below.

Within minutes, a busboy had brought them water with lemon slices, as well as a variety of homemade breads and a small bowl of butter.

When the sommelier brought out the wine list, Juliana said, "I'll just have water. Thank you."

Jason chose a Napa Valley cabernet sauvignon and ordered it by the glass. When they were finally alone, he said, "Thanks for making the trip with me. It's not fun tackling family mysteries on your own."

She smiled. "A trip to a storage unit in San Antonio wasn't in my job description, but it did make for an exciting day."

"What did?" he asked. "Finding the love letters or the art?"

The kiss they shared had been pretty exciting, but she didn't dare mention that. Instead, she said, "I've always enjoyed a good romance novel, but it was fun to find those paintings, too."

"Then I'm glad working for me hasn't been entirely tedious."

"It hasn't. Even when I'm back at the ranch, I enjoy going through the family heirlooms and knickknacks. I almost feel as though I'm cheating someone out of the task."

"Not me. I have far too much to do. So you've taken a lot off my hands. And you've done an awesome job. I'm amazed at how organized you are."

And she was amazed at how generous he was. He'd given her a handsome salary—albeit for only three weeks' time. But he'd also offered to pay for her nursery, which was going above and beyond.

Was it a ploy? An attempt to manipulate her somehow?

Braden thought that Jason might be a charmer, like their father. But Jason didn't seem to emulate the man. Instead, he'd been skeptical of his dad's ability to truly love Camilla. And he didn't respect the man's womanizing.

No, the two men had to be different.

Besides, look how kind he'd been with Shannon. He'd wanted to check on her before leaving today. And he'd offered her his business card, saying he'd make sure she had anything she needed.

How sweet was that?

And while they'd been on the Miller ranch, talking to Shannon, Jason had slipped his arm around Juliana. Not only was that an affectionate gesture, it was also a move that let Shannon know that they were more than a boss and employee. It suggested they were also a couple.

When she'd told him she was pregnant, it hadn't seemed to faze him at all. In fact, he'd seemed to find the idea of her having a baby exciting. He'd gone so far as to touch her growing womb, hoping to feel a kick. He'd also mentioned her expectant glow tonight.

Did that mean he could actually grow to love her *and* her daughter?

Whoa. Juliana quickly took a sip of her icy water, cooling her heated blood and her racing fantasies. She was reading far more into this than was feasible. And she was setting herself up for a major heartbreak.

A waiter brought Jason's wine, interrupting her thoughts. Then the maître d' took their orders. Before long, their conversation resumed with safer topics and better things to think about.

"It's too bad we couldn't see Carly tonight," Juliana said. "She's always wanted to be on the stage, like her mother."

"I know. But I hope a singing career is her dream and not one her mother pushed her into."

It's funny that he'd say that when he'd followed in his father's footsteps. Maybe not in character, but in his career choice. Then again, someone had to take the helm of Rayburn Enterprises now that Charles was gone. And Jason was the one who'd been groomed for it.

After dinner, they ordered dessert—crème brûlée for her and chocolate lava cake for him.

Jason signed the bill and charged it to his room, then he stood and pulled out her chair.

"Thank you for dinner," she said. "It was wonderful."

"You're welcome. But it was the company and the ambience that made it special."

She thought so, too.

On the walk to the elevator she was tempted to slip her arm in his, but she refrained.

When the doors opened, they stepped inside and began the descent to the seventeenth floor. Jason's cologne, a woodsy scent laced with musk, taunted her, and she was again tempted to reach for him. But then what?

Would he expect more from her tonight?

As tempting as it might be to make love with him, she'd made up her mind that she wouldn't have sex again unless she was married. And that wasn't a conversation she was looking forward to having with him, especially since she was coming very close to falling in love with him and feared a discussion like that might scare him off.

And even if he didn't suggest sleeping together, she feared telling him how she felt about him. Her emotions were still too new to trust.

When the doors opened on the seventeenth floor, he took her hand and led her to her room.

"Do you have your key card?" he asked.

"Yes." She dug through her purse and pulled it out. "Right here."

When she let herself in, he followed her.

That didn't surprise her since they'd come out that

door, but things could get a little awkward now. Still, she'd find out just what he was expecting from her—and he'd learn what he could expect from her.

He took a seat on the edge of her bed. Okay, so he wasn't planning on making a mad dash to his room. Did he just expect to have an after-dinner chat?

She hoped so, because if he kissed her again, she just might weaken and forget her resolve about sex before marriage. And then where would she be?

"I've come to care for you," she admitted. "And we definitely have chemistry."

A crooked grin stretched across his face. "I care for you, too. And you're right about the chemistry."

Her heart began pounding in her chest like a runaway locomotive. He hadn't said a word to her about sex—and maybe didn't plan to. So why did she feel so compelled to make a speech?

She ran her hands along her hips, fidgeting just a moment, then pressed on. "Just so you know, I'm not going to make love with a man I'm not married to. I made that mistake once, but I'm not going to do it again."

His smile faded. "I can understand your concern, but I don't need a piece of paper to make a commitment to someone. If we make love, I'm not going to ditch you. I'll be a good lover, and I'll provide well for you."

If he thought that was going to appease her or make her feel better, he was wrong.

"I appreciate that, but it's not enough. I want more than a good lover and provider." She wanted a loving husband and father for her child, but Jason was a smart man. Surely he knew what she meant.

"I'm not the marrying kind," he said.

"Why do you say that?"

He paused for a beat. Was he wondering why he'd made the claim? Or did he want to choose the right words?

"I haven't seen any marriages that have had happy endings. And even if I had, I'm not sure that I have what it takes to make one work."

She appreciated his honesty and hoped that he wouldn't blame her for protecting her own best interests, too. "I'm not trying to force your hand, Jason. I'm just laying things out on the table. So, under the circumstances, I think it's best if I quit working for you. I'm nearly finished with the inventory anyway. So it won't take you—or whoever you get to replace me—long to catch on to my system and complete what I started."

He studied her for a moment, as if he couldn't believe what she was saying.

If truth be told, she found herself wanting to rein in the words, too. But she didn't want to be swept off her feet by a man offering her all the treasures in the world, but none of the promises. She wanted to fall in love with someone who truly felt the same way about her. And how else could she be sure of that?

"I respect your decision," he said. "But will you wait to leave until Braden gets home? I expect him on Monday."

"Sure, I can do that." What would it hurt?

But when Jason walked out of her room, closing both doors between them, her heart ached something fierce.

What would it hurt indeed?

Jason had never been turned down before—not since he was in high school, anyway.

He'd told Juliana that he cared for her, but it was more than that. He wasn't entirely sure how much more, though. Guys like him didn't fall in love.

Hell, he wasn't even sure what kind of a guy he was. Certainly not like his old man. But what if he'd tried so hard to impress his father that he'd become just like him? What if he, too, failed at love and marriage? What if he couldn't love Juliana the way she deserved to be loved?

If he made a commitment to a single mother, he'd be responsible for her baby, too—one way or another. But what if he couldn't provide the kind of loving home and family the child would need? What if he ended up hurting the woman and child he'd come to care about?

That's what concerned Juliana. And that's why she wanted to cut bait now, rather than find out what might happen in the long run.

He probably ought to step back and let her go, but he didn't want to.

Damn. Was this how his father had felt when Camilla left the ranch? If so, it was one hell of a hurt. And one he was going to do his best to ease without compromising himself.

Jason had never cared this much about a woman

in his life. And whether Juliana believed it or not, he wanted more than sex. He wanted to look out for her, to protect her.

He suspected it had something to do with her pregnancy, her vulnerability. But whatever it was, he couldn't help the overwhelming need to make sure she and her baby would be all right. And the only way he could do that was if he kept her close.

That left him in a quandary, though. He wasn't marriage material. He'd never had loving parents to emulate, so what did he know about the kind of work it took to make a long-term relationship last?

Hell, he couldn't even connect with his own brother and sister. So what kind of husband or father would he be?

But he wasn't ready to let Juliana walk out of his life. Not yet.

So he took a seat at the desk in his room, pulled up his contact list and dialed Doug Broderick. After apologizing for calling so late, he said, "Listen, I have a confession to make—and a favor to ask."

"What's that?"

"You remember that change to the artwork I suggested to the marketing department? Well, that idea actually came from an artist who's been helping me at the ranch in Brighton Valley. She's looking for work in the city, and I'd like to offer her a position at Rayburn Enterprises."

"I thought you never got involved with HR decisions," Doug said.

"And I don't actually plan to this time. That's why

I'm calling you. I want you to do it for me—and I don't want her or anyone at the home office to know that I had anything to do with it."

"That's not going to be easy to do."

Jason knew that, but Doug was a spin master. "You'll figure it out. I'll send you her name and number in a text. You can let her know that the marketing department learned that the suggestion came from her. Tell her they were so impressed that they'd like to hire her. Then offer her a full benefit package—a 401(k), health insurance, plus we'll pick up any medical bills that the insurance won't cover. We'll also pay for relocation costs to Houston in a couple weeks, plus a bonus for taking the job."

"That's awfully generous. What kind of experience does she have?"

"Not much, but I'm sure she'll be a great addition to the team."

Doug paused, and Jason had no doubt what he was thinking. But Doug hadn't moved up the ranks as quickly as he had by objecting to a direct order.

"When do you want her to start?" he asked.

"The job will require her to work from the Brighton Valley office for the next few weeks, which is temporarily located at the Leaning R. So once she's finished with the ranch inventory, the marketing team will need to set up some projects she can work on remotely."

"I see."

Did he? Doug might have his suspicions, but he wouldn't know exactly why Jason was so dead set on keeping Juliana around, even after her job was finished. And maybe it was best that he didn't.

"Just make sure the offer comes from marketing—and not from me. I don't want to have anything to do with it. If something doesn't work out, you can be the one to let her go."

"Okay, boss. It's Friday night, so it's going to take a while for me to put things into motion so they'll run smoothly when the news of her hire comes through. I may not be able to contact her until Monday afternoon."

"That's fine."

Doug chuckled. "I have to say, you handled that just the way your father would have."

The praise, which might have caused Jason's heart to soar in the past, left him uneasy. But right now, he couldn't see any other way around it, short of proposing.

And that was out of the question.

Chapter Ten

The ride back to the ranch was quiet and awkward at first, but thanks to satellite radio, country music soon filled the gaps in conversation.

Jason didn't bring up the discussion they'd had last night, and Juliana was glad. Nor did he press her to continue working for him past Monday, when Braden and Carly were supposed to arrive for the family meeting. She was grateful for that, too. The sooner she moved to Houston, got settled and could finally tell her mother about the baby, the better she was going to feel. And if all went according to plan, she'd be able to reveal her secret and ease her mom's mind about how she'd be able to care for her daughter on her own well before she actually gave birth.

When they finally arrived at the Leaning R, Jason

went to find Ian and check on the teenage boys while Juliana entered the house.

As she surveyed the boxes that lined the far wall of the dining room, she estimated that she had at least two-thirds of the inventory listed and packed. By the time Braden and Carly arrived, her job would be nearly done anyway.

And she'd been right. The next two days passed uneventfully, and on Monday morning, when she entered the kitchen, Jason had fixed breakfast—toast and bacon.

"I'm sorry," he said. "I was going to scramble eggs, but we were out of them. I think I'll send one of the boys into town to pick up supplies. He can get groceries, too, if you want to make a list."

She planned to leave this afternoon—or tomorrow morning, at the latest. But she was probably more familiar with the cooking supplies than he was. At least she knew they were out of eggs and milk. "Sure. Send him in before he leaves."

Jason glanced at her expanding waist and smiled. "The baby must have doubled in size these past three weeks. So I figured you wouldn't want to go into town."

"You're right." She hadn't been able to zip her jeans this morning, let alone button them. And her top was stretched snug across her middle. No way did she want to risk being seen in Brighton Valley. There was no hiding her pregnancy anymore.

Come to think of it, her secret would be out the moment Carly and Braden arrived. She'd have to ask

them to keep it to themselves until she had a chance
to tell her mom.

"What time do you expect your brother and sister?" she asked.

"Carly said she'd be here around two, although
Braden will probably get here sooner."

"Okay. I'll be sure to put on a pot of coffee."

"Maybe we should add a dozen doughnuts to that
shopping list. It might sweeten everyone's mood."

"Maybe…" But suddenly, Juliana had a better idea.
She'd go through Granny's recipe box and bake something special. Maybe it would help them remember
their roots and feel like the family they were meant
to be.

There she went again, trying to fix the Rayburns.
But then again, Jason had done a lot for her. The least
she could do was to try and pay him back the only
way she could.

Well, at least it would keep her mind off Camilla
and that romantic mystery.

Jason moved closer and cupped her cheek—the first
intimate gesture he'd made since Friday night. She'd
missed his touch, more than she cared to let on. Yet in
spite of any hesitation she might have had, she placed
her hand over his, holding their momentary bond.

Then, realizing she might be sending mixed messages, she released him.

He didn't object. Instead, he stepped aside, reached
in the cabinet under the sink for the dish soap, then
turned on the faucet.

Odd, she thought. After Friday night, she would

have expected things between them to be awkward, but they weren't. Jason seemed to accept her reason for turning him down, which she found more than a little surprising. She would have thought he might resent her.

He seemed to care about her, though. Did he expect her to change her mind?

Then again, maybe he was more thoughtful and understanding than she'd realized.

"Go on outside," she said. "You fixed breakfast, so I'll do the cleanup."

"Thanks." He tossed her a grin, then headed for the mudroom, where he'd left his boots and his hat.

As she watched the CEO morph into a rancher, albeit a temporary one, she couldn't help but admire his masculine form as well as his work ethic. Would it be wrong to reconsider, to see where a relationship with him might go?

Had that been part of his game plan all along?

Oh, for Pete's sake. Look at how skeptical Alex had made her. Jason had been nothing but a gentleman since she'd met him.

When the back door shut, she snatched a piece of bacon from the plate on the counter and popped it in her mouth.

While the sink filled with warm, soapy water, she pulled out Granny's recipe box from the cupboard. She loved reading the notes written on the back of each card. She would choose a good recipe— something clearly marked as a family favorite—to make today, then check the pantry to see what ingredients she'd need to add to the shopping list.

In the meantime, she glanced out the kitchen window and spotted Jason in the yard.

Maybe she shouldn't have turned him down while they'd been in San Antonio. Maybe she should apologize for not taking him at his word.

And see if he might consider going slow—and giving her another chance.

In spite of what Jason had said, Carly arrived at the ranch before Braden and just after one thirty.

Juliana greeted her in the living room. But when she approached her friend for a hug, Carly put up her hands to stop her from getting too close.

"I feel fine today," Carly said, "so I don't think I'm contagious. But just in case, you better not get near me. I've been sick the past couple of evenings. In the morning, when I wake up, I feel much better. But then at work, it hits me again. I must be pushing myself too hard. Hopefully, with two days off, I can get some rest and kick that bug once and for all."

"I hope so," Juliana said. "I'm sure they don't want you calling in sick too often."

"That's true. They'll let me go and keep my understudy instead." Carly plopped down on the sofa, then glanced at Juliana, her gaze landing on her waistline. "Oh, wow. Look at you."

Juliana placed a hand on her baby bump. "Now you can see why that breakup with Alex was especially unsettling."

"I can't believe he was married and never told you. What a jerk. Does your mom know?"

"Not yet. I don't have the heart to tell her."

"You can't keep your pregnancy a secret forever."

"I don't intend to. I just want to get settled in Houston first. I hope to be able to tell her within the next couple of weeks."

"In person?"

Juliana's cheeks warmed, and she took a seat on the sofa next to Carly. "No, I'll probably do it over the phone. That way I won't have to worry about any of her neighbors seeing me. She can decide when and what she wants to tell them herself. But after I spill the beans, I'll invite her and Gram over for lunch and let them see for themselves that I'm doing fine."

Carly didn't say anything.

"What's the matter?" Juliana asked. "Do you think I'm wrong for not telling her face to face?"

"I'm the last one in the world to point fingers at you. I was seeing a guy recently, and ever since we broke up, I've been avoiding him, too."

"Who is he?"

Carly glanced around the room. After seeing they were alone, she still lowered her voice. "Ian. But don't tell Jason."

"Why not?"

"Because Ian wanted me to live on the ranch and oversee it for the family, but I can't do that and have a career, too. And if Jason knew, he'd pressure me to do the same thing. He can be pretty persuasive when he puts his mind to something. He's like my dad was in that sense, and I'm not going to let him talk me into doing something I don't want to do."

That didn't sound like the man Juliana had gotten to know. "Do you really think Jason would try to force your hand?"

"He's done it before."

At least he hadn't tried to pressure Juliana into having an affair with him. Or to continue working for him longer than she thought was wise. He'd been respectful of her feelings. That had to count for something, didn't it?

She glanced at the boxes she'd packed. "By the way, Ralph Nettles came by and took a look at the ranch. He doesn't think it will take very long to sell. He might even have a buyer who's interested."

"I guess that's good news," Carly said. "I hate to see strangers take over, but not at the expense of my happiness. I've had to live in my parents' shadows all my life, and it's time I did something on my own."

Juliana took her friend's hand. "I understand. Just know that I'm in your corner."

Carly gave her fingers a warm squeeze. "And I'll always be in yours."

At the sound of a vehicle pulling up in the drive, both women got up and looked out the window.

"Braden's here," Juliana said. And Jason was greeting him in the yard. "I'd better put on the coffee."

By the time Jason and his rugged, blond-haired brother entered the living room, the coffee gurgled in the pot and the fresh-brewed aroma filled the air.

Some might consider her tricky, but Juliana didn't care. She'd done her best to create a nostalgic mood by placing Granny's best cups and saucers on the table.

She'd unpacked them earlier today. She would have to wash and repack them after everyone left, but she wanted the siblings to be reminded of their childhood and the woman they'd all loved.

Then she sliced large pieces of the Texas chocolate cake she'd baked. "A real kid-pleaser," Granny had written on the back of the recipe card. "It'll take the fire out of the feistiest old coot."

Just what she needed. Something the kids had loved—and a peace offering, just in case someone wanted to put up a fuss.

Next she filled the creamer and sugar bowl. When she'd set the table, she went out and called the Rayburns to the antique mahogany table in the dining room, where they'd undoubtedly shared many a meal with Granny.

As Carly and Braden each grabbed a chair, Juliana was about to excuse herself, but Jason stopped her. "We can discuss family business later. I'd like to talk about Dad and Camilla first. So why don't you stick around?"

She glanced at Carly, and then at Braden, who both nodded. So she took a seat.

When Carly glanced down at her plate, her breath caught. "Oh, my gosh. Is this Texas chocolate cake?"

"I found Granny's recipe box," Juliana admitted. "And I thought I'd try some of her favorites. I had a little sliver while I was in the kitchen, and I decided it was a great choice. What do you think?"

"This was always my favorite," Carly said as she grabbed her fork. "I was afraid I'd never get to have it again."

"She's right," Braden added. "This is awesome. Would you give me that recipe card, Juliana?"

At his brother's surprising question, Jason leaned forward. "You bake?"

"I've been known to on occasion. Why?"

"No reason." Just that there was another thing he didn't know about his brother. "But I have to tell you, when Juliana found that recipe box, it was a real coup. She's surprised me a couple of times with some of my favorite meals."

Braden winked at her. "Jules is one of a kind."

Jules? So he had a nickname for her. And Jason's nickname had been Bird Legs. Boy, had he missed the mark. She was a jewel, all right.

"So tell me what you know already," Braden said.

"Camilla Cruz was Reuben Montoya's daughter," Jason said. "Dad probably met her here at the ranch and fell for her. But she broke things off and left him."

"She must have stayed here within the past few years," Juliana added, "because there's a portrait of Granny in the bedroom that Camilla painted. And Granny's wearing one of her newer dresses."

"No kidding? I've never seen it." Braden looked at Carly. "Have you?"

"Yes, but I didn't think anything of it. I just figured Granny must have commissioned someone to paint it." Carly bit down on her bottom lip and furrowed her brow. Then she looked at Jason. "But if Camilla was the daughter of the old Leaning R foreman, why did she and Reuben have different last names?"

"Maybe she was married," Jason said. "Or she might have wanted a professional name."

"How did you know that Dad was in love with her?" Braden asked. "That seems like quite a stretch. I'd be more inclined to think that he was obsessed with her because she wasn't interested in him."

Jason told him about the love letter they'd found, about the storage shed, the artwork.

"That puts a different spin on it," Braden said.

Jason leaned forward. "What do you mean?"

"I wasn't aware of the import business. But Dad was looking for her and Reuben when he was in Mexico."

"That's what I don't understand. He even hired a private investigator, but a simple internet search would have told him that Camilla died of breast cancer last year in San Diego."

"That's what I wanted to know. It seems that Reuben's sister was also named Camilla. That might have been the woman Dad was looking for."

"If Camilla, the woman he supposedly loved, was gone, why would Dad go in search of her father and her aunt?"

"Because Camilla had two young children, and Reuben had been looking after them while she went to San Diego for her treatment. And when Reuben passed about four months ago, I think the children were sent to an orphanage. I might be wrong, but my gut tells me that's who Dad was looking for."

"Camilla's kids?" That was certainly possible. "Did he find them?"

"No, but you know how Dad felt about child support and charities that benefited kids—even if he didn't have time to spend with his own. I don't think he wanted Camilla's children to be abandoned to an orphanage."

"So why did you continue Dad's search?" Jason asked.

Braden shrugged. "It's hard to explain. I guess if it was that important to Dad, someone ought to follow through for him. But then my mom called and told me that my grandpa isn't expected to live, so I need to be here for him—and for her."

"Of course," Jason said.

"Do you think Camilla's kids could be the children in that portrait we found in the storage unit?" Juliana asked.

"Who knows?" Jason looked at his brother. "What did you find out about the kids?"

"From what I learned, they're twins—a boy and a girl. I think they'd be about six or seven years old."

Jason's stomach clenched. And after losing both their mother and grandfather, they'd been taken from the only home they knew, the only family they had? Poor kids.

In spite of his obligations at the corporate headquarters, Jason felt compelled to continue the search, although he wasn't sure why.

For Braden? For their father?

Or maybe just for the brother and sister stuck in an orphanage.

It seemed like the right thing to do, even if it wasn't his obligation.

How weird was that?

But somehow, it had become a family quest. And something he was determined to pursue, even if he had to hire the private-investigating firm to continue the search.

The meeting to discuss the sale of the ranch and the division of the heirlooms and furniture seemed to have gone fairly well. At least, Jason shook Braden's hand when it ended. And they all went out to the yard, where Braden got into his pickup.

"Let me know if there's anything I can do for you or your mother," Jason said. "I mean it."

Braden nodded.

Carly climbed into her own car, intending to follow Braden back to his ranch, where she would visit his mom and spend the night. After they both drove off, Jason went out to the barn, leaving Juliana to return to the house.

After she washed, dried and repacked the dishes they'd used earlier, she resealed the box. As she straightened, she again studied the work she'd already completed. She'd told Jason she would leave as soon as the family meeting was over, so she was free to pack and head out.

But did she really want to leave?

What would it hurt to stick it out until the house was completely packed? After all, she'd made a commitment.

She'd also suggested that she wanted one from

him—and after only three weeks. Had that been entirely fair?

Not really. Maybe she should lie down for a while and give it some serious thought.

She'd just returned to the bedroom when her cell phone rang. She didn't recognize the number, but she was glad to see it wasn't Alex trying to contact her again.

"Is this Juliana Bailey?" the male caller asked.

"Yes, it is."

"This is Douglas Broderick of Rayburn Enterprises."

The call took her aback. "What can I do for you?"

"That was a great suggestion you made for the art layout. It made all the difference in the world to the promotional campaign, and the marketing department was very impressed."

She straightened and smiled. "I'm glad I could help, Mr. Broderick."

"So are we. And as a result, we think you'd make a fine addition to Rayburn Enterprises. We're willing to offer you a very generous benefit package, including a 401(k), health insurance, plus we'll pick up any medical bills that the insurance won't cover. We'll also pay for relocation costs to Houston in a couple weeks, plus a bonus for taking the job." He then quoted a starting salary that more than stunned her.

Whoa. Had he said *generous*? The offer was much more than that. It was…mind-boggling. And way over the top. Which made her more than a little suspicious…

"Did Jason Rayburn have anything to do with this?" she asked.

"No, Mr. Rayburn makes it a firm rule not to get involved in any HR decisions. He did, however, mention that you were the person responsible for solving our marketing dilemma. He also gave me your phone number. But the decision to hire you was mine alone."

Without an interview or a background check? And not even a drug test?

"We've needed some new blood and some fresh ideas on our team," he added. "And we believe you're the spark that will put the art department back on track."

While the offer was indeed flattering, it was also a bit unsettling.

"We realize that you're committed to finishing a job, but that's not a problem. We actually have several projects you can handle for us from the remote office Mr. Rayburn has set up in Brighton Valley until your new office is ready for you in Houston."

Seriously? And Jason knew very little about this? Her BS meter was shooting off the charts.

"Can I have some time to think about it?" she asked.

Mr. Broderick paused a beat. "Um, yes. Of course. How much time do you think you'll need?"

"A day or so."

After he gave her the number to his direct line, she ended the call.

You'd think she'd be on top of the world. The offer was way more than she'd ever dreamed of earning. And it would solve all her problems. She'd be able to relocate to Houston, hire a competent nanny and provide well for her baby. But that's what she found so bothersome.

Why would a corporation offer a woman with virtually no experience in the field and only an AA degree a position with a salary and a benefit package like that?

Something wasn't right. And as badly as she needed the job and the money, as flattering and as tempting as the offer had been, she couldn't jump on it. Not without doing a bit of research.

So she used her smartphone, accessed the internet and checked out the employment opportunities at Rayburn Enterprises, as well as the job requirements and the salaries.

It didn't take long for her suspicion to prove true. New hires with only an AA degree weren't given salaries and benefit packages like she'd been offered.

In spite of what Mr. Broderick had told her, Jason had to have had something to do with that call.

Was he trying to manipulate her? He had to be. He was holding that job out to her like a carrot, tempting her to be his lover.

But not his wife.

Like Alex, he wanted her at his beck and call—on his terms, but not on her own.

Well, fool me once, shame on you. Fool me twice, shame on me.

And Juliana was nobody's fool.

Chapter Eleven

After paying the delivery man from Romano's Pizzeria, who'd brought a medium pepperoni and a small vegetarian as well as an antipasto salad, Jason set the table out on the back porch. He figured that would be the best place to have dinner tonight.

He and Juliana had a lot to talk about—and not just the family meeting he'd had with Carly and Braden.

Juliana had disappeared after his brother and sister left, but Doug had said he'd call and make that job offer sometime this afternoon. It was already after five, so she was probably in her room, pondering her good news and making plans for her move.

When she broached the subject, he'd confirm that he never got involved with HR decisions, so he'd had nothing to do with the offer. But he'd admit that he was happy for her—and that he looked forward to having her join the firm.

In most cases—at least 99 percent of them—he considered honesty the best policy. But for now, he'd prefer to let Juliana think the offer had come through because of her own merits. And, in a way, it really had. She'd proven herself to be the kind of woman he wanted to work with—and to be with. So who knew where that might lead?

His father had needed to prove himself to Camilla, but the only person Jason had anything to prove to was himself, because he wasn't sure what kind of man he really was. Or what kind of husband or father he might make. Only time would tell, he supposed.

He glanced at his watch. Juliana had probably received the call from Doug by now, and he couldn't wait to hear what she had to say. He'd feign surprise, of course.

But when she walked outside, carrying her suitcase and her purse, he didn't have a chance to fake his surprise.

"What are you doing?" he asked.

"I'm leaving."

Had Doug screwed up and forgotten that Juliana was to stay here and move to Houston when Jason's time in Brighton Valley was through? Doug usually took notes when Jason gave him an assignment. Either way, Doug would have to tell her there'd been a change in plans or something.

"Where are you going?" Jason asked.

"I'm not sure."

Uh-oh. That didn't seem right. And neither did the cool glare in her eyes. If the call from Doug had come through, she should be happy. "What's wrong?"

She dropped her bag on the ground, crossed her arms and shifted her weight to one hip. "Did you have anything to do with that job Rayburn Enterprises just offered me?"

He'd planned to deny it, but something obviously had gone south, and the only way to rectify the situation was to confess. "Actually, I did. I thought if it came through the proper channels, you might be more apt to agree."

"Then you thought wrong. I'm not going to accept it. In fact, I'm finished here. I quit."

Her words struck him like an undercut to the jaw, and he struggled to catch his breath, let alone speak. "I... I don't understand."

"After everything we've talked about, everything you've learned about me... Jason, what kind of a person do you think I am?"

He thought she was a wonderful woman who'd found herself in a tough situation, and he was trying to help her out. He was offering her a hell of a lot more than she could get job hunting on her own—and not as a charity case. It was because...he cared for her. But she wasn't going to force him to say something he wasn't sure he felt. Something he wasn't sure he was even able to feel.

"I was just trying to help. Did you find that offensive in some way?"

"Help me? Is that what you were trying to do? Or were you trying to buy my affection?"

"You're wrong," he said. "I care for you, but I can't give you what you want. I can, however, give you what you need."

Her frown deepened, and she stooped to pick up her bag. "How in the world would you know that? You aren't even aware of what *you* need." Then she started toward her car.

"What about the money you've earned so far?" he asked.

She continued to walk without turning around. "Give it to Carly. I'll get it from her."

So she wasn't even going to give him a forwarding address? She'd done the same thing when she'd left La Galleria, just faded into obscurity.

"You're a great one for running away from your problems," he said.

At that she did turn. "Don't you dare point out my flaws and shortcomings when you refuse to even consider that you might have any at all. But just for the record, Mr. Rayburn, you have plenty."

Then she opened the car door, tossed in her bag and climbed behind the wheel.

She was barreling down the graveled driveway and kicking up rocks and dust before he could acknowledge that she was right.

Never had he felt so alone in his life—or so much like his father. However, Charles Rayburn had always considered himself a success in all things—women, fame and fortune.

Yet tonight, Jason felt anything but.

For the first mile, Juliana wasn't sure where she was going. And by the time she'd passed the second, the tears welling in her eyes made it difficult to even see the road.

She was two for two when it came to choosing men. What was her problem? Was she wearing some kind of neon sign that flashed *Naive Lover*? *Kept Woman*?

Well, Jason had read her wrong. She could—and would—provide a home for herself and the baby. It might not be anything flashy, but she wouldn't compromise her integrity with a corporate position and salary she hadn't earned.

Ooh. She could throttle him. She'd never been prone to violence, but if he were sitting next to her, she'd throw something at him, although she didn't know what. Her purse was the only thing handy.

"Damn you, Jason Rayburn!"

Yet as her car continued to roll along the country road, she realized he'd had a point. She hadn't wanted to confront her problems, at least when it came to talking to her mother.

Sure, she'd been avoiding the discussion because she didn't want her mom to feel any more embarrassed or hurt than necessary. But in truth, it was more than that. Juliana hadn't wanted to see the look of disappointment on her mom's face, either.

But she was going to see that same expression

whether she waited a week or four more months to tell her. Dragging it on was just causing her unnecessary stress. She might as well get it over with. Besides, she wasn't ever going to be happy until she quit running away from her mistake with Alex and faced it head-on.

So instead of turning onto the interstate that would take her to Houston, she headed to downtown Brighton Valley. Her mom and grandmother would be home having dinner now, which would be the perfect time to tell them both.

Ten minutes later, she parked behind the drugstore, where her mom and grandmother shared the two-bedroom apartment upstairs. She left her bag locked in the trunk, although she might ask if she could spend the night on their sofa bed and drive to the city in the morning. Then she climbed the back stairs to the entrance.

She rapped lightly on the door, and Gram greeted her with a smile. "Julie, what a nice surprise. Come in, you're just in time for dinner. We're having meat loaf and baked potato. Are you hungry?"

"I could eat a little something, if you have enough."

"We have plenty," Gram said as she turned away from Juliana and returned to the small kitchen area.

The two-bedroom apartment was just as she remembered—small, but cozy and clean. The living area opened up to the kitchen, so it was easy to see that dinner was ready.

"Let me set out a plate for you," Gram said, while facing the cupboard. "Your mom is changing out of her work clothes. She'll be out in a minute."

Juliana took a seat at the dinette table, which hid her tummy, and watched as Gram set out a third place setting.

Gram had already shed her business clothes and slipped into a turquoise Hawaiian muumuu. "We've missed having you here, honey. How's the temporary job going?"

Juliana rested her elbows on the table. "It went well, but it's over."

"That's too bad. What's next?"

"Why don't I tell you and Mom together? That's actually why I came. There's something I should have talked you about a few months ago."

"Sounds like bad news."

"Well, I guess that depends on how you look at it. I'd call it good news." Juliana hoped her mother would feel the same way, once she got over the initial shock and disappointment.

The bedroom door swung open, and her mother stepped out wearing a floral blouse and white shorts. She brightened when she saw Juliana. "I thought I heard your voice. Why didn't you call and let us know you were coming? We would have picked up some ice cream or something sweet to have for dessert."

"Actually, I came to make a confession and to share my news."

"Don't tell me," Mom said. "You applied for a job in the city and got it. I knew that was coming. I've been praying you'd find something close, but I guess that wasn't meant to be."

"Is that your confession?" Gram asked, a gray brow

arched, indicating she thought there might be more to it than that.

Juliana took a deep breath, then proceeded to tell them about Alex Montgomery, his lies and how she'd mistakenly gotten involved with him. "And that's the real reason I quit working at the art gallery. I didn't want to be around him anymore. He actually had the gall to think I'd be interested in continuing our relationship—on the sly, of course."

"Why, that ornery rascal," Grandma said. "Shame on him. I don't have any respect for a lying cheater."

"I agree," Juliana said. "But there's more to the story." A *lot* more. She got to her feet and placed her hand on her baby bump. She didn't have to say anything more. Both women could clearly see the part she hadn't mentioned.

"Oh, my," her mother said as tears filled her eyes.

Gram clicked her tongue. "Does the scoundrel know?"

"Yes and no. I told him I was pregnant, which is when he decided to confess that he was married. He asked me to get rid of it."

"Humph." Gram crossed her arms.

"I'm glad you're having the baby," Mom said.

Juliana turned to her, lips parted. "You are? I was afraid you'd be…upset or embarrassed. I mean, you work at the church. What are people going to think if your unwed daughter ran off and got pregnant by a married man?"

"First off," Mom said, "no one needs to know any details. It's none of their business. And second, the folks at church are supposed to be in the business of forgiveness and turning the other cheek. They'll just have to learn to practice what they preach, honey."

Juliana stared at her mother, who was smiling in spite of wiping the tears from her eyes. "Seriously? You're not upset?"

"Well, to be honest, I'm as mad as a wet hen at that man—Mr. Montgomery, I assume? And I'd like to wring his neck." She shook her head. "I'm also heartbroken to think you were betrayed and hurt. It won't be easy to raise a child on your own, but I admire you for it. Babies are a blessing, Julie. I know you'll be a wonderful mama, and Gram and I are here to help you. So what's there for me to be upset about?"

"Well, *I'm* plenty stirred up," Gram said. "What's that fella's name again? I'd like to drive into Wexler and give him a piece of my mind."

No doubt she would, given the chance. Gram was a feisty one. She bowled on Tuesday nights with the American Legion and played softball on the weekends with the Hot Mamas, a league of women, most of whom were twenty or more years her junior. She even kept a Louisville Slugger by the front door to ward off intruders. Of course, that was because Sheriff Hollister had confiscated her pistol last spring when she had a nightmare and fired several shots out the window and into Main Street.

Juliana smiled and gave Gram a hug. "Please don't do that. Haven't you ever heard the old phrase *let sleeping dogs lie*?"

"Hmm," Mom said. "Maybe we should say, 'Let

lying rats sleep.' Either way, I want to know more about my new grandbaby. Do you know what you're having?"

"A little girl," Juliana said.

Mom leaned back and clapped her hands together. "She'll be a winter baby, so I can start knitting blankets and booties." She turned to Grandma. "Won't this be fun, Mother? We have some shopping to do."

It would be fun at that. As the two women began to make plans and discuss baby names, Juliana sat back and marveled at the reception her news had gotten. Maybe she wouldn't need to find a job in Houston after all, which was just as well, she supposed.

The only thing she wouldn't confess was the experience she'd had with Jason. But why tell them about him?

Nothing would become of it. She'd made sure of it when she turned down his job offer and left him standing on the porch, staring at her in disbelief.

Jason had no idea how long he'd stood outside last night, wondering what in the world to do about Juliana. Now that he'd met her, now that she'd shared a small part of his life, he couldn't seem to get her out of his mind.

She'd bewitched him or something. Whatever it was, nothing else seemed to matter other than making things right between them.

But he had no idea how or where to start. He'd certainly botched things up when he'd tried to hire her.

After finally turning in, he'd slept like hell and

woken up early. But still he'd yet to come up with a solution.

It wasn't until he went into Granny's kitchen, poured himself a cup of coffee and cut a slice of leftover Texas chocolate cake that things began to make sense.

For some reason, as he studied the pale blue floral print on the coffee mug and savored that familiar sweet dessert, he could almost hear that sweet old woman pointing him in the right direction, as she'd done so many times when he'd been a boy she'd lovingly nick-named Jay-Ray.

Life isn't all about money. It's about love and fam-ily. Nothing matters until you're willing to put your heart on the line.

Was he willing to do that with Juliana?

His father never had been able to put anyone ahead of his pursuit of financial success. And even though Jason had struggled hard to be his own man, he feared there was just a little too much of Charles in him to be any different.

Could he be the kind of husband and father Juliana and her baby needed?

He thought of her again, remembered her leaning against the doorjamb in the office, stroking the gentle swell of her womb and talking about her baby and its father. *I'm going to teach her to be honest and loving and kind. So even if she ends up looking like her dad, she won't be anything like him.*

Jason's mother had died early, so who'd taught him to be different from his old man?

Granny had tried, but he feared he'd failed her like his father had.

You're a good boy, Jay-Ray. You know right from wrong, so you won't disappoint me like your daddy did.

Would she be disappointed in the man he'd become?

It seemed that everyone thought he'd followed in his dad's footsteps. *You handled that just the way your father would have,* Doug had said.

He supposed he had, but that hadn't been his intent. And his conscience was kicking in, telling him to take corrective action. Didn't that mean something?

I judge a man by his character, the feed store owner had said, *not his bloodlines.*

Maybe it was time for Jason's true character to step up to the plate and for him to lay his heart on the line, no matter what.

Wasn't Juliana worth the risk?

Early the next morning, Jason drove to town. He wasn't sure if Juliana would be at her mother's apartment, but that's where he'd start his search.

When he pulled into the alley behind the drugstore and spotted her car, he parked beside it. Then he climbed the back stairs and knocked at the door.

A woman wearing a blue robe and pink spongy curlers in her silver hair answered. He assumed she was the grandmother.

"Can I help you?" she asked.

"Yes, ma'am. I'm looking for Juliana Bailey."

The elderly woman stiffened. "Julie's in the shower, but she doesn't want to talk to you."

"I understand. And I don't blame her for being upset, but I'd like to apologize—"

The woman lifted a baseball bat that been resting by the door and shook it at him. "Do I need to run you out of here? I have no tolerance for liars."

What in the hell had Juliana told her family about him? He hadn't lied to her. Maybe he'd neglected to tell her the whole truth, but—

At that, another woman—Juliana's mom?—came out of the bedroom wearing a floral robe. "Who is it, Mother?"

"It's that louse who hurt our little girl, and I'm going to knock his head right out of the ballpark if he doesn't get off our stoop."

"You're trespassing," Mrs. Bailey said as she snatched the telephone from its cradle. "If you don't leave right this minute, I'm going to call the sheriff and have you arrested."

Jason had no idea how he could have hurt Juliana this badly. Her mom wanted to have him arrested, and her grandmother wanted to kill him. Didn't this prove that he wasn't any good at relationships?

Yet he didn't want to leave without getting a chance to talk to Juliana personally.

Maybe it would be in his best interest if Sheriff Hollister did come and sort all this out. He was just about to suggest it when Juliana entered the fracas.

"Mom? Grandma? What are you doing?" she asked.

"You told this good-for-nothing rascal to leave you and the baby alone, but he didn't listen," the bat-wielding grandmother shouted. "So I'm going to run him off for good."

"Mother," Mrs. Bailey said as she grabbed the older woman's wrist, "don't hit him with that baseball bat. You'll get arrested for assault, and then look at the trouble you'll be in. Just because you work at city hall doesn't mean you have diplomatic immunity."

"No, but I do have some pull."

"Enough," Juliana's mother said, wrenching the bat from her mother's hands. "I'm calling Sheriff Hollister. We'll file a restraining order against Mr. Montgomery, and he won't be able to bother Juliana again."

Montgomery? So *that's* why they'd called Jason a lying cheat and were so all-fired intent upon running him off. He couldn't say that he blamed them, considering the mistaken identity. "You've got this all wrong. Let me explain."

"No," Juliana said. "Let me. He's not the baby's father."

At that, Grandma's scowl vanished, and she turned to Jason sheepishly. "Then who are you?"

"He's Jason Rayburn," Juliana answered. "My former boss."

"Well, you should have said something sooner," Grandma said. "I could have killed you. I have a batting average of three-ninety in the Hot Mamas League."

Jason offered her a smile and tried to make light of the mistake. "If I'd known that and thought you would have swung, I would have hightailed it out of here."

"Maybe you still should." Juliana crossed her arms.

"Sheriff Hollister knows he'd better hurry over here when Gram thinks she has a prowler."

Apparently, he'd only eased the imminent threat of violence. "Juliana, if you don't mind, I need to talk to you. I'd like to apologize."

"Come on in," Grandma said. "We'd like to hear what you have to say."

We? Surely Juliana would ask for privacy. Wouldn't she?

When all three women stepped aside, he realized he was going to have an audience.

All right then. If that's the way she wanted it… "I'm sorry for offering you the job in Houston. I was wrong for beating around the bush. I should have been more direct, but I was afraid."

"Of what?" Juliana asked. "Having to fire me when you grew tired of having me around?"

When Grandma eased toward Mrs. Bailey, who held the bat, Jason beat her to it, snatching the weapon from Juliana's mother. "I'm sorry, ladies, but I'd feel a lot better if I could hold on to this for a while. Feel free to call the sheriff, though."

He tossed Juliana a smile, but she didn't return it. Okay, then. He'd better get back to the apology. "I was insensitive and selfish, and I'm sorry. I was afraid to admit how I was feeling about you. Over the past few weeks, I fell in love with you, but it scared the crap out of me. I've never felt this way before, and I'm not sure what to do with it. I haven't seen an example of a successful marriage or even a long-lasting relationship before, and what if I suck at it? What if I fail you? I'd not only hurt you, but I'd risk hurting the baby, too."

"You love me?" Juliana asked, her voice softening along with her stance.

"Doesn't that scare you?" he asked.

"Actually, it makes me feel a whole lot better about loving you."

She loved him, too?

"So I'm not alone in this?" he asked.

"No, you're not. And just so you know, I'm not sure what to make of it all, either. It happened so fast. But I *do* love you, Jason Rayburn."

"All right," he said, "then I'd like to apply for a job. And I'm willing to give you my résumé, which is sadly lacking in experience and education. But I'm eager to learn."

"What job is that?"

"I might not be your baby's biological father," Jason said, "but I'd like to apply for the daddy position—if it's available."

Tears welled in her eyes, and her lips quivered as they formed a smile. "The job is definitely open."

"How about the position of husband? I'm afraid I'm lacking in that department, too."

Her eyes widened, and her lips parted. "You want to marry me?"

"I didn't buy a ring yet, which I think was probably my first mistake in Bridegroom 101. So you can see that I have a lot to learn."

Juliana laughed while swiping at the tears streaming down her cheeks. "I don't need a ring."

"Oh, yes, she does," Grandma said. "It doesn't have to be a diamond, but a band of some kind is expected."

Juliana kissed her grandmother. "I know you mean well, and I love you to pieces. But I think it's time Jason and I discussed the rest of these details on our own."

Jason handed the bat to Grandma, trusting she wouldn't use it on him anymore. Then he took Juliana in his arms, burying his face in her hair, savoring her exotic scent and the feel of her in his arms. "I love you, Juliana. We'll work it all out one way or another."

Then he kissed her with all the love in his heart, a silent promise to do whatever it took to be the best husband and father he could, for now and for always.

When the kiss ended, the audience of two broke into smiles, clearly pleased by what had unfolded.

"I'd rather not have a long engagement," he told Juliana. "Unless you want one."

"Are you sure?" she asked.

"I'm more sure with every minute I stand here. So what do you say?"

"Yes, I'll marry you."

At that, cheers broke out.

"Jason," Mrs. Bailey said, "let me be the first to welcome you to the family. Some of us might be a little wild and woolly, especially if we have a pistol or a baseball bat in hand, but we're also very warm, loving and supportive."

"That is," Grandma said, "as long as you're good to our girls—both of them."

"I promise to do my best," he said. And he meant that from the bottom of his heart.

He drew Juliana close. As Granny had said, life was about love and family. And on that, he was willing to lay his heart.

Chapter Twelve

Less than a week after Jason proposed, Juliana stood in front of a floor-length mirror in the choir room at the Brighton Valley Community Church, adjusting her bridal veil.

The past few days had passed in a happy blur, but everything seemed to fall right into place as if they'd planned their small wedding months in advance. Her dress was a simple white satin gown with an empire waist that she'd found in a shop in Wexler. It fit perfectly and hadn't needed a single alteration.

Wanda at Valley Florists played softball with Gram and had given them a deal on the brightly colored flowers—pincushion proteas, peonies and garden roses.

Her mother stood beside her wearing a pale blue

dress, her brown hair pulled up in a twist. "You look beautiful, honey. But then again, I always knew you would be a beautiful bride someday."

Juliana felt beautiful, probably because she also felt loved and cherished. She glanced at her left hand, where Jason had placed a two-carat diamond just five days ago and where he would soon add a matching band.

She'd never been so happy.

"I'm going to make sure everyone is here and seated," Mom said. "Then I'll let Reverend Steuben know that we're ready to begin."

As her mother slipped out of the room, Juliana turned to her maid of honor and soon-to-be sister-in-law. Carly had driven in from San Antonio this morning and had just finished dressing in a light green sundress she'd purchased recently, but hadn't worn. "Thanks for making the trip on such short notice. I know it wasn't easy for you to get the time off."

Carly smiled, her eyes glimmering. "Actually, it wasn't so tough to get away. They let me go yesterday."

Juliana gasped. "I'm so sorry. What happened?"

"It's that stupid flu bug. I can't seem to kick it. One night I'm fine, then the next, I'm sick as a dog. There's no rhyme or reason for it, but the director said that if he couldn't count on me to be one hundred percent for every performance, he had to cut me loose. So here I am."

"I feel guilty for being so happy when your whole world must be falling apart."

Carly grabbed her hand and gave it a squeeze.

"Don't you dare feel sorry for me today. There'll be other singing gigs."

"Are you feeling better now?" Juliana asked.

"I'm fine. Just tired. But I got up early and drove six hours. I just need to get some rest, which I intend to do tonight. But if that doesn't help, I'll see my doctor while I'm in town."

"That might be a good idea. You don't want to take any chances."

"I won't. By the way, do you think Jason would mind if I stayed at the ranch for a while? I let my apartment in town go when I moved to San Antonio."

"Of course he won't mind. We'll be gone on our honeymoon for a week anyway."

Carly glanced in the mirror and fussed with an errant blond curl. "Where are you going?"

"We're spending the night in Houston, then flying to Guadalajara tomorrow morning."

"Why Mexico…?" Carly straightened and turned away from the mirror. "Wait, don't tell me. Jason plans to take over that search for Braden and look for Camilla's kids."

Juliana nodded. "He's determined to check out some of the orphanages and see if he can find them. He wants to make sure they're okay, and I can't blame him."

"What will you do if you find them?"

"He and Braden have been discussing options."

Carly crossed her arms. "That's interesting. And so is the fact that Jason asked Braden to be his best man today."

Juliana laughed. "It's not like they've become best friends yet."

"Still, it's a start."

Yes, it was. And if Juliana had her way, the brothers would grow closer as time went by.

The door opened, and Juliana's mother poked her head inside. "Everyone's here, Julie. Are you girls ready?"

Juliana adjusted her veil one last time. "Yes, we are."

And with that, she swept out of the choir room, ready to marry the man she loved.

While Jason waited with his brother in the church breezeway, ready to walk through the side door along the altar to stand with the minister who would perform the ceremony, his cell phone rang.

"Are you going to answer that *now*?" Braden asked.

Jason glanced at the display, noting that it was Doug at the home office. "This is the last call I'll take. Then I'll power down—or at least, silence it—for the next few days." He swept his finger across the screen. "Hey, Doug. What's up?"

"Stan Wainwright's attorney called again. How do you want me to respond regarding their proposal?"

"Schedule a meeting for the end of next week. I'm getting married today and will be off the radar for the next four or five days."

"That's a surprise. Who's the lucky woman? Have I met her?"

"No, not yet. It's Juliana Bailey."

"The woman you wanted to hire?"

Jason grinned. "Yep, that's the one."

"She turned down the offer I gave her. Did she change her mind about coming to work for us?"

"No, she'll probably enroll at one of the universities instead. She's still thinking about what she wants to do."

Doug blew out a whistle. "Marriage, huh? I never saw that coming. It sure happened quickly. What'd you decide to do? Elope?"

"Pretty much. It's a small guest list—just family and a few close friends."

Counting the bridal party of four, Braden's mom and Juliana's mother and grandmother, the family members only numbered seven. But even with the few friends Karen Bailey and Gram had invited, the church was going to be nearly empty.

Of course, Jason had brought the portrait of Granny and placed it in the front row. It only seemed right that she be there in spirit, although he sensed she would be looking down on them anyway.

"Well, boss," Doug said, "I wish you and your new wife all the best. I'm looking forward to meeting her."

"Thanks, I appreciate that. We'll stop by the office when we get back from our honeymoon."

After disconnecting the line and shutting off the power, Jason turned to Braden. "I won't turn it back on until I call you from Guadalajara."

"What's your first step going to be after you find the kids?" Braden asked.

"I'll look for Camilla's next of kin—or someone who'll provide them with a good home."

"And what if there isn't anyone? Dad wouldn't have left them in an orphanage."

"You're right. So if that's the case, then you and I will have to put our heads together and come up with a solution. Maybe someone in Brighton Valley will want to adopt them. Can you ask around? You might talk to the minister. He'd probably be a good resource."

"That's an idea. I'll see what I can do."

As the organist began to play, Jason nudged Braden's arm. "That's our cue. Come on, let's go."

They walked into the church along the altar and stopped where the Reverend Steuben had instructed them to stand. Then they faced the wedding guests.

Jason's new family sat in the front row. Karen Bailey, who'd soon be his mother-in-law, had told him to call her Mom. He hadn't done so yet, but something told him it wouldn't be long before the good-hearted woman made it seem like the most natural thing in the world for him to do. Next to her sat Jolene Crenshaw, otherwise known as Gram. The spunky old gal was proving to be a real hoot, with stories he might never tire of hearing. Then there was Braden's mom, Shannon Miller. The sweet lady had reached out to Jason years ago, but he hadn't accepted her friendship when he'd been a boy. Things were different now.

He'd grown up—especially these past few weeks. He had a sister and brother he hadn't appreciated until now. And if they were willing, he'd like to get to know them better.

As the organist changed the tune to the bridal march, Carly started down the aisle. His sister had grown into a beautiful young woman. He hoped that she hadn't been as damaged by her parents as he'd been by his. But if so, Jason hoped she found someone special someday, a loving man who touched her heart and soul like Juliana had touched his.

While Carly took her place along the altar, Juliana proceeded down the aisle. His beautiful bride, dressed in a gown of white, nearly stole his breath away. She held a bouquet in front of her belly, where their daughter grew. But she wasn't hiding her secret. Not any longer. They were going to be parents, and his name would join hers on the baby's birth certificate.

As Juliana approached the altar, Jason reached out to her, and she placed her hand in his.

This was it. The day his life would change.

No—the day his life would truly begin.

"Dearly beloved," Reverend Steuben said as he started the ceremony.

Jason could scarcely hear the words. All he could think of was how lucky he was, how glad he was to make Juliana his wife—forever, from this day forward—until death parted them.

Jason hadn't spared any expense when he'd booked the honeymoon suite at The St. Regis in Houston and lined up their catering staff. From the time the valet opened the passenger door until the newlyweds had been escorted to their room, Juliana and Jason were treated like royalty.

Soft music welcomed them into their elegantly decorated suite, where several bouquets of long-stemmed red roses adorned the living area. Platters of chocolate truffles, fresh fruit and a variety of cheeses, as well as a silver champagne bucket and two crystal flutes, sat on the glass-topped table.

"This is amazing," Juliana said.

Jason brushed a kiss on her cheek, then tipped the bellman.

"Why, thank you, sir." After placing their luggage in the dressing room, the bellman stood at the door. "If there's anything you need, Mr. Rayburn, don't hesitate to ask."

Juliet couldn't imagine what that might be, unless he planned to order their dinner from room service.

When they were finally alone, she looked at the ice bucket, which held two bottles rather than one. She placed her hand on her baby bump. "I'm not able to have champagne. Are you going to drink both of those?"

Jason gripped the neck of one bottle and lifted out sparkling apple cider. "I thought we should both toast our marriage tonight."

She placed her hands on her hips and smiled. "Why, Mr. Rayburn. You've turned out to be far more romantic than I realized."

He tossed her a crooked grin. "Should I apologize?"

She moved toward him and slipped her arms around his neck. "Don't you dare. I love romance—and I especially love *you*." Then she kissed him, long and deep.

As their bodies pressed together, Jason's hands slid along the curve of her back and down the slope of her derriere. He pulled her hips forward, against his erection, showing her how badly he wanted her.

She whimpered, then arched forward, revealing her own need, her own arousal.

When she thought she was going to die from desire, she ended the kiss, then slowly turned and lifted her hair, silently asking him to unzip her gown.

As Jason slid Juliana's zipper down in a slow and deliberate fashion, he slipped the fabric over her shoulders and let it fall to the floor. Then he kissed the back of her neck.

Moments later, she turned and stood before him in a white lace bra and matching panties. Her body, petite yet lithe, was everything he'd imagined it to be and more. Even the rounded slope of her belly, where their daughter grew, made her more feminine, more lovely. More alluring.

Today she became his wife, his life partner. And tonight, she had become his lover.

Following her lead, he undressed, too. When he'd removed all but his shorts, he eased toward her.

She skimmed her nails across his chest, sending a shiver through his veins and a rush of heat through his blood. Then she unsnapped her bra and freed her breasts, full and round, the dusky pink tips peaked.

As he bent and took a nipple in his mouth, she gasped in pleasure. He lavished first one breast, and then the other. Fully aroused, she swayed and clutched his shoulder to stay balanced.

Taking her gently in his arms, he carried her to the bedroom and placed her on top of the white goose-down comforter. Her luscious red curls splayed upon the pillow. Never had a woman appeared so lovely, so tempting…

Jason wanted nothing more than to slip out of his shorts and feel her skin against his, but he paused for a beat, drinking in the angelic sight.

"You're beautiful," he said, the words coming out in near reverence. Then he joined her on the bed, where they continued to kiss, to taste and to stroke each other until they were desperate for more.

"I want to feel you inside me," she said, pulling free of his embrace. "We can take things slow later. We have all night."

He didn't want to prolong the foreplay any longer, either. And she was right. They not only had the rest of the night, they had a lifetime ahead of them.

As he hovered over her, she reached for his erection and guided him home.

He entered her slowly, getting the feel of her, the feel of them. And as her body responded to his, she arched up to meet each of his thrusts, their pleasure mounting.

It seemed as though the world around them stood still—the universe, too. Nothing mattered but the two of them and what they were feeling and sharing together.

When Juliana reached a peak, she cried out, arched her back and let go. He released with her in an explosion that left him seeing a blast of comets and swirling stars.

As they lay on the rumpled comforter, lost in the magic of all they felt for each other, they listened to the music in the background, songs that promised true love would last forever.

When their breathing slowed and their heart rates returned to a steady beat, Jason ran his hand along the slope of her womb. "I can't wait until the baby is big enough for me to feel her move."

"At the rate she's growing, that shouldn't be too long.

He smiled. "It's exciting. I can't wait to see her, to hold her."

"What do you think we should we call her?" Juliana asked.

"Would you mind if we named her after Granny? Not Rosabelle, which doesn't sound very modern. But maybe Rose or Belle?"

"How about Bella Rose?" Juliana asked.

"I like that. It's a pretty name—for a little princess."

As they snuggled together, Jason drew Juliana close, savoring the way she fit in his arms, the softness of her skin, the light fragrance of her floral perfume.

"You know," he said, "I used to be afraid of getting this close to someone else."

"Physically?" she asked.

"No, that's not what I mean. It's not about sexual closeness. Strangers can do that."

She placed her hand along his cheek and smiled. "I know exactly what you mean." Then she trailed her fingers down to his heart. "It's a feeling that runs much deeper than sex."

"That's what I was getting at. And now that I have

you, I can't imagine being the loner I used to be. What would I do without you in my life, Juliana?"

"Grow to be a lonely old man?"

"That's true. What an awful thought."

She smiled. "Just think. You no longer have to worry about being lonely. Today you became a husband and father in one fell swoop."

"Don't forget, I also became a son and a grandson. My small family grew exponentially when I married you."

"That's true. I hope you're prepared for what that's going to mean."

"Life won't be boring," he said.

"That's for sure."

"But I didn't expect it to be. Thank you for making my life complete."

Then he kissed his wife again, knowing that he'd spend the rest of his life trying to make her as happy as she'd made him.

* * * * *

The Vineyards of Calanetti

Saying "I do" under the Tuscan sun…

Deep in the Tuscan countryside nestles the
picturesque village of Monte Calanetti. Famed for its
world-renowned vineyards, the village is also home
to the crumbling but beautiful Palazzo di Comparino.
Empty for months, rumors of a new owner are
spreading like wildfire…and that's before the
village is chosen as the setting for the royal
wedding of the year!

It's going to be a roller coaster of a year, but will
wedding bells ring out in Monte Calanetti
for anyone else?

Find out in this fabulously heartwarming, uplifting
and thrillingly romantic new eight-book continuity
from the Mills & Boon® Cherish™ series!

RETURN OF THE ITALIAN TYCOON

BY
JENNIFER FAYE

Published in Great Britain 2015
by Mills & Boon, an imprint of Harlequin (UK) Limited,
Eton House, 18-24 Paradise Road, Richmond, Surrey, TW9 1SR

© 2015 Harlequin Books S.A.

Special thanks and acknowledgement are given to Jennifer Faye for her contribution to The Vineyards of Calanetti series.

ISBN: 978-0-263-25157-9

23-0815

Harlequin (UK) Limited's policy is to use papers that are natural, renewable and recyclable products and made from wood grown in sustainable forests. The logging and manufacturing processes conform to the legal environmental regulations of the country of origin.

Printed and bound in Spain
by CPI, Barcelona

Award-winning author **Jennifer Faye** pens fun, heart-warming romances. Jennifer has won the RT Reviewers' Choice Best Book Award, is a Top Pick author and has been nominated for numerous awards. Now living her dream, she resides with her patient husband, one amazing daughter (the other remarkable daughter is off chasing her own dreams) and two spoiled cats. She'd love to hear from you via her website, www.jenniferfaye.com.

To Michelle Styles, an amazing friend,
who taught me so much, including that the important
part of writing was what I decided to do after the
dreaded "R". Thank you!

CHAPTER ONE

"CAN I SMELL YOU?"

Kayla Hill's fingers struck the wrong keys on her computer. Surely she hadn't heard her boss correctly—her very serious, very handsome boss. "Excuse me. What did you say?"

Angelo Amatucci's tanned face creased with lines as though he were deep in thought. "Are you wearing perfume?"

"Uh…yes, I am."

"Good. That will be helpful. May I have a smell?"

Helpful? With what? She gave up on answering an email and turned her full attention to her boss, who moved to stand next to her. What in the world had prompted him to ask such a question? Was her perfume bothering him? She sure hoped not. She wore it all the time. If he didn't like it or was allergic to it, she thought he'd have mentioned it before now.

Kayla craned her neck, allowing her gaze to travel up over his fit body, all six-foot-plus of muscle, until she met his inquisitive eyes. "I'm sorry but I… I don't understand."

"I just finished speaking with Victoria Van Holsen, owner of Moonshadows Cosmetics. She has decided that her latest fragrance campaign, even though she painstakingly approved it each step of the way, just won't do."

"She doesn't want it?" Kayla failed to keep the astonishment out of her voice.

A muscle in his jaw twitched. "She insists we present her with a totally new proposal."

"But this is a Christmas campaign. Everything should be finalized, considering it's already March." Then, realizing that she was speaking to a man with far more experience, she pressed her lips together, silencing her rambling thoughts.

"Now that information about her competitor's upcoming holiday campaign has been leaked, she wants something more noteworthy—something that will go viral."

"I thought the campaign was unique. I really like it." Kayla truly meant it. She wasn't trying to butter up her boss—that was just an unexpected bonus.

"The fact of the matter is, Victoria Van Holsen is a household name and one of our most important clients. Our duty is to keep her happy."

It was the company's motto—the client's needs come first. No matter what. And if Kayla was ever going to rise up the chain from her temporary detour as the personal assistant to the CEO of Amatucci & Associates Advertising to her dream job as an ad executive on Madison Avenue, she could never forget that the clients were always right. It didn't matter how unreasonable or outrageous their requests might be at times, keeping them happy was of the utmost importance.

"How can I help?"

"Stand up."

His face was devoid of emotion, giving no hint of his thoughts.

She did as he asked. Her heart fluttered as he circled her. When he stopped behind her and leaned in close, an army of goose bumps rose on her skin. Her eyes drifted closed as a gentle sigh slipped across her lips. Angelo Amatucci truly did want an up close and personal whiff of her perfume.

He didn't so much as touch a single hair on her, but she could sense him near her neck. Her pulse raced. If this most unusual request had come from anyone else, she'd swear they were hitting on her. But as Mr. Amatucci stepped to the front of her, his indifferent expression hadn't changed. Her frantic heart rate dipped back to normal.

There had never been any attempt on his part to flirt with her. Though his actions at times could be quite unpredictable, they were always ingenuous. She deduced that his sudden curiosity about her perfume had something to do with the Van Holsen account. But what could he be thinking? Because there was no way she was wearing a Moonshadows fragrance. One ounce of the stuff would set her back an entire paycheck.

"It seems to have faded away." A frown tugged at his lips.

"Perhaps this will be better." She pulled up the sleeve of her blue suit jacket and the pink blouse beneath it before holding out her wrist to him. "Try this."

His hand was warm and his fingers gentle as he lifted her hand to his face. Her heart resumed its frantic tap dancing in her chest. *Tip-tap. Tip-tap.* She wished it wouldn't do that. He was, after all, her boss—the man who held her career aspirations in the palm of his very powerful hand. A man who was much too serious for her.

Still, she couldn't dismiss that his short dark wavy hair with a few silver strands at the temples framed a very handsome, chiseled face. His dark brown eyes closed as he inhaled the fragrance, and she noticed his dark lashes as they swept down, hiding his mesmerizing eyes. It was a wonder some woman hadn't snatched him up—not that Kayla had any thoughts in that direction.

She had narrowly escaped the bondage of marriage to a really nice guy, who even came with her Mom's and Dad's stamp of approval. Though the breakup had been hard, it had been the right decision for both of them. Steven had wanted a traditional wife who was content to cook, clean and raise a large family. Not that there was anything wrong with that vision. It just wasn't what she envisioned for her future. She wanted to get out of Nowhereville, USA, and find her future in New York City.

When Mr. Amatucci released her arm, she could still

feel warmth where his fingers had once been. Her pulse continued to race. She didn't know why she was having this reaction. She wasn't about to jeopardize her rising career for some ridiculous crush on her boss, especially when it was perfectly obvious that he didn't feel a thing for her.

His gaze met hers. "Is that the only perfume you wear?"

She nodded. "It's my favorite."

"Could I convince you to wear another fragrance?"

He was using her as a test market? Interesting. She could tell him what he wanted to hear, but how would that help him develop a new marketing strategy? She decided to take her chances and give him honest answers.

"Why would I change when I've been using this same perfume for years?"

He rubbed his neck as she'd seen him do numerous times in the past when he was contemplating new ideas for big accounts. And the Van Holsen account was a very big account. The fact that the client had the money to toss aside a fully formulated ad campaign and start over from scratch was proof of their deep pockets.

Mr. Amatucci's gaze was still on her, but she couldn't tell if he was lost in thought. "How long have you worn that fragrance?"

"Since I was a teenager." She remembered picking out the flower-shaped bottle from a department store counter. It was right before her first ever school dance. She'd worn it for every special occasion since, including her first date with Steven. And then there was her high school graduation followed by her college commencement. She'd worn it for all the big moments in her life. Even the day she'd packed her bags and moved to New York City in search of her dreams.

"Talk to me." Mr. Amatucci's voice cut through her memories. "What were you thinking about just now?"

She glanced hesitantly at him. In all of the weeks she'd worked as his PA, they'd never ventured into a conversation that was the slightest bit personal. Their talks had always centered around business. Now, he'd probably think she was silly or sentimental or both.

"I was thinking about all the times in my life when I wore this perfume."

"And?"

"And I wore it for every major event. My first date. My first kiss. My—" A sharp look from him silenced her.

"So your attachment to the fragrance goes beyond the scent itself. It is a sentimental attachment, right?"

She shrugged. "I guess so."

She'd never thought of it that way. In fact, she'd never given her perfume this much thought. If the bottle got low, she put it on her shopping list, but that's as far as her thoughts ever went.

"So if our client doesn't want to go with a sparkly, feel-fabulous-when-you-wear-this campaign, we can try a more glamorous sentimental approach. Thanks to you, we now have a new strategy."

She loved watching creativity in action. And she loved being a part of the creative process. "Glad I could help."

He started to walk away, then he paused and turned back. "You were just promoted to a copywriter position before you took this temporary assignment as my PA, right?"

She nodded. What better way to get noticed than to work directly for one of the biggest names in the advertising industry.

"Good. You aren't done with this project. I want you to dig into those memories and write out some ideas—"

"But don't you have a creative team for this account?" She wanted to kick herself for blurting out her thoughts.

Mr. Amatucci sent her a narrowed look. His cool, professional tone remained unchanged. "Are you saying you aren't interested in working on the project?"

Before she could find the words to express her enthusiasm, his phone rang and he turned away. She struggled to contain her excitement. This was her big opening and she fully intended to make the most of it.

This was going to work out perfectly.

A smile tugged at Kayla lips. She'd finally made it. Though people thought she'd made a big mistake by taking a step backward to assume a temporary position as Mr. Amatucci's PA, it was actually working out just as she'd envisioned.

She'd gone after what she wanted and she'd gotten it. Well, not exactly, but she was well on her way to making her dreams a reality. With a little more patience and a lot of hard work, she'd become an account executive on New York's famous Madison Avenue in the exclusive advertising agency of Amatucci & Associates.

Her fingers glided over the keyboard of her computer as she completed the email to the creative department about another of their Christmas campaigns. Sure it was only March, but in the marketing world, they were working months into the future. And with a late-season snowstorm swirling about outside, it seemed sort of fitting to be working on a holiday project.

She glanced off to the side of her computer monitor, noticing her boss holding the phone to his ear as he faced a wall of windows overlooking downtown Manhattan. Being on the twenty-third floor, they normally had a great view of the city, but not today. What she wouldn't give to be someplace sunny—far, far away from the snow. After months of frigid temperatures and icy sidewalks, she was most definitely ready for springtime.

"Have you started that list?" Mr. Amatucci's piercing brown gaze met hers.

Um—she'd been lost in her thoughts and hadn't even realized he'd wrapped up his phone call. Her gaze moved from his tanned face to her monitor. "Not yet. I need to finish one more email. It shouldn't take me long. I think your ideas for the account are spot-on. Just wait until the client lays her eyes on the mock-ups."

Then, realizing she was rambling, she pressed her lips firmly together. There was just something about being around him that filled her with nervous energy. And his long stretches of silence had her rushing to fill in the silent gaps.

Mr. Amatucci looked as though he was about to say something, but his phone rang again. All eyes moved to his desk. The ringtone was different. It must be his private line. In all the time she'd been working for him, it had never rung.

It rang again and yet all he did was stare at the phone.

"Do you want me to get it?" Kayla offered, not sure what the problem was or why Mr. Amatucci was hesitant. "I really don't mind."

"I've got it." He reached over and snatched up the receiver. "Nico, what's the matter?"

Well, that was certainly a strange greeting. Who picked up the phone expecting something to be wrong? Then, realizing that she was staring—not to mention eavesdropping—she turned her attention back to the notes she'd been rewording into an email. She glanced up to see Mr. Amatucci had turned his back to her. He once again faced the windows and spoke softly. Though the words were no longer distinguishable, the steely edge of his voice was still obvious.

She looked at the paper on her desk, her gaze darting over it to find where she'd left off. She didn't want to sit here with her hands idle. No, that definitely wouldn't look good for her.

She was sending along some of Mr. Amatucci's thoughts about the mock-up of an ad campaign for a new client—a very demanding client. The account was huge. It would go global—like most of the other accounts her boss personally handled. Each of his clients expected Mr. Amatucci's world to revolve around them and their accounts. He took their calls, no matter the time—day or night. Through it all, he maintained his cool. To say Angelo was a workaholic was being modest.

As a result, he ran the most sought-after advertising agency in the country—if not the world. Stepping off the elevator, clients and staff were immediately greeted by local artists' work and fresh flowers. The receptionist was bright and cheerful without being annoying. Appointments were kept timely. The quality of the work was exemplary. All of it culminated in Amatucci & Associates being so popular that they had to turn away business.

"*Cosa!* Nico, no!" Mr. Amatucci's hand waved about as he talked.

Her boss's agitated voice rose with each word uttered. Kayla's fingers paused as her attention zeroed in on the man who never raised his voice—until now. He was practically yelling. But she could only make out bits and pieces. His words were a mix of English and Italian with a thick accent.

"Nico, are you sure?"

Had someone died? And who was Nico? She hadn't heard Mr. Amatucci mention anyone with that name, but then again, this call was on his private line. It was highly doubtful that it had anything to do with business. And she knew exactly nothing about his personal life—sometimes she wondered if he even had one.

"Marianna can't be pregnant!" The shouts spiraled off into Italian.

Pregnant? Was he the father? The questions came hard and fast. There was a little voice in the back of her mind that told her she should excuse herself and give him some privacy, but she was riveted to her chair. No one would ever believe that this smooth, icy-cool man was capable of such heated volatility. She blinked, making sure she hadn't fallen asleep and was having some bizarre dream. But when her eyes opened, her boss was standing across the room with his hand slicing through the air as he spoke Italian.

The paramount question was: Who was Marianna?

Angelo Amatucci tightened his grip on the phone until his fingers hurt. This had to be some sort of nightmare and soon he'd wake up. Could it be he'd been working a bit too much lately? Perhaps he should listen to the hints from his business associates to take a break from the frantic pace. That would explain why just moments ago when he'd been examining Ms. Hill's perfume—a scent he found quite inviting—that he'd been tempted to smooth his thumb along the silky skin of her wrist—

"Angelo, are you listening to me?" Tones of blatant concern laced Nico's voice, demanding Angelo's full attention. "What are we going to do?"

Nico was his younger brother by four years, and though their opinions differed on almost everything, the one area where they presented a unified front was their little sister, Marianna—who wasn't so little anymore.

"There has to be another answer to this. You must have misunderstood. Marianna can't be pregnant. She's not even in a serious relationship."

"I know what I heard."

"Tell me again."

"I wanted her to taste the wine from the vineyard. I think it's the best we've ever produced. Just wait until you try some—"

"Nico, tell me about Marianna."

"Yes, well, she has looked awfully pale and out of sorts since she returned home after her year of traveling. I thought she'd done too much partying—"

"*Accidenti!* She wasn't supposed to waste the year partying." Unable to stand still a moment longer, Angelo started to pace again. When his gaze met the wide-eyed stare of Ms. Hill, she glanced down at her desk. He made a point of turning his back to her and lowering his voice. "She was sent to Australia to work on the vineyards there and get more experience in order to help you. If I'd have known she planned for it to be a year of partying, I'd have sent for her. I could have put her to work at the office."

Nico sighed. "Not everyone is like you, big brother. We aren't all driven to spend every last moment of our lives working."

"And you didn't do anything about her being sick?"

"What was I supposed to do? I asked if she needed anything. She said no, that it was some sort of flu bug. What else was I supposed to do?"

Angelo's hand waved around as he flew off in a string of Italian rants. Taking a calming breath, he stopped in front of the windows and stared blindly at the snow. "And it took her confessing she was pregnant for you to figure it out?"

"Like you would have figured it out sooner? What do either of us know about pregnant women...unless there's something you haven't told me?"

"Don't be ridiculous!" Angelo had no intention of getting married and having a family. Not now. Not ever.

"She didn't have any choice but to come clean when I offered her some wine. She knew she couldn't drink it. Hard to believe that you and I will be uncles this time next year."

"Don't tell me you're happy about this development?"

"I'm not. But what do you want me to do?"

"Find out the father's name for starters."

"I tried. She's being closemouthed. All she said was that she couldn't drink the wine because she's eight weeks pregnant. Then she started to cry and took off for her room."

"Didn't you follow? How could you have just let her get away without saying more?"

"How could I? I sure don't see you here trying to deal with an emotional pregnant woman."

How had things spun so totally out of control? Angelo's

entire body tensed. And more importantly, how did he fix them? How did he help his sister from so far away?

Angelo raked his fingers through his hair. "She has to tell you more. How are we supposed to help if we don't even know which man is the father. She isn't exactly the sort to stay in a relationship for long."

"Trust me. I've tried repeatedly to get his name from her. Maybe she'll tell you."

That wasn't a conversation Angelo wanted to have over the phone. It had to be in person. But he was in the middle of overseeing a number of important projects. Now was not the time for him to leave New York. But what choice did he have? This was his baby sister—the little girl he remembered so clearly running around with a smile on her face and her hair in braids.

But a lot of time had passed since he'd left Italy. Would she open up to him? The fact his leaving hadn't been his idea didn't seem to carry much weight with his siblings, who were left behind to deal with their dysfunctional parents. Though he dearly missed his siblings, he didn't miss the constant barrage of high-strung emotions of his parent's arguments and then their inevitable reunions—a constant circle of epic turmoil.

Maybe the trouble Marianna had got herself into was some sort of rebellion. With their parents now living in Milan, there was only Nico at home to cope with their sister. And to Nico's credit, he never complained about the enormous responsibility leveled solely on his shoulders.

Now that their parents had moved on, Angelo didn't have any legitimate excuse to stay away. But every time the subject of his visiting Monte Calanetti surfaced, he pleaded he had too much work to do. It was the truth— mostly. Perhaps he should have tried harder to make more time for his siblings.

Stricken with guilt, anger and a bunch of emotions that Angelo couldn't even name, he couldn't think straight. As the oldest brother, he was supposed to look out for his brother and sister. Instead, he'd focused all of his time and energy on creating a thriving, wildly successful company.

In the process, he'd failed their wayward and headstrong sister.

And now her future would forever be altered.

He owed it to Marianna to do what he could to fix things. But how could he do that when he was so far away?

CHAPTER TWO

THIS ISN'T GOOD. Not good at all.

Kayla pressed Save on the computer. She needed to give Mr. Amatucci some space. She reached for her wallet to go buy a—a—a cocoa. Yes, that would suit the weather outside perfectly.

She got to her feet when her boss slammed down the phone. He raked his fingers through his short hair and glanced at her. "Sorry about that. Where were we?"

The weariness in his voice tugged at her sympathies. "Um…well, I thought that I'd go get some um…cocoa—"

"The Van Holsen account. We were talking about how we need to put a rush on it."

"Um…sure." She sat back down.

Kayla wasn't sure how to act. She'd never before witnessed her boss seriously lose it. And who exactly was Marianna? Was it possible Mr. Amatucci really did have a life outside this office—one nobody knew about? The thought had her fighting back a frown. Why should it bother her to think that her boss might have fathered a baby with this woman? It wasn't as if they were anything more than employee and employer.

Mr. Amatucci stepped up to her desk. "I'll need to go over this with you tomorrow afternoon."

"Tomorrow?"

She knew that he asked for the impossible at times and this happened to be one of those times. He'd caught her totally off guard. It'd take time to think out innovative ideas for the new campaign platform. And she had an important meeting that night, but there was no way she was telling her boss about that.

Mr. Amatucci arched a brow at her. "Is that going to be a problem?"

"Uh…no. No problem." She would not let this opportunity pass her by. "I'll just finish up what I was working on, and I'll get started."

He paused as though considering her answer. "On second thought, it'd be best to go over your ideas first thing in the morning."

"The morning?"

His gaze narrowed in on her, and she wished that her thoughts would quit slipping across her tongue and out her mouth. It certainly wasn't helping this situation. She was here to impress him with her capabilities, not to annoy him when he was obviously already in a bad mood.

"Ms. Hill, you seem to be repeating what I say. Is there some sort of problem I should be aware of?"

She hated that he always called her Ms. Hill. Couldn't he be like everyone else in the office and call her Kayla? But then again, she was talking about Angelo Amatucci—he was unlike anyone she'd ever known.

He was the first man to set her stomach aquiver without so much as touching her. She'd been so aware of his mouth being just a breath away from her neck as he'd sniffed her perfume. The memory was still fresh in her mind. Was it so wrong that she hadn't wanted that moment to end?

Of course it was. She swallowed hard. He was her boss, not just some guy she'd met at a friend's place. There could never be anything serious between them—not that he'd ever even noticed her as a desirable woman.

"Ms. Hill?"

"No, there won't be a…uh…problem." Who was she kidding? This was going to be a big problem, but she'd work it out—somehow—some way.

Her gaze moved to the windows and the darkening sky. With it only nearing the lunch hour, it shouldn't be so dark, which could only mean that they were going to get pounded with more snow. The thought of getting stuck at the office turned her nervous stomach nauseous.

Snow. Snow. Go away.

He gazed at her. "I didn't mean to snap at you—"

"I understand. You've got a lot on your mind."

"Thank you."

His gaze continued to hold hers. The dark depths of his eyes held a mystery—the story of the real man behind the designer suits and the Rolex watches. She had to admit that she was quite curious about him—more than any employee had a right to about her very handsome, very single boss. And that odd phone call only made her all the more curious. Maybe he wasn't as single as she'd presumed. The jagged thought lodged in her throat.

Mr. Amatucci's steady gaze met hers. "You're sure you're up for this project?"

She pressed her lips together, no longer trusting her mouth, and nodded. She'd have to reschedule tonight's meeting for the fund-raiser.

"Good. If you need help, feel free to ask one of the other PAs to take over some of your other work. The Van Holsen account is now your priority."

He gathered his tablet computer and headed for the door. "I've got a meeting. I'll be back later."

"Don't worry. I've got this."

Without a backward glance, he strode out of the room, looking like the calm, cool, collected Angelo Amatucci that everyone respected and admired for his creative foresight. But how he was able to shut down his emotions so quickly was totally beyond her.

What was she going to do about her meeting tonight? It didn't help that she'd been the one to set it up. Somehow she'd been put in charge of the Inner City League after-school program fund-raiser. The program was in a serious financial bind. ICL was a great organization that kept at-risk kids off the streets after school while their parents were still at work.

Kayla had been volunteering for the past year. Helping others was how her parents had raised her. They had always been generous with their spare time and money—not that they had much of either. Kayla may have hightailed it out of Paradise, Pennsylvania, as soon as she could, but there was still a lot of Paradise in her. And she'd swear that she got more back from the kids and the other volunteers than she ever gave to any of them. For a girl who was used to living in a small town of friends, it was a comfort to have such a friendly group to keep her from feeling isolated in such a large city of strangers.

There was no way she could reschedule tonight's meeting. They were running out of time until the charity concert and there was still so much to plan. Somehow she had to make this all work out. She couldn't let down the kids nor could she let down her boss. The thought of Angelo Amatucci counting on her felt good.

Not only was he easy on the eyes, but she really enjoyed working with him, even if he was a bit stiff and withdrawn most of the time. But now that she'd witnessed him emotionally charged, she couldn't help but wonder what it'd be like to get up close and personal with him.

Angelo shook his head.

Marianna pregnant! Impossible.

Okay, so it wasn't impossible, but why had she been acting so irresponsible? It wasn't as if she was married or even considering it. She changed romantic interests faster than he changed ties—never getting too serious—until now. Nico didn't even know the father's name. What was up with that?

"What do you think, Mr. Amatucci?"

He glanced up at his youngest and most promising account executive. This was a meeting to discuss the campaign for a new sports car that was going to be revealed later that year. The car was quite nice and was sure to create a buzz of attention.

But for the life of him, Angelo couldn't keep his mind wrapped around business—no matter how important the account. His head was in Italy at the village of Monte Calanetti—where he should be dealing with his sister's life-changing event.

Angelo glanced down at the presentation on his digital tablet and then back at the account executive. "I think you still have work to do. This presentation is flat. It isn't innovative enough. There's nothing here to sway a twentysomething consumer to take out a sizable loan on top of their college debt in order to have this car. I want the 'must have' factor. The part that says if I have this car all of my friends will be envious. This isn't just a car—this is a status symbol. Do you understand?"

Mike glanced down and then back at Angelo. "But this is what the client asked for."

"And it's your job to push the envelope and give the client something more to consider—to want." Maybe he'd been too quick in his determination that Mike was going to be an asset to Amatucci & Associates—unlike Kayla, who was constantly proving she was an independent thinker. "Try again."

Mike's mouth started to open but out of the corner of Angelo's eye he could see the copywriter give a quick shake of his head. Mike glanced back at Angelo. He nodded his agreement.

"Good. I expect to see something new in forty-eight hours."

Again the man's mouth opened but nothing came out. His lips pressed together, and he nodded. Now if only Angelo could handle his little sister in the same no-nonsense manner. He liked when things were easy and uncomplicated.

But now, with time to cool down, he realized that his only course of action was to return home—to return to Italy. His gut knotted as he thought of the expectations that he'd failed to fulfill. Back in Monte Calanetti he wasn't viewed as someone successful—someone influential. Back home he was Giovanni's son—the son who'd fled his family and their way of life, unlike his younger brother who took great pride in their heritage.

With the meeting concluded, Angelo made his way back to his office. With the decision made to leave first thing in the morning, he had to figure out how to handle his current workload. His clients would never accept having their accounts turned over to anyone else. They paid top dollar for one-on-one attention, and they would accept nothing less.

In order for him to stay on top of everything while traveling abroad, he needed someone who was good in a crisis, levelheaded and an independent worker. Kayla's beautiful face immediately sprang to mind. Could she be the answer?

He hesitated. She did have a habit of being a bit too chatty at times. But this was an emergency. Allowances would have to be made.

More importantly, he was impressed with her work ethic and her attention to details. She was hungry and eager— two elements that would serve her well. And best of all, she had an easy way with people—something that might come in handy on this trip.

He stopped next to her desk. "Ms. Hill." She glanced up. Her green eyes widened. How had he missed their striking shade of jade until now? He cleared his throat, focusing back on the business at hand. "How's the Van Holsen account coming?"

Color pinked her cheeks. "Mr. Amatucci, I... I haven't gotten to it yet. The phone has been ringing and I've been sending out information for some other accounts."

She looked worried as though she'd done something wrong. For the first time, Angelo wondered if everyone who worked for him was intimidated by him. He didn't like the thought of Ms. Hill being uncomfortable around him. He knew he wasn't an easy man to get to know, but he didn't like the thought of striking fear in the hearts of his employees.

"Relax. That's fine. Besides you'll have plenty of time to brainstorm on the flight."

"Excuse me. The flight?"

Since when did he speak without thinking it through first? It had to be this mess with Marianna. It had him off-kilter. "Something urgent has come up. I need to travel to Italy. And I need a competent person to accompany me."

"Me?" Excitement lit up her whole face. Before today, he'd never noticed that behind those black-rimmed reading glasses were not only mesmerizing green eyes but also a beautiful face—not that he was interested in her, or anyone. Ms. Hill clasped her hands together. "I've never been to Italy. I'd love it."

"Good. That's what I was hoping you'd say." But suddenly he wasn't sure spending so much time alone with her was such a good idea, especially now that he'd noticed the unique color of her mesmerizing eyes and her intoxicating scent. He swallowed hard. But it was too late to back out now. "You need to understand this trip will be business only, not a holiday."

"Understood."

"If you go, you'll need to be committed to your work 24/7. We can't afford to miss any deadlines. Is that acceptable?"

She hesitated and, for a moment, he worried that she would back out.

But then Ms. Hill's head bobbed. "I can do it."

"Make sure you are ready to go first thing in the morning."

"As in tomorrow morning?"

He nodded. "And expect to be gone for at least a week—

maybe two." Her mouth gaped and her eyes widened. It was obvious that he'd caught her off guard. But she wasn't the only one to be surprised today—by so many things.

When he'd approved her transfer to be his temporary PA, he'd made it perfectly clear that he demanded 100 percent focus and commitment from his employees. It was that extra push and attention to detail that put Amatucci & Associates head and shoulders above the competition.

If you wanted to be the best, you had to give it your all. And that is what he expected from all of his employees, even if it meant dropping family, hobbies and extracurricular activities in order to focus on the job. What he was asking of Kayla was no different than he'd ask of anyone.

When she didn't jump to accept his offer, he had no patience to wait for an answer. "That won't be a problem, will it?"

From the little he knew about his assistant, she didn't have a family. At least not in the city. And he hadn't seen or heard any hints of a man in her life. Maybe she was more like him than he'd originally thought.

Or was there something else bothering her? Was it the incident with the perfume? Perhaps that hadn't been one of his better moves. He was used to following his instincts when it came to his creative process, but there was something about his assistant that had him leaning a little closer to her slender neck and, for the briefest second, he'd forgotten the reason. His mind had spiraled in a totally inappropriate direction. That wouldn't happen again. He'd see to it.

After all, she wasn't his type. Her nondescript business suits, the way she pulled back her hair and the way she hid her luminous green eyes behind a pair of black-rimmed glasses gave off a very prim, old-fashioned persona. So why was he letting one unexplainable moment bother him?

"I could make arrangements to go, but I have so much work to do on the Van Holsen account—"

"If that's your only objection, then don't worry. The account can wait one day. In fact, take the rest of the day off. I expect to see you at the airport at 6:00 a.m.. Unless you'd like me to pick you up on the way."

"Uh, no." She shook her head vehemently. "I'll find my own way there."

He felt a bit obligated. He was, after all, asking her to drop everything on a moment's notice to help him out. He needed to make a concerted effort to be a little friendlier. "Are you sure? It's really no problem to swing by your place."

"You don't even know where I live."

"True. But since you're going out of your way to help me, I wouldn't mind going out of my way for you."

"Thank you. I appreciate it." She smiled, easing the stress lines from around her mouth.

Angelo found his attention straying to her kissable lips coated with a shimmery light pink gloss. Okay, so not every aspect of her was prim and proper. A fantasy of her pulling off her glasses and letting down her hair played in his mind. Realizing the direction of his wayward thoughts, he halted them.

With effort, his gaze rose over the light splattering of freckles on her pert nose to her intense green eyes. How had he failed to notice her beauty up until today? Had he been that absorbed in his work that he'd failed to see what was standing right in front of him?

He cleared his throat. "I'll pick you up at say five-thirty?"

"Mr. Amatucci—"

"If we're going to travel together, we should at least be on a first name basis. Please, call me Angelo." Now where in the world had that come from? He made a point of keeping his distance from his employees. But then again, he was taking her home with him, where she would meet his family, and that broke all of his professional rules. He reconciled himself with the fact that Kayla's time working for him was limited—soon his regular PA would be back. So maybe he could afford to bend the rules a bit.

"And please call me Kayla." She smiled again, and this time it reached her eyes, making them sparkle like fine jewels.

"We're going to my home in Italy. It's a small village in the Tuscany countryside—Monte Calanetti."

"I'm afraid I've never heard of it, but then again, I've never had the opportunity to travel abroad. Is it big? The village that is?"

He shook his head. "The last time I saw it— granted it has been quite a while—but it was as if time had passed it by. It is rather small and quaint. It is entirely a different world from New York City. Now, are you still interested in going?"

She hesitated and he worried that he'd have to come up with an alternate plan. As of right now, he didn't have one. He needed someone who was familiar with his accounts and wouldn't need a bunch of hand-holding. Kayla was his only viable option. He wasn't one to beg, but at this particular moment he was giving it serious consideration.

Her dimpled chin tilted up. "Yes, I am. It sounds like it'll be a great adventure."

"I don't know about that. The reason I'm going there isn't exactly pleasant, but then again, that isn't for you to worry about. You need to go home and pack."

"Okay. But what should I plan on wearing for the trip? Business attire?"

"Definitely something more casual. There won't be any business meetings, so use your best judgment." He had no doubt her casual attire was as dull and drab as her suits. Not that it mattered to him what she wore so long as she was ready to work.

Kayla gathered her things, and then paused. "Before I leave, should I make plane reservations?"

He shook his head. "No need. We'll take my private jet."

Her pink lips formed an O but nothing came out. And for a moment, he let himself wonder what it'd be like to kiss those full, tempting lips. Not that he would, but he could imagine that one kiss just wouldn't be enough. Something told him that lurking beneath that proper and congenial surface was a passionate woman—

Again, he drew his thoughts up short. The last thing he needed was to notice her feminine qualities. He wasn't about to mix business with pleasure. No way.

CHAPTER THREE

FLUFFY CLOUDS FLOATED past the jet's windows.

They'd soon be touching down in Italy.

A giddy excitement bubbled up in Kayla's chest as she glanced across the aisle at Mr. Amatucci—er—Angelo. She still had a problem remembering to call him by his given name after referring to him as Mr. Amatucci for so long. Being on a first-name basis left her feeling unsettled—not exactly sure how to act around him. If anything, Angelo was even more quiet and reserved than before. Had he sensed her attraction to him?

Impossible. She hadn't said or done anything to betray herself. She smoothed a hand over her gray skirt. She was worrying for nothing.

Just act normal.

She glanced at her boss. "Do you know how long until we arrive?"

Angelo turned in his leather seat to look at her. "What did you say?"

"I was wondering how long we have until we land in Italy."

"Not much longer." His dark gaze dipped to the pen and paper in her lap. "Are you working?"

"I am." Her body tensed as she read over her scribbled notes for the Van Holsen account. She didn't have anything innovative enough to measure up to the Amatucci standard. "I thought this would be a good time to flesh out some ideas."

"And you like doing it longhand?"

"I think better that way." She'd never really taken the time to consider her creative process, but yes, now that she thought about it, she did always start with pen and paper. She didn't move to the computer until she had a fully functioning idea.

"Is that for the Van Holsen account?"

"Yes, I've been doing what you suggested and going with a nostalgic appeal."

"Good. Can I see what you've come up with so far?"

She glanced down at all of her scribbles and half thoughts. And then her eyes caught sight of his name scrolled out in cursive. Her heart clenched. *What in the world?*

She must have done it while she'd been deep in thought. Immediately, her pen started crossing it out. The last thing she needed was for her boss to think she had a crush on him. That would be the end of her career.

"I… I don't exactly have anything solid yet." She was going to have to be careful in the future of what she wrote down just in case Mr. Curious decided to peer over her shoulder.

"I could help you. Let me see what you have." He held out his hand.

She really didn't want to hand over her notepad, but what choice did she have if she wanted to stay in his good graces? She glanced down at the scratched-out spot and squinted. She could still see his name—all fourteen letters. But that was because she knew it was there. She ran the pen over it a few more times.

With great hesitation, she handed over the legal pad. Angelo's acute gaze skimmed over the page. Her palms grew moist. He took his time reading, but he paused as he reached the bottom. That was where she'd vigorously scratched out his name, almost wearing a hole in the page.

"I'm guessing that you've ruled out this idea?" He gestured to the blob of ink.

"Most definitely. It wouldn't have worked."

"Are you sure? Maybe you should tell me what it was,

and then we can see if there's any value in pursuing it?"
He sent her an expectant look.

"Honestly, it's not worth the effort. I was totally off the
mark with it." A man like Angelo, who could have a gorgeous model or movie star on each arm, would never be
interested in someone as plain and boring as herself.

He let the subject go and turned back to her notes while
she sat there realizing just how "off the mark" her imagination had wandered. No way was she going down that
romantic path again, even if it was paved with rose pet-
als. All it'd do was lead her into making a commitment—
having a family—everything she'd left behind in Paradise.
She wanted to be different—she wanted to be professionally successful. She needed to show everyone back in her
hometown that she'd made her dreams come true.

And then Angelo's gaze lifted to meet hers. She should
glance away but the intensity of his gaze held her captive.
Her heart raced. He didn't say anything, which was just as
well, because she doubted she could have strung two words
together. Had he figured out what she'd scribbled on the
page? *Please, not that.* But then again, he didn't look upset.
Instead, he looked like—like what? The breath hitched in
her throat. Was he interested in her?

He glanced away and shook his head. "Sorry about that.
Something you wrote down gave me an idea for the campaign, but then it slipped away."

Silly girl. What made her think he'd ever look at her that
way? And why would she want him to? It'd be the beginning of the end of her rising career—her dream.

Get a grip, Kayla.

"No problem." She held out her hand, willing it not to
shake. "If you let me have the pad back, I'll work on getting my thoughts more organized. Maybe we can discuss
them as soon as we get situated in Italy." She wasn't quite
sure where their accommodations would be since Angelo

had personally handled the travel arrangements, but she was certain they would be nice.

"Sounds good. Just because we're out of town doesn't mean we should fall behind on our work. I don't plan to be here long—just long enough to take care of some personal business. If we're lucky, perhaps I can wrap it up in a day or two."

What had happened to a week—maybe two? Disappointment assailed her. But it would be for the best. After all, it'd get her home sooner to make sure the ICL fund-raiser was moving along without too many snags. But she still couldn't shake the disappointment.

He'd missed this.

Angelo maneuvered the low-slung sports car over the windy roads of the Tuscany hillside toward his home in Monte Calanetti. He was grateful to be behind the wheel. It helped to center his thoughts. On the plane, he'd noticed his assistant in the most unexpected way. With her peaches-and-cream complexion, he'd been tempted to reach out and caress her smooth skin. But it was her green, almost-jade eyes that sparkled and hinted at so much more depth to the woman than he already knew—or would expect to know. The last thing he needed to do was get distracted by his assistant.

Actually, now that he'd noticed her—really noticed her—it was getting harder and harder to keep his mind on business around her. Perhaps bringing her on this trip wasn't his best decision, after all, but it was a necessity. He needed her help. He assured himself that, in the end, it would all work out as long as he stayed focused on the business at hand.

Thankfully, Kayla was just temporary help until his assistant returned from maternity leave. Then life would get back to normal. As far as he was concerned, that wouldn't be soon enough.

"This is wonderful."

The sound of Kayla's excited voice drew him out of his thoughts. He took his eyes off the roadway for just a moment to investigate what she found so fascinating, but he only saw vegetation. "Sorry. I missed it."

"No, you didn't. It's this. The long grass and the trees lining the roadway. It's beautiful."

What? The woman had never been outside of the city? He supposed that was possible. He honestly didn't know much about her other than her excellent work ethic. That, in and of itself, would normally be enough for him, but since they were traveling together, what would it hurt to know a little more?

"Is this your first time outside New York City?"

"I'm not a native New Yorker."

They had something else in common. Still, after all of those years living in New York, it was home to him now. He thrived on the constant energy that flowed through the city. He couldn't imagine living anywhere else. "Where does your family live?"

He could feel her curious gaze on him, but he didn't turn to her. "They live in a small town in Pennsylvania."

"So you really didn't move all that far from home."

"That's not what my parents think."

He glanced at her and saw she'd pressed her lips together in a firm line. Something told him that she hadn't meant to share that bit of information. But why? What else was she holding back?

"Your parents aren't crazy about the big-city life?"

There was a moment of hesitation as though she were trying to figure out how to answer him. "It's not New York so much as the fact that I'm not in Paradise anymore. They had my whole life planned out for me, but I rejected it."

"You must have had one of those chopper mothers I've heard about."

Kayla laughed. The sound was melodious and endearing. In that moment, he realized that he'd never heard her laugh before. He really liked it and hoped she'd do it more often, but for the life of him, he had no idea what he'd said to cause such a reaction.

"Do you mean a helicopter mom?"

He shrugged. "I guess. I knew it was something like that."

"My mom wasn't too bad. I know friends that had mothers who were much more controlling. But my mom is pretty good."

Wait. Something wasn't adding up. He pulled to a stop at an intersection. If he went straight ahead, it'd lead them up the hill to the village. But if he veered to the right, it'd take them to Nico's boutique vineyard—their childhood home.

Checking the rearview mirror and finding no traffic behind them, he paused and turned to her. "So if your mother is so great, why did you flee to the big city?"

Kayla shifted in her seat as though she were uncomfortable—or was it that he was digging too deep into personal territory? He knew what that was like—wanting to keep a firm lid on the past. But he couldn't help himself. There was just something about Kayla that intrigued him—and it went much deeper than her beauty. He was genuinely interested in her as a person.

Her voice was soft when she spoke, and he strained to hear. "I didn't live up to my parents' expectations."

That was so hard to believe. He was a very particular employer, and Kayla lived up to and in some areas exceeded his expectations. "Do they know what a wonderful job you've done at Amatucci & Associates?"

Her gaze widened. "You really think so?"

Angelo didn't realize he'd kept his approval of her work under wraps. Then again, he wasn't the sort of man to go on about someone's performance. Yet, in this moment, something told him that Kayla really needed to hear his evaluation of her performance.

"I think you've done an excellent job—"

"You do?" She smiled brightly and practically bounced in her seat before clasping her hands together.

"I do—"

A horn beeped behind them.

The interruption was a welcome one. This conversation was getting a little too emotional for his comfort. He thought for a moment that in her glee she might throw her arms around him. He didn't do hugs—no way—and certainly not with an employee. He couldn't—wouldn't—let the lines between them blur.

Angelo eased the car forward, focusing once again on the road and his destination. He urged himself to ignore the funny feeling Kayla's obvious excitement had given him. He trained his thoughts on the scene he'd be walking into at the vineyard. His fingers tightened on the black leather steering wheel.

On second thought, maybe he should have dropped Kayla off at the hotel before venturing out here. But he hadn't exactly been thinking straight—not since Nico had dropped the bombshell that their little sister was about to have a baby. Angelo was about to become an uncle. He wasn't sure how he felt about that. He'd worked so hard to distance himself from his family—from his emotionally charged parents and their chaotic marriage. But now that they'd moved, what excuse did he have to stay away from his birthplace—the home of his brother and sister?

"Is this the way to the village?" Kayla sat up a little straighter.

"No, this is the way to my brother's vineyard."

"Oh, how exciting. I've never visited a vineyard. I can't wait to see it. I bet it's beautiful like those magazine photos. Will we be staying there?"

"No." Angelo's tone was brusquer than he'd intended, but her endless chatter combined with his pending reunion had him on edge.

He chanced a glance her way and found her eyes had widened in surprise. He couldn't blame her, but how did he explain his family dynamics to her? Then again, why did he feel a need to explain his family at all?

"It'll be best if we stay at a hotel in the village. I'm not sure if the internet at the vineyard has been updated." There, that sounded like a valid reason for them to have some space between him and his siblings.

"Oh, I hadn't thought about that. I know the Van Holsen account needs to be updated as soon as possible. I already contacted the art department and let them know that a whole new strategy will be coming their way."

"Good. I want everything to move ahead without delay."

Whether he liked it or not, he'd been right to bring Kayla along on this trip. She was efficient and quite good at her job. Now, if only he could be just as professional and keep his mind from meandering into dangerous territory. However, the more time he spent around her, the more he found himself being anything but professional.

CHAPTER FOUR

THE CAR TURNED to the right and lurched forward. Kayla
grabbed for the door handle. She had no idea that the vineyard would be so far out in the country, but then again,
this was her first trip to Italy. In fact, other than one business trip to Canada, this was her first expedition out of
the country.

"Welcome to Calanetti Vineyard."

Kayla glanced around, taking in the neat lines of grapevines. "Does all of this belong to your brother?"

"No. His vineyard is just a small portion of this land,
but he produces some of the highest quality wine in the
country."

"And you grew up here?"

"I did." Angelo pulled the car to a stop in front of a two-
story villa. The home featured earth tones that blended
in well with the land. "My brother will be expecting us. I
phoned him from the airport."

As if on cue, the front door of the villa swung open
and a man stepped out. Kayla did a double take—it was
like looking at a slightly younger version of Angelo. The
man approached the car wearing an easy smile. His eyes
were dark brown like his brother's, but there was an easiness in them. They were quite unlike Angelo's dark and
mysterious eyes.

When Nico opened the car door for her and held out his
hand, she accepted his offer. Then she noticed the biggest
difference of all. Instead of her stomach quivering with nervous energy in response to Nico's touch, she had no reaction
at all. What did that mean? How could two men who looked
so much alike have her reacting in such opposite ways?

It had to be that Angelo was her boss. That must be it. There was simply no other reasonable explanation for the electric charge that Angelo gave her every time she felt his gaze on her or when their fingers brushed as they passed papers back and forth.

"Benvenuta." Nico's voice carried a thick, warm Italian accent. When she sent him a puzzled look, he smiled. *"Scusi.* Welcome."

She smiled back, immediately liking Angelo's brother. "I'm so glad to be here."

"My brother doesn't bring many visitors home. In fact, you are the first. You must be special—"

"Nico, this is my assistant." Angelo frowned at his sibling.

Nico's dark brows rose and then a knowing smile pulled at his lips. "I hope my brother doesn't work you too hard while you're in Italy. There's so much to see. I'd love to give you a tour of the vineyard—"

"She doesn't have time for that stuff. She's here to work." Any hint of the easiness Angelo had displayed in the car was gone—hidden behind an impenetrable wall. "Now where is Marianna?"

"I don't know."

"What? Didn't you tell her that I was on my way?"

"I did." Nico folded his arms over his broad chest and lifted his chin. "I think that's the reason she left so early this morning without even bothering to grab a bite to eat. I haven't seen her since, but then again, I haven't looked for her, either."

"You let her walk away—?"

"What did you want me to do? Lock her in her room?"

"Maybe if you'd have done that a while ago, we wouldn't be in this mess."

Nico's arms lowered and his shoulders straightened. "You're blaming me for this?"

Angelo's body visibly tensed. "Yes...no. If only I'd have known something was wrong, I could have..."

"Could have what?"

Kayla's gaze darted between the two men who glared at each other. It was time to do something and fast. "This certainly is a beautiful place you have here." She acted as though she were totally oblivious to the torrent of undercurrents. "Angelo told me you produce some of the finest wine in Italy."

At last, the brothers quit glaring at each other. Nico turned to her. "My brother got that much right. I'd be happy if you'd sample some while you're here."

"I'd be honored."

This palpable tension certainly wasn't what she'd been expecting for a family reunion, but then again, after overhearing the heated conversation when Nico had phoned the office, she shouldn't be too surprised. She turned her attention to her always-in-control boss, who looked as though he was about to lose his cool edge and have a meltdown. *Intriguing.* There was definitely a lot more to him than what she'd witnessed so far.

"I should have come back before now." There was a weary, pained toned to Angelo's voice. "I let the past keep me away."

Nico turned back to his sibling. "What happened to you was a long time ago. It wasn't right, but a lot has changed since then. You no longer have an excuse to stay away."

"But I still have a company to run. I don't have time to drop everything and travel halfway around the globe to check up on things. As far as I knew, everything was all right."

"Maybe if you didn't work all the time and bothered to call occasionally, you'd know how things were going around here."

Questions crowded into Kayla's mind—questions that were absolutely none of her business. But that didn't stop her from wondering what had happened to drive Angelo away from his family. He obviously loved them or he wouldn't have let his cool composure slide. And what caused him to keep his emotions under lock and key in the first place?

Angelo raked his fingers through his hair. "Maybe I should have called more."

"Yes, you should have."

The thud of a door slamming shut punctuated Nico's words. Kayla hesitantly glanced off in the distance as a young woman marched toward them. Her brown hair was wild and curly as it fluttered in the breeze. Her lips pressed into a firm line and her eyes narrowed in on the two men. This must be Marianna.

"Enough!" The woman came to a stop between Angelo and Nico. "You two are being ridiculous. Anytime you both want to quit with the overprotective-brother routine, we can talk."

Though she was at least a foot shorter than her brothers, Marianna certainly didn't hesitate to step between them. Something told Kayla that little sister wasn't a shrinking violet with these two as her brothers. She'd definitely have to be strong-willed. Silently Kayla cheered her on.

Angelo's broad chest puffed up before he sighed. When he spoke, his voice was much gentler. "Marianna, if only I'd known—"

"Stop." The young woman pressed her hands to her hips and pulled back her slender shoulders. "Neither of you are to blame for my choices."

Angelo's brows drew together in a formidable line. "But—"

"I'm not done." Her shoulders remained ramrod straight. "I'm a grown woman, if you hadn't noticed. But then again, you've been off in the States and missed the fact that I've grown up. Maybe if you'd spent more time here, you'd have realized this."

Kayla's heart went out to Angelo. He'd obviously made mistakes where his family was concerned, and they weren't shy about calling him out on it. In his eyes, she could see pain and regret. Beneath his hard, protective shell lurked a vulnerable man.

Angelo's stance eased and his head lowered. "I know I should have been here for you—"

"No. This isn't what I want." Marianna shook her head, sending her hair flying. "I don't need you feeling guilty. I need you to understand that I can make my own decisions."

"See, I told you," Nico piped in. "Trying to deal with her isn't as easy as it sounds."

Angelo turned to his brother. "Maybe if you'd have told me sooner—"

Nico's dark brows drew together in a formidable line. "Told you—I tried calling you but I always got your voice mail. And you didn't call back."

"I… I was getting around to it."

Nico shook his head in disbelief. "I'm glad to know where I fit on your list of priorities."

"You don't understand." Angelo rubbed the back of his neck. "You don't know what it's like to have a lot of people relying on you to produce cutting-edge promotions and other people looking to you for a paycheck. It's not as easy as it sounds to run a successful company."

Nico expelled a disgusted sigh. "And you think turning this place into a renowned boutique vineyard has been easy? Yet I still found time to call you."

"Your message never said it was important."

"Stop!" Marianna pushed Angelo back. "You aren't helping anything by coming here and fighting with Nico."

Angelo took a deep breath and blew it out. "I know I wasn't here when you needed me, but I'm here now. Let me help."

Kayla watched all of this in utter amazement. She never would have guessed her boss was capable of such a wide range of emotions. So then why did he strive at the office for such an unflappable persona? What was she missing?

Kayla was about to introduce herself to Marianna, when the young woman stared up at Angelo and said, "And I wish you weren't here now. Not like this. Not with all of the fighting." When Angelo's brows rose and his mouth opened but nothing came out, Marianna added, "I don't want to play referee." Her hand moved protectively to her still-flat stomach. "It isn't good for the baby."

Angelo and Nico looked at each other as though neither had considered how their fighting would stress their sister—their pregnant sister.

Marianna moved to look at both of her brothers. "I'm fully capable of taking care of myself."

Nico rolled his eyes. Angelo crossed his arms but refrained from saying anything.

"I hope you'll both give me some space."

Angelo's brows rose. "But first, we want to know the name of the father."

"That's none of your business."

Nico stepped forward. "It is our business if he thinks he's going to get our sister pregnant and then just walk away."

Marianna's face filled with color.

Angelo pressed his hands to his sides. "We deserve the right to speak to this guy. He needs to know that we expect him to step up and do his part—"

"And I expect you both to mind your own business." Marianna started for the house.

Enough was enough. The time had come to make a hasty exit. It was obvious that Marianna was in over her head and that her brothers were only making the situation worse.

When Angelo turned to follow his sister, Kayla moved swiftly in front of him. "I'm not feeling so good." It wasn't totally a lie—her stomach was in knots watching the Amatucci siblings squabble. "Could you take me to the hotel?"

Angelo's worried gaze moved from her to his sister to her. "Sure." He turned to Nico. "We need to talk more."

"I figured as much."

"I'll be back after we get settled."

Nico shrugged. "I'll be here. I can't speak for Marianna."

"I don't think she needs anyone to speak for her. She certainly does have a mind of her own. Even if it gets her in trouble."

"She always was strong-willed. I think she's a lot like Mama."

"Agreed."

At last the two had something they agreed on—their little sister's character. And now that things were on a good note, it was definitely time to say goodbye.

Kayla cleared her throat, hoping to gain Angelo's attention. When he didn't turn her way, she proceeded to say, "Angelo, are you ready to go?"

She'd have rather had a tour of the vineyard and stretched her legs, but not under these strained circumstances. She couldn't help but wonder if it was the situation with their sister that had them at odds or if they had a history of not getting along.

Angelo glanced her way. "It was a long trip. I suppose you would like to lie down for a bit."

"That would be nice." She turned to Nico, who was still eyeing his brother with obvious agitation. "It was so nice to meet you. I hope that we'll see each other again."

"I suppose that'll depend on my brother and whether he trusts you with me—"

"Nico. Enough." Angelo's voice held an obvious note of warning. "We'll be staying at the Hotel Villa Bellezza. If Marianna cools down, phone me."

Angelo quietly followed her to the car and opened the door for her. "I'm sorry you had to witness that."

"Don't be." She searched for words of comfort. "Families are messy. It's what happens when people love each other. And I saw a lot of love back there."

"You did?"

"Most definitely." She stepped past him and got in the car.

She'd never met anyone who could get under her boss's skin like Nico. The man appeared to have needling his big brother down to a fine art. There was so much more to the polished, successful businessman standing next to her than she'd ever imagined. And she was anxious to know more.

CHAPTER FIVE

KAYLA GRIPPED THE armrest tightly.

The line of cypress trees was no more than a blur as Angelo accelerated away from the vineyard. He didn't say a word as they zigzagged through the valley before starting their ascent up a hillside. The vegetation was so green and lush that she couldn't imagine there was a village, much less a five-star hotel, within miles of here.

"I need to apologize." Angelo's voice broke the awkward silence. "I didn't mean to have you witness our family drama."

"It's okay. I know how families can be." She couldn't help but want to know more about him and his family. "Your parents, do they live around here?"

He shook his head, keeping his eyes on the road. "They left the vineyard to us kids and moved to Milan. It was best for everyone."

Kayla wasn't sure what to say to that. Obviously there wasn't a close relationship between him and his parents. Did she even want to know why? It'd just move them further from boss and employee and into a new relationship— one that she didn't want to examine too closely.

Angelo downshifted for a curve. "I know that you come from a close-knit family, so it'd be hard for you to understand a family that functions better apart than together."

Kayla was surprised that he kept talking about his private life when she hadn't even asked him anything. It was as if these thoughts were pent up inside him, and he needed to get them out if he was to have any peace.

She searched frantically for words of comfort. "Every family is different. Not better. Not worse. Just different."

"But this is my fault." His palm smacked the steering wheel. "I shouldn't have left for New York to go to college. I should have found a way to stay here. Marianna was so young when I left, and my parents—well, they were so consumed with each other that they didn't have time to worry about anyone else."

"I'm sure they did their best."

He shook his head. "You don't know my parents. They are the most passionate people I know. And not in a good way. One minute they love each other and the next they are getting divorced. That's the end. They never want to see each other again. To say our childhoods were unstable is putting it mildly."

Kayla struggled to keep her mouth from gaping open. Her parents were the most mild-mannered couple. Their voices were rarely raised to each other, and they still gazed lovingly at each other like a couple of starstruck teenagers. Kayla knew they wanted her to experience the same sort of love and happiness. That's why she didn't hold it against them for trying to guide her life. It's just that she was different. There was so much more to life than love, marriage and babies. And she wanted to experience all of it.

Angelo cleared his throat, but his voice still rumbled with emotion. "I just couldn't take any more of their fighting and making up. It was so unnerving to never know if my parents were passionately in love or on the verge of calling their divorce attorneys. And there was no way I could take Nico with me—not that he'd have gone. He has this unbreakable tie to the vineyard—to the village. He never would have done what I did. And maybe he's right. Maybe if I'd stayed then Marianna wouldn't be alone and having a baby."

"It's not your fault." Kayla resisted the urge to reach out to him. "Your sister is a grown woman. She has to be allowed to make her own choices. Right or wrong. You couldn't have prevented this."

"But maybe if I'd been here, she'd have felt like she still had a family that loves her. Then she wouldn't have taken off on this trip of hers only to let some smooth-talking guy take advantage of her." Angelo's body noticeably stiffened.

"I'm fairly certain that no one could take advantage of your sister. She seems quite strong, like her brothers. She just needs some time to sort things out."

He sighed. "I'm sure she's plenty confused. And I suppose Nico and I did nothing to help by arguing. It's just that every time my brother and I get together, we disagree. We are very different. That's why I reserved us a suite at the hotel. I knew staying at the vineyard would just lead to more drama, and that's the last thing any of us need."

"But you two didn't argue at the end."

"That's because we both agree that Marianna needs both of us—whether she likes it or not."

"Good. Maybe you can build on that."

"Perhaps."

She decided that enough had been said for now on that subject. Angelo needed time to calm down. "Is the hotel far from here?"

"No. It's just at the rise of the hill." His voice had returned to its normal reserved, unemotional tone.

"Really. I never would have guessed. I can't wait to see the village." But if Angelo was serious about this being a productive trip, she wasn't sure that she'd get to see much of Italy. The thought dampened her mood. "Do you think I'll have some time to look around the village?"

He glanced at her before turning back to the road. "There really isn't much to see."

She'd beg to differ with him. Everything about Italy was special for this American girl. This was the biggest adventure of her life. How could he think this place was anything but special?

"I… I've never been here before. I was just hoping to sneak in some sightseeing."

"As long as you get your work done, I don't care what you do with your free time."

Oh, good!

As the car climbed the hill, Angelo pulled to the side for an older truck that was barreling toward them. Once back on the road, the car's tire dropped into a rut and bounced Kayla. The seat belt restrained her, but her bare thigh brushed against his hand as it gripped the gearshift. Heat raced up her leg, under her skirt and set her whole body tingling.

"Sorry about that." He quickly moved his hand back to the steering wheel.

Had he noticed their touch? Had it affected him, too? Was that why he'd moved his hand? Or was she just being ridiculous? Definitely being ridiculous. She knew when men were interested in her, and Angelo certainly wasn't. A frown pulled at her lips.

So why then did it bother her? Sure, he was the most handsome man she'd ever laid eyes on. But, he was her boss—the key to her career. She wouldn't—she couldn't—let some ridiculous crush get in her way after everything she'd sacrificed to get here.

Time to think about something else.

"I didn't have time to do any research before we left New York. What should I see while I'm here?"

He shrugged. "Honestly, there's nothing special about Monte Calanetti. It's just small and old."

"I'm used to small towns. I grew up in one. And there's always something special about them."

He glanced her way and his dark brow rose. "What was special about your town?"

"A number of things." She wasn't sure that she wanted to delve into this subject with him. She'd finally got past her homesickness. The way she'd done that was by not thinking of her hometown and what made it special.

"Such as?"

She shook her head. "Never mind."

Before he could question her more, she spotted what she thought was the edge of Monte Calanetti. "Are we here?"

"We are."

She stared out the windshield, not exactly sure what to expect. There was a tall wall. As they eased past it she found rustic buildings of earth tones similar in color to Nico's villa. People stopped and glanced their way as though trying to figure out if they should know them.

As more and more people turned to stare, Kayla couldn't hold back her curiosity any longer. "Why are they staring?"

He shrugged. "It must be the car."

"The car?"

"Yeah, you know because it's a sports car. They probably don't see many around here."

"Oh." She glanced over at him. Was he sitting up a little straighter? And was his chin tilted just a little higher? *Interesting.* "The village looks quite intriguing. And small enough to explore on foot."

Angelo didn't say anything. He just kept driving. And sadly he didn't offer her a guided tour. She forced herself not to frown. Then again, why should he bend over backward for her? She was, after all, merely an employee. They weren't even friends. Though little by little, she was getting to know Angelo better and better. In fact, she'd learned more about him in the past forty-eight hours than she had in the past two months while working as his assistant.

The car slowed as they eased through a wrought iron gate and up the short paved drive to a two-story building. The outside was plain but there was an elegance in its simplicity. Beneath a black awning, a bronze plaque off to the side of the front door read: Hotel Villa Bellezza. The place looked old but well kept. It reminded her of maybe a duke's grand house. She couldn't wait to check out the inside.

A young man in a black uniform rushed outside and opened her door for her. He smiled at her before his gaze moved to Angelo. The smile dimmed. She had the feeling that the young man had jumped to the wrong conclusion—that she and Angelo were a couple, here for a romantic tryst. Nothing could be further from the truth. But for the first time, she imagined what it might be like if Angelo were to look at her as a woman—a woman he desired. The thought rolled around in her mind at a dizzying pace.

Angelo moved to her side and spoke softly in her ear. "Are you okay?"

His voice drew her from her thoughts. She swallowed and hoped she succeeded in composing herself. "Yes."

"Are you sure? You're a little pale."

She patted his arm, not a good move as her fingertips tingled where they made contact. "I'm fine. Honest."

Or she would be, once she quit fantasizing about her boss. He obviously wasn't attracted to her. He saw her as nothing more than his temporary assistant, and that's the way it'd have to remain if she hoped to convince him of her talents.

While Angelo took care of registering them, she took in her surroundings. The modest exterior had not prepared her for the beauty of the interior. The floor was gleaming marble while the walls and ceiling were masterpieces of art with ornate parquet. Kayla had to force her mouth to remain closed instead of gaping open. She'd never stayed anywhere so fancy.

She couldn't even imagine how much this visit would cost Angelo. And the fact that he could afford to stay in a place such as this without even batting an eye impressed her. They sure didn't have anything like this back in Paradise. Wait until she told her mother and father about this.

CHAPTER SIX

THERE WAS NO time for fun and games.

Angelo didn't get to the top of his profession by taking time off. Now that they were settled into their suite and Kayla had rested for a bit, they needed to get back to work. As he waited for her to join him, he couldn't help but wonder what she made of his clash with his brother. He shouldn't have taken her to the vineyard. What had he been thinking?

Yet on the car ride here, she hadn't seemed to judge him. Instead, she'd acted as though she cared. It was as if she understood him. Her reaction surprised him. He wasn't used to letting people into his personal life. But from the moment he'd asked her to join him on this trip, the lines between personal and professional had become irrevocably blurred.

Kayla entered the common room between their bedrooms. Her auburn hair was loose and cascaded down past her shoulders. Her glasses were off and she was no longer wearing the drab gray business suit. Instead, she was wearing pink capris and a white cotton sleeveless top, which showed off her creamy shoulders and slender arms.

The breath hitched in his throat. Who was this gorgeous woman? And what had happened to his nondescript assistant?

"I hope you don't mind that I changed?"

Wow! All he could do was stare. It was as if she were some sort of butterfly who'd just emerged from a cocoon.

Kayla settled on the couch with her laptop. She gave him a strange look as though wondering why he had yet to say a word. The problem was he didn't know what to say. Ever since they'd left New York, the ground had been shifting under his feet. Now it was as though a fissure had opened up and he was teetering on the edge, scrambling not to get swallowed up.

She didn't appear to be too disturbed by his standoffishness, which was good. Before he took a seat anywhere near her, he had to get a hold on his rambling thoughts. Kayla wasn't just any woman. He couldn't indulge in a romantic romp with her, and then go about his life.

He was her boss and, more important, he couldn't afford to lose her because she was good—really good at her job. He'd already had ideas of promoting her, but he wasn't sure that she was ready to be advanced quite yet. He wanted to see how she handled the Van Holsen account, since he'd given her a lot of room to show him her stuff.

The tight muscles in his chest eased and he was able to breathe easier. Concentrating on work always relaxed him and put him back in his groove. Work was logical for the most part and it lacked emotions, again for the most part, depending on the client. But since he was the boss, he was able to hand off the more excitable clients to other account executives.

That was it. Focus on business and not on how appealing he found her. "How's the Van Holsen account coming?"

She glanced over the top of her laptop. "Thanks to your help, I think I've come up with some innovative ideas. Would you care to take a look?"

His gaze moved to the cushion next to her on the couch and his body tensed. He was being ridiculous. She wasn't the first beautiful woman that he'd been around. What in the world had got into him today? It had to be his return home. It had him feeling out of sorts.

Time to start acting like Angelo Amatucci, the man in charge. "Sure. I'll have a look."

He strode over to the couch and took a seat. Kayla handed over the laptop and their fingers brushed. Hers were soft, smooth and warm. A jolt of awareness zinged up his arm and the air hitched in his lungs. *Stay focused.* He didn't dare turn to look at her. Instead, he focused his gaze on the computer monitor.

He read over her ideas for the new fragrance campaign and was truly impressed. Not only had she taken his ideas and expanded upon them, but she'd also inserted some of her own. He loved her initiative. Kayla was exactly the kind of innovative person that he wanted at Amatucci & Associates. Talented people like Kayla were the assets that would keep his company one of the most sought-after advertising agencies in the world.

"This is really good." He turned to her. When her green gaze met his, the rest of his thoughts scattered.

"You really like it?"

He nodded. His line of vision momentarily dipped to her pink frosted lips before meeting her gaze again. He struggled for a nonchalant expression. "I think you've captured a touching nostalgic note with a forward-thinking view. This should capture both the new and old consumer."

Her tempting lips lifted into a broad smile that lit up her eyes. "Now we just have to hope the client will approve."

"I wouldn't worry about that. Send this along to the art department and have them start working on some mock-ups."

Her smile dimmed a bit. "You're sure about this?"

"Of course I am. Don't look so surprised. You don't think you got the position as my assistant just because you're beautiful, do you?"

Now why in the world had he gone and said that? But it was the truth. She was stunning. In fact, he was considering changing the dress code at the office. He really enjoyed this different look on her. Then again, if she looked this way in the office, he'd never get any work done.

Color bloomed on her creamy cheeks. "You think I'm beautiful?"

He stared back into her eyes longer than was necessary.

In that moment, his ability to speak intelligently was debatable. He merely nodded.

"No man has ever called me that."

At last finding his voice, Angelo said, "I'm having a hard time believing that."

"Steven was more matter-of-fact and sparing on compliments. It wasn't that he was a bad man. In fact, it's quite the opposite. He was really good to me. He just wasn't good with flowery words."

"This Steven, he's from Paradise, too?"

She nodded. "High-school sweethearts."

"The man must need glasses badly to have missed your beauty. Both inside and out. Is he still your boyfriend?" Part of Angelo wanted her to say yes to put a swift end to this surreal moment, but a much stronger part wanted her to be free.

"We…we broke up before I moved to New York."

The field was wide-open. Exhilaration flooded through Angelo. His hand reached out, stroking the smooth, silky skin of her cheek. The backs of his fingers skimmed down over her jaw, and then his thumb ran over the plumpness of her bottom lip. Her sudden inhale drew air over his fingers.

In her eyes, he noted the flames of desire had been ignited. She wanted him as much as he wanted her. And in that moment, he didn't want to think—he just wanted to act. He wanted to forget everything and enjoy this moment with the girl with wavy red hair.

His heart pounded as he leaned forward. He needed her and her understanding ways more than he imagined possible. Their lips met. He was a man who knew what he wanted and he wanted Kayla. Yet he fought back the urge to let loose with his mounting need. Instead, his touch was tentative and gentle. He didn't want to do anything to scare her away—not now that he had her exactly where he wanted her.

Kayla's lips were rose-petal soft. And when she opened them up to him, a moan grew deep in his throat. She tasted sweet like chocolate. He'd never been a fan of candy until this moment. Now he couldn't get enough of her sugary sweetness.

His arms wrapped round her curvy form, pulling her close. The gentle scent of perfume wrapped around them— the teasing scent that he hadn't been able to forget since that day in the office. It was as though she'd cast some sort of magical spell over him.

In the next instant, his phone vibrated in his pocket, zapping him back to his senses. He pulled back and Kayla's confused gaze met his. He couldn't blame her. He was just as confused by what had happened.

He held up a finger to silence her inevitable questions— questions for which he had no answers. Because there was no way he was falling for her. Getting involved with her— with anyone—meant dealing with a bunch of messy emotions. The last thing in the world he wanted to do was end up like his parents. Just the memory of their turbulent life had Angelo immediately working to rebuild the wall between him and Kayla. He just couldn't—wouldn't—subject anyone to such miserable instability.

Angelo glanced down at the screen to see his brother's name pop up. Hopefully his sister had confessed all. Angelo couldn't wait to confront the man who'd walked away from his responsibilities.

Angelo lifted the phone to his ear. "Nico, do you have a name yet?"

There was a distinct sigh. "Is this how you answer your phone these days? Too important for a friendly greeting before diving into the heart of the matter?"

Angelo's back teeth ground together. He quickly counted to ten, okay maybe only to five, before addressing his sibling. "Hello, Nico. What did Marianna say?"

"Nothing."

He was losing his patience. "But why did you call?"

"You and Kayla need to return to the villa. Now. I'll explain everything when you both get here." The line went dead.

Angelo slipped the phone back into his pocket. He turned to Kayla, whose face was still filled with color. "We have to go."

"What happened?"

"I don't know. That was Nico and he summoned us back to the villa. It must be Marianna. I just pray there aren't complications with the baby." Before they left he needed to clear the air about their kiss that never should have happened. "Listen, about the kiss, I crossed a line. I... I don't know what I was thinking."

A myriad of expressions crossed over her face. "It's forgotten."

He didn't believe her. "Can we talk about it later?"

"I'd rather not. There's nothing to say. Besides, you have more important things to deal with." She jumped to her feet and moved away from him. "You should get going. I'll be fine here."

"Nico requested you, too." Angelo held back the startling fact that he'd feel better facing this crisis with her next to him.

Kayla pressed a hand to her chest. "But why me?"

"I don't know. But we have to go."

"Okay. Just let me grab my shoes and purse." She rushed back to her room.

Angelo got to his feet and paced back and forth. Of course he was worried about his sister, but there was something else fueling his inability to sit still—Kayla's off-the-cuff dismissal of his kiss.

The women he was used to spending time with never brushed off his advances, though each of them knew his rules in advance—nothing serious. So why did that rule not apply here? Probably because Kayla was off-limits. She was his assistant. He couldn't forget that going forward—no matter how much his personal life spun out of control while in Italy.

From this point forward, Kayla was off-limits.

CHAPTER SEVEN

HER THOUGHTS RACED so fast that it unsettled her stomach.

Kayla stared out of the passenger window as she clasped her hands tightly together. Angelo expertly guided the rented sports car along the narrow, tree-lined road. How in the world had she lost control of the situation?

She inwardly groaned. As fantastic as that kiss had been, it couldn't have come at a worse time. Angelo at last had noticed her work and complimented her professionally. And what did she turn around and do, stare at him like some lovesick teenager—encouraging him to kiss her.

Sure, she was wildly attracted to him. What woman with a pulse wasn't? He was gorgeous with that short, dark hair, olive skin and dark, sensual eyes. But he was her boss—the man in charge of her professional future—her dreams.

She couldn't afford any more blunders. She had to remain aloof but professional. Surely it wasn't too late to correct things between them. At least he hadn't mentioned anything about sending her back to New York on the next plane, but then again they'd rushed out of the hotel so quickly that he didn't have time to think of it. His thoughts were on his sister.

Kayla sure hoped there wasn't anything wrong with Marianna. This was the first time Kayla had ever witnessed Angelo visibly worried. He obviously cared a great deal for his family though he never let on at the office—when he was working he was 100 percent professional—

So then what happened back there at the hotel?

Angelo pulled the car to a skidding halt in front of the villa. Before she could summon an answer to that nagging question, Angelo had her car door opened. She would figure it out later. Right now, she would offer her support in whatever capacity to Angelo's family.

Nico rushed into the drive. "About time you got here."

"We came right away." Angelo frowned at his brother. "What's the matter with Marianna?"

"Marianna?" Nico's brows drew together in a questioning look. "This has nothing to do with our sister."

"Then why in the world did you have us rush over here?" Angelo's voice took on a sharp edge.

Kayla breathed a sigh of relief. She had no idea what Nico wanted, but she was fully relieved that mother and baby were okay. However, she did have to wonder why Nico wanted her here? Was he hoping that she'd play referee?

Nico's eyes opened wide and his face became animated. "You are never going to believe this—"

"I might if you'd get to the point."

Nico smiled in spite of his brother's obvious agitation. "What would you say if I told you that I was just approached by representatives of Halencia? Monte Calanetti has just made the short list of locations for the royal wedding of Prince Antonio and Christina Rose."

Angelo rolled his eyes. "Nico, this is no time for joking around—"

"I'm not. I'm perfectly serious."

Kayla's mouth gaped open. A royal wedding. Wow! She really was in Europe because nothing like this ever happened back in the States. Wait until she told her family. They would never believe it.

Her gaze moved to Angelo. He still wasn't smiling. In fact, he didn't look the least bit excited about this news. She had absolutely no ties to this village and she was over-the-moon happy for them. So why was he so reserved?

Angelo pressed his hands to his trim waist. "You called us back here to tell us this?"

"Brother, you're not understanding. The royal family of Halencia wants us to make a pitch as to why Monte Calanetti should be the location for the soon-to-be king and his intended bride's wedding."

"And?"

Nico shook his head. "What aren't you understanding? This is where you come in. You and Kayla. This is what you two do for a living—pitch ideas, convince people to go with the products you represent. That's what we need."

Nico wanted Angelo and her to help? Really? For a royal wedding?

The breath caught in her throat as she held back a squeal of excitement. If she'd ever wanted a chance to stand out and gain a promotion, this was a prime opportunity. Plus, it'd mean continuing to work with Angelo. But once they got back to New York, away from this romantic countryside, things would go back to normal. Wouldn't they?

Surely they would. This project was huge. It was amazing. An honest-to-goodness royal wedding. She didn't even know where they'd begin, but she couldn't contain her excitement. She'd show Angelo how good an ad executive she could be. Just wait and see.

Pitch a wedding to royalty?

Angelo had never done such a thing. Weddings weren't his thing. He knew nothing about love and romance. He was highly unqualified for this project. But he wasn't about to admit any of this to Nico. No way. So how was he supposed to get out of this?

Nico smiled as he led them straight through the modestly decorated villa that still looked much the same as it did when he'd been a child. Once everyone was situated on the veranda with cold drinks, Nico turned to him. "So what do you think?"

"About what?"

"You know, coming up with a pitch for the village?"

Angelo wanted to tell his brother that he was too busy and that he couldn't possibly fit it into his schedule. He highly doubted his brother would hear him. Nico had selective hearing when he wanted something bad enough—like Angelo being a silent investor in the vineyard.

Angelo turned to Kayla to see what she thought about the idea, hoping she'd make some excuse to get them out of this situation. But her green eyes sparkled with excitement. How wrong could he have been to look to her for support? Was there a woman alive who didn't get excited about weddings? Or was it the part about pitching it to a real-life prince that had caught her full attention?

Angelo's gut tightened when he thought of Kayla being starstruck over the royal prince. He shrugged off the uneasy sensation. It was none of his concern. Besides, it wasn't as if she was attracted to him. She couldn't dismiss their kiss fast enough.

His jaw tensed as he recalled how easily she'd brushed off their moment. He could have sworn she'd been as into him as he was into her. It just showed how little he understood women.

He drew up his thoughts, refusing to dwell on the subject. In the meantime, Kayla had engaged his brother in light conversation about the vineyard and how it'd been their childhood home. Angelo looked around the place and was truly impressed by what his brother had done to bring this place back to life. It looked so different than when they were kids, when the place was dying off.

Angelo had actually thought that his brother was crazy for wanting to devote his time and money into reviving the vineyard, but with Nico's determination, he'd made a go of the place. In fact, this boutique vineyard might not produce a large quantity of wine, but what it did produce was of the finest quality. Angelo kept his private wine collection stocked with it. Calanetti wines impressed a great number of influential guests that he'd entertained.

The chime of Kayla's laughter drew his thoughts back to the moment. Nico was entertaining her with a tale from when they were kids. As the oldest, Angelo had always been put in charge of his siblings while his parents went out. But this one time, Angelo hadn't been paying attention and they'd sneaked off. What Nico failed to add, and what he probably didn't know, was that had been one of Angelo's scariest moments—not knowing what had happened to his brother and sister.

"Are you telling them about the royal wedding?" Marianna joined them. Her face was a bit on the pale side and there were shadows beneath her eyes.

Nico leaned back in his chair. "I just told Angelo about it. He's thinking it over."

Marianna turned to Angelo. "You have to think it over? But why? This will be the biggest thing you've ever done."

"You really want me to do the pitch?"

She nodded. "Please. It would be so wonderful for everyone. Couldn't you just this once help your family?"

Guilt landed squarely on his shoulders with the force of a full wine barrel. He owed his brother and sister this. It'd put Monte Calanetti on the map. And the benefits the village would reap from the royal wedding taking place here were countless.

But he was already fully obligated. And he couldn't do it all on his own. He'd need help. A good copywriter. His gaze strayed to Kayla. He'd already witnessed just how talented she was with words and images. He could easily imagine her taking on some more of his workload, allowing him time to work on the wedding proposal.

They'd have to work closely together—closer than ever. There was no way he'd let her loose with the company's most important clients. But would they be able to manage it after the kiss?

"So what do you say, Angelo?" Nico looked at him. "The village is all abuzz with the news, and you know that pitching a wedding isn't my area of specialty."

"Please Angelo, will you do it?" Marianna looked at him, openly pleading with him with her eyes.

He'd never been good at telling her no. And now that she was standing there carrying some stranger's baby—some man that his sister wouldn't even introduce to their family—his resistance to her plea was nonexistent. If playing host to a royal wedding made her happy, how could he deny it to her? The decision for once was quite simple.

"Okay. I'll do it."

"You will?" The words echoed around the patio.

"Why does everyone sound so shocked? It'll be good publicity for the firm." But that wasn't his reason for agreeing—it was to see the smiles on the two women in his life... and his brother.

Marianna launched herself into his arms. Warmth swelled in his chest. He may not have been here to protect her and watch over her as he should have been, but at least he could give her something to look forward to while she sorted out the rest of her life.

Marianna pulled back and sent him a watery smile. "Thanks."

He turned to Kayla. She looked like an excited kid on Christmas Eve. "How about you? Are you up for taking on some more responsibility?"

Kayla didn't waste a moment before uttering, "Definitely. Just tell me what needs done."

"Good." He turned to his brother. "It looks like you've hired yourself a team. I'll get started on the pitch as soon as we get back to New York."

"New York?" Nico's brows gathered together.

"Yes, that's where we work. I'll send through what I come up with, but it's going to take me a little time. I have a rush project that I—we—have to wrap up—"

"This can't wait. You have to get started on it right away."

Angelo didn't like the worried tone of his brother's voice. "Why? What haven't you told us?"

Nico got to his feet. "Does anyone need anything else to drink?"

Angelo knew a stalling tactic when he saw one. "Nico, spit it out. What is the catch?"

After Nico finished refilling Kayla's iced tea, he turned to his brother. "The catch is the pitch has to be completed in no more than three weeks' time."

"Three weeks." Angelo leaned back in his chair. "You sure don't give a person much time."

"And—"

"There's more?"

Nico nodded. "The presentation has to be given to the royal family at the palace in Halencia."

Nico sank down into his chair while Angelo charged to his feet. "This changes everything. I wasn't planning to stay in Italy for three weeks. Nico, don't you understand? I have a business to run."

"You're the boss. Can't you put someone else in charge while you're here?"

Angelo never sloughed off his work on other people. He stayed on top of things. Some people called him a control freak. He considered it the only way to keep the company on track. "That's not the point. There are certain things only I can do."

"The point is that when we need you, you're never here." Nico got to his feet and faced him. "Why should I have thought this would be any different?"

His brother's words were pointed and needled at his guilt. "That's not fair. I've lent you money for the vineyard—"

"This isn't about you writing out a check. I'm talking about you personally investing yourself—your time—in something that's important to your family."

Angelo turned to Marianna, looking for support, but she moved to Nico's side. When he sought out Kayla, she was busy studying her iced tea glass with such intensity that it was as if she'd never seen glassware before. He was alone in this. He knew what he should do, but it was so hard to just hand over the reins of the company he'd built from the ground up.

Three weeks was a long time to be away. And yet it wasn't much time to create a compelling campaign for a wedding—a royal wedding. It had just started to sink in what a big deal this really was for his brother and sister, and the village, plus it would be amazing for his company— that is if they won the pitch.

Angelo raked his fingers through his hair. Letting go of the reins at Amatucci & Associates went against every business instinct. Yet, he couldn't turn his back on his siblings again. "Okay. I'll stay."

Marianna turned to Kayla. "Will you stay, too?"

"Yes, Kayla," Nico chimed in. "Will you help my brother? I get the feeling that he won't be able to do it without you."

Kayla's eyes flashed with surprise. "I don't know that I need to stay in Italy to do it."

"It'd be most convenient," Marianna pointed out. "I'm sure Angelo will need your input. After all, we're talking about a wedding. And my brothers, well, they aren't exactly romantic."

"Hey!" Nico and Angelo protested in unison.

Both women burst out in laughter. Angelo supposed the dig was worth it as his sister's face broke into a smile. And when he turned to Kayla, the happiness reflected in her eyes warmed a spot in his chest. She was a very beautiful woman. Why, oh, why did it have to be now when they were practically attached at the hip that he truly realized his attraction to her?

When she caught him staring, the breath hitched in his throat. He should glance away, but he couldn't. He was in awe of her. Was it being away from the office that had him more relaxed about the proper conduct between employer and employee? Nonsense. He knew what he was doing. He could keep this together.

He gazed directly at the woman who took up more and more of his thoughts. "Well, don't keep us in suspense. Will you remain in Italy and lend a hand?"

CHAPTER EIGHT

THIS WAS A very bad idea.

But it was so tempting. How could she let such a rare opportunity pass her by?

Kayla worried her bottom lip. Though she wouldn't be working directly on the royal wedding, she'd be close at hand. Perhaps she could add an idea here and there. Oh, what she wouldn't give to actually work on the project itself. Yet, she understood with the magnitude of a royal wedding that only the best of the best would work on the project, and that meant Angelo.

But she was needed back in New York. The ICL fund-raiser was quickly approaching, and seeing as it was her idea—it was her responsibility to make sure it went off without a hitch. However, she had put Pam, an associate at the after-school program, in charge while she was gone. And how much could possibly go wrong in three weeks?

"Please say you'll stay." Marianna looked so hopeful. "I could use someone on my side against my brothers, who think they know everything."

That sold her. Marianna could definitely use some help keeping her brothers in line while she figured out her next move. "Okay, I'll stay."

Everyone smiled except Angelo.

Aside from the fund-raiser, there was nothing waiting for her back in New York, not even a goldfish. When she wasn't at the office, she was at the after-school program helping kids with their homework followed by a game of dodgeball or basketball or volleyball. She wasn't very good at any of the games, but she gave it her best effort.

For the moment, she was giving herself permission to

enjoy Italy before she set to work. And this was the perfect place to start. She'd love to see more of the vineyard, and it'd give Angelo some private time with his siblings.

"Would you mind if I had a look around the vineyard?" Kayla's gaze met Nico's.

"My apologies. I should have offered to give you a tour earlier. I've had other thoughts on my mind—" his gaze strayed to his sister and then back to her "—with uh…the royal wedding."

"That's okay. I totally understand." Kayla got to her feet. "I've never been to a vineyard before. I'll just show myself around."

"Nonsense. Angelo can give you the grand tour while I make some phone calls and spread the good news. And make sure he shows you the chapel." Nico turned a smile to Angelo. "You can handle that, can't you, brother?"

Angelo's jaw tightened, but he didn't argue. Kayla took that as progress between the brothers. Not wanting to give Angelo time to change his mind, she set off for the vines, hoping Angelo would follow.

He did, and he proved to be quite an insightful guide. He explained to her the difference between a larger vineyard and this boutique vineyard. While Nico produced fewer barrels of wine—less than five thousand cases a year—it was carefully processed to the highest quality with the least amount of oxidation.

As much as the history and current production of wine interested her, it was the bell tower in the distance that drew her attention. She headed for the weathered building that sat on the other side of the wall that lined the edge of the vineyard. "Is this the chapel your brother mentioned?"

"Yes. Nico and I explored it as kids. We considered it our castle. I was the king and Nico was the daring knight fighting off dragons." Angelo smiled at the long-forgotten memory.

"You and your brother must have had a lot of fun."

"Now that I think about it, we did have some good times."

She smiled. "This looks like a great place for an adventure. Can we go inside the chapel?"

"It's nothing you'd be interested in."

"Sure I would." Her steps grew quicker as she headed for the opening in the wall that led to the little chapel. Maybe this was her chance to let Angelo know that she'd be more than willing to help with the wedding pitch—in fact, this was the opportunity of a lifetime. Now, how did she broach the subject with Angelo?

She stopped next to the four steps that led to two tall, narrow wooden doors. It looked as though time had passed it by. Okay so it needed a little TLC, but it had a charm about it that transcended time. "Your brother is so lucky to have this piece of history on his land. Imagine all of the weddings and christenings that must have taken place here."

"Technically it's not on Nico's land." Angelo pointed over his shoulder to the wall. That divides the vineyard. The other side is Nico's."

"So who owns this land, then?"

"This is Palazzo di Comparino. Its owner, Signor Carlos Bartolini, recently passed away. From what I understand, there's a young woman staying there now."

"You know this chapel gives me an idea—it'd be perfect for the royal wedding."

"I don't know." Angelo rubbed his chin. "It needs work."

She pulled open one of the doors and peered inside at the rows of pews. The place was filled with dust and cobwebs. "It's nothing that can't be done rather easily." This was her chance to put herself out there. "You know I could help you with the pitch."

Angelo didn't immediately respond. The breath hitched in her throat as she waited—hoping that he'd latch on to her offer. The experience from working on such a prestigious project had immeasurable potential, from a promotion at Amatucci & Associates to making her résumé stand out—head and shoulders above the rest.

"I don't think so. You'll have enough to do with the other accounts that need looking after." The disappointment must have filtered across her face because his stance eased and his voice softened. "I appreciate the offer, but I don't want you getting overwhelmed."

It teetered on the tip of her tongue to ask him if this had anything to do with the kiss, but she hesitated. She couldn't bring herself to tarnish that moment. The memory of how his eyes had devoured her before his lips had claimed hers still made her heart race.

If it wasn't the kiss, why was he turning away her offer of help? Was it just as he said, not wanting to give her too much work? Or did he feel she wasn't up to the task of working on something so important?

With the wind temporarily knocked out of her sails, she turned back to the villa. She wasn't giving up. She would show Angelo that she was invaluable.

What was the problem?

Two days later, Angelo paced around the hotel suite. He needed a fresh approach to the wedding. It had to be something amazing—something unique to Monte Calanetti that would appeal to a prince and his intended bride. But what?

He was stuck. This had never happened to him before. He inwardly groaned as his mind drew a total blank. This was ridiculous. He clenched his hands into tight balls. He had absolutely nothing. And that was so not like him.

He liked to think outside the box. He liked to push boundaries and experiment, but all he could think of was why would anyone would want to get married in Monte Calanetti? What special qualities did they see in the village for it to make the royals' short list?

He poured himself a cup of the now-lukewarm coffee.

The silence of the suite was getting to him. Kayla had cleared out early that morning, claiming she wanted some fresh air while she worked on the mock-ups for the Van Holsen account and answered emails. She'd been great about taking on additional responsibilities, allowing him time to brainstorm. Not that it was helping him much.

In fact, she'd done such an exceptional job that maybe he should see what she could do with this wedding stuff. After all, she was a girl, and didn't they all dream about their weddings?

Suddenly the image of Kayla in a white dress formed in his mind. His body tensed. As quickly as the image came to him, he vanquished it. She'd be a beautiful bride, but for someone else. He wasn't getting married—ever.

Determined to stay on point and to get her input on the wedding, he headed downstairs to the pool area. He opened the door and stepped outside, momentarily blinded by the bright sunlight. Once his vision adjusted, he glanced around, quickly locating his assistant. She was at a shaded poolside table. She lifted her head and smiled, but it wasn't aimed at him.

She wasn't alone. A young man stood next to her table. Angelo's gut knotted. He told himself that it was because she was supposed to be working, not flirting. His only interest was in her getting her work done in a timely fashion. But as the chime of her laughter carried through the gentle breeze, Angelo's mouth pulled into a frown.

He strode toward the table. Kayla didn't even notice him approach as she was captivated by the young man.

Angelo cleared his throat. "Hello, Kayla."

Both heads turned his way. Kayla's eyes opened wide with surprise. The young man drew himself up to his full height as though he was about to defend his right to be flirting with Kayla. The guy had no idea that Angelo had no intention of challenging his right to gain Kayla's attention. After all, it would be for the best if she was interested in someone—as long as it wasn't him. But that would all have to wait, because right now she was on the clock. And he needed her help.

Angelo used his practiced professional voice, the one that let people know that he meant business. "How's the Van Holsen account coming?"

"Uh, good. Dino was just asking about the royal wedding."

"He was?" Angelo stepped between Kayla and the young man. "What do you want to know?"

The young man glanced down, not meeting Angelo's direct gaze. "I... I was just curious if the rumor was true that they might pick Monte Calanetti for the wedding."

"It is. Is there anything else?"

Dino shrugged his shoulders. "I guess not."

"Good. Kayla has work to do now. If you'll excuse us."

"Uh, sure." Dino leaned to the side to look at Kayla. "I'll see you around."

"Bye."

Angelo took a seat next to Kayla. "It seems you've found yourself an admirer."

"Who? Dino?" She shook her head. "He was just interested in what I knew about the royal wedding, which wasn't anything more than he's heard through the grapevine. How's the pitch for the wedding coming?"

"Good." *Liar.*

He wasn't about to admit that he, Angelo Amatucci, couldn't come up with a dynamic pitch that would turn the prince's and his bride's heads. No way. What would Kayla think of him? No. Scratch that. He didn't want to know what she'd think. She'd probably laugh at him.

"I'm glad to hear it's going well. I know that I'm not the only one who's anxious for the pitch. Imagine a royal wedding. The whole world will be watching it and you'll have played a big part in it."

"Not a big part."

"You're too modest. You're like the village hero now."

Just what he needed was more pressure. He swallowed down his uneasiness. "You're assuming that the prince will choose this village, and that's a big leap."

"But why wouldn't they pick Monte Calanetti? From the little I've seen, I think it's a lovely village."

"That's just because you didn't grow up here."

Her green eyes widened. "You really didn't like living here?"

He shook his head, but he wasn't going to get into the details of his childhood or his strained relationship with his parents. Kayla had already been privy to more about his private life than anyone else ever. But something told him that his family secrets were safe with her.

Not in the mood to talk anymore about this village or dwell on the fact that he'd wasted two days without coming up with anything striking or fascinating, he decided to turn the conversation around. "How is the work going?"

CHAPTER NINE

COULD SHE PRETEND she hadn't heard Angelo?

Kayla had spent a large chunk of time at this poolside table. With most of the guests either off sightseeing or attending other engagements, it was a peaceful place for her to jot out more ideas for the Van Holsen account. But after going back and forth between the art department and the very demanding client, they were still missing the mark.

It didn't help that her ideas for the Van Holsen account had stalled. For the past half hour or so, she'd been jotting out ideas for the fund-raiser back in New York. The event was their last hope to keep the after-school program going for so many at-risk kids and it was weighing heavy on her mind. There were still so many details to iron out.

And as exciting as it was to be working with Angelo Amatucci on what could be the project to catapult her career, she couldn't forget the children. They were relying on her to make their lives a little better by raising money to keep their facility open.

"Kayla, did you hear me?"

The sound of Angelo's voice startled her back to the here and now. "Sorry. I just had a thought."

"About the account?"

She nodded. "It's coming along."

"Why don't you tell me what you have so far and we can work on it together?"

She glanced down at her closed notebook. "That's okay. I know you have more important things to concentrate on. I've got this."

Angelo's dark brows drew together. "Listen, I know that

things haven't exactly been right between us since, well, you know…the kiss. If that's still bothering you—?"

"It's not." Yes, it was. But not the way he was thinking. The kiss had been better than she'd ever imagined. And she knew that it could never happen again. She had too much on the line to risk it all by fooling around with her boss.

The truth of the matter was the pad of paper also contained her thoughts for the benefit concert. Angelo had a strict policy about not taking on charity accounts—he believed there were too many good causes and not enough time to help them all. Kayla couldn't understand his stance, but then again she'd never been in charge of a large company. Maybe there was more to it than what she knew.

The one thing she did know was that she couldn't let Angelo find out that she was organizing a fund-raiser while on this trip. She didn't want him to have a reason not to consider her for a promotion or worse yet to have her replaced as his assistant. She wasn't sure how he would handle the situation. In all of her time at Amatucci & Associates, she'd never witnessed anyone going against company policy. Angelo was a man no one wanted to cross.

"I'm just jotting out some ideas. Nothing specific yet." She caught herself worrying her bottom lip, hoping he wouldn't take exception to her not coming up with something more concrete. After all, they were on a timetable and the clock was ticking. "I spent the morning on the phone with the art department and Mrs. Van Holsen—"

His brows drew together into a formidable line. "Why didn't you get me?"

"I… I didn't want to disturb you. I'm supposed to be here to lighten your load."

He shook his head. "I can't spend all of my time on one campaign. That isn't fair to the other clients. I have to stay on top of everything. Next time you speak with a client, I expect to be in on the call. Understood?"

"Yes."

He let the subject go as he continued on with some other business items. "By the way, while I was on the phone with the office I mentioned that we'd been unavoidably detained in Italy, but I didn't go into specifics. I don't want any rumors starting up that we put off longtime clients in favor of this royal wedding pitch. I won't risk my company's reputation for something that is never going to happen."

Kayla's mouth gaped before she caught it and forced her lips together. "Is that really what you think?"

He nodded. "Pretty much."

"But why?"

"Well, I can't see what a royal couple would find so endearing about Monte Calanetti. I think everyone, including my brother and sister, are getting worked up over something that will never happen."

"I don't understand. If that's truly what you think then why go to all of the bother to delay your return to New York and work on a campaign that you're certain will fail?"

He shrugged. "It's an obligation that I owe them." He raked his fingers through his hair. "I owe it to Nico and Marianna—you know, for skipping out on them. For letting them fend for themselves with parents who were more wrapped up in their marital drama than worrying about their children."

"I'm sorry—"

"Don't be. I didn't tell you any of that so you'd feel sorry for me. In fact, I don't know why I mentioned it at all."

"I'm glad you did. I'd like to think that we've become more than coworkers." When she met his drawn brows, she realized that she'd said more than she should have. "I… I don't mean about the kiss. I just thought we might be friends, too."

A wave of relief washed over his face easing the stress lines. "I would like that."

"You would?"

Slowly he nodded, and then a smile tugged at his lips. "Yes, I would."

She couldn't help but smile back. She noticed how the worry lines bracketing his eyes and mouth smoothed. She'd never seen him look so worried before. Why would that be? He was amazing at creating winning pitches. He was amazing in a lot of ways.

Realizing that she was staring, she turned away, but by then, her heart was beating faster than normal. Images of the kiss they'd shared clouded her mind. She'd tried to put it out of her head, but the memory kept her awake late into the night. What had it meant? Had it meant anything? Because there was no way that a wealthy, successful businessman who could have his choice of women would fall for his assistant.

Kayla reached for a tall, cool glass of iced tea. "Would you like something to drink? I could go and get you something."

"Thanks. But I'm all right." He looked at her as though studying her. "Can I ask what direction you think the wedding pitch should take?"

"Really?" She sat up straighter. "You want my input?"

He nodded. "I thought you might have some ideas that I hadn't thought of."

"I do…have ideas, that is." She struggled to gather her thoughts.

"I'm listening."

She'd done a lot of thinking about this—probably too much, considering she hadn't even been invited to help with the royal pitch until now. "I'm thinking that regardless of whether they go big or small, they're going to want elements that play into an elegant yet traditional event."

"That's true. If they wanted a contemporary feel, they certainly wouldn't come to Monte Calanetti." He rubbed the back of his neck.

"What's bothering you?"

"I'm just trying to figure out why this village made the short list for the royal wedding. I mean, there's nothing special here. I've gone round and round with this, but I still have no answer. It's not like it has amazing history like Rome or the heartbeat of the nation like Milan or the stunning architecture of Venice. This is a little, old village."

"And it's tripping you up when you're trying to come up with a unique pitch."

Angelo hesitated as though he wasn't sure whether or not to confide in her. Then he sighed. "Yes, it's giving me a bit of a problem. No matter which way I go at it, I just can't find that special quality that will put Monte Calanetti head and shoulders above the other locations."

Kayla smiled and shook her head. "You just don't see it because you take this place for granted. It's your home, but to outsiders, it's something special."

His gaze met hers. "You think it's special?"

She decided a neutral stance was best. "I haven't made up my mind yet."

"Then how can you tell me that I'm blind to what's in front of me when you haven't even made up your mind?" His voice held a disgruntled tone.

She smiled, liking the fact that she could get past his polished persona and make him feel real genuine emotions. "I mean that I need to see the village." When he opened his mouth to protest, she held up her hand, stopping him. "And driving straight through it to get to the hotel does not count. It was more of a blur than anything."

"What are you saying?"

"I'm saying that tomorrow you and I will start exploring Monte Calanetti. You can tell me all about it. You know, the little things that a tourist wouldn't know—the parts that make the village special."

"Don't be too disappointed when it doesn't live up to your expectations."

"I think you'll actually end up surprising yourself."

His gaze narrowed in on her. "You really want to walk all through the village?"

She nodded. "If you want to come up with a winning pitch to make all of the citizens, not to mention your brother and sister very happy, you're going to have to see it differently."

"I'm not sure that's possible. But if you insist on it, I will give you the grand tour."

"I would like that."

"Now, if you'll excuse me, I promised to swing by my brother's villa. He wants to show me the latest improvements at the winery." He got to his feet. "Of course, if you'd like to accompany me, you're welcome."

Kayla glanced down at her rather sparse list of notes. "I think my time would be better spent here doing some research."

"You're sure?"

She nodded. "I am. But thank you for the invite."

The truth was, she and Angelo were getting along a lot better than they had in the office. She'd been working for him for weeks now and they'd only ever addressed each other with mister and miss, but now they were on a first-name basis. And then there was that kiss...er...no she wasn't going to think about it. No matter how good it was or how much she wished that he'd kiss her again—

Her thoughts screeched to a halt. Did she want him to kiss her again? She turned to watch his retreating form. His broad shoulders were evident in the linen suit jacket. His long, powerful legs moved at a swift pace, covering the patio area quickly.

Yes, she did want to be kissed again. Only this time she wanted him to kiss her because he wanted her and not because he was exhausted and stressed after a run-in with his siblings. But that couldn't happen. She needed this job.

A quick fling with her boss in the warm sunshine of

Tuscany wasn't worth throwing away her dreams—the rest of her life. No matter how tempting Angelo might be, she just couldn't ruin this opportunity.

And she couldn't return to Paradise as a failure.

CHAPTER TEN

WHY EXACTLY HAD he agreed to this?

The last thing Angelo wanted to do was take a stroll through Monte Calanetti. It was like taking a walk back through history—a history that he preferred not to dwell on. Still, he had to admit that having Kayla along would make the journey back in time a little more tolerable, but he still didn't see how it was going to help him create a winning pitch.

He paced back and forth in the hotel lobby, waiting for Kayla to finish getting ready for their outing. He'd also wanted to check with the front desk to make sure that extending their stay wouldn't be an issue.

"Mr. Amatucci, you're in luck." The concierge strode up to him. "We've just had a cancellation. And with a bit of juggling we've been able to keep you and your assistant in your suite of rooms." The young man, who was polished from the top of his short cut hair down to his spiffed-up dress shoes, looked quite pleased with himself. "Is there anything else I can do for you?"

"Actually there is." Angelo wasn't sure it was a good idea, but he decided that Kayla deserved a night out for being such a good sport. "I've heard that Mancini's is quite a popular restaurant."

"Yes, it is. We're so lucky to have had Raffaele Mancini return to the village. Mancini's is so popular that they only take reservations."

That's what Angelo suspected. "Would you mind making a reservation for myself and my assistant for tomorrow evening?"

The concierge's face creased with worry lines.

"Is there a problem?"

"Well, sir. They're usually booked well in advance."

Angelo wasn't used to being put off. Even in New York he didn't have a problem getting into the most popular restaurants. How in the world was it that he was being turned down in little old Monte Calanetti? Impossible.

"Do you know who I am?"

The young man's eyes opened wide, and then he nodded.

Angelo got the distinct impression that the young man didn't have a clue who he was or what power he wielded outside of the Tuscany countryside. He felt as though he'd stepped back in time, becoming a nobody who faded into the crowd. With his pride pricked, he gave the young man a pointed look. But he knew that he was letting his past get the best of him. He swallowed down the unwarranted agitation. Of course the young man didn't know him. The concierge wasn't much more than a kid.

Angelo decided upon a new approach. "Forgive me. My tone was uncalled-for just now. When you call for the reservations, tell them that the owner of Amatucci & Associates is requesting a table as we are considering including them in the pitch for the royal wedding."

Maybe he had put it on a little thick just now, but he wanted—no, he needed to prove to everyone including himself that he had far surpassed everyone's expectations of him—especially his father's. Angelo's gut churned at the memory of his father turning to him in anger and saying, *You'll never amount to anything.*

"Yes, sir." The concierge attempted a nervous smile. "I'll do that right away. I had no idea, sir—"

"It's okay." Angelo tipped the young man handsomely to make up for his brusqueness. "I just need you to know that this dinner is very important." But suddenly Angelo was no longer talking about business or proving himself to the villagers or even the royal wedding. His mind was on Kayla. He liked making her happy, and he was hoping this dinner would earn him another smile or two.

"I'll get right on it, sir."

"Thank you. I appreciate it."

Angelo moved over to the small sitting area in the lobby to wait for Kayla. Just about to reach for the newspaper to find out what was going on around the world, Angelo caught a movement out of the corner of his eye. Curious to see if it was Kayla, he turned.

His gaze settled on her slender form. He stood transfixed as he took in her beauty. Kayla's auburn wavy hair hung loose and flowed down over her shoulders. A pair of sunglasses sat atop her head like a hair band. Her face was lightly made up and her reading glasses were nowhere in sight. A sheer tan cardigan covered her arms while beneath was a lacy white tank top. She looked so stunning that all of the villagers would be too busy trying to figure out if she was a movie star to take any notice of him.

"Is everything all right with the suite?" She stopped next to him.

He swallowed hard and glanced away, telling himself to relax. This was still the same Kayla that he'd been working closely with for weeks. He gazed at her again, trying to see her as the levelheaded assistant that he'd come to rely on. Spending the day with her, leisurely strolling about was going to be a struggle. He just had to keep in mind that they had a mission to accomplish—a royal wedding to brainstorm.

"Angelo?" She sent him a concerned look.

"Um…sorry. Yes, the suite is ours for the duration."

She pressed a hand to her chest. "That's good. You had me worried for a moment there."

"Nothing at all to worry about. Are you ready for your grand tour?"

She smiled and nodded. "Yes, I am. I'm really looking forward to it."

Without thinking, he extended his arm to her. Surprise lit up her eyes but in a blink it was gone. She slipped her arm in his. He didn't know why he'd made the gesture. It just felt right. So much for the promise he'd made himself to remain professional around her. They hadn't even left the hotel and he was already treating her like...like... Oh, whatever.

Angelo led her out of the hotel into the sunshiny afternoon. He had to admit that it was nice to get away from the stress of the wedding pitch. The whole project had ground to a complete halt. He sure hoped this outing would refill his creative well. If nothing else, maybe it would help him relax so he could start brainstorming again.

He glanced over to find Kayla taking in their surroundings. "I thought we would walk since the village isn't far from here."

"Sounds fine by me. I've been cooped up in the hotel long enough. Back in New York, I'm used to doing a lot of walking."

"Really. Where do you walk?" He didn't know why but he was truly interested.

"I walk to the subway and then to the office. Sometimes, if the weather is right, I will duck out at lunch and stretch my legs."

"So you truly like to walk."

She nodded. "It sure beats eating like a bird. If you hadn't noticed, I do enjoy food." She rubbed her flat abs. "Especially pasta."

"Would you like to try some of the best Italian food in the region?"

"Definitely."

"Good. From what I've heard, you should be impressed with the restaurant I've chosen."

"Is it far from here?"

"Not at all. In fact, it's right here in Monte Calanetti. We have reservations for tomorrow night."

"I can't wait."

"Good. Consider it a date."

When her fine brows rose and her eyes glittered with unspoken questions, he realized he'd blundered. But he didn't take back the words. He liked the thought of having a friendly date with her.

They walked a bit before Kayla spoke. "What's it called?"

"Mancini's. It's an exclusive IGF-starred restaurant on the outskirts of the village. The chef is a friend of my brother's."

"This friend of your brother's, is he from around here?"

"Yes, he grew up here. After Raffaele achieved international success with his cooking, he returned to open his own restaurant. I suspect he was anxious to try running his own place, but I'm surprised he didn't start his business in one of the cities like Rome or Milan."

"Perhaps he just wanted to be home again. Have you really never considered moving back here?"

Angelo gave a firm shake of head. "Not even once."

"Don't you like it here?"

"It…it has a lot of memories. Not all of them good ones."

Angelo remembered how he'd been turned away from his home and told not to return. The buried memories came flooding back to him. The loud arguments between his parents. His brother and sister upset. And then there was the last time he came to his mother's defense. He'd experienced many a row with his father before that life-altering one—the one where his father threw him out of the house, telling him that he was old enough to make it on his own.

When Angelo had turned a pleading stare to his mother, she'd told him that he was a smart, strong young man and that it was time to make his way in life. That was when he'd had no choice but to follow his dreams. With the aid of his inheritance from his grandfather combined with his meager savings, he'd set out for New York.

Though he hated to leave his brother and sister, he didn't have a choice. His father was a stubborn man who wouldn't back down from an argument. And Angelo wasn't about to live any longer with his parents and their dysfunctional relationship. In fact, he hadn't even come back to Monte Calanetti to visit until his mother and father had moved to Milan. He had no intention of seeing his father again.

"I'm sorry. I didn't mean to upset you."

Kayla's voice drew him out of his thoughts. "What? Um…oh, you didn't."

She sent him an I-don't-believe-you look but said nothing more. They continued toward the village in silence. It felt so strange to be back here—when he'd left all of those years ago, he'd sworn that he'd never return. And he hadn't for a long time.

The truth was he missed his brother and sister. But he rarely made the journey home. It was too hard. There were too many unsettling memories lurking about, and he just didn't have the same draw to this place that his brother and sister did. He didn't understand Nico's need to cling to their heritage, not when there were so many adventures outside of Monte Calanetti to experience.

"This is beautiful." Kayla stood at the crumbling rock wall that surrounded the village, which was perched high upon a hill. "What an amazing view. What's with the wall?"

"The village is centuries old and used to be a stronghold against attacks."

"I couldn't imagine there being unrest here. I mean, did you ever see anything so peaceful?" There was a distinct note of awe in Kayla's voice. "There's something almost magical about it."

"I used to think that, too."

"You did?"

He nodded, recalling days of long ago. "I used to come to this spot when I was a kid." What he failed to mention is that he came here to get away from his parents' arguing.

"I'd pretend that I was the defender of the kingdom. Many sword battles took place where you're standing."

"Really? So you were Sir Lancelot?" She eyed him up as though imagining him in a coat of armor.

He was no knight—not even close to it. He'd just been a kid trying to escape the battlefield between his parents, but he didn't want to get into any of that. A gentle breeze rushed past them and he willed it to sweep away the unsettling memories. He didn't want the past to ruin this day.

"Look." She pointed to a flock of little birds as they took flight. They soared up into the sky, circled and swooped low before rising again. "Aren't they beautiful?"

He was never a bird-watcher, but he had to admire the symmetry of their movements. He couldn't help but wonder what else he'd been missing. His gaze strayed back to Kayla. How had he missed noticing how amazing she was both inside and out?

"And listen."

He did as she asked. "I don't hear anything."

"Exactly! There's nothing but the rustle of the leaves. It's so freeing."

Now that he could agree on. He'd been searching for quietness like this ever since he'd moved to New York, but he'd never been able to find it—until now. "It clears the mind."

"Good. We want clear heads when we tour Monte Calanetti." She turned and pointed off in the distance. "I just love the rows of grapevines. I wonder how they get the lines so straight."

"I'm betting if you were to ask Nico that he'd tell you anything you want to know about running a vineyard. He's very proud of his work."

"You mean all of that is Nico's land?"

Angelo nodded. "It has been passed down through the family. When my father couldn't make a go of it, they passed the land down to us kids. I was already working in New York and Marianna was too young, so Nico stepped up. He's worked really hard to rebuild the vineyard and make a name for the wine."

"Hardworking must be a trait of the Amatucci men."

"Some of them anyhow." His father wasn't big on work, which was evident by the poor condition of the vineyard when he'd handed it over to his children. "Come on. I thought you wanted to see Monte Calanetti."

"I do."

With Kayla's hand still tucked in the crook of his arm, Angelo took comfort in having her next to him. This was his first stroll through the village since that dreadful day when his father cast him out of their family home. These days when he returned to Italy, he either stayed in the city or at the villa. He just wasn't up for the curious stares or worse the questions about why he left.

As they strolled through the village, Angelo warned himself not to get too comfortable with Kayla. Soon this vacation illusion would end, and they'd be back in New York, where he'd transform back into Mr. Amatucci and she'd once again be Ms. Hill. Everything would once again be as it should.

CHAPTER ELEVEN

NEVER ONE TO lurk in the shadows, Angelo led Kayla into the center of Monte Calanetti. Their first stop was at the *caffè* shop. He'd never met a woman who loved coffee as much as Kayla. She savored each sip before swallowing. He loved to watch her facial features when she'd take her first sip—it was somewhere between total delight and ecstasy. He longed to be able to put that look on her face…and not with coffee…but with a long, slow, deep, soul-stirring kiss.

He'd given up the futile effort of fighting his lustful thoughts for Kayla. He couldn't lie to himself. He found her utterly enchanting. And as long as he stuck with his daydreams of holding her—of kissing her passionately— they'd be fine. It wasn't as if she could read his mind.

They stepped out of the shop and onto the busy sidewalk. As they started to walk again, he reminded himself not to get too caught up in having Kayla by his side. She was the absolute wrong person for him to have a dalliance with beneath the Tuscany sun. He was her escort—her friend— nothing more. He forced his thoughts to the quaint shops that offered such things as locally grown flowers and to-die-for baked goods. There was a little bit of everything. And he could tell by the rapt stare on Kayla's face that she was enthralled by all of it.

"Angelo, is that you?"

They both stopped at the sound of a woman's excited voice. Angelo glanced over his shoulder to see an older woman rushing toward them. She looked vaguely familiar.

"It is you." The woman couldn't be much more than five feet tall, if that. She beamed up at him. "I knew you'd come back."

It took him a moment, but then the woman's gentle smile and warm eyes clicked a spot in his memory—Mrs. Caruso. He hadn't seen her since he was a teenager. Back then, she'd had long dark hair that she kept braided over one shoulder. Now, her dark hair had given way to shades of gray, and instead of the braid, her hair was pinned up.

Kayla elbowed him, and at last, he found his voice. "Mrs. Caruso, it's good to see you."

"What kind of greeting is that?" She grabbed him by the arms and pulled him toward her. When he'd stooped over far enough, she placed a hand on either side of his head, and then kissed each cheek. "You've been gone much too long. You've been missed."

She pulled him back down to her and gave him a tight hug. He hugged her back. Heat warmed his face. He wasn't used to public displays of affection…no matter how innocent they might be. This would never happen back in the States. But then again, Monte Calanetti was a lifetime away from New York City, and the same rules didn't seem to apply here.

They chatted for a bit as she asked one question after the other about what he'd been doing with himself. The years rolled away as she put him at ease with her friendly chatter. The best part was that she really listened to him—as she'd done all of those years ago when he was a kid. Mrs. Caruso and her husband ran the local bakery. They'd never had any children of their own. Angelo always suspected that it wasn't from the lack of wanting or trying. Without little ones of her own, she'd doted on the kids in the village.

"You are going to do the royal wedding pitch, aren't you?" She smiled and clapped her hands together as though she'd just solved the world's problems.

"Nico asked me to work on it. My assistant and I just extended our stay here in order to work up a presentation for the royal family."

"Wonderful!" Mrs. Caruso beamed. "Now I'm more

certain than ever that the village will host the wedding.
Everyone will be so grateful to both of you."

"I don't know about that—"

"You're just being modest. You always were." Mrs. Caruso's gaze moved to Kayla. "Now where are my manners?
Angelo, introduce me to your girlfriend."

His girlfriend? Hadn't she heard him say Kayla was his
assistant? His gaze moved from her to Kayla, who was
smiling. Why wasn't she correcting the woman? Was she
just being polite? Or should he be concerned that she was
taking this friendly outing far too seriously?

"Hi, I'm Kayla." She held out a hand while Angelo struggled to settle his thoughts. "I'm actually Mr. Amatucci's
assistant."

Mrs. Caruso's brows rose as her gaze moved back and
forth between them. "I could have sworn that you two
were— Oh, never mind me. I'm just so glad that you're
both here to help with the wedding."

They promised to stop by the bakery soon and moved on
down the walkway. He still didn't know why Mrs. Caruso
would think they were a couple. Then he glanced down to
where Kayla's hand was resting on his arm. Okay, so maybe
from the outside the lines in their relationship appeared a
bit blurred, but they knew where they stood. Didn't they?

He swallowed hard. "I'm sorry about back there with
Mrs. Caruso jumping to conclusions about us."

"It's okay. It was a natural mistake."

A natural mistake? Wait. What exactly did that mean?

He glanced over at Kayla. "But you know that you and
I…that we're, um…that nothing has changed. Right?"

She smiled up at him. "Relax. We're just two business
associates enjoying a stroll through the village. It's a mission. We have to learn as much about this place as possible so that you can do some brainstorming about the pitch
when we return to our suite."

She said all of the right things, but why did they sound

so wrong to his ears? Maybe he was just being hypersensitive. He took a deep breath and blew it out. "Exactly." Now he needed to change the subject to something a little less stressful. "Mrs. Caruso certainly seemed hopeful about the royal wedding."

"She did. It seems as if the whole village is buzzing with excitement about it."

"I just hope they don't end up disappointed."

She lightly elbowed him. "They won't be. You'll see to that."

At this particular moment, she had a lot more faith in his abilities than he did. "I don't know if I'm that good. This is just a small village and we're talking about a royal wedding—the sort of thing they write about in history books."

"And who better to sell the royal couple on the merits of Monte Calanetti?" She gazed up at him with hope in her eyes. "You just need to loosen up a bit and enjoy yourself."

"I am relaxed." As relaxed as he got these days.

She sighed and shook her head. "No, you aren't. Let down your guard and enjoy the sun on your face."

"Why is this so important to you?"

"Because I want you to really see Monte Calanetti and get excited about it." Her gaze met his and then dipped to his mouth. "I think if you're passionate about something it will show."

The temperature started to rise. He knew what she was thinking because he was thinking the same thing. He zeroed in on her inviting lips. He was definitely feeling passionate. Would it be wrong to kiss her again?

Someone bumped his shoulder as they passed by, reminding him that they were in the middle of the village. Not exactly the place for a passionate moment or even a quick peck. Besides, he couldn't give her the wrong impression. He didn't do relationships.

Before he could decide if he should say something,

Kayla slipped her arm in his and they started to walk again. They made their way around the piazza, taking in the various shops from a shoe boutique to a candy shop. Monte Calanetti offered so much more than he recalled.

Maybe it wasn't quite the small backward village he'd conjured up in his memory—the same village where he'd once got into a bit of mischief with harmless pranks. Those were the carefree days that he hadn't known to appreciate as they flew by.

"What are you smiling about?" Kayla sent him a curious look.

He was smiling? He hadn't realized his thoughts had crossed his face. "I was just recalling some antics I'd gotten into as a kid."

"Oh, tell me. I'd love to hear."

"You would?" He wouldn't think something like that would interest her. When she nodded, he continued. "There was this one time when I glued a coin to the sidewalk outside the market. You wouldn't believe how many people tried to pry it free."

Her eyes twinkled. "So you didn't always play by the rules."

He shrugged. "What kind of trouble did you get into?"

"Me? Nothing."

"Oh, come on, confess. There has to be something."

She paused as though giving it some serious consideration. "Well, there was this one time the neighborhood boys attached some fishing line to a dollar. It was similar to what you did. They'd lay it out in front of my parents' market, and when someone went to pick up it up, they'd tug on the line."

"See, I knew you weren't as innocent as you appeared."

"Hey, it wasn't me. It was them. I… I was just watching."

"Uh-huh." He enjoyed the way her cheeks filled with color. "It's good to know you have some spunk in you. That will come in handy in this business."

* * *

Kayla was in love—with the village, of course.

Brilliant sunshine lit up the heart of Monte Calanetti. The piazza was surrounded by a wide range of small shops to satisfy even the most discerning tastes. But it was the large fountain in the center of the village square that drew Kayla's attention. She tugged on Angelo's arm, leading them toward it.

The focal point of the fountain was a nymph draped in a cloak. She held a huge clamshell overhead. The sunshine sparkled and danced over the fine billowing mist from the continuous jets of water. Kayla stopped at the fountain's edge. She smiled, loving the details of the sculpture that included a ring of fish leaping out of the water.

"I take it you like the fountain." Angelo's deep voice came from just behind her. "You know there's a tradition that if you toss a coin and it lands in the shell, you get your wish."

Her gaze rose to the clamshell—suddenly it didn't look quite so big. "You'd have to be awfully lucky to get it all the way up there."

"Why don't you give it a try?"

"I… I don't think so. I was never good at those types of things."

Angelo held a coin out to her. "Here you go." His fingers pressed the money into her palm. "I made a wish once and it came true."

"Really?" She turned to him. "What was it?"

He shook his head. "You aren't supposed to tell your wish."

"But that doesn't apply if your wish has already come true. So, out with it."

The corner of his very inviting lips lifted. "Okay. I wished that someday I'd get to travel the world."

"Wow. It really did come true." She thought really hard, but was torn by what she should wish for. She could wish for the fund-raiser to be a huge success. Or she could wish for her promotion to ad executive. But fountains should be for fanciful dreams.

"Don't look so worried. Turn around."

She did as he said. The next thing she knew, his body pressed to her back—his hard planes to her soft curves. His breath tickled her neck. Her heart thumped and her knees grew weak. Thankfully he was there holding her up.

His voice was soft as he spoke. "You make the wish and I'll help you get the coin in the shell. Ready?"

She nodded. Together with their hands touching, they swung. The coin flipped end over end through the air.

Let Angelo kiss me.

Plunk! The coin landed in the clamshell.

"We did it!"

At that moment, Angelo backed away. "Did you ever doubt it?"

"I couldn't have done it without you." She turned around, hoping her wish would come true.

"Did you make your wish?"

Disappointment washed over her. Of course he wasn't going to kiss her. She'd let herself get caught up in the moment. That wouldn't happen again.

"We should keep moving." She turned to start walking. "We don't want to miss anything."

"Wait." He reached out for her hand. "Aren't you going to tell me what you wished for?"

"Um...no. I can't." When he sent her a puzzled look, she added, "If I tell you, it won't come true."

"Well, we wouldn't want that to happen."

Her hand remained in his warm grasp as they continued their stroll. Was it her imagination or was Angelo's icy professional persona melting beneath the Tuscany sun? She smiled. He was definitely warming up.

CHAPTER TWELVE

SIMPLY *CHARMING*.

At this particular moment, Kayla had no better word for it. And she wasn't just talking about the village. She gave Angelo a sideways gaze. Handsome, thoughtful and entertaining. "Quite a combo."

"What?"

Oops! She hadn't meant to vocalize her thoughts. "I... I was just thinking Monte Calanetti has quite an amazing combination of old-world charm and modern day functionality."

They meandered away from the fountain. On the edge of the piazza, they passed by a well that she was certain had seen its days of women gathering to fill their buckets. While waiting for their turn, she imagined they'd shared the happenings of the village—the historic form of gossiping around the water cooler. It was so easy to envision how things used to be. Something told Kayla that this village hadn't changed a whole lot over the years.

The sunshine warmed the back of her neck, but it was Angelo's arm beneath her fingertips that warmed her insides. She resisted the urge to smooth her fingers over his tanned skin. She was in serious danger of forgetting that he was her boss—the key to her future promotion.

As the bell towers rang out, Kayla stared at the cobblestone path that wound its way between the brick buildings. A number of the homes had flower boxes with red, yellow and purple blooms. There were also flowerpots by the various shaped doors painted in every imaginable color. In other places, ivy snaked its way along the bricks. This area was quite picturesque and made Kayla forget that she was in the center of the village.

A rustling sound had her glancing upward. She craned her neck, finding fresh laundry fluttering in the breeze. She couldn't help but smile. It was a lovely, inviting sight. But as much as she liked it, it was the man at her side that she found utterly captivating.

Angelo Amatucci might be icy cool in the office, but she'd found that once he thawed out, he was a warm, thoughtful man. Not that she was falling for his amazing good looks or his dark, mysterious eyes. Her priority was her career—the reason she'd left her home in Paradise. And she wasn't about to ruin her future by throwing herself at her boss.

She chanced a quick glance his way. But then again—

No. She pulled her thoughts up short. This wasn't getting her anywhere.

She was supposed to be touring Monte Calanetti to get ideas for the wedding pitch. If they were going to sell the royal couple on this location for the wedding, she needed to know as much about it as possible. And of what she'd seen so far, she loved it. This village and its occupants would give the wedding an old-world feel with lots of heart.

The villagers sent puzzled glances their way as though they should know who Angelo was but couldn't quite place his face. And then there were a few people that ventured to ask if he was indeed Angelo. When he confirmed their suspicions, he wasn't greeted with a simple hello or a mere handshake; instead, he was yanked into warm hugs. She could see the frown lines etched on his face, but to his credit he didn't complain. There were even a few tears of happiness from the older women who remembered him when he was just a young boy.

Angelo took her hand in his as though it were natural for them. Kayla liked feeling connected to him—feeling his long fingers wrapped around hers.

"I'm sorry about that." Angelo started walking again. "I didn't expect anyone to remember me."

"You must have spent a lot of time in the village as a kid."

"I did. It was my escape from the monotony of working around the vineyard." His jaw tensed and a muscle twitched.

"I take it that's why you let your brother have the run of Calanetti Vineyards?"

He nodded. "Nico is as passionate about the winery as I am with advertising. How about you? Do you have any brothers or sisters?"

Kayla shook her head. "My parents wanted more children, but that didn't work out. So with me being an only child, they heaped all of their hopes and dreams onto me."

"Hmm...sounds a bit daunting for one person."

"It is. That's why I had to leave Paradise."

"Somehow I just can't imagine life in Paradise could be such a hardship."

She shrugged. "It's great. The people are wonderful. It's the perfect place to raise kids."

"But you weren't ready for kids?"

The thought of taking on that sort of responsibility still overwhelmed her. "I have to figure out me first and accomplish some things on my own before I can be there 24/7 for others. And my parents, as much as I love them, didn't understand this."

"They wanted you to graduate high school and settle down."

She nodded. "They had it all planned out. I'd get married, have lots of kids and when the time came my husband and I would take over the family store."

"Doesn't sound so bad."

"No. It isn't. But I always had a dream of going to college and making a name for myself. I wanted to move to the city. I wanted to climb the corporate ladder. I wanted to—"

She bit off her last words. Heat rushed up her neck and warmed her face. She couldn't believe that she'd gotten so comfortable around Angelo that she'd just rambled on about her dreams. For a moment, she'd forgotten that she was talking to her boss.

Not good, Kayla. Not good at all.

She freed her hand from his. It was time she started acting like his employee, not his girlfriend. The time had come to get back to reality.

Angelo stopped walking and turned to her. "What aren't you saying? What do you want to do?"

"Um…nothing. It's no big deal. Let's keep going. I want to see the whole village." She turned to start walking again.

Angelo reached out, catching her arm in his firm grip. "Not so fast." She turned back, glancing up at his serious gaze. "Kayla, talk to me." His hand fell away from her arm. "I've told you all sorts of things that I don't normally share with people. I'd like to know what you were about to say and why you stopped. Surely by now you know that you can trust me."

Could she trust him? She supposed it depended on the subject. With her safety—most definitely. With her dreams—perhaps. With her heart— Wait, where had that come from?

"Kayla, what is it?"

She wasn't good at lying so that left her with the truth, but she didn't know how Angelo would take it. "I came to New York because I wanted…er… I want to be an ad executive."

His brows scrunched together. "And?"

She shrugged. "And that's it."

"That's what you didn't want to tell me?"

Her gaze moved to the cobblestone walkway. "It's just that I got comfortable around you and forgot to watch what I was saying."

"Oh, I see. Since I'm the boss, you feel like you have to screen what you say to me?"

She nodded.

"How about this? For the duration of this trip, I'm not

your boss. We're just business associates or how about friends? Would you like that?"

Her gaze met his and she found that he was being perfectly serious. "But what about when we return to New York?"

"Obviously things will have to change then, but for right now, I'd like to just be Angelo, not Mr. Amatucci. I'd forgotten what it's like just to be me again."

"And I like you calling me Kayla." Her gaze met his. Within his eyes she found a comforting warmth. "Consider yourself a friend."

He held out his hand to her. She accepted it. A shiver of excitement raced up her arm. They continued to stare deep into each other's eyes, even though it was totally unnecessary. She knew she should turn away. She knew that it was the proper thing to do with her boss. But as he'd just pointed out they were friends—for now.

His voice grew deeper. "I couldn't think of a better friend to have."

Her heart fluttered in her chest. What had just happened?

Angelo turned and tucked her hand back in the crook of his arm. Why did it suddenly feel as though their relationship had just taken a detour? How would they ever find their way back to just being boss and employee now?

Monte Calanetti is a diamond in the rough.

Had that thought really just crossed his mind?

Before he'd left the hotel a few hours ago, he'd envisioned Monte Calanetti as he had when he was a child— suffocating with its traditional ways and its resistance to growth and to modernization. But somehow, with Kayla by his side, he'd seen the village from a different perspective —he'd seen it through her very beautiful, very observant eyes. With her passion and romantic tendencies, she might just be the key he needed to pull this wedding pitch together. But did he dare ask for her help?

Sure, she had talent. He'd witnessed it firsthand with the Van Holsen account. But did he trust her with a project that was so important to his family? After all, his brother and sister, not to mention the entire village, were counting on him to represent them properly to the royal couple. But how was he supposed to do that when he kept hitting one brick wall after the other?

They walked some more before Kayla turned to him. "Thank you for showing me your hometown. I love it."

"Really?" He failed to keep the surprise from his voice.

"Of course I do. How could you not? Not only that but it has the most delicious aromas and it's so peaceful." Just then two scooters whizzed by them. "Okay, so it isn't totally peaceful."

"You'll get used to them. Scooters are very popular around here."

A couple more scooters zoomed down the road causing Kayla to step into the grass. She took a moment, taking in her surroundings. "Is this where you went to school?"

Angelo glanced at the back of the building off in the distance. The years started to slip away. "Yes, it is."

"I bet you were a handful back then."

As a young kid, he'd been the complete opposite of the way he is now. "I believe the word they used was *incorrigible*."

Now why had he gone and admitted that? Letting down his defenses and opening up about his past would only lead to confusion and misunderstandings, because sharing was what people did when they were getting serious. And that wasn't going to happen. He refused to let it happen. No matter how ripe her lips were for a kiss. Or how her smile sent his pulse racing.

"You probably picked on all of the girls and pulled on their ponytails."

He shook his head. "Not me. I didn't have time for girls, not until I was a bit older."

"And then I bet you broke a lot of hearts."

He wasn't sure about that, but there was one girl, Vera Carducci, and he'd had the biggest crush on her. He hadn't thought of her in years.

"See. I was right." Kayla smiled triumphantly.

"Actually, I was the one who got dumped."

"That's so hard to believe—"

"It's the truth." Why did he feel the need to make Kayla believe that his life was far from idyllic? What was it about her that had him letting down his guard? He had to do better. He couldn't let her get too close. It'd only cause them pain in the end.

Kayla walked over to a tree in the school yard. Her fingers traced over the numerous carvings from initials to hearts. "Was this the kissing tree?"

He nodded, suddenly wishing they were anywhere but here.

"I bet your initials are here…somewhere." Kayla's voice drew him back to the present. "Want to point me in the right direction?"

"Actually, they aren't here."

Her eyes opened wide. "Really? I thought for sure that you would have been popular with the girls."

He shrugged, recalling his fair share of girlfriends over the years. But he'd never kissed them here. Not a chance.

"Surely you stole a kiss or two." Her gaze needled him for answers.

"Not here."

"Why not?"

Oh, what did it matter if he told her? It wasn't as if there was any truth to the legend. It was all a bunch of wishful thinking.

"There's some silly legend attached to the tree that says whoever you kiss here will be your soul mate for life."

Kayla's green eyes widened with interest. "Really? And you don't believe it?"

He shook his head. "It's just an old wives' tale. There's nothing to it."

"And yet you've made a point not to kiss anyone here." She stepped closer to him. "If you don't believe in such superstitions, prove it."

His pulse kicked up a notch. Why was there a gleam in her eyes? Was she challenging him? Did she really expect him to kiss her here?

Instead of the idea scaring him off, it actually appealed to him. His gaze dipped to her lips. Kayla was the only woman he had ever contemplated kissing here—wait, when did that happen? He gave himself a mental jerk, but it didn't chase away the tempting thought.

What was it about Miss Kayla Hill that had him wishing there were such things as happily-ever-afters instead of roller-coaster relationships? He'd had so much turbulence in his life that he couldn't stand anymore. But Kayla was different. She had a calming presence.

This wasn't right. He should make it perfectly clear that he was no Romeo, but the way she kept staring at him, challenging him with her eyes, filled him with a warm sensation. He didn't want it to end. What would it hurt to let her remain caught up in her romantic imaginings?

Without thinking about the pros and cons of what he was about to do, he dipped his head and caught her lips with his own. Her lips were soft and pliant. He wrapped his arms around her slender waist and pulled her to him. She willingly followed his lead. Her soft curves pressed to him and a moan swelled deep in his throat. How in the world was he ever going to let her go? He'd never felt anything this intense for anyone—ever.

He wanted to convince himself that it was because she was forbidden fruit—his assistant. But he couldn't buy that. There was something so special about her that he couldn't diminish the connection with such a flimsy excuse. He knew as sure as he was standing there in a lip-lock with her that if their situation were different and he wasn't her boss that he'd still desire her with every fiber of his body.

His mouth moved over hers, slow at first. Yet when she met him move for move, the desire burning in him flared. Her mouth opened to him and she tasted sweet like the sun-ripened berries she'd sampled back in the village. He'd never tasted anything so delectable in his life. He doubted he'd ever experience a moment like this again.

There was something so special about Kayla. It was as though no matter what he did, she could see the real him. But could she see his scars, the ones that kept him from letting people get too close?

Her hands slid up over his shoulders and wrapped around the back of his neck. Her touch sent waves of excitement down his spine. He wanted her. He needed her. But his heart and mind were still guarded.

If he let her get any closer, she'd learn of his shame—of his ultimate pain—and then she'd pity him. Pity was not something that he could tolerate. He was Angelo Amatucci. A self-made man. He needed no one's sympathy. He needed no one.

Anxious to rebuild that wall between them, he braced his hands on her hips and pushed her back. Her eyes fluttered open and confusion showed in them.

"We should head back to the hotel. I… I have work to do."

Disappointment flashed in her eyes. "Oh. Okay."

He retraced their steps. "I have a conference call this afternoon."

Kayla fell in step beside him. He should say something. Explain somehow. But he didn't know what to say because that kiss left him utterly confused by the rush of emotions she'd evoked in him. Somehow, some way, she'd sneaked past his well-placed barriers and with each smile, each touch, she was getting to him. That wasn't part of his plan.

Unable to decide what to do about his undeniable attraction to his assistant, he turned his attention to something much less stressful—the village. For the first time, he saw its charms. Kayla had opened his eyes to everything he'd blocked out, from the amazing artisans, to the detailed architecture, to the warm and friendly people. He had so much to work with now. The pitch would be amazing if he could pull it all together, even though he was still unsure about the wedding aspect.

Still, Monte Calanetti had some of the best food in the world. It was sure to impress even the royal couple. And to be truthful, he was quite anxious to try Raffaele's restaurant—if the rumors were anything to go by, it was out of this world.

Although his desire to go to dinner had more to do with Kayla than the food. He hungered for more of her melodious laugh and her contagious smiles. Though he shouldn't, he'd come to really enjoy her company.

As productive as they were, working as a team, he was enjoying getting to know her on a personal level. After all, it wasn't as if this thing, whatever you wanted to call it, would carry over to New York. He'd make sure of it. But what would it hurt to enjoy the moment?

CHAPTER THIRTEEN

ANGELO SWIPED HIS key card and opened the suite door for Kayla. When she brushed past him, he noticed the softest scent of wildflowers. He inhaled deeply, enjoying the light fragrance as he followed her into the room, wishing he could hold on to her delicate scent just a little longer.

When she stopped short, he bumped into her. He grabbed her shoulders to steady her. She turned in his arms and gazed up at him with those big luminous green eyes. His heart pounded in his chest.

"Wasn't the afternoon wonderful?"

Was it his imagination or was her voice soft and sultry? And was she looking at him differently? Or was it that he wanted her so much that he was projecting his lusty thoughts upon her?

He swallowed down the lump in his throat. "Yes, it was a really nice day."

"Thank you so much for spending the day with me. I promise to pay you back." She stood up on her tiptoes and leaned forward.

She was going to repeat their kiss. His heart pounded. His brain told him that it shouldn't happen, but his body had other thoughts. He started to lean forward—

Buzz. Buzz. His phone vibrated in his pocket, breaking the spell.

He pulled back. After retrieving the phone from his pocket, he checked the screen. "It's the conference call. I have to take it. Can we talk later?"

He moved to his room to take the call in private. He actually welcomed the interruption. It gave him time to figure out how to handle this change of dynamics with Kayla.

The phone call dragged on much longer than he'd anticipated. When he finally disconnected the call, he found Kayla was still in the suite working on her laptop.

He cleared his throat and she glanced up, but her gaze didn't quite reach his. "Sorry about the interruption."

"No problem." Her voice didn't hold its normal lilt. She lifted her reading glasses and rested them on her head.

As much as he'd like to pretend that the kiss hadn't happened, he couldn't. It was already affecting their working relationship and that was not acceptable. "I need to apologize. That kiss…back at the tree, it shouldn't have happened. You must understand that it can't happen again."

"Is that what you really want?"

"Yes. No. I don't know." He raked his fingers through his hair. "Maybe I was wrong about this. Maybe it'd be better if you flew back to New York."

"What?" She jumped to her feet. Her heated gaze was most definitely meeting his now.

"This isn't going to work between us." He glanced away, knowing he'd created this problem. "We can't keep our hands off each other. How are we supposed to concentrate on all of the work we have to get done?"

She stepped up to him and poked him in the chest. "You're not firing me. I won't let you—"

"Wait. Who said anything about firing you?" He wrapped his hand around her finger, fighting off the urge to wrap his lips around it. "Certainly not me. You are very talented. Do you honestly think that I'd sack you over a kiss or two—kisses that I initiated?"

"Then what?" She pulled her finger from his hold as though she'd read his errant thought. "You don't think you can keep your hands to yourself around me?"

"Yes… I mean, no." He absolutely hated this feeling of being out of control—of his emotions or whatever you called it ruling over his common sense. "You confuse me."

"How so?" Her gaze narrowed in on him. When he didn't answer her, she persisted. "Tell me. I want to know."

He sighed. "It's nothing. Just forget I said anything."

"What is this really about? It has to be about more than just a kiss."

His gaze lifted and met hers head-on. How could she understand him so well? No other woman had ever seen the real him—they'd always been more interested in having a good time. But then again, he'd gone out of his way to hook up with women who didn't have serious, long-term plans where he was concerned.

His strong reaction to Kayla was due to a lot more than just the kiss. She made him feel things—want things—that he had no business feeling or wanting. And the way she'd moved him with that passionate kiss hadn't done anything to settle him. It had only made him want her all the more. What was up with that? He'd never desired a woman with every single fiber of his being. Until now.

Kayla stepped closer and lowered her voice. "Angelo, I think we've grown close enough on this trip that you can talk to me and know that it won't go any further. Tell me what's eating you up inside."

He knew what she was after—the secrets of his past. But was he ready for that? Did he have the courage to peel back those old wounds? Was he ready to deal with her reaction? Could he stand having her think less of him?

The answer was a resounding no.

Angelo inhaled a deep breath and blew it out. He wasn't prepared to open that door. It wasn't as if they were involved romantically. They didn't have a future, just the here and the now.

But there was something else…

He needed her—well…er…her help. He couldn't do this wedding pitch alone. The admission twisted his gut in a knot. He was not a man accustomed to reaching out to others.

He made a point of being the man handing out assignments, making suggestions and overseeing operations. He was never at a loss for how to accomplish things—especially an advertising pitch. This was supposed to be his area of expertise—his specialty.

What was wrong with him? Why couldn't he come up with a solid pitch? And what was Kayla going to think of him when he made this request? Would she think less of him?

Wanting to get it over with, he uttered, "I need your assistance."

"What?" Her brow creased. "Of course I'll help you. That's what I'm here for." She took a seat on the couch. "What do you need?"

His gaze met hers briefly, and then he glanced away. "I... I'm having issues with this pitch. Weddings and romance aren't my thing." That much was the truth. He avoided weddings like the plague—he always had a prior business engagement. "I thought maybe you'd have some experience with them."

"Well, um... I have a bit of experience." Her cheeks took on a pasty shade of white.

"You don't look so good. I'll get you something to drink."

"You don't have to wait on me. I can get it."

She started to get up when he pressed a hand to her shoulder. "I've got this."

He retrieved a bottle of water from the fridge and poured it in a glass for her. This was his fault. He'd had her gallivanting all around Monte Calanetti in the sun. She must have worn herself out.

He moved to her side and handed over the water. "Can I get you anything else?"

She shook her head. "Thanks. This is fine."

He sat down beside her as she sipped at the water. "I'm sorry if I pushed you too hard in the village. I should have brought you back here sooner—"

"No, that's not it. The visit was perfect. I wouldn't have changed anything about it." She sent him a smile, but it didn't quite reach her eyes.

"I don't believe you. There's something bothering you." He stopped and thought about it. "And it started when I mentioned the wedding pitch. Do you feel that I'm expecting too much of you?"

"That's not it." She placed a hand on his knee. The warmth of her touch could be felt through his jeans. "I'm just a bit tired."

"Are you sure that's all it is? It doesn't have anything to do with your broken engagement?"

Her eyes widened. "That's been over for a long time. I've moved on."

Moved on? Surely she wasn't thinking those kisses— that they'd somehow lead to something. He swallowed hard and decided it was best to change topics. "Have you made many friends since you moved to New York?"

"I haven't had much time. But I made a few at the after-school program." She pressed her lips together and turned away.

He was missing something, but he had no idea what that might be. "What do you do at this after-school program?"

She shrugged. "It's no big deal. So what can I do to help you with the wedding pitch?"

"Wait. I'd like to hear more about this program. What do you do? And how do you have time?" It seemed as if she was always in the office working long hours without a complaint.

"I do what is necessary. It all depends on the day and how many volunteers show up. Sometimes I help with homework and do a bit of tutoring. Other times I play kickball or a board game."

"You do all of that on top of the overtime you put in at the office?"

"It's not that big of a deal." She toyed with the hem of her top. "I don't have anything waiting for me at home, so why not put my spare time to good use?"

"You shouldn't dismiss what you do. There are very few people in this world who are willing to go out of their way for others. It's impressive."

Her eyes widened. "You really think so?"

"I do. Why do you seem so surprised?"

"It's just that at the office you've banned employees from taking on charitable accounts."

"It has to be that way." He raked his fingers through his hair. "There are only so many hours in the workday. I write out enough checks each year to various organizations to make up for it."

Kayla nodded, but she certainly didn't seem impressed. Uneasiness churned in his gut. Maybe she would be more understanding if she knew the amount of those checks.

"I'm sure those organizations appreciate the donations."

Guilt settled over him. What was up with that? It wasn't as if he didn't do anything. He just couldn't afford the time to take on more accounts—especially for free. He was still working on growing Amatucci & Associates into the biggest and the best advertising firm. Speaking of which, he needed to get moving on this pitch. Time was running out before his trip to Halencia.

"I need to ask you something."

She reached for the glass of water. "Ask away. Then I need to go check my email. I'm waiting on some responses about the Van Holsen account."

He shook his head, thinking this was a bad idea. "Never mind. You have enough to deal with."

She arched a thin brow at him. "You can't back out now. You have me curious."

He just couldn't admit to her that he had absolutely no direction for the pitch. Three wasted days of jotting down ideas and then realizing that they were clichéd or just plain stupid—certainly nothing that he would present to the royal family.

"If it doesn't bother you—you know, because of your broken engagement—I wanted to ask you some wedding questions."

She reached out and squeezed his hand. "I appreciate you watching out for my feelings but talking about weddings won't reduce me to tears. I promise. Let's get started."

His gaze met hers and his breath caught in his throat. He was going to have to be really careful around her or he just might be tempted to start something that neither of them was ready for. And once he got something started with her, he wasn't sure he'd ever be able to end it when reality crashed in around them.

CHAPTER FOURTEEN

THIS IS IT!

At last, it was her big break.

Kayla grinned as she sat by the pool the next day. She could hardly believe that at last her plans were all coming together. If only she could keep her attraction to Angelo under wraps. Was that even possible at this point?

Who'd have thought that the wish she'd made at the fountain would actually come true?

Angelo had kissed her—again.

Her eyelids drifted closed as her thoughts spiraled back to their amazing day beneath the Tuscany sun. The day couldn't have gone any better. She'd always treasure it. And then there had been that mind-blowing, toe-curling kiss—

"And what has you staring off into space with a smile on your face?"

Kayla glanced up to find Angelo gazing at her. "Um… nothing. I… I mean I was thinking about the wedding."

"How about the Van Holsen account? We don't want to forget about it."

"Of course not. I've sent out the new concepts to the art department."

"Good." He took a seat next to her. "You know if you're having problems you can talk to me?"

Was he referring to personal problems? Or business ones? Since they'd arrived in Italy the lines had blurred so much that she wasn't sure. But she decided that it was best for her career to take his comment as a purely professional one.

"I understand." She smoothed her hands down over her white capris. "And so far the accounts are all moving along.

I should have some drafts back from the art department this afternoon to run by you."

"Sounds good. Can I see what you've come up with so far for the royal wedding?"

She pushed her notebook over to him. "Go ahead."

The seconds slowly passed as his gaze moved down over the first page. "But this is all about Monte Calanetti." He shoved aside the pages. "There's nothing here about the wedding itself. Nothing sentimental or romantic."

Oh, boy.

This was not the start she'd imagined. She swallowed a lump in her throat. To be honest, she wasn't ready to present her ideas to him. They were only partial thoughts—snippets of this and that.

She'd have to think fast on her feet if she wanted him to keep her on this account, because she wasn't about to let this opportunity slip through her fingers. She leveled her shoulders and tilted her chin up, meeting his frown. "I think the main focus should be all about the location."

"You do?"

She nodded. "The royal couple have already been taken by the village's charm." Kayla lowered her voice and added, "I was taken by it, too. It'd be the perfect backdrop for a wedding. And that's the part I think we should exploit."

Angelo's eyes widened and he was quiet for a moment as though considering her words. "What issues do you have with basing the pitch on the wedding itself? You know with all of the pomp and circumstance. We could even throw in a horse-drawn carriage for good measure."

Kayla smiled, loving the idea of six white horses leading a shiny white carriage with gold trim. And then her imagination took a wild turn and there was Angelo next to her in the carriage. Her insides quivered at the thought. Then, realizing that she was getting off point, she gave herself a mental jerk.

"We don't know anything about what the bride wants for the actual ceremony. But we need to show them that no matter whether it is a big, splashy affair, which seems most reasonable considering it's a royal wedding, or whether they want something smaller and more intimate, that Monte Calanetti can be quite accommodating."

Angelo leaned back and crossed his arms as he quietly stared at her. He was taking her suggestions seriously. She inwardly cheered. Not about to lose her momentum, she continued. "No matter what the size of the ceremony, we need to show them that we are willing to work with the bride. We need to show them that the whole community will come together to make it a day that neither of them will ever forget."

"So you think our approach should be two-pronged, showing the village both as intimate and accommodating."

Kayla nodded. "The tour you gave me was a great start. But if we are going to sell the royals on the virtues of this village, I think we need to dig deeper."

Angelo nodded. "Sounds reasonable. What do you have in mind?"

Before she could continue, her phone vibrated on the table. She'd turned off the ringer, not wanting to bother anyone else who was around the pool.

"Do you need to get that?" Angelo's gaze moved from her to the phone.

"Um…no."

Angelo cocked a brow. "It could be the office."

"I already checked my voice mail and sorted everything that needs attention." She wanted to get back to their conversation, but he kept glancing at her phone. Knowing he wasn't going to let up on this subject until he found out why she was so hesitant to answer, she grabbed her phone and checked the ID. Just as she'd suspected, the call was from the States but it wasn't the office—it was Pam, the woman handling the fund-raiser while Kayla was in Italy.

"It's nothing urgent." Kayla would deal with it later.

"Are you sure?"

"I am." This wasn't Pam's first call of the day nor would it likely be her last.

Why was Angelo looking at her that way? It was as though he could see that she was holding something back. And the last thing Kayla needed was for him not to trust her. Because this royal wedding was the opportunity of a lifetime. She planned to grasp it with both hands and hold on tight. Having Angelo make her an official part of this pitch would be the validation she needed to show her parents that she'd made the right decision with her life. At last, they'd be proud of her and her choices.

"Okay." He waved away the phone and grabbed for her notebook again. "You need to add more detail to these notes."

"I will, but I was thinking we need to visit each of the establishments in the village again. I could write up very specific notes about their specialties—things that will be hard to find elsewhere—items that the village is especially proud of."

His eyes lit up. "And I know exactly where we'll start."

"You do?" She smiled, knowing he liked her ideas. "Where?"

"Mancini's. You did bring something pretty, formal— Oh, you know what I mean."

"A little black dress?"

"Yes, that will do nicely. We have reservations at seven. Consider it a research expedition during which I want to hear more of your thoughts."

Her mounting excitement skidded to a halt upon his assurance that this evening would be all about business. She didn't know why she should let it bother her. This is what she wanted—for things to return to a business relationship. Wasn't it?

* * *

Time flew by far too fast.

A week had passed since their dinner at Mancini's. Angelo had been quite impressed with the service and most especially the food. What Raffaele was doing spending his time here in the countryside was beyond Angelo. The man was a magician in the kitchen. He could head up any restaurant that he set his sights on from Rome to New York. Although, it was lucky for Angelo, because Mancini's award-winning menu was going to be the centerpiece of the pitch.

Angelo stood in the middle of the hotel suite. He really liked what he saw. His gaze zeroed in on Kayla. They'd had a couple of tables brought in. The room had been rearranged so that the area loosely resembled an office more than a relaxing, posh hotel room. And it seemed to be helping them to stay on track.

Feeling the pressure to get this right, Angelo had relented and had Kayla pass along some of their other accounts to his top ad executive. Their attention needed to be centered on the wedding, especially since he'd already lost time spinning his wheels. One of the accounts they had retained was Victoria Van Holsen's account. The woman simply wouldn't deal with anyone but himself or Kayla. Victoria, who was quite particular about who she dealt with, had surprisingly taken to Kayla's sunny disposition. It seemed no one was immune to Kayla's charms—him included.

There was so much more to Kayla than he'd given her credit for when he'd hired her as his temporary assistant. Sure, her résumé had been excellent and her supervisors had nothing but glowing reports about her. Still, he was so busy rushing from meeting to meeting, cutting a new deal and approving the latest cutting-edge promotion that he never had time to notice the girl behind the black-rimmed glasses and the nondescript business suits.

While in Italy, he'd witnessed firsthand her passion for her work. She invigorated him to work harder and dig deeper for fresh ideas to top her own, which was nearly impossible as she came up with ideas for the wedding that never would have crossed his mind. To say she was a hard worker was an understatement. She was amazing and it wasn't just her work ethic that fascinated him.

Her smile lit up his world like the golden rays of the morning sun. And when he would lean over her shoulder, he'd get a whiff of her sweet, intoxicating scent. It conjured up the image of a field of wildflowers in his mind and always tempted him to lean in closer for a deeper whiff.

Then there were times like now, when she was concentrating so hard that her green eyes grew darker. She lifted her hand and twirled a long red curl around her finger. He noticed that she did this when she was unsure of something. He wondered what was troubling her now.

He moved closer. "Need some help?"

She glanced up with a wide-eyed stare as though she'd been totally lost in her thoughts. "Um...what?"

This wasn't the first time she'd been so lost in her thoughts that she hadn't heard him. "I said, would you like some help?"

"Sure. I was contemplating the piazza. I'm thinking it should play a prominent part in the wedding processional."

Her words sparked his own imagination. They made a great couple...um, team. He couldn't remember the last time he'd felt this invigorated. "How about having a horse-drawn carriage circle the fountain, giving the villagers a chance to cheer on the future queen?"

"I don't know. The bride will be a bundle of nerves. I don't know if she'll want to spend the time waving at people—"

"Sure she will."

Kayla sent him a doubtful look. "What would you know about weddings?"

"Nothing." His jaw tightened. And he planned to keep it that way. "You're forgetting one important thing."

"And what's that?"

"The villagers are the part that makes the village special."

A smile eased the worry lines on her face. "I'm glad you were paying attention while on our tour. And if the bride is willing, I think the villagers should play a prominent role in the festivities."

"And along the route there could be large royal flags waving in the breeze—"

"No. That's too impersonal." Her eyes sparkled. "What if we hand out small complimentary flags to the onlookers to welcome the newest member of the royal family?"

Angelo paused as he considered the idea. "I like it. It'll be a sea of color."

"I also think the chapel should be included in the pitch." Before he could utter a word, she rushed on. "The place is so beautiful. Sure it needs some work, but it has such a romantic feel to it. Just imagine it filled with roses— No, make that lilies. And the glow of the candles would add to the magic. Can't you just imagine it all?"

"No." He didn't believe in magic or romance. They were just fanciful thoughts. "I can't imagine anyone wanting to get married in such a dump—"

"It's not a dump!"

He ignored her outburst. "Besides, you're forgetting that I talked to the new owner and she wants nothing to do with the wedding."

"And that's it...you're just giving up? She could change her mind."

What was Kayla getting so worked up for? He wasn't making up these problems. "The chapel is crumbling. We are not putting it in the pitch. The royal couple would laugh us out of the room if we presented it—"

"They would not." Her words were rushed and loud. "They'd love its charm."

His muscles tensed. He hated conflict. "We're not using it!"

Her fine brows drew together as she crossed her arms. "You're making a mistake!"

He wasn't used to people challenging his decisions and they certainly didn't raise their voice to him. This argument was ending now. "This is my company—my decision! We're not including the chapel." When she went to speak, he added, "End of story."

She huffed but said nothing more.

For a while, they worked in an uncomfortable silence. He kept waiting for Kayla to rehash their disagreement, but she surprised him and let it go. He didn't know how much time had passed when they started to communicate like normal again.

Angelo rubbed his jaw. "Perhaps our best option is to take all of these photos and do a workup of each setting. We can have sketches made up of how each wedding scenario would work. Nothing sells better than letting the client see it with their own eyes. I'll have the art department start on it right away. They'll be on solid overtime until our meeting with the happy couple."

"You never said— Where is the meeting? At Nico's villa?"

"No. The meeting is in Halencia. It's an island not far from here."

"Oh, how exciting. You must be nervous to be meeting a real prince and his bride."

"Me? What about you?"

"What about me?"

"You're part of this team. You'll be going, too. I hope you have something in your suitcase suitable for a royal meeting. If not, perhaps you can find an outfit or two in the village."

Kayla's mouth gaped open and he couldn't help but chuckle. She looked absolutely stunned. Surely she didn't think that he'd put her to all of this work and then leave her behind. He was never one to take credit for another person's work, and he wasn't about to start now. Kayla deserved this honor.

But he sensed something else was on her mind. He could see the subtle worry lines marring her beautiful complexion when she didn't think he was looking. He had no doubt she was still smarting over his unilateral decision to scrap the chapel proposal. She had to accept that he knew what he was doing.

Just then a cell phone vibrated, rattling against the tabletop. Not sure whose phone it was, Angelo headed for the table in time to witness Kayla grabbing her phone and turning it off without bothering to take the call. She'd been doing it a lot lately.

He cleared his throat. "You know, just because I'm here doesn't mean you can't take a phone call from home now and then."

She shook her head. "It…it was nothing."

"Are you sure about that? I get the distinct feeling that the call was definitely something."

"I told you it's nothing important." Her voice rose with each syllable. "Why are you making such a big deal of it?"

"I just thought it might be important."

Her gaze didn't meet his. Her voice was heated and her words were rushed. "It's nothing for you to worry about. Besides, we have work to do."

He'd never witnessed Kayla losing her composure—ever. What was wrong with her? And why wouldn't she open up to him?

"Kayla, if you need a break—"

"I don't." She ran her fingers through her long red curls before twisting the strands around her fingertip. "Can we get back to work?"

His jaw tightened. These heated exchanges reminded him of his parents, and not in a good way. Kayla had just reinforced his determination to remain single. He wanted absolutely nothing to do with a turbulent relationship.

"Work sounds like a good idea." He turned to his laptop. Before he could even type in his password, Kayla softly called out his name. In fact, her voice was so soft that he was sure he'd imagined it. He glanced over his shoulder to find her standing next to him.

Her gaze was downcast and her fingers were laced together. "I'm sorry for snapping. I didn't mean to grouch at you. I... I—"

Before she could go any further, he uttered, "It's okay. We're both under a lot of pressure, working night and day to get this pitch perfected."

Her eyes widened in surprise. "Thanks for understanding. It won't happen again."

He didn't doubt that she meant it, but he was a realist and knew that blowups happened even in the best of relationships. So where did they go from here?

When he didn't immediately say anything, she added, "The phone call was a friend. I'll deal with it later."

Not about to repeat their earlier argument, he let her comment slide. "Then let's get back to work. We have the menu to work into the layout."

He didn't miss the way she played with her hair—the telltale sign she was nervous. Oh, that call was definitely something important. All of his suspicions were now confirmed. So what could be so important that it had her jumping for the phone, and yet she refused to take the call in front of him? A boyfriend? But she'd already stated categorically that she didn't have one, and he believed her.

So what had her nervous and fidgeting with her hair? What didn't she want him to know? And why was he more concerned about her blasted phone calls and mysterious ways than he was about this presentation that was quickly approaching?

He really needed to get his head in this game or Monte Calanetti would lose the pitch before they even gave their presentation in Halencia. But with Kayla so close by it was difficult at times to remember that she was here to work and not to fulfill his growing fantasies.

Moonbeams danced upon the window sheers as Kayla leaned back in her chair. They'd been working on this pitch night and day, trying to make it beyond amazing. A yawn passed her lips. Not even coffee was helping her at this point.

"You should call it a night." Angelo stared at her over the top of his laptop. "I've got this."

Not about to let him think she wasn't as dedicated to this project as he was, she said, "If you're staying up, so am I."

He sent her an I-don't-believe-you're-so-stubborn look. "If you insist—"

"I do." She crossed her arms. Even that movement took a lot of effort.

He arched a brow, but he didn't argue. "How about we take a break? I'm starved."

"Sounds good to me, but I don't think there's any room service at this hour."

"Who needs room service? There's still half of a pizza in the fridge."

"Oh. I forgot."

In no time, Angelo warmed them each a couple of slices in the microwave in their kitchenette. After handing her a plate, he moved to the couch. "Sorry, I can't provide you anything else."

"This is plenty. It reminds me of my college days. Leftover pizza for breakfast was a common staple in the dorms."

Angelo leaned back, kicked off his loafers and propped his feet up on the coffee table. There was no longer any boss/employee awkwardness between them. Being closed up in a hotel suite, no matter how fancy, left no room for cool distances. In fact, they'd shared some passionate disagreements over the pitch, which only led them to better, outside-the-box ideas. But it was far too late for any passionate conversations—at least the professional ones.

"I'm surprised your parents let you go to college." Angelo's voice roused her from her exhaustion-induced fantasy.

"Why?"

"Because they had your life planned out to be a wife, to be a mom and to take over the family business. Why spend the money and time on an advanced degree if you weren't going to use it?"

The fact that Angelo Amatucci, star of Madison Avenue, was truly interested in her life sent her heart fluttering. "It was hard for them to object when I won an academic scholarship. Plus, they knew I had my heart set on earning a degree. My guess is they thought I'd go, have fun with my friends for a few years and eventually realize my place was with them in Paradise." Her gaze met his. "Didn't your parents expect you to return to Italy after you graduated college?"

He glanced away as he tossed his plate of half-eaten pizza onto the table. "My family is quite different from yours. Their expectations weren't the same."

"I have a hard time believing that, after seeing how much your brother and sister miss you. Maybe you can slow down and fly here more often."

"I don't know." He rubbed the back of his neck. "I'd have to find someone to help with the special accounts—someone the clients would trust."

"Do you have anyone in mind?"

His steady gaze met hers, making her stomach quiver.

"I have an idea or two. And how about you? Is Amatucci & Associates just a stepping-stone for you? Do you have other plans for your future?"

"I'm exactly where I want to be."

His gaze dipped to her lips and then back to her eyes. "That's good to know. I want you here, too." He glanced away. "I mean at the company. You've become really important to me." He cleared his throat. "To the company. You know, it's really late. Let's call it a night and pick up where we left off tomorrow. You know, with the pitch."

Kayla sat there quietly as her normally calm, composed boss tripped and fell over his words. She wanted to tell him to relax because she liked him, too—a lot. The words teetered on the tip of her tongue when he jumped to his feet and moved across the room to shut down his computer.

Disappointment settled in her chest. Shouting her feelings across the room just didn't seem right, nor did she have the guts to do it. And by the rigid line of his shoulders, he wasn't ready to hear the words. She had to accept that the fleeting moment had passed—if it had truly been there at all.

She tried to tell herself that it was for the best. Taking a risk on revealing her feelings to Angelo was putting all of her hopes and dreams on the line, but she wasn't much of a gambler. She liked sure bets. At the moment, the odds were really good that she'd gain a promotion if they pulled off this royal pitch. And that's what she needed to focus on—not on the way Angelo's intense gaze could make her stomach do a series of somersaults.

CHAPTER FIFTEEN

THIS COULDN'T BE HAPPENING.

Two days before Angelo's private jet was scheduled to sweep them off to the Mediterranean island of Halencia, Kayla received yet another phone call from Pam. However with Angelo hovering so close by and forever checking over her shoulder to see the progress she was making with their pitch, she couldn't answer the call. No way. No how.

Kayla sent the call to voice mail before returning to the email she was composing. But a thought had been nagging at her that perhaps after their talk Angelo might have changed his stance on the company doing some charity work. There were so many worthy causes out there that really could use the power of Amatucci & Associates to make a difference. And she wasn't just thinking of her beloved after-school program.

There were countless other organizations that were worthy of a helping hand. Perhaps it was worth a shot. What was the worst that could happen? He would tell her to drop the subject and get back to work? Because surely at this point he wouldn't fire her, would he?

"You've done a really good job with this pitch." And she meant it. Angelo was very talented and creative. If he weren't, he wouldn't be at the top of his game. "It might be a nice idea if you'd considered implementing a charity program at the office. I know a lot of people would be willing to help—"

"No."

Just a one-word answer? Really? Kayla tried to accept it as his final word, but she was having problems swallowing such a quick dismissal. Why did he have to be so close-minded? Was he that worried about his bottom line?

She stared at him. How was it possible that the same man who had escorted her around the village and had shared some of his childhood memories with her could be opposed to helping charities? There had to be something more to his decision.

Maybe if she understood, she could change his mind—make him see that charities needed his special kind of help. Not everyone was gifted in getting the word out in so many different capacities from tweeting to commercials and radio spots. Not to mention that Angelo had an army of contacts in Hollywood willing to help him when needed.

"Why are you so opposed to the idea of helping out charity organizations?"

"You just aren't going to let this go, are you?"

She shook her head. How could she be honest with him about what had her distracted when she knew that it would put her job in jeopardy? Maybe if she understood his reasons, it would bridge the divide. "Explain it to me."

He raked his fingers through his hair and pulled out a chair next to her. "When I came to the States, I was alone. I didn't know anyone. And I'll admit that it wasn't easy and there were a few scary moments."

This certainly wasn't the explanation that she was expecting, but she liked that he was opening up to her, little by little. "I can't even imagine what that must have been like for you. I mean, I moved to New York City and I didn't know a soul here, but I was only a car ride away from my family. You practically moved halfway around the world."

"I didn't have a choice." His lips pressed together into a firm line as though stopping what was about to come out of his mouth.

"What do you mean?"

"Nothing. It's just that when I was in school, I got caught up in the football team and my dream of graduating college started to fade into the rearview mirror. Now granted, that isn't the same as working for a charitable organization, but

I learned a valuable lesson—if I wanted to be the best at whatever I decided to do, I had to commit myself 100 percent. I couldn't let myself get distracted."

Was that happening to her with the fund-raiser? Was she spreading herself too thin? Was she trying to cover too many bases?

She didn't want to accept that she was setting herself up to fail. He had to be wrong. "Couldn't you have done both in moderation?"

"You're not understanding me—I had to succeed—I had to be the best to get anywhere in New York City. Competition is fierce and if I failed, I couldn't go home."

"Sure you could have—"

"You don't know what you're talking about." His intense stare met hers, warning her not to delve further into that subject. "The point is that I know what happens when people become distracted for any reason—no matter how good the cause. They lose their focus. Their ambition dwindles. And that can't happen to Amatucci & Associates. I hate to say it, but it's a cutthroat business. If we lose our edge, the competitors will swoop in and steal away our clients."

Between the lines she read, if she lost her edge—if she didn't give 100 percent—she'd lose her dream. She'd fail and return to Paradise with her tail between her legs. Her stomach twisted into a queasy knot.

She clasped her hands together. Knowing all of this, there was no way she was about to confess to Angelo that she was spending every free moment handling a fund-raiser that seemed to hit one snag after the next. He'd think she wasn't dedicated to her career—that couldn't be further from the truth.

She cleared the lump from the back of her throat. "And that's why you compromise and write generous checks each year to the various organizations?"

He nodded. "I didn't say I wasn't sympathetic. But the office policy stands. End of discussion."

She was more than happy to change subjects, and he'd touched upon one that she was most curious about. "And your parents—"

"Are not part of this discussion."

They might not be, but that didn't mean that she didn't understand a whole lot more about them now. At last, the pieces of his family life started to fall into place. She had wondered why they weren't at the villa to greet Angelo. Nor were they around to help their daughter cope with her unplanned pregnancy. There was definitely discord, and it must run quite deep if Angelo still wasn't ready to broach the subject.

Something told her that he'd closed himself off from that part of his life and focused on his business not so much because he was worried about losing focus, but rather because he found his business safe. It lacked the ability to wound him the way family could do with just a word or a look. That was why he was so cold and professional most of the time. It was his shield.

That was no way to live. There was so much more in life to experience. And she desperately wanted to show him that…and so much more.

But how was she to help him if he wasn't willing to open up?

"Help! I don't know what to do. Everything is ruined."

Kayla's heart lurched at the sound of Pam's panicked voice. She gripped the phone tightly and reminded herself that Pam tended to overreact. Things with the ICL fundraiser had been going pretty well. Ticket sales were still lagging but the radio spots were helping. What could be wrong now?

"Pam, slow down."

"But we don't have time."

"Take a deep breath. It can't be as bad as you're thinking."

"No, it could be worse." Pam sniffled.

Okay. What had happened this time? Did Pam lose another file on her computer? Or misplace the phone number for the manager of the headline band? Pam did blow things out of proportion.

"Pam, pull yourself together and tell me what happened." While Kayla hoped for the best, she steeled herself for a catastrophe.

"They canceled."

Kayla sat up straight, knocking her empty water glass over. Surely she hadn't heard correctly. "Who canceled?"

"The band." Pam started to cry again.

Impossible. "The band quit?"

"Yes! What are you going to do?" She hiccupped.

"But they can't just quit. We have an agreement—a contract."

"That…that's what I said. They said there was a clause or some sort of thing in there that let them back out."

Kayla rubbed her forehead. This couldn't be happening. What was she supposed to do about it all the way in Italy?

"I… I just can't do this anymore. Everyone is yelling at me." The sniffles echoed across the Atlantic. "I can't."

Oh, no. She couldn't have Pam backing out on her, too. "Calm down." Kayla's hands grew clammy as she tightened her hold on the phone. "You can't quit. The kids are counting on us. We can't let them down."

"But what are you going to do? You have to fix this. I can't."

Kayla wanted to yell that she didn't know but that the whining wasn't helping anyone. "I don't know yet. What did the band say was the problem?"

"They got a contract with some big band to be the opening act on a cross-country tour. They leave before the concert."

It'd certainly be hard to compete with a national tour.

Most likely this was the band's big break and Kayla's heart sank, knowing that wild horses couldn't hold them back. And to be honest, she couldn't blame them. This was what they'd been working toward for so long now. But none of that helped her or the fund-raiser.

Kayla struggled to speak calmly. "Just sit tight. I'll think of something."

"You know of another band that can fill in at the last minute?"

She didn't have a clue where to find a replacement. In fact, she'd totally lucked into that first band. A friend of a friend knew the band manager, who liked the idea of free publicity. Where in the world would she locate another band?

"I need time to think." Kayla said, feeling as though the world was crumbling around her.

"But what do I tell people?"

"Tell them that we'll have an announcement soon."

Kayla ended the call. Her mind was spinning. She didn't know how she was going to save the event. The enormity of the situation was only beginning to settle in. With no headline act, there was no point. The tickets would have to be refunded. The Inner City League after-school program would cease to exist.

All of those at-risk kids would be turned away.

No! She refused to fail them. Visions of Gina's smiling face, Patrick's pout when she didn't have time to throw the ball with him and Lilly's anxious look as she'd handed Kayla a new drawing filled her mind. And there were so many more faces—all counting on her to come through for them.

Something splashed her hand. Kayla glanced down to see a tear streak down the back of her hand. She lifted her fingers and touched her cheek, finding it damp. At that moment, she heard the door to the suite open. She took a deep calming breath and dashed the back of her hands across her cheeks.

"I'm back." Angelo's deep voice echoed through the large room. "Did I miss anything?"

Talk about a loaded question. "Um…no." She struggled to sound normal as she kept her back to him. She blinked repeatedly and resisted the urge to fan her overheated face. "Nothing much happened around here."

"You were right about approaching my brother." He paused. "Kayla?"

"Yes."

"Is there a reason I'm talking to the back of your head?"

She shook her head. "I'm just finishing up an email."

"Do you want to hear this?"

"Um…yes. Of course. I can do two things at once."

There was an extended pause as though he was deciding if she were truly interested or not. "Well, I asked Nico for permission to offer up his vineyard as one of the sites for the wedding. The photographer from the village is stopping by tomorrow to take some professional photos."

"I'm glad the meeting went smoothly between you and your brother. What about the new owner of the neighboring vineyard? What did you say her name was?"

"Louisa something or other." He rubbed the back of his neck. "I talked to her about using her vineyard, since it's larger than Nico's place, but she was adamant that she wants absolutely nothing to do with the wedding."

"Really? How odd."

"Not as odd as this."

"What do you mean?" Kayla hated putting on this pretense, but she knew that he would never abide her splitting her work hours between the royal wedding and a charity event. He'd already made that abundantly clear.

"You won't face me and there's something off with your voice." His approaching footsteps had her body tensing. He knelt down next to her. He placed a finger beneath her chin and turned her face to his. "Now tell me, what's got you upset?"

His voice was so soft and comforting. All she wanted to do in that moment was lean into his arms and rest her face in the crook of his neck. She wanted to feel the comfort and security of his strong arms holding her close. She wanted him to tell her that everything would be all right—that they would work together to find a solution.

But none of that could or would happen. Angelo would never understand how she'd knowingly gone behind his back to work on this fund-raiser instead of focusing solely on the royal wedding. She'd never be able to justify her actions to his satisfaction.

"I'm fine." Her gaze didn't meet his.

"You're not fine. Not by a long shot." As though he'd been privy to her thoughts, he reached out and pulled her to him.

She shouldn't do this. It wasn't right. But her body had other thoughts and willingly followed his lead. Her cheek pressed against the firmness of his shoulder and she inhaled the spicy scent of his cologne mingled with his male scent. It was quite intoxicating.

Her eyes drifted closed and for a moment she let go of everything. The silent tears streamed down her cheeks. She took comfort in the way Angelo's hands rubbed her back. It wove a spell over her and relaxed muscles that she hadn't realized were stiff.

"I'm sorry for working you too hard."

She dashed her fingers over her cheeks and pulled back. "You aren't making me work this hard—I want to do it. I want to do everything to make our pitch stand out."

He ran his hands up her arms, sending goose bumps racing down her skin. "But not to the point where you've worn yourself to a frazzle. Look at you. You've gotten yourself all worked up."

She shook her head. No matter how much she wanted

to open up to him, she couldn't. They only had two days until they had to catch a plane to Halencia, and they still didn't have a completed pitch. And what they had didn't sparkle. And it didn't scream "pick me." There was something missing, but she just couldn't put her finger on it. And now, add to it the problem with the fund-raiser and she was at a total loss.

"Kayla, if you won't talk to me, how can I help?"

Her gaze met his, and she saw the worry reflected in his eyes. "You can't."

"Why don't you give me a chance?"

He just wasn't going to let this go. His eyes begged her to open up to him—to trust him. But she couldn't give up her dream of being the sort of person that Angelo Amatucci would want as an ad executive—she'd given up everything to follow this dream. She couldn't return to Paradise and face her parents as a failure.

"The truth is I... I have a headache." And that wasn't a lie. The stress of everything had her temples pounding.

He studied her for a moment as though weighing her words. "Did you take anything for it?"

"I was about to, but I hadn't made it there yet."

Angelo nodded as though he knew what needed to be done. "Go lie down on the couch and rest—"

"But I have stuff that needs done—"

"Later. Right now, you're going to rest. I'll get some medication for you."

His thoughtfulness only made her feel worse—about everything—most especially that she couldn't open up to him. She was certain that he would have some amazing suggestion that would save the fund-raiser, but she just couldn't risk everything she'd worked for. Instead, she'd have to pray for a miracle.

CHAPTER SIXTEEN

HE WAS AS ready as he would ever be.

Angelo kept telling himself that, hoping it would sink in.

As the royal limo ushered them through the streets of Halencia toward the palace, Angelo stared out the window. Mounting tension over this meeting had his body stiff. This sort of reaction was unfamiliar to him. Usually he was calm, cool and collected. He was the expert when it came to marketing. But ever since he'd let his guard down around Kayla, he'd lost that cool aloofness that he counted on when doing business.

She'd gotten past his defenses and had him connecting with his emotions. He just hoped he hadn't lost his edge— the confidence needed to execute a pitch and sell the buyer on his—er—their ideas.

The flight had been a short one as Halencia was just a small island nation not far off the coast of Italy. Angelo had noticed how Kayla kept to herself, working on her computer. He had no idea what she'd been working on because at that point the pitch had been locked in. They had the talking points nailed down and the graphics were in order. He'd made sure to include what he considered the key element—a sample menu from Raffaelle's restaurant. All combined, he hoped this pitch would clinch the royal couple's interest.

Kayla had even insisted on bringing along some of the baked goods for the royal couple to sample. They were fresh baked that morning and delivered to their hotel suite. He'd tried to taste them, but Kayla had smacked his hand away with a warning glance. Everyone in Monte Calanetti was excited and more than willing to do their part to help.

But Kayla had him worried. She'd been so quiet on the flight here. And now as she leaned against the door of the limo with her face to the window, the bubbly woman who toured Monte Calanetti was gone. He didn't recognize this new person.

He cleared his throat. "Are you feeling all right?"

Kayla turned to him, the dark circles under her eyes were pronounced. His gut tightened.

She smiled, but her lips barely lifted at the corners. "Sure. I'm fine."

He wasn't going to argue the point when it was obvious that she was anything but fine. "You did an excellent job preparing the pitch."

She shrugged. "I don't know. I guess it all depends on what the royal couple says."

He shook his head. "It doesn't matter whether they chose Monte Calanetti or not for the wedding, I know for a fact that you went above and beyond for this project." He hated how his praise seemed to barely faze her. She'd worn herself out and he'd been so busy trying to tie up all of the loose ends for this pitch that he'd failed to notice.

On the flight to Halencia, he'd been mulling over how to recognize Kayla's tremendous effort. He decided to share part of it with her now. "And when we get back to New York, you'll be rewarded for your accomplishments not only with the royal pitch but also with the success of the Van Holsen account."

Her eyes widened. "Really? I... I mean thank you."

Before she could say more, her phone buzzed. She swiped her finger over the screen and frowned. Her fingers moved rapidly over the touch screen as her frown deepened.

Even Angelo had his limits. Work could wait. They were almost at the palace and having her upset was not going to be a good way to start their meeting with the royal couple. He reached out and snagged her phone from her.

She glanced up and her mouth gaped open. Then her lips pressed together into a firm line and her gaze narrowed.

She held out her hand. "It's important."

"It can wait."

"No, it can't."

The car slowed as they eased through the gates leading up the drive to the palace. "We're here. Forget the rest of the world and enjoy this adventure. It isn't every day you get a royal invitation to a palace."

Kayla turned to the window as they wound their way up the paved drive lined with statues and greenery. It was very prestigious and yet it wasn't overly pretentious. In fact, he found it quite a fitting reflection of their nobility. He just hoped that they'd find the prince and his bride to have the same unassuming demeanor.

When the palace came into view, Angelo was taken by surprise at the enormity of it. The palace stood three stories high and appeared to be a large square with towers at each corner. The outside was painted a sunny yellow while the numerous windows were outlined in white. Grand, sweeping stairs led the way to a large patio area with two enormous doors in the background that granted access to the palace.

There weren't that many things in life that still took Angelo's breath away, but he had to admit that this palace was an amazing piece of architecture. And with the abundance of greenery and bright flowers, it was definitely like stepping into paradise. He couldn't even imagine what it must be like calling this place home.

The car swung up the drive and stopped right in front of the palace. To one side was a garden with a fountain in the center. It was quite inviting. He could easily imagine taking Kayla for a stroll through it after dinner as the setting sun cast a watermelon hue over the sky. They'd stop to admire a flower and she'd turn to him. The breeze would rush through her hair as her gaze would meet his. Then his attention would move to her lips. No words would be necessary as they'd lean into each other's arms.

"Angelo, this is amazing."

Kayla's voice jerked him from his daydream, which was in fact amazing. "Um...yes. This is quite beautiful."

"Is this your first visit?"

"It is. I've never done business in this part of the world before." Though he had done business in a great many other countries.

As beautiful as the grounds were, Angelo's attention was drawn back to Kayla. He had plans for her. A surprise after their big presentation. At first, he'd been hesitant, but now, seeing how weary she was, he was certain that he'd made the right decision. He just hoped she would relax long enough to enjoy it.

He still had the feeling that she was keeping something from him—something that was eating at her. But what was it? Was she worried that he'd make another move on her?

The thought left him feeling unsettled. Granted, he wasn't that good at reading women. They were forever a mystery to him, but he'd swear that she was into him and his kisses. She'd come alive in his arms. He was certain that he hadn't imagined that. So then, what had her putting an unusually big gap between them in the limo?

He was impressive.

Kayla sat in one of the plush chairs in the palace's state room. Instead of taking a closer view of the ornate ceiling with large crystal chandeliers, the red walls with white trim, the huge paintings of historical figures or the priceless statues on pedestals, her entire attention was focused on Angelo as he stood in the front of the room in his freshly pressed navy suit and maroon tie. Every inch of him looked as if he'd just stepped off the cover of a men's magazine. He was definitely the most handsome man she'd ever laid her eyes on.

And his presentation was truly impressive. If this didn't sell the royal couple on the benefits of holding the royal wedding in Monte Calanetti, then nothing would. Angelo's talk was informative while containing bits of entertainment. Sure, he'd gone over it with her back in Italy, but somehow here in front of the royal prince and his bride, it seemed so much more special—more dynamic.

"Monte Calanetti offers a variety of services from a world-renowned chef to the most delicious bakery." Angelo moved off to the side while Kayla started the slideshow presentation on a large high-definition screen. "You can see here an overview of the village—"

With the slideshow up and running, Kayla's thoughts spiraled away from the presentation she knew verbatim. Instead, she was amazed by the man making the presentation. Though he didn't have the best one-on-one people skills, he was truly amazing when he was selling an idea. His voice was strong, sure and unwavering. His tone was cajoling. And his posture was confident but not cocky. No wonder he was the best in the business.

So then how in the world was he so inept when it came to dealing with people—people like his family? People like her? Why did he have to make it so tough to get close to him?

Why couldn't he let his guard down and take a chance on love like the crown prince and his Cinderella bride? Kayla's gaze moved to the soon-to-be couple, envious that they seemed to have it all—success, stability and most of all love.

But as they sat there surrounded by their staff, Kayla didn't see any telltale signs of love. There were no clasped hands. No loving gazes when they thought no one was looking. No nothing.

Kayla gave herself a mental jerk. She was overthinking things. Of course they were being all businesslike. This was their wedding—a wedding that would have all of the world watching. That had to be their focus right now.

Still, there was something that nagged at her about the couple, but she brushed it off. Whatever it was—bridal nerves or such—it was absolutely none of her business. She had enough of her own problems.

He'd nailed it.

Angelo wore an easy smile. The presentation had gone without a hitch. Everything had fallen into place just as he'd practiced it over and over again with Kayla in their hotel suite. He had a good feeling that Monte Calanetti would be in serious contention for the site of the royal wedding.

After the slideshow presentation was over, Angelo asked, "Are there any questions?"

"Yes." The bride, Christina Rose, sat up straight. "I didn't see anything in your presentation about the chapel. I'm particularly interested in it."

Angelo's gut knotted. He'd been wrong. His gaze sought out Kayla. He was certain that she'd be wearing an I-told-you-so look. But her chair was empty? Where had she gone? The next thing he knew Kayla was standing next to him. What in the world?

"Hi. I'm Kayla." She sent him an I've-got-this smile. "The chapel is my part of the presentation."

He moved away and went to take a seat. What in the world did Kayla have up her sleeve? He thought they'd settled this back in Monte Calanetti—no chapel presentation. His back teeth ground together as he remembered that call had been his.

Angelo leaned back in his chair while Kayla put photos of the chapel up on the screen with a pitch that he'd never heard before, but it sounded like music to his ears. So the little minx had gone behind his back and done exactly what he'd told her not to do.

And he couldn't be happier.

After Kayla finished her short presentation, the bride

spoke up again. "The chapel—you mentioned that it had just switched ownership—the new owner—have they approved the use of it for the wedding?"

Seriously? That had to be the first question. Kayla's gaze momentarily strayed to him. He had no help to offer her, but he was anxious to see how she handled the question.

Kayla laced her fingers together. "At this moment, we have not obtained a release for the use of the chapel." The bride's face creased with frown lines. That was definitely not a good sign. "Knowing the chapel is of particular interest to you, we will make it a priority to secure its use for the wedding."

The young woman's eyes lit up, but she didn't say anything as she glanced over at the crown prince. He didn't speak to Kayla, either, but rather conversed softly with his advisors, who had a list of questions.

Kayla handled the inquiries with calm and grace. Angelo couldn't have done any better. She certainly was full of surprises, and he couldn't be happier having her by his side.

It wasn't until much later that Angelo walked with her toward their rooms. This was their first chance to talk privately since the presentation. As they strolled along the elegant hallways, Kayla waited anxiously to hear Angelo's thoughts on how she'd handled her part of the meeting. She hoped he wasn't too upset about her ignoring his dictate about the chapel.

Angelo stopped and turned to face her. "Stop looking so worried. You did an excellent job today."

"I did?"

He nodded. "I owe you an apology for not listening to you and a thank-you for being so prepared."

"Really? Even though I didn't do what you said?"

He gazed deep into her eyes. "I think you have excellent instincts and the courage to follow them. You've got what it takes to have a very bright future."

In her excitement, she threw her arms around him. He had no idea how much she needed this one perfect moment.

Coming back to earth, she grudgingly let go of him and stepped back. "Thank you for the opportunity."

"You earned it. And you did well by knowing all of the answers to their questions. And you took notes of things that particularly interested them. I couldn't have done any better."

"You really mean that? You're not just saying these things to make me feel better."

He chuckled. "Did anyone ever tell you that you don't take compliments well?"

She shrugged. "I guess I'm still wound up."

"We make a great team."

It was the first time he'd ever referred to them in that manner and she liked it. She really liked it. More than that, she liked him a lot—more than was wise. But that didn't stop her heart from pounding in her chest when he gazed deeply into her eyes.

He was going to kiss her—again. She should turn away. She should pretend she didn't know that he was interested in her. But her body had a will of its own, holding her in place. She knew that nothing good would come of it, but she wanted him to kiss her more than she wanted anything in that moment.

Angelo turned and continued down the hallway. The air that had been caught in her lungs rushed out. What had happened? It took her a second to gather her wits about her, and then she rushed to catch up to him.

They continued on in silence until they stopped outside her bedroom door. He turned to her again. "Thank you for everything. If I had done this alone, I wouldn't have stood a chance of winning their favor. You were my ace in the hole."

His gaze caught and held hers.

"I… I was?"

He nodded and stepped closer. "How could anyone turn you down?"

Her heart pitter-pattered harder and faster. She didn't want this moment to end—not yet. It was her very own fairy tale. "Do you want to come inside?"

He tucked a loose curl behind her ear. Then the back of his fingers grazed down her cheek. "I don't think that would be a good idea. We're expected at dinner with the royal couple. It wouldn't look right if we were late."

The hammering of her heart drowned out her common sense. Because when he was looking at her that way and touching her so sweetly, all she could think about was kissing him—

She lifted up on her tiptoes and pressed her lips to his. He didn't move at first and she wondered if there was some way that she had misread the situation. But then his arms wrapped around her and pulled her hard against him. She'd been here before, but it never failed to excite her. He was thoughtful, sweet and kind. Nothing like her boss at the office. This was a different side of him, and she found him utterly irresistible.

Angelo braced his hands on her hips, moving an arm's length away. "We need to stop now or we are never going to make it to that dinner."

"Who needs dinner?" There was only one thing she was hungry for at that moment and she was staring at him.

"Don't tempt me." He smiled at her. "I don't think that would help our pitch." He pressed a kiss to her forehead and proceeded down the hallway to his room.

In that moment, Kayla felt lighter than she had in days. Suddenly anything seemed possible. Maybe she'd given up on the fund-raiser too soon. She pressed a hand to her lips. Perhaps everything would work out in the end, after all.

She sure hoped so.

CHAPTER SEVENTEEN

"I DON'T UNDERSTAND."

Kayla's gaze narrowed in on Angelo as they stood beneath the crystal chandelier in the marble foyer. He'd been acting mysterious ever since they'd given their pitch to the royal couple the day before. Was it the kiss? It couldn't be. He hadn't been distant at the royal dinner. In fact, he'd been quite attentive—even if the evening hadn't ended with any more kisses.

"Trust me." His dark eyes twinkled with mischief. "You will understand soon enough."

"It'd be easier if you'd just tell me where we're going. If this has something to do with the pitch, you should tell me. I would have brought my laptop. Or at least I could have grabbed my tablet."

"You don't need it." He took her hand and guided her out the door, down the palace steps and into an awaiting limo. "Trust me."

"But how do I know if I'm dressed appropriately. The only formal clothes I have with me I wore yesterday for the pitch and then the dinner with the royal couple. I thought that we'd be leaving today."

"I've delayed our departure."

He had? She didn't recall him mentioning anything to her. Then again, she'd been so caught up in her thoughts lately that she might have missed it.

"Don't worry. I ran it past your boss." He winked at her. "He's fine with it."

"He is, huh?" She wondered what Angelo was up to and why he was in such a good mood. "But why aren't we flying back to Italy? I thought you'd be anxious to wrap things up there before we return to New York."

"It can wait."

She had absolutely no idea where they were headed. The curiosity was eating at her. But the driver knew. She turned to the front to ask him.

"Don't even think of it," Angelo warned as though he knew exactly what she intended. "He's been sworn to secrecy."

Her mouth gaped open. Angelo really did know what she was thinking. Thankfully he didn't know everything that crossed her mind or else he'd know that she'd gone against his express wishes and worked on the fund-raiser during work hours.

And worst of all, her efforts were for naught. She'd reached out to everyone she could think of, but she had yet to come up with another big-name band on such short notice. But ever the optimist, she wasn't canceling the event until the very last minute. There just had to be a way to help the kids.

"Hey, no frowning is allowed."

She hadn't realized that her thoughts had transferred to her face. "Sorry. I was just thinking of all the work I should be doing instead of riding around with you."

"You'll have plenty of time for work later. In fact, when we return to New York I imagine that you'll have more work than you'll ever want."

She sent him a quizzical look. Was he trying to tell her something?

"Quit trying to guess. You aren't going to figure out our destination."

The car zipped along the scenic roadway. Angelo was totally relaxed, enjoying the terrific view of the tranquil sea. But she couldn't relax. Not yet. Not like this. Not with the fate of the fund-raiser hanging over her head.

Kayla desperately wanted to ask Angelo for help, but she just couldn't bring herself to trust him, knowing his adamant stance on such matters. But if she didn't ask Angelo for help, what did that say about their relationship? Did it mean what they'd shared meant nothing?

The thought left a sour taste in her mouth. The Angelo she'd got to know so well here in Italy put his family above his own needs even at the risk of one of his most important accounts. But that was his family? And she was what?

She had absolutely no answer.

Realizing that he was still holding her hand, her heart thumped. She was certainly more than his assistant—but how much more?

He turned to her. Their gazes caught and held. Her heart started to go *tap-tap-tap*. Oh, yes, she was definitely falling for her boss.

But what would happen when this trip was over? What would their relationship be like when they returned to the reality of their Madison Avenue office? Or worse yet, what if he found out that she'd been working on the fund-raiser instead of devoting all of her attention to her work?

"Relax. Everything will be okay." Angelo raised her hand to his lips and pressed a gentle kiss to the back of her hand.

Her stomach shivered with excitement. Throwing caution to the wind, she uttered, "When you do that, relaxing is the last thing on my mind."

"In that case..." He pulled her close and with her hand held securely in his, he rested his arm on his leg. His voice lowered. "You can get as worked up as you like now."

His heated gaze said a hundred things at once. And all of them made her pulse race and her insides melt. He wanted her. Angelo Amatucci, the king of Madison Avenue, was staring at her with desire evident in his eyes.

If she were wise, she would pull away and pretend that none of this had happened. But her heart was pounding and her willpower was fading away. She'd been resisting this for so long that she was tired of fighting it—tired of denying the mounting attraction between them.

Maybe this thing between them wouldn't survive the harsh glare of the office, but that was days away. They were to remain in Italy until the royal couple had all of the inquiries answered and their decision made. In the meantime, what was so wrong with indulging in a most delightful fantasy?

Once again, Angelo seemingly read her mind—realizing that she'd come to a decision. He turned to her and leaned forward. His lips were warm as they pressed to hers. Her eyes drifted closed as her fingers moved to his face, running over his freshly shaved jaw. His spicy aftershave tormented and teased. It should be illegal for anyone to smell so good. A moan bubbled up in the back of her throat.

The car stopped, jostling them back to the here and now. Angelo was the first to pull away. Disappointment coursed through her. Her eyes fluttered open and met his heated gaze.

"Don't look so disappointed. There will be time for more of this later." He smiled and her discontentment faded away. "Remember, I have a surprise for you."

"Did I forget to tell you that I love surprises?"

He laughed. "I was hoping you would."

She glanced out her window, finding nothing but lush greenery, flowers and trees. She struggled to see around Angelo, but with his arm draped loosely around her, she couldn't see much.

"I can't see." She wiggled but his strong arm kept her next to him—not a bad place to be, but she was curious about their location. "Where are we?"

"My, aren't you impatient? You'll soon see."

She couldn't wait. Though she still had problems to resolve, for just this moment she let them shift to the back of her mind. She might never have this kind of experience again, and she didn't want to miss a moment of it. And it had nothing to do with the surprise that Angelo had planned for her.

It had everything to do with the man who could make her heart swoon with those dark, mysterious eyes.

Mud. Seriously.

Angelo frowned as he sat submerged in a mud bath. He felt utterly ridiculous. This was his first trip to a spa, and though he'd set up the appointment for Kayla, he'd thought he might find out what he was missing. After all, Halencia was known for its world-renowned spa. It ought to be renowned for the exorbitant prices and, worse yet, the cajoling he had to do to get an appointment at the last moment. He'd finally relented and name-dropped—the prince's name certainly opened up their schedule quickly. But it had been worth it when Kayla's face lit up.

He glanced sideways at her as she leaned back against the tub's ledge with her eyes closed. Her long red wavy hair was twisted up in a white towel, safe from this muck. She definitely wasn't the prim-and-proper girl that he'd originally thought her to be when he'd hired her as his temporary assistant. No, Kayla definitely had a bit of a naughty, devil-may-care attitude. And that just intrigued him all the more.

"I'm sorry." Angelo didn't know what else to say. "I guess I should have done more research before making the reservations, but we were so pushed for time with the royal pitch that it just slipped my mind."

Kayla lifted her head. "It's really no problem. I'm enjoying myself."

"But how was I to know that they would set us up for a couple's spa day?"

Her eyes lit up. Her smile stretched into a grin and her eyes sparkled with utter amusement.

"Hey, you aren't inwardly laughing at me, are you?"

"Who? Me? No way." She clutched her bottom lip between her teeth as her shoulders shook.

He wasn't used to being the source of entertainment, but she certainly seemed to be enjoying herself. He supposed that made it worth it. Although, when he'd found out what was involved in the deluxe package, he did think that she was going to balk and walk away. But he'd been worried for no reason.

Kayla wasn't shy. In fact, she could be quite bold. The memory of her in hot pink lacy underwear before she'd stepped into the mud had totally fogged up his mind. Although, when he'd had to strip down to his navy boxers, he'd been none too happy. How could he have overlooked the need to bring swimsuits? Talk about taking down each other's defenses and getting down to the basics.

"What are you thinking about?"

He turned to Kayla, finding her studying him. "Nothing important. So, are you enjoying your trip?"

"Definitely. But…"

"But what?"

"I get the feeling that you aren't enjoying it. Why is that? Is it because of your sister's situation?"

He shrugged. "I suppose that has something to do with it."

"What else is bothering you? I'd think after being gone for so long that you'd be happy to be back in Italy."

"And you would be wrong. Returning to Monte Calanetti and interacting with my siblings and villagers is one of the hardest things I've ever had to do."

She arched an eyebrow and looked at him expectantly.

Why had he opened his mouth? He didn't want to get into this subject. It would lead to nothing but painful memories. And he couldn't even fathom what Kayla would think of him after he told her the truth about his past—about how he ended up in New York.

She reached out her hand and gripped his arm. "You know that you can talk to me. Openness and honesty are important to a relationship—even a friendship or whatever this is between us. Besides, I'm a really good listener."

Even though they were submerged in this mineral mud

stuff, her touch still sent a jolt up his arm and awakened his whole body. After telling himself repeatedly that she was off-limits, he wanted her more with each passing day. He turned and his gaze met hers.

She was the most beautiful woman he'd ever laid his eyes on and it wasn't just skin-deep. Her beauty came from the inside out. She was kind, thoughtful and caring. She was everything he would ever want in a woman—if he were interested in getting involved in a serious relationship.

But he wasn't. He jerked his gaze back to the large window that gave an amazing view of the Mediterranean Sea, but it wasn't the landscape that filled his mind—it was Kayla. She consumed far too many of his thoughts.

"Angelo, talk to me." Her voice was soft and encouraging.

For the first time in his life, he actually wanted to open up. And though his instinct was to keep it all bottled up inside, he wondered if that was the right thing to do. Maybe if Kayla, with her near-perfect home life, were to see him clearly she wouldn't look at him with desire in her eyes.

But could he do it? Could he reveal the most horrific episode in his life? More than that, could he relive the pain and shame?

He gazed into Kayla's eyes, finding compassion and understanding there. He swallowed hard and realized that perhaps he had more strength than he gave himself credit for. Though taking down his ingrained defenses to expose the most vulnerable part of himself would be extremely hard, he firmly believed it would be for the best. If it would put an end to this thing between him and Kayla, how could he hold back?

He cleared his throat. "Remember when I told you that I left Italy to go to school in the States?"

She nodded. "It's the bravest thing I've ever heard. I couldn't have done it—"

"But the thing is… I didn't do it because I wanted to."

Her brows drew together. "What are you saying?"

"My father and I didn't get along and that's putting it mildly." Angelo's body tensed as his mind rolled back in time. "My parents have always had a rocky relationship. On and off. Divorcing and remarrying." He shook his head, chasing away the unwelcome memories. "It was awful to listen to them."

He stopped and glanced at Kayla, whose expression was one of compassion. And then she did something he didn't expect. She reached over, grabbed his arm again and slid her hand down into the mud until she reached his hand. She laced her fingers tightly around his and gave him a big squeeze.

He exhaled a deep breath and continued. "My father is not a small man and he can be quite intimidating. When I'd had enough and my mother needed help with his temper, I... I'd step between them. My father did not like that at all."

"You don't have to tell me this."

"Yes, I do." He'd started this and he was going to see it through to the end. "It didn't matter what I did, it was never up to my father's expectations. I don't think there was anything I could have done to please him. And by the time I graduated school, I was done trying. And he was done trying."

"One day he blew up at me for not doing something in the vineyard. His bad mood spilled over to my mother— this was one of their good periods, so she didn't want to ruin things with him. When I tried to intervene between him and her by trying to soothe him, my father...he...he threw me out."

Kayla's fine brows rose. "But surely he calmed down and let you back in."

Angelo shook his head as he stared blindly out the window. Suddenly he was back there on that sunny day. His father had pressed a meaty hand to Angelo's chest, sending him stumbling out the front door. His mother's expression was one of horror, but she didn't say a word—not one thing—to contradict her husband. Instead, she'd agreed with him. Angelo's hurt had come out as anger. He'd balled up his hands and lifted them, taunting his father into a fight. But his father had told him that he wasn't worth the effort. How did a father do that to his son? How did he turn his back on him?

Angelo blinked repeatedly. "He told me that I was worthless and that I would never amount to anything. And then he told me to never darken his doorway again. He closed the door in my face."

"But your mother—"

"Wanted to make her husband happy. Don't you get it? Neither of them…they…didn't want me." His gut tightened into a knot and the air caught in his lungs as he fought back the pain of rejection.

This is where Kayla would turn away—just like his parents. She would know he was damaged goods. Not even his own parents could love him. He couldn't face Kayla. He couldn't see the rejection in her eyes.

"So you just left?" Her voice was soft.

He nodded. "I wasn't about to go back."

"But you were just a kid."

"I was man enough to make it on my own. I didn't have a choice. I couldn't live with him after that. And he didn't want me there. Nico brought my clothes to me, and with the money I'd saved from odd jobs over the years and my inheritance from my grandfather, I left. If it wasn't for Nico and Marianna, I'd have never looked back."

"And this is why you avoid serious relationships?"

He shrugged. "There isn't any point in them. The relationship will fail and somebody will get hurt. It's best this way."

"Best for who? You? You know that not everyone will treat you like your parents."

Suddenly he turned to her. His gaze searched her eyes. What was she saying?

Her warm gaze caressed him. "You can't keep yourself locked away from love because you're afraid. Some things are worth the risk."

She is worth the risk.

He leaned over and dipped his head, seeking out her lips. Every time he thought he'd learned everything there was to know about Kayla, she surprised him again. What did he ever do to deserve her?

He deepened the kiss. She responded to his every move. Her heated touch was melting the wall of ice inside him that he used to keep everyone out. Every second with their lips pressed together and their fingers intertwined was like a soothing balm on his scarred heart.

He needed her. He wanted her. He...he cared oh, so much about her.

A person cleared their throat in the background. "Do you need anything?"

Yeah, for you to leave.

Fighting back a frustrated groan, Angelo pulled back. If it wasn't for their attendant, he might have continued that kiss to its natural conclusion. Yes, he'd have definitely followed her into the shower and finished it.

In what seemed like no time, they were ushered from the mud bath into a shower and then into a private Jacuzzi. Angelo didn't know what to do with his hands. Well, he knew what he wanted to do with them, but with their attendant floating in and out, those plans would have to wait for later. For now, he stretched his arms along the rim of the tub and pulled her close to him. He just needed to feel that physical connection.

"Are you enjoying yourself?" He just had to be sure.

"This is perfect. Thank you."

"Well, not quite perfect. I did overlook the need for swimsuits." The heat of embarrassment crept up his neck.

"And miss seeing you in your boxers?" She waggled her brows at him. "I think it worked out perfectly."

"But you had to ruin your…um, clothes. They're all stained now."

"Oh, well. It was worth the sacrifice."

"Don't worry. I'll make sure to replace your…things." Why did he get so tripped up around her? It wasn't like him. But then again, everything was different when he was around Kayla.

"Will you be picking them out yourself?" Her eyes taunted him.

"Sure. Why not?"

"Do you have much experience with women's lingerie? And exactly how will you know what sizes to get?"

Boy, this water was starting to get hot—really hot. "Fine." His voice came out rough, and he had to stop to clear his dry throat. "I'll give you the money and you can get what you need."

She grinned at him. "I never thought of you as the kind to take the easy way out."

He had the distinct feeling there was no winning this conversation. No matter which way he went, he was doomed. "I'll make you a deal."

"Oh, I like the sound of this. Tell me more."

"We'll go together. I'll pick them out, but you have to promise not to wear them for anyone else."

Her eyes widened and then narrowed in on him. "Why, Mr. Amatucci, are you hitting on me?"

"I must be losing my touch if it took you this long to figure it out." He didn't even wait for her response before his head dipped and he caught her lips with his own.

Their relationship was unlike anything he had known previously—he never tired of Kayla. In fact, he missed her when she wasn't next to him. And her kisses, they were sweet and addicting.

What was wrong with him? He never acted like this.

And he never took part in flirting. He never had to. Normally women gravitated to him and things were casual at best. But with Kayla it was different—he was different. He barely recognized himself. It was as if he'd let down his shield of Mr. Angelo Amatucci, Madison Avenue CEO, and could at last be himself.

However, Kayla had taught him that a relationship didn't have to be turbulent like his parent's relationship. She'd opened his eyes to other possibilities. She'd shown him through her patience and understanding that, with openness and honesty, things didn't have to be kept bottled up inside until they exploded.

She hadn't been afraid to voice her disagreement over ideas for the wedding pitch. Nor had she been shy about vocalizing her objection to his no-charity-projects rule at the office. And though he hadn't agreed with her on some of the things, he'd been able to communicate it without losing his temper. Was it possible that he wasn't like his parents? Or was Kayla the key to this calm, trusting relationship?

He wasn't sure what it was, but the one thing he was certain about was that he wanted to explore this more—this thing that was growing between them.

When their attendant entered the room, they pulled apart. Disappointment settled in his chest. But the thought of picking up where they'd left off filled him with renewed vigor. This wasn't the end—it was just the beginning.

"I just have one question." Kayla gave him a puzzled look. "What exactly are we supposed to wear when we leave here? Please don't tell me that we're going commando."

He burst out laughing at the horrified look on her face.

"Hey, this isn't funny."

"Relax. I have another surprise waiting for you."

The worry lines on her face eased. "You do? Aren't you a man of mystery today?"

"I try."

"So tell me what it is."

He shook his head. "Just relax and let the water do its magic. You'll learn about your next surprise soon enough."

CHAPTER EIGHTEEN

CINDERELLA.

Yep, that's exactly how Kayla felt as she stepped out of the limo. Her nails were freshly manicured, her face was done up by a makeup artist and her hair was swept up with crystal-studded bobby pins. And that was just the beginning.

Angelo had surprised her with a gorgeous navy blue chiffon dress. Wide satin straps looped over her shoulders while a pleated bodice hugged her midsection. The tea-length skirt was drawn up slightly in the front while the back of the skirt flirted with her ankles. The thought that Angelo had picked it out for her and that it fit perfectly amazed her.

And there was lingerie—she wasn't even going to ask how he got all of her sizes right. Heat tinged her cheeks. Some things were best left unknown. Her silver sandals, though a bit tight, looked spectacular. And he'd even thought to present her with a sparkly necklace and earrings. The man was truly Prince Charming in disguise.

She looped her hand through the crook of his arm as he escorted her into a very posh restaurant. Tall columns, a marble floor and white table linens greeted them. Palms grew in large urns. The soft lighting and instrumental music made the ambience quite romantic. When the maître d' led them to the back of the restaurant and out a door, she wondered where they were going.

She soon found them standing on the terrace overlooking the Mediterranean Sea. A sweet floral scent filled the air. Kayla glanced up to find a wisteria vine woven through an overhead trellis. The beautiful bunches of delicate purple flowers were in full bloom. Lanterns hung from chains and gave off a soft glow. The whole setup was just perfect for a first date—this was a date, wasn't it?

Her gaze strayed to Angelo. What exactly had been his intention in giving her this magical day? Suddenly she decided she didn't want to analyze it—she just wanted to enjoy it.

The maître d' stopped next to a table by the railing. The view was spectacular, but even that word didn't cover the magnificence of the sight before her. The sea gently rolled inland, lapping against the rocks below the balcony. The glow of the sinking sun danced and played with the water, sweeping away her breath. She didn't know such a beautiful place existed on earth.

"If this is a dream, I don't want to wake up."

Angelo smiled at her. "Trust me. I'm having the same dream and I have no intention of waking up anytime soon."

"You have made this a day I'll never forget."

"Nor will I."

She continued to stare across the candlelit table at Angelo, who was decked out in a black tux that spanned his broad shoulders—the place where'd she'd been resting her head not so long ago. Even his dark hair was styled to perfection. Her fingers itched to mess up the thick strands while losing herself in another of his kisses. But that would have to wait until later. It would be the sweetest dessert ever.

The maître d' presented the menus and explained the wine list to Angelo before walking away. Everything sounded delightful.

Angelo peered over the menu at her. "I hope you brought your appetite."

She nodded, eating him up with her eyes. This was going to be a very long dinner.

However much Kayla wanted to throw caution to the wind, there was still a small hesitant voice in the back of her mind. And try as she might, it was impossible to ignore. She'd worked so hard to get to where she was at Amatucci & Associates—did she really want to jeopardize her dreams? And worse yet, if she did continue to thrive there, would she always wonder if her flourishing was due to the fact that she'd had a fling with her boss?

"Did I tell you how beautiful you look?" The flickering candlelight reflected in his dark eyes as he stared across the table at her.

"You don't look so bad yourself."

"You mean this old thing?" He tugged on his lapel. "I just grabbed it out of the back of my closet."

His teasing made her laugh. Maybe she'd worry about all of the ramifications tomorrow. "Is it possible that we never have to go back to New York? Couldn't we just live here in this little piece of heaven and never let the moment end?"

"Mmm… I wish. I've never enjoyed myself this much. But we can make the most of our time here." His eyes hinted at unspoken pleasures that were yet to come. "You know if we weren't in public and there wasn't a table separating us, I'd finish that kiss we started back at the spa."

Her stomach shivered with the anticipation. "Then I guess I have something more to look forward to."

"We both do."

Like Cinderella swept away in her carriage…

The limo moved swiftly over the darkened roadway back to the palace. All Kayla could remember of the dinner was staring across the table at her date. Angelo had presented one surprise after the other, and somewhere along the way, she'd lost her heart to him.

She didn't know when her love for him had started. It was a while back. Maybe it was when she first witnessed how much Angelo cared about his family. Or maybe it was when he'd given her a tour of his village and told her about pieces of his past—finally letting down that wall he kept between them. Then somewhere, somehow, Angelo Amatucci had sneaked into her heart.

Kayla loved him wholly and completely.

The revelation shook her to her core. Part of her wanted to run from him—from these feelings. They had the power to destroy everything she'd built for herself back in New York. But how did she turn off the powerful emotions that Angelo evoked in her? And did she want to?

Just a look and he had her heart racing. Her body willingly became submissive to his touch. And she reveled in the way he'd looked at her back at the spa. He had no idea that her insides had been nothing more than quivering jelly when she stripped down to her undies. But when his eyes had lit up with definite approval and then desire, her nervousness was quickly forgotten.

In his eyes, she saw her present and her future. She saw a baby with Angelo's dark eyes and her smile. Startlingly enough, the thought didn't scare her off. In fact, she liked it. Maybe it was never the idea of a family that frightened her, but rather she'd had her sights set on the wrong man.

"Hey, what has you so quiet?" Angelo reached out and pulled her to his side.

"Nothing." *Everything.*

"I hope you had a good day."

"It was the best." She turned her head and reached up, placing a kiss on the heated skin of his neck. There was a distinct uneven breath on his part.

His fingers lifted from her shoulder and fanned across her cheek. "No, you're the best."

They both turned at once and their lips met. There was no timidity. No hesitation. Instead, there was a raw hunger—a fiery passion. And it stemmed from both of them. Their movements were rushed and needy. Their breath mingled as their arms wrapped around each other. Reality reeled away as though it was lost out there in the sea.

Right now, the only thing Kayla needed or wanted was

Angelo. If they were to have only this one moment together, she wanted it to be everything. She wanted memories that would keep her warm on those long lonely winter nights back in New York.

Angelo moved his mouth from hers. His hands held her face as his forehead rested against hers. His breathing was ragged. "I don't want to leave you tonight."

She knew her response without any debate. "I don't want you to go."

For once, she was going to risk it all to have this moment with the man she loved—even if he didn't love her back.

The limo pulled to a stop at the foot of the palace's sweeping white stairs that were lit with lanterns trailing up each side. Angelo didn't follow protocol. He opened the door before the driver could make it around the car. Angelo turned back and held out his hand to help her to her feet.

With both of them smiling like starstruck lovers, they rushed up the steps and inside the palace. Brushing off offers of assistance from the staff, hand in hand they swiftly moved to the second floor. They stopped outside her bedroom door and Angelo pulled her close. His mouth pressed to hers. He didn't have to say a word; all of his pent-up desire was expressed in that kiss.

When he pulled back, he gazed into her eyes. "Are you sure about this?"

She nodded and opened the door. She'd never been so sure about anything in her life. She led the way into the room. This would be a night neither of them would ever forget.

CHAPTER NINETEEN

WHAT IN THE world had he let happen?

Angelo raked his fingers through his hair, not caring if he messed it up or not. He'd already messed things up bigtime with Kayla. In the bright light of the morning sun, he stood on the balcony of his suite in the royal palace. He'd woken up in the middle of the night after a nightmare—a nightmare he'd thought he'd done away with long ago.

After leaving Italy, he'd had nightmares about his father turning him out—of his father throwing his clothes out in the drive and telling him that he was not welcome there ever again. In his dream, and in real life, his mother had cried, but she didn't dare go against her husband's wishes even if it meant sacrificing one of her own children.

But last night his nightmare had been different. It was Kayla who'd turned him away. She'd told him that she never wanted to see him again. He'd begged and pleaded, but she'd hear none of it. Her face had been devoid of emotion as she slammed the door in his face. With nowhere to go, he'd walked the dark streets of New York. When a mugger attacked him, Angelo had sat up straight in bed. His heart had been racing and he'd broken out in a cold sweat.

Angelo gave his head a firm shake, trying to erase the haunting images. Of course, he knew that he wasn't going to end up homeless, but he also knew that the dream was a warning of looming trouble. If his own parents could turn him out, why couldn't Kayla? How could he risk getting close to her, knowing how unreliable relationships could be? After all, his own parents were quite familiar with the divorce courts as they broke up and got back together on a regular basis. Angelo's chest tightened.

The only thing he could do was end things with Kayla—quickly and swiftly. There was no way to put the genie back in the bottle, but that didn't mean that they had to continue down this road—no matter how tempted he was to do just that. He couldn't put his tattered heart on the line only to have it shunned again. The price was just too high.

A knock at his door alerted him to the fact that their car was waiting to take them to the airstrip. It was time to return to Italy. More than that, it was time to face Kayla. He didn't know what to say to her—how to explain that everything they'd shared was a big mistake.

By the time he made it downstairs, Kayla was already in the car. Not even the clear blue sky and the sight of the beautiful gardens could lighten his mood. He was in the wrong here. Things had spiraled totally out of control yesterday, and it had been all his doing.

"Good morning." He settled in the seat next to her, making sure to leave plenty of room between them.

Her face was turned away. "Morning."

That was it. The only conversation they had as his luggage was loaded in the rear. Time seemed suspended as he waited for the car to roll down the driveway. This was going to be a very long trip back to Italy. And a very quiet one.

It wasn't until they were on his private jet and airborne that he realized ignoring the situation wasn't going to make it go away. They still had to work together.

"We need to talk."

Kayla turned to him. "Funny you should pick now to talk."

"What's that supposed to mean?"

"It means that you didn't have time to talk last night. You had one thing on your mind and now that you've gotten it, you want to give me the big kiss-off."

"Hey, that's not fair. I didn't set out to hurt you. You were as willing for last night as I was."

"You didn't even have the decency to face me this morning. You slunk away in the middle of the night."

"That's not true." Not exactly. "I couldn't sleep and I didn't want to wake you up." The truth was that he'd never gone back to sleep after that nightmare. He just couldn't shake the feeling of inevitable doom.

She eyed him up. "So then I jumped to the wrong conclusion? You weren't trying to get away from me?"

The hurt look in her eyes tore at him. This was all about him, not her. She was wonderful—amazing—perfect. He just wasn't the guy for her. But how did he make that clear to her?

He got up from his seat and moved across the aisle and sat beside her, still not sure what to say. Somehow, someway he had to say the right words to make her realize that she was amazing, but they just weren't going to have more than they'd shared yesterday.

He resisted the urge to pull her into his arms and kiss away the unhappiness written all over her face. Instead, he took her hand in his. "Kayla, you are the most wonderful woman I have ever known. And yesterday was very special. I will never ever forget it—"

"But you don't want to see me again." She jerked her hand away.

"No—I mean yes." He blew out a breath. "I'm not the man to settle down into a serious relationship."

"Is that what you tell all of your women?"

"No. It's not." She eyed him with obvious disbelief reflected in her eyes. "I'm telling you the truth. I never let anyone get this close to me."

She crossed her arms. "Then why me? Why did I have to be the one that you let get close only to reject me after one night?"

Frustration balled up in his gut—not at her, at himself for being unable to explain this properly. He'd been a scared young man with no one to turn to for help. Thank goodness for his inheritance or else he never would have been able to make it in the States. But did either of his parents care? No. Did they ever write or phone? No. Not until he'd made it on his own did he hear from his mother—she was marrying his father again and she wanted him to be there. Angelo didn't bother to respond. The only family he acknowledged these days was his brother and sister.

He didn't need a romantic relationship. Love was overrated. His business gave him happiness and a sense of accomplishment—that was all he'd ever need.

And somewhere along the way, he'd stumbled upon his explanation to Kayla. "You have to understand that for years now the only thing I've had to count on in my life was my career, and then it was my business. I've put everything I am into it—"

"But what does that have to do with me—with us?"

He reached out as though to squeeze her arm, but when her eyes widened, he realized that he was making yet another mistake and pulled back. "One of the reasons that Amatucci & Associates was able to grow so rapidly into a top advertising firm is that I gave it 110 percent of my attention—to the point of spending many nights on the couch in my office."

Her eyes grew shiny and she blinked repeatedly. "So what you're saying is that your company is now and will always be more important to you than me."

Is that what he was saying? It sure sounded much harsher when she said it. His gut twisted in a painful knot, knowing that he couldn't be the man worthy of her heart.

"You have to understand. I'm losing my edge. I fumbled this wedding pitch. If it wasn't for you, it would have been a disaster. The thing is I don't fumble accounts. I always maintain my cool. I keep my distance so that I am able to view projects objectively. But since we've been in Italy—since that first kiss—I haven't been able to maintain a professional distance. I've been all over the place, and that can't happen—I can't lose focus. It's what keeps me ahead of my competitors."

He did his best work when he relied on his head and not his heart. It was all of the talk about romance and weddings that had him thinking there was something between him and Kayla. That was all. Exhaustion and too much talk of love.

"I really need to work now." Kayla's voice was icy cold and dismissive.

"Do me a favor." He wanted to say something to lighten her mood.

"Depends."

"Remind me to stay far, far away from any other accounts where there's a wedding involved."

She didn't smile. She didn't react at all. Her head turned back to her computer.

He felt compelled to try again to smooth things over. Was that even possible at this point? "Is there anything I can help you with?"

Her narrowed gaze met his straight on. "You've helped me quite enough. I can handle this on my own. I'm sure you have something requiring your objective view and professional distance."

He moved back to his seat on the other side of the aisle. The fact that she was throwing his own words back in his face hurt. But he deserved it and so much more. He'd lost his head while in Halencia and now Kayla was paying the price.

For the rest of the flight, Kayla didn't say a word, and though he longed for her understanding—he had to accept that it was too much for her to take in. There was a part of him that wasn't buying it, either. It was the same part of him that couldn't imagine what his life was going to be like without her in it.

He leaned back in his seat, hearing the wheels of the plane screech as they made contact with the tarmac. Instead of returning to Italy, he longed to be in New York—a return to a structured, disciplined work atmosphere.

Back at the office there'd be no cucumber waters with sprigs of mint and the most adorable woman dressed in nothing more than a white fluffy robe that hid a lacy hot pink set of lingerie. His mouth grew dry as he recalled how Kayla had stared at him over the rim of her glass with those alluring green eyes.

He drew his thoughts to a sharp halt. He reminded himself that his regular PA should be returning from her maternity leave soon—real soon. If he could just keep it together a little longer, his life would return to normal. But why didn't that sound so appealing any longer?

It doesn't matter.

Kayla kept repeating that mantra to herself, wishing her heart would believe it. Three days had passed since she'd woken up alone after a night of lovemaking. How could Angelo just slip away into the night without a word? Did he know how much it would hurt her? Did he even give her feelings any consideration?

It doesn't matter.

Today was the day they learned whether their royal wedding pitch had been accepted or not. Kayla replayed the presentation in her head. She couldn't help wondering—if she hadn't been so distracted by the problems with the fundraiser and with her growing feelings for Angelo could she have done more? She worried her bottom lip. For months and months, she'd done everything to be the best employee, and now that it counted, she'd lost her focus. She'd let herself fall for her boss's mesmerizing eyes, devilish good looks and charms.

It doesn't matter.

Dismissing their time together was his choice. Why should she let it bother her? She didn't need him. She squeezed her eyes shut, blocking out the memories of being held in his arms—of the tender touch of his lips. How could such a special night go so terribly wrong? Had she totally misread what Angelo had been telling her?

None of it matters!

She had important work to do. Angelo had just departed for his brother's villa to speak to him about their sister. Kayla had declined his stilted offer to take her with him. She may have made a mess of things with Angelo, but there was still time to pull together the after-school program fund-raiser.

Kayla focused on the email she was composing to the manager of another New York City band. She could only hope they had a cancellation because the most popular bands were booked well into the future. With her name typed at the bottom, she reread it, making sure it contained plenty of appeals to the man's generous side. After all, who could possibly turn down a group of needy kids? She sure couldn't. Once she was certain there weren't any typos, she pressed Send, hoping and praying that this appeal to the Spiraling Kaleidoscopes would turn things around.

Her thoughts immediately turned to her faltering career at Amatucci & Associates. She grabbed frantically for some glimmer of hope that there was a way to get back to their prior boss-employee relationship. But every time Angelo looked at her, her heart ached and her mind went back in time to those precious moments they'd spent together, wondering if any of it was real.

Ending things now was for the best. It was all of this talk about a wedding that had filled her head with these ridiculous romantic notions. And after working so closely with Angelo these past few weeks, it was only natural that she would project them onto him. The truth was that she wasn't ready to fall in love with him—or anyone. She didn't want to settle down yet. She still had her dreams to accomplish and her career to achieve.

A message flashed on the computer screen. She had a

new email. Her body tensed and she said a silent prayer that it would be good news.

She positioned the cursor on the email and clicked, opening the message on to the screen:

To: Kayla Hill
From: Howard Simpson
RE: Spiraling Kaleidoscope Booking
Thanks so much for thinking of us for your fund-raiser. I am sorry but we are already booked solid for that weekend, in fact, we're booked for the month. Next time consider booking well in advance.

The backs of Kayla's eyes stung. She continued to stare at the email, wishing the letters would rearrange themselves into an acceptance letter, but they refused to budge. This was it. She was out of ideas and out of time. No other band at this late date was going to be available.

Another email popped into her inbox.

To: Ms. Kayla Hill
From: Ms. Stephanie Dyer, Public Relations, Paper Magic Inc.
RE: ICL after-school program fund-raiser
It has recently come to our attention that the fund-raiser no longer has a headline performer. And it is therefore with great regret that we will have to pull our sponsorship...

Her vision blurred. She'd made a mess of everything. And she had no idea how she was ever going to face the children of the after-school program and tell them that she'd let them down—that the doors of the center were going to close.

Just then the door of the suite swung open. It must be the maid. Kayla swiped a hand across her cheeks and sniffled.

She was a mess. Hopefully the cleaning lady wouldn't notice. And if she did, hopefully she wouldn't say anything.

"I'll just move out of your way." Kayla closed her laptop, preparing to move down to the pool area to work.

"Why would you have to get out of my way?"

That wasn't the maid's voice. It was Angelo's. He was back. But why?

When she didn't say a word, he moved to her side. "Kayla, what's the matter?"

She didn't face him. "I… I thought you were the maid."

"Obviously, I'm not. I forgot my phone so I came back. I didn't want to miss a call from the royal family about the pitch."

"Oh, okay." She kept her head down and fidgeted with the pens on the table.

"Kayla, look at me."

She shook her head.

"Kayla." He knelt down next to her.

Oh, what did it matter? She lifted her face to him. "What do you need?"

"I need you to explain to me what's wrong." The concern was evident in the gentleness of his voice. "I thought we had everything worked out between us."

"Is that what you call it?" He really wanted to know? Then fine. She'd tell him. "I call it ignoring the big pink elephant in the middle of the room."

But that wasn't the only reason she'd been crying. It seemed in the past few days that everything she cared about was disintegrating.

"Kayla, talk to me."

His phone chimed. Saved by the bell so to speak. He checked the caller ID and then held up a finger for her to wait. He straightened and moved to the window, where he took the call.

This was her chance to escape his inevitable interrogation. She didn't know where she would go. Suddenly gelato sounded divine. So what if she was wallowing in her own misery? She deserved some sugary comfort—until she figured out what to do next.

She moved to her room to splash some water on her face, repair her makeup and grab her purse. When she was ready to go, there was a knock at her door. She knew it was Angelo. She sighed. Why couldn't he just leave well enough alone?

"Kayla, we need to talk."

CHAPTER TWENTY

"No, we don't." Kayla moved to the door and swung it open. "Not unless it's about work. Other than that we have nothing to say."

Frown lines bracketed Angelo's face. "Did I hurt you that much?"

She glared at him. He really didn't expect an answer, did he? "Please move. I'm on my way out."

He moved aside and she passed by. She'd reached the exterior doorknob when he said, "Kayla, that was the prince's representative on the phone."

That stopped her in her tracks. Her heart pounded in her chest. *Please don't let the wedding fall through, too.* She turned and scanned Angelo's face. There were no hints of what had transpired on the phone.

"And…"

"The royal couple is steadfast in their decision that the chapel must be a part of the wedding. The bride was totally taken with the place. From what I understand that's the reason Monte Calanetti was placed on the short list."

"Did you try again to talk Louisa into letting them use it?"

His face creased with worry lines. "I did. And no matter what I said, she wanted no part of the wedding."

Kayla worried her bottom lip. This wasn't good. Not good at all. "This is all my fault. I shouldn't have let the royal couple believe we could deliver something that we obviously can't."

"It's not your fault. I thought that Louisa would change her mind. What I don't understand is why she's so adamant to avoid the royal wedding. Aren't all women romantics at heart?"

"Obviously not. And it's my fault. Everything is falling apart because of me."

Kayla's chin lowered. How could this be happening? Instead of helping everyone, she was about to let them all down. Most of all, she was about to let down the man she loved—correction, the man she worked for.

Angelo stepped up to her and grabbed her by the shoulders. "I've had enough of the riddles. There's more going on here than the royal wedding. I want to know what it is. Let me help you."

Her heart wanted to trust him. It wanted to spill out the problems so that they could work together to solve them. Perhaps it was time she let go of her dream of being an ad executive at Amatucci & Associates.

The price for her career advancement was far too steep. In her haste to escape her home and make a name for herself, she feared that she'd lost a part of herself. Now she realized that deep down where it counted, she still had the same principles that she'd been raised with. Her caring hometown and loving family had shown her what was truly important in life.

And the fact was she could never be happy as an ad executive, knowing she'd stepped over other people's hopes and dreams to get there. It was time to put her faith in Angelo's kindness and generosity.

She needed his help.

Why wouldn't she let him in?

Why did she insist on refusing his help?

Then Angelo remembered how their night of lovemaking had ended. His jaw tightened as he recalled how badly he'd handled that whole situation. No wonder she didn't trust him. If the roles were reversed, he'd feel the same way. But he couldn't give up. He couldn't just walk away and leave her upset.

"I know you don't have any reason to trust me, but if

you'll give me a chance, I'd like to help." His tone was gentle and coaxing. "I did my best for Nico and Marianna when they asked me—"

"But they are family. And…and I'm, well, just an employee."

His thumb moved below her chin and tilted her face upward until their gazes met. "I think you know that you're much more than that."

It was in that moment the air became trapped in his lungs. In her worried gaze he saw something else—something he hadn't expected to find. And it shook him to his core.

He saw his future.

It was in that moment that he realized just how much she meant to him.

He, the man who was intent on remaining a bachelor, had fallen head over heels, madly, passionately in love with his assistant. She was everything he'd been trying to avoid. Excitable, emotional and compassionate. The exact opposite of the cool, collected businessman image he'd created for himself.

The how and the when of these emotions totally eluded him. The startling revelation left him totally off-kilter and not sure what to say or do next. All that kept rolling through his mind was…

He, Angelo Amatucci, loved Kayla Hill.

"Angelo, what is it?"

"Um…nothing. And don't try changing the subject. We were talking about you and what has you so upset."

She breathed out an unsteady breath. "It's the emails."

"What emails? From the office?"

She shook her head. "Emails from the band's manager and the sponsors. Everyone's pulling out and…and it's in shambles—"

"Whoa. Slow down. I think we better take a seat and you need to start at the beginning."

Once seated on the couch, everything came bubbling to the surface. She told him about how she was involved with the after-school program. It came out about how the program was about to lose their lease unless they could come up with money to cover a hefty increase in the lease. And then she told him that she was heading up a fund-raiser—a big fund-raiser.

In fact, he'd heard about the fund-raiser. It was all over the radio and the papers. At the time, he'd been surprised his company hadn't been approached for a donation, but now he knew why.

"And this fund-raiser, you've been organizing it while you were here in Italy?"

She nodded. "I didn't have a choice."

So this is what she'd been hiding from him. "And you didn't think to mention it?"

"I thought about it." His mouth opened to respond but she cut him off. "And don't you dare blame this on me. I tried." Her voice rose and her face filled with color. "Every time I mentioned helping a charitable organization, you didn't want any part of it. Me not telling you before now is as much your fault as mine. I couldn't risk my job."

His voice rose. "You thought I'd fire you?"

She shouted back. "Wouldn't you have? Correction, aren't you going to now that you know?"

What he wanted to do was leave. Kayla was loud, emotional and making him extremely uncomfortable. She had him raising his voice—something he avoided at all costs. In that moment, he had flashbacks of his parents' endless arguments. He refused to end up like them.

He started for the door. The walls started to close in on him.

"Where are you going?"

"Out." His head pounded.

"And my job?"

"I don't know." He honestly didn't. He was torn between

his newfound feelings for her and the fear that they'd end up miserable like his parents. The pain in his temples intensified.

He stormed out the door, covering as much ground as he could cover with no destination in mind. He just had to get away from the arguing.

Over the years he'd worked so hard to control as much of his life as possible—keeping it the exact opposite of his emotional, turbulent parents. And then in one afternoon, he found himself back exactly where he'd started—in the middle of a heated relationship. That was unacceptable. His home and his office were kept orderly and on an even keel. Everything was how he wanted it—so then why couldn't he control his own traitorous heart?

CHAPTER TWENTY-ONE

HAD SHE BEEN FIRED?

Impossible.

But she was resigning from Amatucci & Associates effective as soon as she completed this one final task. Kayla sat across from Louisa Harrison on her patio. The Tuscany sun beamed bright overhead, but Louisa had the white table shaded by a large yellow umbrella. The woman was quiet, reserved and poised. Not exactly the easiest person to get to know.

"Thank you so much for taking the time to see me." Kayla fidgeted with the cup of coffee that Louisa had served just moments ago.

"I'm new here so I don't get much company."

Kayla gazed up at the huge palazzo. "Do you live here alone?"

Louisa nodded.

"You must get lonely in this big place all by yourself." Kayla pressed her lips together, realizing she'd once again said too much. "Sorry. I shouldn't have said that. Sometimes I don't think before I speak."

"It's okay. Most people probably would get lonely." Louisa played with the spoon resting on the saucer. "I moved here to get away from the crowd in Boston."

So Louisa wanted to be alone—perhaps that was the reason for her refusing to host a royal wedding that would bring a huge crowd of onlookers, not to mention the press. So was Louisa an introvert? Or was there another reason she preferred a quiet atmosphere?

First, Kayla had to build some friendly bridges. Hopefully she'd do a better job of that going forward. She genuinely liked Louisa. And she felt sorry for the woman, being so secluded from life.

And then a thought struck Kayla—if she wasn't careful and didn't stop pushing people away, she might end up alone just like Louisa. First, she'd shoved away her ex because she just didn't share his vision of the future. And now, there was Angelo, who had given her one amazing opportunity after the next. And how did she repay him but by having an utter meltdown.

She hadn't spoken to him since he'd stormed out of their suite that morning. He'd never returned. And she'd been so busy losing her cool that she never did get to ask him for help with the fund-raiser.

At the moment, though, she had to focus on Louisa. "You know, we have something in common. I'm new here, too. Except I'm not staying. I'm only here on a business trip with my boss, Angelo Amatucci."

Louisa's cup rattled as she placed it on the saucer. "I met Mr. Amatucci. I suppose he sent you here to convince me to change my mind about the royal wedding?"

Kayla could hear the obvious resistance in Louisa's voice. She'd have to tread lightly if she were to learn anything. "Actually, he didn't send me. He doesn't even know I'm here."

Louisa's eyes widened. "Then why have you come?"

"I need to be honest with you. I am here about the use of the chapel."

Louisa's mouth pressed together in a firm line and she shook her head. "I haven't changed my mind. I told Mr. Amatucci numerous times that I wouldn't agree to it."

"But I was wondering if there was something we could do to make the idea acceptable to you. The fact of the matter is this event could really help the village's economy. And the royal couple is adamant about using the chapel. If it's not available, they'll move on to the next village on their list."

Surprise reflected in the woman's eyes. "It's really that important?"

Kayla nodded. "I haven't lied to you so far. I need you to believe me now."

Louisa's light blue gaze met hers. "I do believe you. As much as I'd like to help, I just can't do it."

Kayla leaned forward. "If you tell me the problem, maybe I can find a way around it."

"I… I just can't have all of those people and reporters poking around here."

Something told Kayla that Louisa had spent more time in front of the paparazzi's cameras than she preferred. Her sympathy went out to the woman, but there had to be a compromise. "What if I make it my personal mission to ensure that you aren't photographed or even mentioned in the press coverage?"

Louisa's eyes opened wide. "You can do that?"

"Remember, we are dealing with royalty here. They have far-reaching hands. I'll let them know about your stipulation, and I'm sure they'll be able to handle the press."

There was a moment of silence. "If you're sure. I suppose it'd be all right."

Kayla resisted the urge to reach out and hug the woman, not wanting to scare her off. Instead, she leaned forward and squeezed Louisa's arm.

"Thank you." Kayla sent her a smile. "Now, if you don't mind, I'd love to hear more about your plans for this place. It's absolutely beautiful here."

Kayla sat back and sipped her coffee. She was happy that she could provide Angelo with this parting gift. With her resignation already typed up on her laptop, it was time for her to print it out.

That evening, Angelo had plans to dine with his brother and sister. While he was off having some family time, she would catch a plane home. Her moment beneath the Tuscany sun was over, and it was time to face the harsh reality of being jobless and heartbroken.

CHAPTER TWENTY-TWO

THIS HAS TO WORK.

Angelo sat in the back of a limousine outside Kayla's apartment. He'd been trying to call her ever since he'd found her resignation letter and the hotel suite empty, but she wasn't taking his calls. He'd just arrived in New York earlier that day after wrapping things up in Italy. Thanks to Kayla, Monte Calanetti was hosting the royal wedding.

He'd have left earlier but he couldn't. Nico and Marianna had been counting on him to stay until the royal decree was announced. Now that he and his siblings had achieved a peaceful relationship, it was as if they were truly a family again—something Angelo hadn't known how much he'd missed. And though Marianna still refused to divulge the name of the father of her baby, she knew without a doubt that both he and Nico were there for her—to support her no matter what decision she made about her future.

He'd returned to New York with orders from his brother and sister to track down Kayla and sweep her off her feet.

Since she'd been gone, he'd had time to realize how black-and-white his life was without her in it. He'd overreacted when he realized that he loved her. But now that he'd come to terms with the depth of his emotions, he hoped what he had planned was enough for her to give him—give them—a second chance.

Thanks to Kayla's very helpful assistant, who was a romantic at heart, he and Pam had secretly been able to piece the fund-raiser back together. And Kayla had been notified that a very special sponsor would be sending a car to escort her to the event.

He hated waiting. It seemed like forever since he'd last

laid his eyes on her. He wanted to march up to her apartment and beg her forgiveness, but he couldn't take the chance that she'd slam the door in his face. Worst of all, she'd end up missing her big night at the fund-raiser. He couldn't let that happen.

Instead, he'd stayed behind in the limo and sent up his driver with instructions not to mention that he was waiting. He needed a chance to talk to Kayla face-to-face. There was so much that he wanted to say—to apologize for—but he still hadn't found the right words.

The car door swung open and Kayla slid in the car next to him. She wore the navy dress he'd given her for their date in the Mediterranean. It hugged all of her curves and dipped in just the right places. It left him speechless that any woman could look so good.

When her gaze landed on him, her eyes opened wide. "What are you doing here?"

"What does it look like?"

Her gaze scanned his dark suit. "It looks like…like you're set for a night on the town."

"And so I am."

"Well, it can't be with me. I'm quite certain that it goes against your rules to date an employee."

"Ah, but what you're forgetting is that you're no longer an employee of Amatucci & Associates." He sighed. "We need to talk."

"Now's not the time. I have a fund-raiser to attend. Alone." She reached for the door handle, but before she could open it, the car started moving.

"And it looks like I'm your ride."

Her gaze narrowed in on him. "Angelo, there's nothing left to say. You said it all back in Tuscany."

"Not everything. Why did you quit without even talking to me?"

"First, I have a question for you. I thought it was strange when an internationally acclaimed rock band wanted to play for our fund-raiser on short notice. No one would tell me how Slammin' Apples heard about our need for help. Now I know. It was you, wasn't it?"

He wasn't so sure by the tone of her voice if this was going to go his way or not. "I was the one who called in a favor or two to have the band show up tonight."

"That isn't just any band. They are amazing. They've won national awards."

Angelo was going to take this all as a good sign. "I'm glad that you are pleased."

Her brows gathered together. "I didn't ask for your help."

"Kind of like how I didn't ask for your help with gaining permission from Louisa to use the chapel."

She shrugged. "I don't quit in the middle of projects."

He hoped this news would thaw her demeanor. "And thanks to you, Monte Calanetti is the official host of the royal wedding."

"Really?" A big smile bowed her lips and eased her frown lines. "I mean, I'm really happy for them."

"I knew you would be. Nico and Marianna send along their sincerest thank-yous." This was his chance to fix things. "I'm sorry about what was said in Tuscany. I never ever meant for you to quit. I need to make things right. You're far too talented to let go."

The light in her eyes dimmed. He'd obviously not said the right thing. For a man who made his fortune coming up with just the right words to turn people's heads and convince them to buy certain products or ideas, why was he messing this up so badly? Why couldn't he find the words to tell Kayla what she truly meant to him?

And then he knew what it was—what was holding him back. He was afraid that she wouldn't feel the same. He didn't want her to close the door on him as his parents had done so many years ago.

But still, he had to do it. He had to put himself out there if he ever wanted to win Kayla back. And that was something

he most definitely wanted. After their month in Tuscany
—he couldn't imagine another day without Kayla's sunny
smile or her beautiful laugh.

Yet before he could sort his thoughts into words, the
car pulled to a stop. Without waiting for the driver, Kayla
swung the door open.

"Kayla, wait."

Without a backward glance, she faded into the sea of
people waiting to get into the convention center. Though
he rushed to get out of the car, by the time he did so she'd
vanished—lost in the excited crowd.

He'd lost his chance to speak his piece. Maybe showing her how he felt would be better. He just hoped that his
other surprise worked, because he just couldn't lose her
now, not after she'd shown him that there was a different
way to live—one with love in it.

CHAPTER TWENTY-THREE

KAYLA'S HEART ACHED.

She bit down on the inside of her lower lip, holding in the pain. Her legs were on automatic pilot as they kept moving one after the other, weaving her way through the throng of people. She didn't have a particular destination in mind. She just needed to put distance between her and Angelo before she crumbled in front of him.

After all they'd shared, how could Angelo look at her and see nothing more than an Amatucci & Associates asset? Was that truly all she was to him? The thought slugged her in the chest, knocking the breath from her.

And the sad thing was, for the longest time that's what she thought she'd wanted—Angelo to look at her and see her for all of her creative talent. But now things had changed—they'd changed considerably. Now she wanted him to see oh so much more—to see the woman that loved him with all of her heart.

After passing through security, she made her way to the front of the hall where the stage was set up. The kids of the ICL after-school program rushed up to her.

"Ms. Hill." Her name was repeated in chorus.

"Hi." With so many happy, smiling faces looking at her, it was like a temporary bandage on her broken heart. She forced a smile to her lips. "Is everyone here?"

"Yeah!"

The parents made their way up to her, shaking her hand and thanking her. She wanted to tell them that she hadn't done this, that it had been Angelo, but every time she opened her mouth to explain someone else thanked her.

And then her parents stepped in front of her. Her mother's eyes were misty as she smiled at her and her father looked at her. "You've done us proud."

They drew together into a group hug—something she'd grown up doing. No matter how old she got, some things didn't change.

Kayla pulled back. "But what are you two doing here?"

"Honey—" her mother dabbed at her eyes "—you don't think that we'd miss this after the invitation you sent."

Invitation? That she had sent? Something told her that Angelo had orchestrated this, too. Suddenly she wasn't so upset with him. For him to listen to her and give her this chance to show her parents what she'd accomplished while in New York touched her deeply. She wished he was around so that she could apologize for overreacting in the limo. More than that, she wanted to thank him.

The lights dimmed and one of the security guards approached her. They guided her through the barrier, around the stage and up a set of steps. When she stepped on the stage, she was awed by the number of people in the audience. She wondered if Angelo was out there somewhere or if he'd given up and gone home. The thought of him giving up on her left her deeply saddened.

Oh, boy. This wasn't good. She couldn't think about Angelo. Not here. Not now. She had to keep it together for all of the excited faces in the audience who were counting on her to pull this off. She'd made it this far—just a little longer.

And then as if perfectly timed, pink-and-silver balloons fell from the ceiling, scattering across the stage. *What in the world?*

The head of the outreach program stood at the microphone. Mr. Wilson was an older gentleman who'd already raised his family. Now he and his wife spent their time helping the children enrolled in the program.

"Kayla, join me." He turned to the audience. "Everyone,

please give the mastermind behind this amazing event a round of applause."

The clapping and cheers were unbelievable. And it would have been so much better if Angelo was standing next to her—after all, he'd been the one to save the fundraiser. Not her.

As she peered at the countless smiling faces, her gaze connected with Angelo's. Her heart picked up its pace. What was he still doing here?

When quiet settled over the crowd, Mr. Wilson continued. "Kayla, would you like to say something?"

Though her insides quivered with nerves, she moved up to the microphone. Back at her apartment, she'd planned out what to say, but now standing here in front of thousands of people, including Angelo, the words totally escaped her.

She swallowed hard and relied on her gut. "I want to say a huge thank-you to everyone who helped with this event. Those people who helped with the planning and the organizing, please stand." Afraid to start naming names and forgetting someone, she stuck with generalities. "This was most definitely a group effort, and what a fabulous group. So please give them a round of applause."

She handed the microphone back to Mr. Wilson before she herself started clapping. Her gaze moved back to the last place she'd seen Angelo, but he was no longer there. She searched the immediate area but saw no sign of him. Her heart sank.

And then a familiar voice came across the speaker system. "Kayla, I know I say everything wrong when it comes to you. But I want you to know that I think you are the most amazing woman I've ever met."

Just then Angelo stepped on the stage and approached her. Her heart pounded in her chest. He stopped in front of her.

"What are you doing?" Heat flamed in her cheeks.

"Kayla, you've opened my eyes and my heart to the way

life can be if I let down my guard." He took her hand in his and gave it a squeeze. "I couldn't imagine doing that with anyone but you."

Kayla's eyes grew misty. It was a good thing that Angelo was holding her hand or she might have fallen over, because everything from her neck down felt like gelatin.

He handed the microphone back to Mr. Wilson as the band started to play. "Can I have this dance?"

He wanted to dance right here? Right now? In front of everyone?

Surely this all had to be a dream. If so, what did it matter if she accepted? She nodded and he pulled her into his arms as the band played a romantic ballad.

Angelo stared deeply into her eyes. "I never thought it was possible for me to feel this way, but I love you."

A tear of joy splashed on her cheek, a trait she inherited from her mother. "I love you, too."

"Does that mean I can rip up your resignation?"

"You still want me?"

"Always and forever."

EPILOGUE

Three months later...

"Do you have time for a new account?"

Kayla turned from her computer monitor to face Angelo. Was he serious? It was hard to tell as he was smiling at her. Ever since the charity concert, Angelo had been a different man in the office. He'd let his guard down and put on a friendly face, but one thing that hadn't changed was that he still expected perfection—or as close to it as anyone could get with their work.

"I don't know. Since we succeeded with the royal pitch, we've been flooded with new accounts. It really put Amatucci & Associates heads and shoulders above the competition."

"Yes, it did. And I couldn't have done it without you."

She knew that praise from Angelo didn't come willy-nilly. He truly had to mean it or he wouldn't say anything. "Thank you. But you were the driving force behind it."

"How about we just settle for 'you and I make a great team'?" He approached her and held out his hand to her.

She placed her hand in his, all the while wondering what he was up to. He pulled her gently to her feet, and then his hands wrapped around her waist. What in the world was up with him? He never acted this way at the office —ever.

"About this account—" he stared deep into her eyes, making her heart flutter "—if you decide to take it, it'll be all yours."

The breath hitched in her throat. Was he saying what she thought he was saying? "It'll be my first solo account?"

He smiled and nodded. "I thought that might get your attention."

As much as she wanted to spread her wings, she also didn't want to mess up. "Are you really sure that you want to give me so much responsibility?"

"I'm quite confident that you'll handle it perfectly. You are amazingly talented in so many ways." His eyes lit up, letting her know that his thoughts had momentarily strayed to more intimate territory.

She lightly swiped at his arm. "We aren't supposed to talk about those things at the office. What if someone overheard?"

"Then they'd know that I'm crazy about you."

She couldn't hold back a smile as she shook her head in disbelief at this side of Angelo, which had been lurking just beneath the surface for so long. "Now tell me more about this account. I'm dying to hear all about it before I make up my mind."

"It's a wedding."

"Are you serious?" He nodded and she rushed on. "I don't know. Don't you remember all of the headaches we had with the royal wedding? I couldn't imagine having a nervous bride lurking over my shoulder. I don't think I'd be good at mollifying a bridezilla."

"I don't think you give yourself enough credit. Look at how you handled me and opened my eyes to a thing or two."

"I know. Talk about a lot of hard work to get past your stiff, cold shell—"

"Hey!" His mouth formed a frown, but his eyes twinkled, letting her know that he was playing with her. "There's no need to throw insults."

"I wasn't. I was just stating the obvious." She grinned at him, letting him know that she was playing, too. "We could take an office poll and see which boss they like best—pre-Italy Mr. Amatucci or post-Italy?"

"I think we'll pass on that idea. Besides, you're going

to be too busy for such things now that you have this very special account."

"Special, huh? How special are we talking?"

Angelo reached into his pocket and pulled out a box. He dropped down to one knee. "Kayla, I love you. Will you be my bride?"

With tears of joy in her eyes, she nodded vigorously. "Yes. Yes, I will. I love you, too."

* * * * *

0815_23_MB514

MILLS & BOON®

Cherish™

EXPERIENCE THE ULTIMATE RUSH OF FALLING IN LOVE

A sneak peek at next month's titles...

In stores from 21st August 2015:

- **A Wedding for the Greek Tycoon** – Rebecca Winters
  and **The Cowboy and the Lady** – Marie Ferrarella

- **Reunited by a Baby Secret** – Michelle Douglas
  and **An Officer and a Maverick** – Teresa Southwick

In stores from 4th September 2015:

- **Beauty & Her Billionaire Boss** – Barbara Wallace
  and **The Bachelor Takes a Bride** – Brenda Harlen

- **Newborn on Her Doorstep** – Ellie Darkins
  and **Destined to Be a Dad** – Christyne Butler

Available at WHSmith, Tesco, Asda, Eason, Amazon and Apple

Just can't wait?
Buy our books online a month before they hit the shops!
visit www.millsandboon.co.uk

These books are also available in eBook format!